THE MOON THIEF SERIES

MOON
THIEF

RACHEL SHINNICK

Moon Thief

Future House Publishing
www.futurehousepublishing.com

Cover image copyright: Future House Publishing

Text © 2024 Rachel Shinnick

Paperback ISBN: 978-1-950020-85-0
eBook ISBN: 978-1-950020-84-3

Editing by Kelly A. Taylor

To Lysander, Emma, and Fletcher, whose impact reached far beyond the days they lived.

CHAPTER ONE

Ilis gripped the helm firmly, her mind made up.

The darkness of the night was thick about her. The sea-salted wind pulled at her hair and whispered in her ears, adding to the cacophony of her thoughts. Steadying her breathing, she listened to the captain's pounding footsteps as he retired to his cabin. When she heard the click of his door closing, she made her move. She had convinced Captain to leave her at the helm, telling him he should rest while he could.

Captain should have known better than to trust her; she didn't trust herself.

With a careful eye on the Stars, she turned the wheel and slowly shifted their course westward, letting the sparkling lights lead her to redemption. She did her best to make her movements minuscule and match them with the breaks of the waves that crashed upon the side of *Maribor* in a steady beating rhythm.

The only other pirate now above deck with her was Skinner Merton in the crow's nest, but as he was known for falling asleep on his watch, she doubted he would notice their course change. For once, something in her favor.

Her hand fell to rest upon the hilt of her sword, *Dawnbringer*, and sorrow flooded her heart. Chances were high that with the dawning of the Sun, she would have to part with it—the sword that was the only remaining physical reminder of her deceased mother; the sword that Ilis had mastered her swordsmanship with; the sword that she had slain a sea dragon with; and the sword that she had pinned up Skinner's trousers with many a time in pranks. She caressed the pommel, an ache building in her heart at even the thought of it sinking to the depths of the ocean.

A few more months and she would have reached her late teen years, an occasion marked on the seas by the taking of one's sword's name into one's own. As long as she could remember, she had dreamt of being Ilis *Dawnbringer*. Ruefully, she added that dream to the long list of others that would never be.

She glanced up at the Stars again, focusing on Canthares, the constellation most useful in seafaring navigation. Captain had taught her how to navigate by the Stars, and she was fairly certain she was doing it right. And right now, fairly certain was all she needed, for any change in their course for an hour or two would prevent them from making their intended rendezvous with Baroness Elida's ship.

Captain wanted to rid the baroness of the jewels she was transporting from the Sanhildin. It was a decent heist, to be sure, but Ilis needed to be elsewhere.

Perhaps if the crew realized they were already too far off course to catch the baroness before her ship reached the shore, Ilis would have a chance of convincing them to simply let her go, and then she need not part with *Dawnbringer*.

But to do that, she had to portray confidence. It would be so much easier if she could convince them she could do this.

It would be so much easier if she could convince herself.

But regardless, she would go. She had to.

Ilis shook her head and tried to redirect her thoughts. She focused on the cool night about her and smiled, thankful for the few hours of escape from the heat. For the past few decades, the Sun had slowly eaten up more and more of their days until night only laid claim to four hours.

Her smile turned into a scowl as she thought of the destruction that the Sun was bringing upon them. Rumors had it that soon the entire ocean would dry up, and while Ilis was wise enough not to believe everything she heard, she had seen coasts grow with her own eyes as the water level dropped. Captain used to joke that one day they would have to cease travel over the Edge and remain in the Under, the belly side of their flat world, to escape the Sun's heat. At least the Under still had a vast sea on which to sail.

No one knew why the Sun now reigned and burned their side of the world with such ferocity. Some said that it was the Under's doing, and some that the Sun herself was intent upon the world's destruction, while others thought it was because the fabled Moon no longer ruled the night sky.

Ilis looked up at the dark sky, scattered with Stars, and tried to imagine it with the mystical Moon. She scoffed, realizing that the idea of the Moon even existing once was beyond ridiculous.

When the Sun dawned a few short hours later, Ilis found the shore of Basileia already in sight. And right as she saw it, apparently so did Skinner from the crow's nest.

"Wai . . . What? Oh no, no, no . . ." came Skinner's mumbled cries from above, followed promptly by the ringing of the bell poised in the crow's nest.

Maribor awoke with the haste that only a pirate ship can.

Pirates poured forth from below deck, swords at the ready and eyes scanning for trouble. Footsteps and frantic shouts filled the air as everyone tried to figure out what was going on.

Captain lumbered out of his cabin shirtless and with a cutlass in hand. His thick brown beard, dusted with the occasional rogue white hairs, covered up the tattoo that Ilis had held his hand while getting. Gaze swift, his brown eyes went to Ilis first. He straightened to his full imposing height, sword raised and ready to fight anyone putting her in danger. A look of relief washed over him when he found her out of trouble. However, with one look at the shoreline, his eyes fell back on Ilis as he realized she was the trouble.

The eyes of the crew swiveled back and forth from Ilis to the captain, waiting to see what sort of doom he would pronounce over the young girl.

"ILIS!" Captain bellowed, his face twisting in rage. He pushed through the crew and up to the quarterdeck.

With a glance, Ilis found Almanzo beside her, his black hair pulled back in a short braid, and his silver earring in the shape of a sea dragon glinting in the morning light. His long fingers, fingers so useful in the art of thievery, took the wheel from Ilis. A small, kind smile spread upon his long face as he moved his long frame behind the wheel so Ilis could step away. The look cast a pang of guilt down deep in her chest.

"Blasted blow horns, if I find you've ruined my plans again, I'll have your hide!" the captain yelled.

Convince them you're confident, Ilis told herself, focusing on the present. *Convince them you can do this.*

She shoved all her doubts and shame aside and played the part of the spirited young Ilis they knew of old.

Spreading her hands out reassuringly, she forced a cocky grin to splay on her face while backpedaling away from the assault of words and down to the main deck. "But Captain, when have I ever *really* ruined your plans?"

"The Heist of '62?" offered Ulrich, grateful for a chance to partake in a lighthearted parry of words.

Captain's boots pounded on the deck as he rushed toward Ilis with his blade still in hand.

"The Conquest of Conor's Island," suggested Hawk. He leaned up against the railing to watch, a playful glint in his eyes.

Ilis ducked a savage sweep at her head from the captain and made her way toward the bow.

"Oh, and then there's always the time with Garland Smyth," Skinner reminded them, dangling from the rope ladder to the crow's nest.

Captain swung at her again, but this time Ilis merely hopped out of reach. She leapt to the bow of the ship and walked backwards along the spine of the carved dragon.

"But, gentlemen!" Ilis coaxed, using the title that always got under their skin. "Let's not forget the end of those tales." The captain did not have the best balance when he was mad, so she knew she had roughly thirty seconds on the dragon's back to calm him down.

Don't think about the last heist, Ilis told herself. *Just feign boldness.*

Remember what it was like before.

Ilis looked at Ulrich. "'62 was our most prosperous year." She pointed to herself. "All because of your favorite little miss." She tapped the sword sheathed at her side and faced Hawk. "And whose swordsmanship clearly conquered Conor's Island in the end?

"And as for old Garland . . ." Ilis shrugged in defeat. "I'll admit that one was my fault." She stepped off the dragon's back and seemed to plunge straight into the water until she reached out one arm, hooked it on the dragon's tongue, and flung herself back onto the ship's railing, right beside Captain. Ilis looked up at him with doe eyes. "But wouldn't you do the same if it meant you could see the infamous Iron Fists without his wig or wits one more time?"

The captain stared at her. He took three deep breaths to calm himself before replying. "In view of our most recent heist, I think it wise for you to take a break from scheming."

Silence broke out upon the deck. Eyes that had been jovially watching the fun quickly turned away. Suddenly, blades needed inspecting, ropes needed loosening, and the crew's fingernails became very fascinating. The only sounds were the waves crashing on the side of *Maribor* and the occasional creak of her deck.

Ilis chewed her lip. She felt tears beginning to brim in her eyes but willed them away.

"Actually, our last heist is the very reason I am embarking upon this next one without you all," Ilis said. She was shocked to find her voice didn't crack. "Perhaps the last one would have succeeded if I had gone alone."

She forced herself to maintain eye contact with the captain. They both knew her words were *far* from the truth.

But as she locked eyes with Captain, her gaze resolute, she willed him to understand.

This quest could right her wrongs.

"Please," she added softly. "Just let me go and do this."

Captain's face went stone cold. "No, what you need to do is stay out of trouble."

He took another breath to calm himself, sheathed his sword, and nodded—as if that settled the matter. Someone threw him a shirt and he pulled it on in one motion. Spinning on his heel, he began making his way back to the helm.

"Starboard bound! Release the main sails!"

His bellowing voice made Ilis cringe.

"But wait!" Ilis called. She rushed to keep up with him. She took the steps back up to the quarterdeck two at a time, the rising Sun already beginning to make her sweat. "You are already too late to intercept Baroness Elida. Can it truly hurt to let me try?"

Pausing mid-step, Captain glanced down at her and didn't even answer.

Ilis grimaced but continued. "I'm sure you can find another way to steal the baroness's jewels; I just need to be let off somewhere else first."

Captain stepped up to the wheel. Almanzo passed the helm off and avoided eye contact.

Ember, the only other female on board, stood leaning up against the railing near the helm, her hand resting on her sword. "And what, pray tell, do you hope to do all by your lonesome self?" she asked.

Ilis watched as those within earshot tried to inconspicuously listen in. "Steal the Crown Jewel."

Snickers escaped from the crew. Ilis tried not to cringe at the sound.

The Crown Jewel was the most sought-after prize on this side of the world, as well as the most mysterious. No one knew where the Crown Jewel was hidden or even what it was. But all that mattered to Ilis was the buyer: someone she knew was willing to give riches beyond belief in exchange for it.

"And you were thinking about doing it all alone?" Skinner asked incredulously.

Ilis nodded. *Don't let them see how terrified you are.* "My plan will only work if I go alone."

"The Crown Jewel isn't an easy prize to obtain," said Ulrich wearily—and he was one to know, seeing as he had lost his hand in a venture to simply gain information about its whereabouts.

"All I ask is you sail a little closer to the shore and save my arms from some rowing. Once ashore, I'll head for Mount Oros and arrive in plenty of time for the youngest prince's ball."

Captain just shook his head.

Ulrich dragged his hand down his face. "Ilis," he groaned, "is this about that Royal Thief title again? I know it would permit you to snoop about Mount Oros and look for the Crown Jewel, but . . ." He looked at her pleadingly. "They're not gonna give it to a pirate."

Ilis lifted her chin. "Oh, I bet they will."

Ember looked at her skeptically. "Why?"

"'Cause I'll steal the king's crown," Ilis said.

With a sigh that seemed to escape from his very bones, Captain returned the wheel to Almanzo, grabbed Ilis by the arm, and led her away from the crew.

"Ilis, the answer is no," he said fiercely. "I am not going to let you go off and kill yourself, you hear me?"

She faced him, forcing herself to lift her head high. "I won't let the crew baby me for the rest of my life, nor will I let them resent me for the consequences they face because of me. I can fix this. I'll become the Royal Thief, act as the kingdom's resident thief and spy, and while doing so, find the Crown Jewel. That will fix everything."

"The crew doesn't resent you," Captain said.

"Maybe not now! But when the seas on this side of the Edge dry up and the only waters on which to sail are in the Under where they can't go because of the bounty on their heads? What will they think of me then?"

"If they have a problem with it, they can deal with me."

Ilis shook her head. "You can't fight all my battles."

"I can try."

Ilis turned and faced the sea, leaning out over the ship's railing. "What if *I* need this?" she said softly. "I still have nightmares of that day. How am I supposed to escape the guilt of almost leading the entire crew to their deaths? At least with this, I can give them back their freedom." She looked back up at Captain. "Please, I have to try."

Captain sighed and leaned over the railing beside Ilis. He was slow to respond. His eyes were fixed out upon the great waves on which he had lived his years.

"I know it probably feels like the world is falling apart for you, but this won't fix that. I can't let you go risk your life like this. We will get through this the way we always have—together. We are a crew. Your place is here with us."

"I was afraid you'd say that," Ilis said sadly. "This would have been less painful if you had just let me go."

She stepped away from him and toward the middle of the deck. In one swift move, she leapt onto a barrel and raised her voice.

"I evoke Oathdeath."

Silence hit the deck like a savage slap to the cheek.

"I lay down my sword and hereby declare that this is my last day as a crew member of *Maribor*. I demand my release from any obligations to be loyal to you and release you all from any obligations to be loyal to me. I will leave these decks and . . ."

Her voice faltered. She forced herself to lock eyes with Captain. Tears stung behind her eyes, but she forced them down.

"I will leave these decks and never return."

The silence on deck was deafening. But this silence was tinted with sorrow and betrayal. She found the crew staring at her with disbelief.

Almanzo, who had trained her in going unseen even under a bright Sun; Hawk, who had taught her to be the best swordswoman on the seas; Ulrich, who she considered an uncle; Ember, the closest thing she had to a mother—each of them stared at her. Their faces held enough shock and sorrow that she almost relented right there.

I'm doing this for them, Ilis reminded herself. *They would have hated me anyway after long. At least this way there is a chance for redemption.*

Captain stormed toward her, his face red. "Ilis, you can't. I won't allow it."

Ilis jumped off the barrel and stared up at Captain with a fire in her eyes. Her jet-black hair caught in the wind. "Am I or am I not currently a crew member of the *Maribor*?"

Captain clenched his jaw for a long moment.

"Of course you are," he finally relented with a grimace. "But—"

"But what?" Ilis spat.

Pain echoed across Captain's face. "But you are my daughter. I can't just let you leave."

Ilis's face softened. She stepped up and placed her hand over his heart, right where her name was etched into his skin in ink. "And your daughter I will always be, but . . . but you will no longer be my captain."

"Ilis, don't do this. Please."

Ilis stepped away and threw her shoulders back. "You gave me no choice. I will restore *Maribor's* freedom on the seas . . . even if I'm no longer a part of it."

With shaky breaths, she looked down at *Dawnbringer* and slid it from its sheath. Before she could lose her nerve, she slammed it down into the ship's deck.

"I forfeit my belonging to this crew and demand my release. Today I lay my sword at your feet."

Not even Captain had any more words to try and persuade her otherwise.

Forcing herself to look away, she reached under some ropes and pulled out a bundle of belongings that she had stashed the night before. She slung them over her shoulder and moved toward the side of the deck. The rowboat was secured over the water on the side of *Maribor*.

With a leap, she was over the railing and into the rowboat.

Maribor was still forging full speed ahead, and thus the waters below were rushing quickly. When Captain made no move to pull in the sails, Ilis began lowering herself down with the rope pulley system. The rowboat lowered a whole of one foot before Captain's voice boomed out like a death sentence.

"Ilis of the Seas, crewmate of *You are no longer a part of the crew of Maribor.* since birth, we honor Oathdeath. You are released from your bindings to this ship and this crew. You are no longer a part of the crew of *Maribor*."

He plucked *Dawnbringer* from the deck. With a heave, he launched the sword into the air and over the side of *Maribor*. They all watched as *Dawnbringer* fell into the water with a sickening splat and then slowly drifted down into the unknown of the ocean below. Her sword was lost forever to the great depths, just as she was now lost forever to this crew.

Captain and Ilis locked eyes for a long moment—father with pained love etched upon his face, daughter with unknown tears streaming down her own.

"Pull in the sails!" Captain bellowed. "And steer a little closer to shore." And with that, he turned and walked away.

When Maribor had reduced in speed, Ilis lowered herself down into the water and rowed—away from the ship she once called home, away from the crew she once called family, and toward a desperate attempt at redemption.

CHAPTER TWO

The crew of *Maribor* were some of the most feared pirates on the seas. In decades past, it had been so because they were some of the deadliest. They had pillaged. They had plundered. They had done all the things expected of pirates.

But then came the birth of Ilis.

They had made the choice to turn from their murderous ways and instead took up a less deadly profession—that of master thieves.

"She's too precious to risk losing," Captain had said, tears in his eyes as he held the little bundle. "We've got to be better for her. We've got to be better for my daughter."

Now, the *crew* of *Maribor* were still some of the most feared pirates upon the seas—but in a different way. They had become known and notorious for stealing that which was never expected, doing so in a way which was never seen coming, and escaping with the general public only ever seeing what they wanted them to see. And somehow, pirates who planned heists of extraordinary proportions had ended up being pirates that people feared all the more.

However, even before the birth of Ilis, the crew of *Maribor* stood apart with the Right of Oathdeath. Their pirate kin held no qualms about killing any who even hinted at betraying the loyalty of the seas, but not the captains of *Maribor*. From the very beginning, an old captain whose name is perhaps completely forgotten decided that he wanted those on his crew to be loyal by choice, not by fear of death. And thus, the right of evoking Oathdeath was written into existence. Any pirate who wished to leave the crew could do so, but it meant the surrender of their sword and never again being a part of the crew.

This was now Ilis's fate.

She didn't look back as she rowed toward the shore. She couldn't. She feared if she did, all her resolve would be lost.

Instead, she focused on the shoreline before her, which had drastically altered over the past ten to twenty years, receding further and further from its original place. During Ilis's lifetime, it had withdrawn almost a mile, leaving a long stretch of barren beach. It was toward that dry and wasted shore that Ilis rowed.

Reaching the shore, she hauled the rowboat up on land toward a small outcropping of rocks, pulled out the bundle she had stashed inside, and set her eyes toward Mount Oros.

The knowledge that her crew—or rather, *the* crew of *Maribor*—were sailing within sight behind her burned in her mind. The ache to look back one last time welled up within her, but she simply stepped forward. She could not afford to be sentimental. Not now.

She walked along the dry shoreline decorated with skeletons of fish and small rodents for over an hour before reaching one of the cities settled on the coast.

Oar's Rest used to exist with the waves of the shore lapping right up to its borders. Now, it had docks stretched out over the mile of shore to get to and from the bustling port city.

It was in this city that Ilis hired a horse to take her to Mount Oros. She would simply return it to a stable on the mountain upon arrival. Slinging herself into the saddle, Ilis patted the horse on its neck and set off through the bustling roads of the city.

Horses pulled carts of fish out of the port. Women began to set up booths alongside the street to sell their wares: wooden utensils, cloth, vegetables, and more.

Ilis picked up bits of conversation as she passed through.

"Did you hear about the phoenix spotted by Murkwell? I heard it almost burnt down the entire town!"

"I heard a dragon was spotted on the other side of Maydover Run."

She shook her head. Beasts of such sorts had been lying dormant for decades. It was only in the past several months that sightings of them had begun to pop up.

Even though it had hardly reached five in the morning, the Sun was up and scorching. Ilis felt sweat begin to drip down her back.

Urging her horse into a trot, she exited the town. On the open road, Ilis let her thoughts drift. It would be a few hours of travel before she reached another major town, and the roads were mostly empty at this time of the morning.

Ilis considered the journey before her. The path up to Mount Oros, Basileia's capital, was well known. While she had never spent too much time *in* Mount Oros, she and her crew had made the trek a few times for some heist or another.

This was, however, her first time alone.

She thought back to her bold boasting on the ship . . . it was easy to be bold with the crew. It was easy to be confident among her family of thieves. It was easy to be who they had created her to be when they were by her side.

She tried to remind herself why she could be confident. Why, her heists were known upon land and sea! Through her daring feats, she had made a name for herself—but then again, she could hardly take credit for the victories. Each and every success had more to do with her crew making something good out of a harebrained idea than it did with her. She thought back to their playful mocking this morning: they were right—the one thing she was truly good at was ruining Captain's plans . . . That, and almost getting herself—and others—killed.

Her heart picked up speed at the thought, remembering their last heist. She rubbed the scar on the back of her neck. Perhaps the very act of doing this alone would be her downfall. But she could see no other way.

Ilis took a steady breath, the hot breeze pulling at wisps of her black hair. Closing her eyes, she let her horse have its head as they cantered on, the steady clomping of the hooves calming her raging thoughts.

She lifted her chin. She needed to try and fix her mistakes.

And this time, she would be the only one to suffer if things went wrong.

***

As she rode, Ilis picked out Mount Oros and its twin, Mount Eros, from the mountain range. Mount Oros stood slightly taller than its counterpart, with Twin Peaks Valley nestled high up on the mountain range between them.

She passed through forests with trees that were beginning to look dry and withered. The change the Sun had caused throughout their land over the past few decades had been slow but devastating. She wondered how much longer the world would last like this.

As Ilis and her horse continued up the mountain, they came upon various travelers and tradesmen from the surrounding area, but they paid her no mind. She kept an eye on the horizon, watching the twin mountain peaks that were tucked up in the clouds. Every once in a while, she thought she caught sight of the Oval Window, the pride and joy of Mount Oros. From this distance, it was a mere shining spot on the mountainside, but she knew that up close, it was so much more.

Just as she reached the base of the mountain, the Sun set, marking it as ten o'clock. For once, she was grateful for the extended hours of light the Sun offered. She camped, caught a quick four hours of sleep, and then awoke with the Sun. From her bundle of belongings, Ilis pulled out a bright red coat stolen from a Royal Messenger a few years back. Slipping it on, she threw her hair into a braid and tucked it under a cap. Pulling out her satchel from the bundle, she checked to see if the fake letter and seal were still there.

Once everything was in order, she continued her journey.

A few hours later she reached a point where the mountain's incline increased exponentially. Ilis pulled her horse to a stop and looked up at Needle's Twist: the most treacherous portion of the journey. The road was carved into a sheer cliff in a zigzagging pattern. She had no idea how this path had been carved, but she was grateful for it; the only other route up meant adding hours to the journey and cutting through Garen's Well, a city she was infamous in for stealing their city bell.

It was in Ilis's best interest to avoid visiting Garen's Well for a few more years.

Her horse shook its head—as if to say, "Let's get this over with."

Up they went, the horse's hoofs clipping along the stone pathway beneath in a clear beat. She let her horse take its time, trusting it to go at a steady pace. Midway up, she looked down and gulped.

Ilis was not one to fear heights, but even this view turned her stomach slightly. Looking down, she could see the scattered remains of carts that had not made it up the trek. Hawk once told her that he had tried to impersonate an ambassador from a neighboring land and attempted to make the journey up in a fancy carriage. The carriage had not made it. Hawk was told afterwards that all royal officials and family members rode horses from this point onwards, even the women.

Ilis forced herself to control her breathing as her horse clomped its way up the narrow path one step at a time. Relief flooded her when they finally reached the top. She urged her horse into a trot as the path leveled out. This last portion they could cover quickly. A little over an hour later, she came into a clearing, and the wall of Mount Oros appeared. Glancing up at the Sun and its lopsided rotation of their land, she guessed it was almost noon.

Mount Oros was heavily fortified. The capital of Basileia had been built on Mount Oros to be fortified against an attack from the Under. There were rumors of tunnels connecting the two sides of the flat world; therefore, to be as far away as possible, the Basileians had built their capital on the tallest mountain in the land. The walls around Mount Oros were thick. Some sections were made out of large blocks of stone, while others were carved straight out of the mountainside and thus were jagged but impenetrable.

Over the walls, Ilis could see other parts of the capital built into the top of the mountain. She spotted the infirmary, nestled halfway in the mountain and halfway out, with its tall precipice sticking up like a beacon of hope to the ill. The palace sat all the way at the top of the mountain, though at the moment it was mostly hidden by the clouds.

And then she saw the Oval Window. While it looked like just a large window built into the mountainside, it was also the entrance to the Oval Library—and a marvel to behold, even from afar. Every time she saw it, her breath caught, though she wasn't quite sure why.

To her left sat Twin Peaks Valley, though getting there from the main trail was near impossible. The area directly before her around the gate of Mount Oros was cleared grassland, but toward the left were jagged cliffs until the ground leveled out again for Twin Peaks Valley.

"They sure did pick a well-fortified spot," she said to her horse. She thought through how else she could enter the capital city . . . One either went through the Main Gate, which was well guarded, or scaled up a mountainside and entered the East Gate. Ilis doubted if even Almanzo Leviathan—her trainer in the art of sneaking—could scale those cliffs.

Realizing that she and her steed had stopped to stare at the mountain, she clicked her heels and urged her horse back into a canter.

The gatekeepers spotted her from a distance and started shouting commands with haste—one does not delay the king's messenger, and thanks to her coat, that's exactly who she appeared to be. The outermost gate was a drawbridge that was let down over a natural crevice in the mountainside. Ilis reached it just as it was lowered into place. The innermost gate was enormous, thick, and wooden but was already open when she went across the deadly cliffs of Mount Oros.

The art of sneaking lies in the ability to not look like you are sneaking. You don't even have to hold a true purpose in your doings. All you have to do is look purposeful. And Ilis was good at pretending.

Ilis showed a letter to one of the guards—a letter bearing the seal of Naval Officer Conburn, who had yet to figure out that the crew of *Maribor* had made a copy of his seal the very night he thought he was about to catch "the Ghosts of the Seas." With a nod, the guard let her through.

The gate let out right in the middle of the marketplace. Ilis led her horse to the left through carts, stalls, and shoppers toward the stables by the East Gate. People moved aside for the king's messenger riding with speed.

Reaching the stables, she slipped off her horse and took off at a run toward the palace, just as was expected of a messenger.

She took a detour into an alley, and no one noticed when she did a quick wardrobe change and stashed a bundle in a hidden nook underneath someone's back steps. When she emerged, she was a palace attendant with her leather satchel still on her side.

As Mount Oros was both a city and a mountain, Ilis had to practically hike to get from the stables near the city wall to the palace at the peak. She slipped through alleyways and stayed in the shadows until she reached the part of the mountain at the base of the palace. From here she would have to climb with careful movements to reach her destination.

She had been to Mount Oros only once. When Ilis was seven, Almanzo had taken her up to the castle and shown her around some of his favorite spots. She was heading to just one of those spots.

The palace, like many other structures in the capital, was built into the mountain itself. Therefore, the path she scaled was one of sheer mountainside. She remembered asking Almanzo if he thought the royals were worried that people would climb into their palace this way. Almanzo replied that they most likely thought it was impossible to climb. This made Ilis chuckle, as last time, Almanzo had climbed it with her on his back. However, her chuckle died on her lips as she remembered that she would never see him again. But if she succeeded here, at least he could have his freedom back.

The climb was painstakingly slow and rather precarious, but she was determined. She was doing this on her own this time, and it felt so good.

About halfway up, Ilis reached a point that *did* seem impossible. Her legs, arms, and fingers ached from the act of exerting muscles not often used, and she couldn't find another solid handhold, let alone a foothold.

Her thoughts went back to her last heist. She could almost feel her fingers slipping as they had then . . . almost see herself falling . . . almost feel the sickening blow of her body hitting stone—only to be swarmed by guards and taken to be executed . . .

With a shake of her head, she was back: muscles on fire but clinging for dear life to the cliff. She would *not* fail again.

Gritting her teeth, she set her gaze on a groove in the mountainside far out of her reach. Almanzo would scold her for such a risky maneuver at this height, but she didn't care. She would succeed. Or die trying.

With a burst of effort, Ilis shoved herself up wildly toward the hold. Her fingers latched on and she scrambled to find a place for her feet. After a slice of eternity, she found sound footing and let out a sigh of relief.

A breeze came up the mountain and warmed her skin. She groaned. Even the breeze was hot right now. Ilis glared at the Sun in its blistering reign. She sighed, wishing she could steal the Sun and save the land from this heat. She cocked her head. *Now there was a thought*—though, perhaps, a thought for another day.

Just when her muscles felt like they would give up, she reached the window Almanzo had shown her when she was young. She pulled out a knife and slid it between two of the glass panels. Almanzo had done all the hard work for her, so all she had to do was scrape out his temporary sealant and carefully remove the panel. Inside the window was an alcove that sat above a hallway, so she carefully placed the glass panel in the shelf around the alcove. It was just large enough to climb through.

Perched in the alcove, Ilis replaced the glass panel and waited. The alcove peaked up in a dome-like formation, allowing Ilis to perch hidden with one leg on each side to hold her up.

The king's crown only ever came off his head while he slept. And as she hoped to be announced as the Royal Thief at that night's festivities, she did not have the option of merely breaking into the king's bedroom and stealing it while he slept. Plus, that would have been too easy.

Stealing the crown off an awake king was a much better challenge.

When Ilis heard the telltale sounds of long strides, she knew the king was almost to her.

She loosened her snag lines. Skinner had taught her how to use a snag line at age five by having her use the slick string with a loop at the end to catch fish. Granted, she had only ever caught one fish this way . . . but surely a crown would be much easier than that.

Ilis held one snag line in her left hand and two in her right, as she would have to simultaneously catch the crown's prongs in three different spots in order to lift it off the king's head without him feeling anything.

You can do this, she told herself. Taking a deep breath to calm her nerves, she tried not to think about her previous ill fortune in stealing crowns.

The king came into view. He walked with his head held high and almost a bored look upon his face. While he looked just as tall as Captain, he was a good deal thinner and less muscular—which Ilis supposed made sense given their different occupations. Upon a head of brown curls speckled with gray sat the crown that was Ilis's prize.

It was a circlet made of fine strands of gold interwoven with rubies. Above each ruby the strands of woven metal protruded upward to form a cross. Out of all of the royal crowns, the king's was the least impressive in terms of outward beauty. But while its physical weight was little, the weight of its story balanced the scale.

The first king of Basileia, King Isten, had the crown formed by Firespeakers of old with the rubies that had been found in Mount Oros. The crown had been passed down from generation to generation without alteration.

And today, Ilis was grateful that it did not weigh much.

She lowered the snag lines, forcing herself to breathe softly, and guided the three loops toward some of the small crosses on the crown. She was putting a great deal of trust in two things: one, in the rumor that the king used a lot of wax in his hair to keep the curls just so, and two, that the crown was light enough that when she raised it off of his hopefully stiff curls, he wouldn't feel the difference.

The loops hooked upon the crosses, and then, in a moment, it was over.

The king continued his confidant gait down the halls while Ilis hastily pulled the crown upward. She clutched the crown to her chest, waiting until she could no longer hear his footsteps. It had worked! She was tempted to wear it but thought that might be going too far.

Instead, she hid her satchel and tools in the alcove, slipped back through the window, down the crevice, and back down the mountain, retracing her steps with the crown tucked in her coat. When she reached the marketplace, she lifted the crown above her head and shouted: "I stole the king's crown!"

She neither wanted nor needed to be subtle at that point.

CHAPTER THREE

A shockingly short time later, Ilis sat in a cold cell in the barracks, rather annoyed.

"Why am I here?" she asked.

"Because you stole the king's crown!" the guard yelled through Ilis's rusty cell door, wondering at the foolishness of the child.

"Yes," Ilis said slowly. She had known this was a potential outcome but hadn't thought it probable. She gripped the metal bench upon which she sat. "But why *here?*"

"If you mean as opposed to the gallows, I honestly don't know." The guard started to stroll away and she hopped to her feet, wincing as the shackles rubbed against her skin. The heat of the cell was sickening, causing her clothes to stick to her flesh.

"No, I mean as opposed to the palace."

Bewildered, the guard turned and looked at her tiny face framed by the metal bars. Ilis pulled one of the tacked-up notices that had been all over the nation for the last few months from her sweat-soaked pocket and pointed:

"Whoever steals an item of most value will be knighted Royal Thief." Ilis turned to the guard. "And what is more valued by the king than his crown?"

The guard looked at her as if she were a lunatic. "The king was looking to fill his coffers, you little fool, not to find a handy thief."

Ilis shuddered. She had considered that, but thought if she brought enough attention to herself, it wouldn't matter. A king could hardly ignore a thief who stole his crown right from over his nose.

"Why did you think he would ever trust you with such a title?" the guard asked, suddenly curious. "Royal Thieves are considered the High Spies of the kingdom. They steal secrets from the king's enemies and are trusted with the knowledge that no one else is. And you thought they would trust you with that?"

"I figured no one ever truly trusts a Royal Thief . . . I figured they would want to keep their enemies close."

The guard stared at her blankly, marveling at her confused logic. Finally, he shrugged. "Well, then I guess he does not find you that dangerous of an enemy."

As the guard marched off, Ilis pondered this. If that were the case, there was only one thing to do.

***

In Basileia, the firstborn carried the responsibility of ensuring that their family legacy was not forgotten. As a symbol of this weight and honor, the crown prince's crown was lavish beyond belief—so lavish, in fact, the crown prince only ever wore it on the most special of occasions.

Being as it was around lunchtime, Ilis guessed the prince would be in the royal dining quarters while his crown would be resting securely in the royal treasury. Ilis had heard tales that it was so heavy, the crown prince had to do exercises to have neck muscles capable of wearing it for hours on end. Personally, she thought it foolish to have a crown so grand you couldn't wear it all the time; but then again, she found many things the Basileians did foolish.

She mused that she probably should have just gone to the royal treasury in the first place, but breaking into the treasury was said to be impossible . . . And Ilis's odds with the impossible weren't very high these days.

Since the palace was located at the top of Mount Oros, the layout naturally took a rounded shape, and right in the middle sat the royal treasury. It only had one entrance, guarded by twenty-four guards, and twelve layers of doors with different locks to which only the king and crown prince had the keys. It also happened to be the one place of importance in the palace she had not been into . . . because Almanzo had never been inside.

But it wasn't even the guards or the locked doors that were the real problem. The real problem was that the entrance was situated behind a glass wall that looked out upon the main hallway of the palace.

It would be possible to distract or disable twenty-four guards and then pick the locks of twelve doors—but to do so without being noticed by the hundred or so onlookers who would pass by in that time . . . That was the real problem.

Ilis paced the floor of her cell in short shackled steps. Her brain assessed what she knew of the treasury.

Entrances: Only one known. Heavily guarded.

Structure: Walls and floor carved from the mountain itself. The roof, the floor of the king's quarters, also made of mountain stone.

Arrowslits: Four, one in each direction. But only six by six inches. Secured with wire. And high up in the walls. It was just enough to let a breeze come through and ward off any sickness that was said to grow on the feared dragon gold.

Ilis stopped her pacing and cocked her head. "Now that could work," she muttered to herself.

Locks had never been a problem for Ilis, at least, given enough time. She was raised on a pirate ship after all. The moment the guard was out of earshot, Ilis slipped off her boot and pulled out a strand of wire tucked in the heel that was made to look like part of the shoe's design. She snapped the wire in half and used the two pieces to pick the lock.

With silent footfalls, she slipped through the prison and back out into the hot mountain air. Scowling at the Sun, she made her way up to the palace yet again, retracing her steps from earlier this morning. Scaling back up the side of the palace, her muscles complained from the constant use. She had to pause often, letting her body rest before going on, and this time, she found another route where she didn't have to risk her life in a frenzied leap. Slowly but surely, she made her way upward. When she reached the alcove, she paused only to reopen the window and retrieve her satchel and tools before continuing toward the small window on the east side of the royal treasury.

When she reached the tiny window, she found two good footholds in the mountainside and then peered down into the treasury. Sure enough, right in the middle of the room was the crown.

"Huh," she mused, "they weren't lying when they said it was large." The crown held more jewels than Ilis had ever seen at one time, and that was saying something.

Out from her pocket, she pulled a thick rubber cord, which she tied to each side of the metal wiring of the tiny window. Then she retrieved from another pocket a spool of sturdy twine—hopefully sturdy enough to lift the crown—and a small metal arrow as long as her hand. Ilis tied the twine to the arrow, set the arrow in the rubber cord, and pulled it back.

The doubts tried to enter, but she shook them away. She didn't have time for them. Instead, she lifted her lips in a smirk as she thought of the insanity of this scheme. Not only did she have to shoot the miniature arrow through the metal wiring on her side, but in order for this to work, she also had to get it to fly through the wiring on the other side.

She stopped thinking, let out a breath, and let the arrow fly.

The arrow passed soundlessly through the window on the other side. She tugged on the twine and the arrow caught upon the wire, forming a line of twine from one window to the next.

A silent huff of laughter escaped from her lips as she slipped a hook on the line. The hook was the size of her thumb and had been used to reel in a swordfish larger than she was. Surely it could hold the crown.

With a flick of her finger, she sent the hook away from her on the line and then let the weight of the hook pull the twine downward. If the Basileians hadn't placed the crown in the exact center of the room, this never would have been possible. So in all actuality, what happened next was their own fault.

When the line was lowered enough, the hook snagged the crown, and then she slowly started hauling in the line. It was a slow and arduous process that caused her muscles to protest yet again. The weight of the crown alone was a feat to lift, but with every successive pull, the weight intensified because of the angle. She continued drawing in the line until she deemed it high enough to be out of sight from any guard who might enter.

And every good thief knows there is safety in heights, for few ever remember to look up. She indulged in another silent huff of laughter as she tied off the line securely to the window.

Her father's words rushed to her memory: *Sometimes, the art of a great heist is not necessarily removing an item from its location as much as it is about convincing everyone else that you have done so.*

The words brought sorrow flowing back into her heart like a flood.

"I am doing this for them," she reminded herself. "I will regain their rights upon the seas."

Heist accomplished, Ilis retraced her steps yet again and locked herself back in her prison cell. She figured that was the best way for them to find her—and the second stolen crown—again.

***

An hour later, she found herself kneeling in the throne room, just as she had planned. True, she had been shoved to her knees, and a guard now held a dagger to her throat, which she found a bit much . . . but, who was she to complain?

"Where is it?" the crown prince growled. He had the same dark brown hair as his father, though cut shorter so Ilis couldn't tell if he had matching curls.

Ilis looked up at him innocently. "Where is what?"

"My crown, you fool!" the prince shouted back.

The king raised his hand, silencing the prince. He turned to Ilis.

"You cannot expect to plead your innocence, child. You are the only person in a century to steal something of such great value. I highly doubt another thief with your skills has come out of the woodwork within the course of a day."

Ilis's lips quirked. She had no intention of feigning innocence.

"Then you admit I have stolen the item of the greatest value." She paused, her eyebrow raised in a question.

In a stride, the crown prince had crossed the floor and slapped her across the face. "Street scum, everyone knows that my crown is second only to the Crown Jewel."

Though her cheek stung, Ilis smirked. "Then shouldn't you name me the Royal Thief?"

"Why, you little oaf!" the prince roared. "I'll have you hung by your toes for this!"

But the king remained calm and simply stared at her.

"I mean, that is what you said. Is it not, Your Majesty?" Ilis tried to hide her smug grin as she asked the king, "Or is your word not your bond?"

The crown prince's scowl deepened, but the king chuckled.

"You're a witty thing, I'll admit," the king said, stroking his beard. "But how could I ever trust a thief like you?"

"You couldn't," Ilis stated plainly, shaking her head. She let herself smirk openly. "But you might learn to appreciate me nonetheless."

The king looked at her, expressionless. The crown prince, on the other hand, was still red in the face.

"After she tells us where the crown is hidden, give her ten lashes," the king finally said.

Ilis felt her heart plummet. So much for her plan.

Her brain began searching for a way out. They would take her back to the dungeons again, but she still had another wire in her other heel she could use to pick the locks as long as they didn't find it. Maybe she could steal something on her way there just in case, but hide it where? Swallowing things was notoriously dangerous, but maybe . . .

She almost missed what the king said next.

"And then, have her bandaged up and dressed for the prince's ball." The king locked eyes with her. "Consider it your initiation."

Ilis felt a wave of relief sweep over her, but outwardly she scowled.

"Simply go into the treasury and look up," Ilis muttered.

"Excuse me?" the crown prince roared.

Ilis faced the crown prince and lifted her chin before the guards dragged her out of his presence with no small amount of force.

MOON THIEF

***

They dragged her from the palace, down through the marketplace, and to a clearing in front of the infirmary. She supposed that this was an efficient decision, as she would definitely need medical care after this. A crowd of onlookers had gathered, but Ilis tried to ignore them.

While it was not the first time Ilis had been whipped, it was the first time she had not fought her way out of the lashing. With each successive lash, Ilis had to admit that sitting through torture was far worse than fighting for freedom through torture. Truth be told, all Ilis wanted to do was shout at them to stop so she could crawl into a ball until Captain came to rescue her.

Only he wouldn't come to rescue her. She had gone painfully far out of her way to make sure this mission was a solo one. She needed this success. For once in her life, she needed to do something right. With all her outward bravado, inside she was still just a quivering girl who yearned for self-confidence.

Ilis tried to recount her reasons for concocting this scheme as the lashes burned across her back. To regain the crew's freedom upon the seas of course; but also, she felt she needed some kind of redemption to escape the guilt that had been chasing her like a swarm of angry tree flies.

And she was curious to see what life on land was like. She wanted to understand life in Oros, the capital of the Kingdom of Basileia. She wanted to understand Basileians' fascination with books and why they feared dragons more than pirates.

But it wasn't just that. She needed to prove herself—show that she was capable of accomplishing something on her own. So far, all she had proved to the crew was that her very presence brought about a lot of headaches . . . some so severe that they almost lost the very heads that were aching. She needed to prove that she was worth it—worth all the time and care they had given her.

She needed to prove that she was worth her mother dying for.

She would become the Royal Thief, steal the Crown Jewel, trade it for the crew's freedom to sail again in the Under, thus making sure they had seas to be pirates upon even with the scorching Sun, and then . . . Well, to be honest, she didn't know. If she could pull off the heist without anyone being suspicious of her, perhaps she could live on the mountain. Or she had connections in the Under. Maybe she could work with them. All she truly hoped was that she could find a life free from that ever-present guilt.

Having finished dealing out her sentence, the guards cut her bonds and threw her to the ground. She tried to break her fall, but there was no easing the pain that shot up her back like a lightning bolt. Ilis blinked and tried not to pass out.

So maybe she was questioning that desire to see what life on land was like.

Land was hard. Land hurt. But land would not break her.

Ilis gritted her teeth and tried to stand. Her back felt like it was on fire, and the pain seemed to spread to each and every one of her limbs.

A strangled cry escaped from her gritted teeth, but she managed to stand. Her vision began to black out, but before it was gone completely, Ilis saw a blonde nurse rush from the crowd to her aid.

The young lass ordered some foot soldiers to put Ilis on a stretcher. It took all of Ilis's willpower not to pass out while they moved her from the square into the infirmary.

The soldiers set down her stretcher on a table in a whitewashed room. Ilis lifted her head to see what was going on, but even that movement sent tendrils of pain down her back.

"Take it easy for a few days," the young nurse said. Ilis laughed and groaned all in one at the nurse's ironic remark. Ilis was about to tell the nurse that resting wasn't an option when a redheaded soldier entered and did it for her.

Bearing a hefty bundle in hand, the soldier stopped before the nurse. Ilis guessed that they were both about her age, which set her wondering: at what age did people take on their work roles on Mount Oros? Ilis also seemed to notice a conversation being told in their eyes that she couldn't understand. She tried to lift her head and better observe, but then felt like she was about to pass out again so gave up.

Ilis closed her eyes and focused on breathing shallow breaths. How many hours were there until the ball? Her stomach turned at the thought of having to stand, much less dance, and endure the pain.

After their silent conversation, the soldier briskly addressed the nurse and instructed her to help Ilis into her gown and ready her for the ball. He deposited the bundle into the nurse's arms.

"You don't mean she is to attend tonight's celebrations!" the nurse replied, scandalized by the prospect.

The soldier's firm expression never changed. "If the king does not see her on the dance floor tonight, he will assume she has forfeited her chance at the title of Royal Thief and gone back to the gutter from whence she came." He clicked his heels and walked away.

The nurse muttered something under her breath and then instructed Ilis to wait and left the room.

As if I'm going anywhere, Ilis thought grimly. She turned her head, ignoring the pain, and found a small C-shaped crevice in the floor. She tried to focus on that and not on the ache.

"I would have thought by now you'd be used to the pain, Ilis, me lass," Ilis moaned, trying to use her father's often-said words to comfort herself. She failed.

Tonight was going to be miserable.

When the young nurse came back, she held a green jar clutched close against her chest and wore a determined look on her face.

"This is dragon blood from the Dragon Age." The lass paused and looked down at the jar. "It will sting like fire and scar like it too, but it will ease the pain." She paused again and cast a coy smile at Ilis. "Perhaps just enough for you to dance and prove the worth of us guttersnipes."

Ilis looked into the girl's pale blue eyes and nodded, understanding both the nurse's sacrifice and the fire behind her voice.

When the dragon's blood mixed with her own, Ilis screamed like a siren. But when the red haze of pain subsided, she found she could look upon the nurse and smirk again.

"They wanted a thief. So a thief they shall get."

Chapter Four

It was Basileian tradition to start balls after sunset so as to show off the brilliance of the Oval Window. Not even the shifting of the Sun would alter this tradition. Close to eleven o'clock, Ilis found herself walking up to the heart of the mountain—the Oval Library. The air had chilled slightly with the setting of the Sun but not enough to warrant a cape.

The heart of the mountain was like the heart of the Basileian people: filled with books. And yet, as Ilis looked up at the grand masterpiece, she still had a hard time imagining that something as magnificent as this could be the wall to a mere library.

But it wasn't just a wall; it was a giant oval window created of a thousand panels, two of which were the entrance to the library.

Ilis stood grounded in the middle of the stairs outside, forcing guests to go around her but unable to take another step. The sight before her stole her breath and gave her life all at once.

Tales about the Oval Library of Mount Oros came flooding back to her. The tales spoke of how its oval opening was made of diamonds melted into glass by the Firespeakers of olden times. Whispers revealed how it held the ability to shine light upon the rooms inside without fading a single page. A whole family was said to be employed year-round to clean and maintain the glass which spanned seven stories high and about half that distance wide. She had even heard how candles were lit in a hundred of the window panes, making the great windows shine bright in the few dark hours their world now offered. The Stars seemed dull in light of this brilliance before her.

No matter how many times she saw it, her awe and reverence for the sight never faded. It seemed to fulfill a longing in her heart she didn't know existed.

Shaking herself out of her daze, she forced herself to walk up the stone steps. Two large and sparkling panels of the lower portion of the Oval Window opened wide for the guests of the youngest prince's celebration ball. Excitement thrummed through her veins as she walked through the doorway. Her one heist to Mount Oros had not given her reason to go *into* the Oval Library.

She walked slowly, trying to calm her emotions. She realized excitement was not the only emotion welling up inside of her. Curling up in her belly, like a baby dragon curled up in its shell, sat a nervous fear. Ilis pushed it away. She wouldn't fail again. She couldn't this time.

Ilis reminded herself to stay focused.

The main room, bright by the light of a thousand candles, was walled from floor to ceiling with *books*. Ilis craned her neck to look all the way up, gaping at the seven stories worth of bindings, knowing that those she saw were not even a drop in the bucket compared to the whole collection. Rumor told that the library ran through the heart of the mountain and came out the other side.

Ilis tore her eyes away from the books and took in her surroundings, chiding herself for not doing so sooner. The only public exit seemed to be the doors through which she came, but she spotted thirteen doors along the walls of the first floor and eight for every accompanying floor, all of which could house ways to escape. Though, as she counted the stories, she realized that only five balconies were visible instead of all seven she had heard were a part of the Oval Library. The top two floors—*if they truly existed*—must be located on a level separate from the rest.

The grand room was filled with men and women dressed in their finest. Beneath her feet was white marble with streaks of gray that ran like rivers across the floor. With a start, she realized that there were no lines in the marble tiles. This was not tiling at all, but the mountain itself, carved and shined to perfection.

White banners hung along each of the five-story balconies, falling down like the branches of a willow tree. A fifty-piece orchestra sat in the second-story balcony and played lively songs to which many lords and ladies danced, making the center of the room a show of bopping hats and swooping skirts. The king sat on his throne in the back of the room, up on a dais so he and his sons could look out upon the festivities.

Lifting her chin, Ilis strode toward the throne to make her presence known. Briefly, she wondered what the king would think of her small rebellion in regard to her dress. Suffice it to say, the dress she wore was not the dress provided to her by the king. He had supplied her with a gown of pale blue and white frills which looked as dainty as could be.

Ilis nearly snorted when she saw it and subsequently excused herself from her nurse to gather her own dress. She had hidden it under someone's back steps near the Main Gate and had to steal a horse to retrieve it in time. The horse was returned to his rightful owner a half hour before the ball began, which gave Ilis just enough time to thread her long jet-black hair into a braid and slip into her dress.

It was the dress Ember had sewed for her when the crew hit a funeral last year, but it had become her favorite. Its top was simple with a black lace collar and quarter-length sleeves. A plain black silk ribbon fastened around her waist, and the thick silk bottom was long enough to cover her toes. Despite its simpleness, and perhaps morbidness, the dress was unmistakably beautiful in its own dark and silent way.

Eyes followed her as she wove through the crowd, her dress a stark contrast to the pastel colors of the ladies around her. While sticking out was not her first intention with wearing this gown, she would be lying if she called it an unwanted effect.

As she walked, her eyes drank the royals in, finding them a rather fascinating sight. The king sat tall, as he had every right to, his red cape spilling down the steps ascending to his throne. To his right sat the crown prince, whose sour face she knew well, and whose sparkling crown she knew even better. To his left sat the king's youngest son, who was the cause of this celebration. Ilis knew there was a middle prince, but his throne sat empty. He must have been off dancing.

The kingdom always came together in celebration of each of the three princes' birthdays. The king was also said to give a gift of extraordinary value to his sons for the occasion, which piqued Ilis's interest only slightly more than the youngest prince himself, who was currently gaping at her as if she were a long-lost friend . . . or a long-lost enemy. The look could have gone both ways. But then, in an instant, it was replaced with a polite smile.

Rumors about the youngest prince were abundant, but Ilis had her suspicions as to which were true and which were smoke on the wind. Rumor held that he had once jumped off of a cliff with a makeshift parachute (by Ilis's guess, this was true enough), wrestled with a bear and come out with a single scrape down his arm (Ilis called this one a bluff—her personal guess was that it was actually an overexcited beaver), and escaped from bloodthirsty assassins (Ilis had no opinion on this one, other than questions as to who would even want to kidnap the youngest prince). Even with all the false mixed in with the truth, everyone agreed that his daring feats had made a name for him beyond that of just being the king's son.

He would have made a good pirate.

She looked him over, noticing that he, too, seemed to share his father's confidence. His chest was puffed out, brandishing the medals that sat upon it. He was of average height and build for a young man, and his head was held high, as if daring anyone to miss the crown upon his head. It was silver, engraved with the faint outline of mountains and studded with emeralds that matched his eyes. He had a head full of thick chestnut brown hair which almost curled around his crown and a face that some might say was handsome. Ilis reminded herself that she was not one of the "some."

She reached the throne and curtsied before the king.

The king raised his eyebrows at the sight of her but made no comment about her dress.

"So, you are a tough one, I see," spoke the king in his deep voice. As it seemed to be a statement and not a question, Ilis chose to remain silent while the king continued to look her over.

"We have never before had a Royal Thief so young." He paused and let that statement hang over her. "But I am willing to let you try, provided you pass through some training first."

A weight seemed to lift off Ilis's chest at his words.

"You will be enrolled in Oros Academy to be instructed in our ways. You will also need to pass a few trials before you officially gain your title." The king looked her over once more and nodded in approval.

"Malcolm," the king said, turning to his youngest son. "Take our new thief for a turn on the dance floor. Keep her close; it is good to have a Royal Thief in your pocket."

Ilis found two emotions at war inside of her: the desire to escape to the shadows, and a piqued curiosity about this prince. She tried to squash the second emotion. Now was not the time to get distracted.

A wisp of a smirk appeared on the prince's face, but he controlled it well. He stood tall in a navy blue suit with golden buttons running down the front. Ilis eyed the buttons, wondering if they could have been his gift and she had already missed them being presented as such but decided against it. Surely the gift would be something more than . . . buttons.

"Of course, Father." Prince Malcolm turned to Ilis. "May I?"

It's not as if I have much of a choice, Ilis thought. But she merely bowed and accepted his hand.

The prince whisked her off to the dance floor, making her heart beat a smidge louder in her chest. When they had fallen into the rhythm of music, their steps matching each beat, the prince cleared his throat.

Oh dear, Ilis thought, and now he is going to try and make conversation.

"Have you often been to Mount Oros? I cannot say I have seen you at the past festivities."

Ilis lifted her chin. "I have been here enough, and if I did not want you to see me, I can guarantee you that you would not have. I am quite adept at being invisible when I want to."

"Somehow I find that hard to believe."

Ilis glared, trying to decide if he had just flirted with her or insulted her—and which outcome she found more repulsive.

"Well, I suppose I should be grateful that it is not you I had to prove my worth to, but your father, and he found me up to the task."

Ilis looked around, ready to end this dreadful dance and do anything but be in the arms of a prince. She found herself having a hard time breathing steadily—which was unnerving, to say the least.

The prince drew her attention back to him. "What makes you think that it was the king you had to convince?"

Ilis sighed. "What, are you saying stealing two crowns was not impressive enough for you?"

"To be fair, you only truly stole one crown . . . The other, you just pretended to steal."

Ilis raised an eyebrow. Passion for her trade sparked inside her. "But that is the brilliance of it! In order to steal something, you don't have to remove it from its original location; you just have to convince the previous owner of your doing so."

The prince seemed to think this over. "But how can it be truly stolen if it is never in your possession?"

"Who's to say it wasn't? The crown most assuredly was not in your brother's possession, and seeing as I knew the location of it, was it not then more mine than his?"

The prince blinked and then laughed. "Well, I suppose that is one way of thinking of it."

He turned his attention to her dress and picked at her black sleeves. Ilis looked up at him challengingly. "Your Highness?"

"I must say, black is not quite the usual choice for a girl of your age," he said.

Ilis cocked her head. "And your blunt words are not quite the usual choice for a prince your age," she replied. When his face showed all the shock of being rebuffed by a mere peasant, Ilis could not hold back a smirk. "What did you expect of a thief?" she said, referring to more than just her words and dress.

The prince seemed to think about this as he continued to lead her in the dance.

"I suppose I did not expect you to be a thief, but simply a girl," he admitted while leading her in a complicated series of steps. Ilis put on her best carefree expression, one she had worked hard to master. She smiled, pretending to enjoy the music, pretending to enjoy the dance, and pretending not to notice his careful examination.

As he stared intently into her eyes and she stared boldly back, she laughed out loud, realizing what others must think. To the average onlooker, it no doubt looked as if the prince, with his intense green eyes, was trying to woo the young new thief.

But Ilis knew better.

She knew how to read a challenge in a foe's eye.

"Who are you really?" he asked.

"Not all answers are ready to be heard," Ilis answered. She searched his eyes, trying to decipher what exactly his challenge was.

Their feet flew underneath them as he led her faster and faster in the steps, but her mind whizzed at an even greater pace. The skirt of her dress flicked at her ankles. Lifting her chin, she danced by his side, her eyes never leaving his. Pain from her lashes crept up her spine, but she paid it no mind. When the music slowed to a stop, she bowed her head and curtsied low.

The prince bowed in turn, signifying the end of the dance, and began to march off. Pausing briefly, he turned back and said, "I expected more of you, Thief . . . even if you are just a child."

Ilis lifted an eyebrow and showed a glimmer of a grin. The subtle challenge written on her face caused the prince to tilt his head slightly in a question.

From one pocket she pulled out his topcoat button, from another his watch, and from a third his medals marking his prestigious achievements. Then she stepped forward, knelt before the prince, and pulled a crown from within the folds of her dress—*his* crown.

An audible gasp swept through the room.

Ilis wondered if stealing three crowns in one day was a bit excessive. But the redemption sure did feel good. She had a sudden undeniable ache to tell the crew about her day, an ache that felt all the hollower when she realized she would never have a chance.

The prince before her reclaimed her attention as he appraised her with a slight smile on his lips. He stepped up to her and took his crown back from her outstretched arms. With a flick of his wrist, he threw it up in the air, causing it to spin round and round before catching it again and placing it back upon his head.

"Now that's a thief I'm glad to know," he said, nodding his head. "Yes, I think you will do." He offered her his hand, and they joined in the next dance.

The words of his father rushed back to her. She looked at him, eyes narrowed. "What did your father mean earlier? It almost seemed like he thought he was giving you a gift by letting you dance with me."

The prince smiled at her, as if he had a secret he was about to share.

Ilis's mind beat him to it. "The notices are pinned up around town," she said, suddenly breathless. "Your father was looking for the greatest thief—" She pushed herself away from him. "For you." Her brow furrowed. "I'm your birthday gift?"

The irony was terrible.

The prince laughed at her outrage. "You showed up just in time." He paused. "Though I must apologize for the lashings. That was not a part of the plan. It seems you angered my elder brother so much my father felt some form of punishment was needed."

"Why did you ask for a thief?" Ilis asked.

He stared back at her, calm in the midst of her bewilderment. "Because I need to steal something."

"Steal what?"

"Not all answers are ready to be heard," said the prince, stealing her words. Then he turned on his heel and began to walk off. The crowd of suits and dresses parted for him. After a shocked heartbeat, Ilis picked up the dark folds of her dress and ran after him.

"Eh . . . Your Highness?" Ilis questioned.

He turned, and she pulled from her pocket his other belongings that she had yet to hand back to him.

"I am sure you will find a way to return them to me," the prince said over his shoulder.

Ilis slowed and watched the prince disappear in the crowd, only to realize all eyes were on her. So Ilis did what she did best. Throwing her shoulders back, she sauntered into a shadow and disappeared.

***

Ilis wandered until she found an open window where the mountain breeze called to her. With a glance around to make sure no one was watching, she climbed through the window and out onto a small alcove on a cliff off to the side of the Oval Window. The night's brisk chill kissed her cheeks and the gentle howl of the wind replaced the ballroom's music. All was dark around her, and she reveled in it. She was invisible in the night, her dark hair mimicking the sky, her eyes the Stars.

Her thoughts once again found themselves sailing among the seas with her family. She found herself shaking, and the realization was shocking. She was not one to get stage fright.

But I suppose I have never had a solo, Ilis thought. *Today was my first true heist on my own.* She tried to let that realization bolster her courage. But while the sores on her back from being whipped were only dull aches—thanks to the dragon blood—the pain from the lashings echoed fiercely in her memory. *My first heist on my own, and I got the scars to prove it.*

Part of her realized that she should also celebrate, as she had indeed completed the first step of her plan. Somehow though, she didn't feel in the mood for reveling. The completion of this heist did not mean she was safe from danger. In fact, with this batch of royals, it just might have placed her closer to it.

When she heard voices, she shook herself out of her thoughts and climbed along the mountainside toward them. She soon found that the voices were coming from another open window—based on the placement, Ilis guessed that it was a window from one of the rooms within the Oval Library.

"Do you think our new Royal Thief could truly be her?" one voice asked.

"She is the right age and skill set."

"It almost feels like too much to hope for."

"If it is her, she will have a special connection to it. We will know for certain after the heist."

There was a sigh.

"What if she is the wrong one? Our plan rather revolves around her being the right one."

"There is part of me that hopes I am wrong and that she doesn't exist."

There was silence. "See, I think I understand you until you go off saying things like that."

One of them chuckled lightly.

And then there was silence.

Ilis's thoughts ran amok. What had she just overheard? Who did those voices belong to . . . The one with all the questions almost sounded like Prince Malcolm, but who was the other? And what heist did they have planned? Why was she such an important part of their plan? None of it made sense.

It was perhaps an hour before she felt herself again and returned to the ball. But, having lost her appetite for dancing, she stayed along the walls, looking over the books but not seeing anything. She wandered up to the second-story balcony and was staring blankly down at the dancers below when a voice broke through her thoughts.

"Excuse me, miss?"

Ilis recognized that voice.

Ilis turned to find a young man, of the gangly tall sort, standing before her. He looked a few years older than her, with round, owlish blue eyes and the voice of the person she had just overheard talking to the prince. He smelled like a memory. Ilis took his posture, his brown hair falling loosely about his shoulders, and green waistcoat to be proof of his aspired profession: Forester. They were the hidden soldiers of the Hearing Tribe of the Kingdom of Basileia.

When he merely stared at her, looking dumbfounded, Ilis asked, "Yes?" What was it with people staring at her tonight? Taken with the conversation she had just overheard, it felt as if everyone knew something about her that she didn't.

He snapped out of it quickly, replacing the wondering look with one completely void of expression. "Prince Malcolm sent me to escort you to your room if you are ready."

Ilis agreed to this proposition. The day had been long, and she was eager to see its end.

The Forester, who introduced himself as Neil, led her out of the grand entryway, down the steps, and along a wide cobblestone path that wrapped around the mountainside of Oros. The path lit by the occasional lantern wound around various buildings tucked in the cliff face as they trekked along, the hot breeze ever around them. When they reached the south side, Neil pointed to the grand building before them that was built into the mountain itself. It was made of the gray stones of the mountain and pocketed with large windows.

"That is Oros Academy. You will report there in the morning to Professor Owlistare at eight o'clock. The king has insisted that you be enrolled as a student to have a proper mountain education, so you shall be taught alongside other students your age who are being instructed in their various trades."

Ilis looked sideways at the young man who stood beside her. He pointed again toward the building. "See that tower off to the right?"

Ilis had to peer through the darkness but thought she did see a shadowy tower off in the distance.

"That's where we are headed."

They hiked up further toward Oros Academy, reaching the courtyard in front of the building and passing by a statue of a griffin that stood guarding the area. Neil led her to a set of stone stairs that led them up past Oros Academy and to the base of the tower he had pointed to before.

The door at the base of the tower opened with a creak and led to a spiral staircase. When they had gone up four flights of stairs, and dust had become thick along the stone floor, they reached a door that looked like it hadn't been opened in years. A dirty window sat to its left.

"Here you are," Neil said. He looked at the door before him and shrugged. "I would unlock it for you, only no one has been able to get through this door since the last Royal Thief." He tried the handle to prove it to her and then shrugged again. "I am told that getting into your room will be another test. If you can't get in, you are instructed to head home."

Ahh, to be loved and wanted, Ilis thought ruefully. She knelt before the lock.

"I'll get in."

She pulled out two hairpins and stuck them into the lock, feeling around. When Neil continued to stand behind her, she added, "Three words to watch."

"Did you ever wonder why the Basileians of old decided to name our currency after marks of literature?" Neil asked. His voice was soft and thoughtful. When Ilis busied herself with the lock and ignored him, he continued, "I mean, think about it, it does not take seven letters to make a word in real life, so why make it so in our currency?"

Ilis turned around and eyed the young man before her.

"They say seven is the number of completion. Perhaps they hoped it would be a mark of favor. And even if that math is off, letters do make up words; words do make up sentences; and sentences, paragraphs; and paragraphs, books; so at least that much was true."

Neil shrugged, but there was a glimmer in his eye that Ilis could not decipher.

Ilis raised an eyebrow. "So, you paying or leaving?"

With a light chuckle, Neil was gone, leaving the lantern with her.

Ilis twirled her lock picks once more around the insides of the lock before confirming her suspicions. It was fake, with no locking mechanisms to unlock. Standing, Ilis brushed off her dress and removed her makeshift glowstone torch from her left stocking. Ilis had made it herself from four triangular pieces of mirror attached to a hilt with a glowstone sitting in the middle of the mirror pieces. When not in use, the mirror pieces could be folded inward to form a pyramid that concealed the glow and then simply unfolded again when one wanted to magnify the glow of the small glowstone. Glowstone was a rock of high value on the seas, known for its mystic ability to glow without any power source.

Opening the window, Ilis shone the glowstone torch outside to take in her surroundings. The tower was built in the ordinary stone and mortar of most of the castle mountain, which meant there was just enough room in between stones for her small feet to climb.

Sticking the glowstone torch between her teeth, Ilis swung herself out of the window and climbed around the tower. Being careful where she placed her feet, Ilis scaled around the tower until she reached the window of the Royal Thief's room. She shone the glowstone torch at the window and found it locked from the inside with a large chain.

Craning her neck, Ilis could see what appeared to be a rope hanging down from the tower's roof. She climbed over to it and gave it a good tug. While it did feel pretty old, it seemed to hold under her weight. Sticking her glowstone torch back in her stocking, Ilis climbed until she was right under the roofing and needed the rope to pull herself over. Grabbing the rope in her fist, Ilis began to pull herself up. The rope creaked under her weight. Just as she was almost up, the rope snapped, and Ilis found herself falling.

CHAPTER FIVE

Ilis grabbed the side of the roof, but barely.

She could feel her fingers slipping. Instinct kicked in, and Ilis swung. Just as she lost her grip, she propelled herself through the window below. Glass and wood shattered around her in a deafening crash.

She found herself lying on a wooden floor, staring up at the dark ceiling. Lying there, she took a few deep breaths, just like Captain had taught her: one to clear the senses, one to clear the nerves, and one to think of something witty to say.

"Smashing entrance," Ilis muttered.

Sitting up, she pulled her glowstone torch from her stocking. From its soft glow, Ilis took note of herself and her surroundings.

She had a good gash on her left arm, but nothing that seemed to require stitches, though landing so did make the lashes on her back burn anew. Beneath her was a burnt orange woolen carpet that was now covered with glass and wooden splinters. The roof above her was peaked, in typical tower fashion, and there was a ladder built into the east side of the room leading to a hatch door (which must have been what the rope led to).

The walls were lined with books. In fact, as Ilis surveyed the room, pretty much all of the room was . . . books. *Typical Basileian,* Ilis thought. There was a large table in the middle of the small room, covered with maps (and open books of course); a chair poised by one of the bookshelves (as if someone short had needed it to reach the higher shelf); a grandfather clock facing north; a washbasin tucked in a corner; and two long chests, one sitting on the east side and the other the west—but other than that, it was all books.

Ilis stood and brushed her fingers against the leather bindings, breathing in the scent. There were the factual: *The Butterbumble: A History of the Evolution of the Butterfly and the Bumblebee*, *The War of the Nymphs and the Dryads*, *101 Uses for a Unicorn's Horn*, *The Woodland Penguins: Who Are They and Where Are They Now?*, *How to Speak Eagalinez*, *The Fate of Mad King Isten*, and *A Natural History of Forest Whales*.

The mythical tales, too, had their place on the shelves: *Elephants and Other Beasts of Folklore*, *The Myth of Electricity*, *Visiting Outer Space*, and *The Moon: Fabled King of the Night*. Ilis's eyes landed upon *Living Upside Down: The Biography of an Underling*—at which Ilis snorted, knowing by its title that it must have been written by an Upperlander.

After taking in her new room, Ilis moved to lie down on the bed, only to realize that there was none.

"What, don't Royal Thieves sleep?" Ilis said to herself.

Glowstone torch in hand, Ilis moved to the door which had given trouble to all who had attempted to open it. She laughed out loud when she saw how it was locked.

The locking mechanism was near the floor and seemed to be activated by a simple press.

Ilis opened the door and let it close behind her with a click. Standing before the door which no one had been able to unlock in years, Ilis pressed the left bottommost part of the door with the tip of her boot. There was a click, and the door swung open. With a smirk, Ilis grabbed the lantern and sauntered into her room.

As she reentered, her eyes landed on something hanging from the rafters.

"Oh. My. Stars," Ilis exclaimed. "Whoever you were, Royal Thief, I love you!"

Above her head hung a hammock.

***

It was a knock that woke her.

Ilis had climbed into the hammock and fallen asleep before even changing out of her dress. Squinting in the light of the Sun, she wondered what time it was. Since the Sun rose around two in the morning nowadays, judging by its placement it looked like it was around six or seven in the morning. One glance at the clock confirmed it.

She swung from her hanging bed and landed on the floor with a thump and some crunching. Eyeing the glass still on the floor, she made a mental note to try and track down a broom.

Ilis opened the door to find a gaggle of girls in front of it. She suddenly wondered at the state of her hair. With all the smoothness of a thief, she reached up and found it at least mostly respectable—only to remember that she was still in her gown from last night.

Ilis lifted her chin and dared the girls to comment on her wrinkled gown.

"We heard there was a new girl on the mountain," spoke a blonde with a smile that didn't seem to reach her eyes. She stood in front, with a brunette right beside her.

"So we thought we would come and introduce ourselves," finished the brunette, her voice delicately high-pitched. The three girls who stood behind them all nodded.

"I'm Dianne of the Understanding Tribe," said the blonde who had spoken first. Dianne reached out her hand, but Ilis just stared at it. She wasn't here to make friends, and she wasn't sure these girls were the type she wanted to be friends with anyway.

After a pause that had every potential for being awkward, Ilis smiled and shook the hand offered to her, deciding that friends might come in handy at some point.

"Ilis, Royal Thief of Basileia."

Dianne chuckled. "I heard you were a cocky one." Her eyes darted up and down Ilis, no doubt taking in the wrinkled ball gown with glass still lining its hem. "Crown Prince Magnus said you were still in training, so I wouldn't go brandishing that fancy title just yet. One would hate to think *you* brash."

The other girls chittered behind her. Ilis couldn't help thinking that these girls reminded her of a flock of birds—the kind that wake you up before you want to be awake and try and sing to you when all you want is silence.

Deciding that she would be better off without these girls as friends after all, Ilis gave a curt nod.

"Well, nice to meet you, but I should go get ready." Ilis put on a very fake smile. "I would hate to be late for my first day of class."

Dianne put on her own fake smile. "We would be glad to wait for you to . . . clean yourself up," she said, with yet another long look at Ilis's gown. "We were on our way to the dining hall now. We would be delighted to show you the way."

Ilis blinked. "I think I'll pass." With a wave, she said, "See you in class!" and shut the door in their faces.

As soon as the door clicked closed, Ilis shook the smile from her face and groaned. She had heard about the Understanding Tribe, as they were called, but they were even worse in person!

Understanders were the type of people who rose to power because of their heritage, not because of their own achievements. Their blood gifted them with a phenomenal memory as well as the ability to tell when people were lying. Understanders did not easily forget any words spoken to them. Knowledge is power, and with their memory, the Understanders had lots of knowledge.

A shiver ran down Ilis's back as she thought of the power Understanders held in Basileia. They might be powerful allies, but were they worth the snobbery she had seen in Dianne? However, on the flip side, they would be terrible enemies.

Eyeing the chests in her room, Ilis hoped the former Royal Thief had some spare clothes her size; if not, she was going to have to go out and swipe some. Popping open the chest on the western wall, Ilis was not surprised to find an assortment of weapons, spyglasses, and other tools. While her fingers itched to try out her new finds, she told herself there wasn't time.

She tried the chest on the east wall and was relieved to find it stocked to the brim with dresses. She lifted one up, only to find it almost perfectly her size.

"It's a little long, but other than that!" Ilis said aloud in awe. She almost wondered if the prince had found a way to put them up here but dismissed the thought when she had to shake out a layer of dust from the dress.

So the last Royal Thief was female, she thought with satisfaction. Filing this information away for future use, she decided to ask around for more information about her predecessor.

The dress was a dark amber. It would need a few adjustments, but it was good enough for today. Ilis scanned the room for a mirror.

After a bit of rummaging, she had a mirror up and was doing her hair in a bun as many of the other girls on the mountain did. Today, she intended to blend in and not draw any more attention to herself than necessary. She would go to the academy, pass whatever tests the prince threw her way, and look for the location of the Crown Jewel. Simple as swordplay.

Ilis figured she had a pretty good shot at finding the Crown Jewel now that she was here . . . though perhaps she wouldn't get close enough until she was officially the Royal Thief. But she figured she had a pretty good shot at making Royal Thief . . . as long as they didn't find out that she was a pirate . . . more specifically, one who had connections with the Under, Basileia's most feared enemies—never mind that those connections were not pleasant ones.

Ilis had to swallow her nerves at the thought. She could just feel the wood around her neck, locking her in place on the chopping block . . . but that wouldn't happen . . . not again. She rubbed the scar on the back of her neck. Not if she kept her identity a secret and made her skills of value to the king—or the prince, she supposed, since she was his birthday gift.

She groaned at the thought.

Ilis gave the room one more glance in search of some sort of bag. The guards had confiscated her last one. Her eyes landed on a leather satchel leaning against one of the table's legs. Snatching it up, she threw in the prince's trinkets and dashed down the stairs in search of breakfast.

She scampered down the steps of the tower, back out into the blazing light of the morning, hiked the steps that traced up and around the mountain to the front of Oros Academy, and entered through the main entrance.

She passed through the foyer of Oros Academy, whose walls were unsurprisingly lined with books, and made her way toward the dining hall. Due to the smells wafting through the halls, it was not hard to find; due to the sea of faces, it was not hard for Ilis to slip in, grab some food, and slip out.

Breakfast roll in hand, Ilis strolled through the halls of Oros Academy, looking for Professor Owlistare's classroom. After passing through two stories' worth of classrooms, as well as finishing off her breakfast, she finally found it and was still a half hour early.

With silent footfalls, she slipped through the classroom door and scanned the area. Looking for the exits, she found three options: the wooden door in the side wall at the front of the room through which she had entered, another door on the opposite wall, and several high windows at the back of the room.

The seats rose higher in the back of the classroom and curved around so that each seat faced the center where the professor would stand. Ilis thought this room seemed more like an auditorium than a classroom, but perhaps that was the intent. Either way, the windows in the back would be a challenge to slip out of unnoticed—but it was a challenge Ilis felt she could manage under the right circumstances.

In the front of the classroom, toward which all of the seats were facing, sat a large wooden desk with ornate carvings along each of its four legs. Ilis stepped closer and knelt down, running her finger along the carvings, finding them to be vines with small berries growing on the stems. She let out a little huff of wonder at the sight. Rarely had she seen something as commonplace as a desk with carvings of such detail. Pondering this, Ilis wondered what sort of professor would care so deeply about his workplace—as this was clearly an item of great expense.

To the right of the desk sat a wastebasket. It was mostly empty except for a sheet of paper noting various meetings for the upcoming week.

Behind the desk sat a black chalkboard, which had left a light dusting of chalk upon the stone floors. A clock ticked steadily from its perch to the right of the chalkboard.

Her eyes landed on the door opposite to the one she had entered, curious as to what lay behind it. A glance at the clock told her she still had plenty of time. Ilis looked back at the wooden door she had come through and then at the other door. They were the same size and structure, only the one at the far end of the room had been painted a very foreboding shade of black.

Crossing the room to the black door, Ilis placed her ear against it and listened for any sounds of movement. Hearing nothing, she tried the handle and found it locked. A sly grin grew upon her lips. Pulling two pins from her hair, she inserted them into the lock, fiddled around for a moment, and lifted her chin as the door swung open. Almanzo would be proud.

Peering into the darkness, Ilis removed her glowstone torch from her stocking and shone it down the corridor. It was long, and the air was musty. Bending down, she swept a finger across the floor, finding a thick layer of dust.

Curiosity piqued, she closed the door behind her to explore the hall, following its downward slope. Not even her new satchel made a noise as it rubbed against her side with each step. She grinned at the attention to detail of her predecessor.

Soon she reached a fork in the tunnel. Though all she wanted to do was explore further, she opted to head back to class so she could claim her seat and study the other students as they arrived. And thus, she retreated from the mysterious tunnels as silently as she had come, bidding them goodbye—but only until she could escape again to search them further after class.

Thankfully, not even the professor had arrived in the classroom yet, so she was able to reenter without being noticed. Assuming the confidence of a pirate, she ascended the eight rows of seats to hide in her perch.

As the other students began to enter, Ilis remained blissfully unnoticed by her fellow classmates. Over a hundred students meandered into the room, their voices crowding the space comfortably. As Ilis looked around, she found that young people from every tribe were represented.

The Moving Tribe, the feet of the body of Basileia, were mainly soldiers. The Moving Tribe distinguished themselves by their strong build and their strut that made them look like they already had a row of medals on their chest. Ilis spotted the redheaded soldier who had brought her the pale and unused dress yesterday. She decided to do her best to stay away from him.

The Understanding Tribe were mostly diplomats in training. They wore light-colored robes with draping sleeves and seemed to float as they walked, as if the ground were too simple a thing to bother with. Dianne and her friends entered with lifted chins and sat down with their other classmates of this tribe.

The Speaking Tribe held two main tracks: public speakers and animal speakers. Public speakers were dressed in vibrant colors, such as orange and purple, while those who possessed the talent of speaking with animals were dressed in browns and calmer colors. For both tracks, the girls had their hair loosely braided, while the boys' hair hung long and was tied back by a simple leather cord.

The Serving Tribe, the hands of the body of Basileia, had several tracks. There were the inventors (who rattled as they walked because of the gears in their pockets), the honorable scribes (with their ink-stained hands and prestigious duties, such as making copies of the Great Books and recording the history of the kingdom), and the cooks (who smelled of mouthwatering spices).

The Hearing Tribe were known as Foresters, as they were the ears in the forest and lowlands. They often served as soldiers to the king or peacekeepers in local towns and villages. They were a quiet lot who knew the land well and were deadly with a bow and arrow. Ilis saw Neil, the Forester attendant who had shown her to her room, sitting in the front row with a stack of papers in his lap. It almost looked as if he were assisting in teaching—which would make sense, as he seemed to be a good few years older than the rest of the class; though why a Forester would be assisting any class was beyond her. That seemed oddly out of his expertise.

The Feeling Tribe, the beating heart of Basileia, were enrolled either in the medical field or as bookkeepers, working with the Serving Tribe to organize Basileia's library—a great feat, considering every member of the kingdom was required by law to write at least one book in their lifetime. Most of the time, these books were kept in the family, the wisdom of the elders being preserved and passed down to future generations. But those whose works were more prestigious had to be hand copied to be kept in the Oval Library. This was the work of the Feeling and Serving Tribes.

The Seeing Tribe provided most of the scouts and guards, as their phenomenal eyesight enabled them to see leagues away. It was said that, with their astounding peripheral vision, they might as well have eyes in the back of their head. Many of the Seeing Tribe also ended up being teachers and counselors in their old age, as all they saw gave them valued wisdom.

Just before class, the young blonde nurse who had given her the dragon's blood slipped in and took a seat beside the redheaded soldier. Ilis turned from the pair to Neil and Dianne and wondered if it was just a coincidence that the handful of people who had interacted with her as of yet were all in her class.

Then through the doorway strolled Professor Owlistare. Conversations ceased mid-sentence, the rustling of papers and scuffling of shoes stopped as students froze and stealthily slid into their seats, and suddenly the only thing Ilis could hear was the clock ticking on the wall. Ilis turned to inspect this professor who demanded such respect without ever opening his mouth.

He was a tall, elderly man with a slight hunch—as if he had carried too many burdens over the years. His beard was stark white and so long and typical for a professor it seemed almost out of place. If his name had not already given it away, his purple-hued eyes confirmed his Tribe: Seeing Tribe. Ilis dismissed any hope of escaping through the back windows unnoticed. But his eyes were soft and not sharp, an oddity for one of the Seeing Tribe. He wore a long light-purple robe with a silver rope belted around his waist, and he seemed to walk with a grace about him, almost as if the ground had no hold on him.

He took a seat at his desk, pulled out a pair of spectacles, and began looking over his notes. Still, not a lick of sound came from the classroom. Ilis looked around in awe. This was an obedience that did not come from stern lectures; this was an obedience that came from love.

Ilis leaned back in her chair, comfortable with her assessment of her classmates and professor. Before the professor had entered, all the students seemed satisfied with their own group of friends, so there was little danger of being noticed. She felt invisible and loved the feeling, as being invisible when she wanted to was something she prided herself in.

Then the prince walked in.

He shattered the beautiful silence by apologizing to the professor for being late with some excuse about national security and then scanned the classroom. Ilis wondered briefly why the prince would be in the same class as her, but her thoughts were cut short.

The prince saw her and grinned smugly. Ilis's heart dropped.

Here was the only one capable of shattering her invisibility. He passed by seven rows of seats—all of which had plenty of good seating options— and plopped down right next to her.

Every eye in the room settled on the new girl in the back who, suddenly, was starkly visible.

"Hey, Pirate," the prince said, loudly enough for all to hear.

His words simultaneously sparked two very different emotions in her. One, a grief for the life she had lost. She could no longer claim the title of "pirate." That title was a thing of the past. Its absence ached like a real wound.

The second was fear. For the second time that day, Ilis had that vivid picture of herself on the guillotine. Surely, he didn't know . . .

Did he?

The prince spread his books out before him. "I thought you would have the decency to return all that stuff you stole from me, but I suppose that was too much for me to expect from you." He grinned at her.

The grin confirmed it; he was just teasing. No way a prince would grin so at a pirate. No way he would grin so if he knew what she had done.

Princes beheaded the likes of her, and she knew it. The fact that they whipped her just to appease the crown prince proved it.

Whether he was plotting her death or not, all Ilis wanted to do was knock the air out of him who dared to tease her so. She barely had the self-control not to. Instead, she settled for glaring at the professor, desperately hoping that he would start talking and get all of the students' eyes off of her.

But the gray-haired man was writing something on the board, and the students seemed very comfortable staring at her now. The prince kept chatting on and on to her about the expectations that were upon her now that she was attempting to be the new Royal Thief. All the rest of the class was respecting the professor by keeping quiet; why could the prince not show the same respect? Ilis rubbed the scar on the nape of her neck, feeling frustrated at the weight of all the stares.

". . . I mean, stealing things from the prince you need to impress and not giving them back is just bad form!"

Finally, Ilis spun and glared at the prince. She lowered her voice and tried to control her words.

"For the record, I *tried* to give you back all your trinkets." She pointed a finger at him. "*You* left."

"I did not leave. I simply headed back to the king's side, as is customary. Leaving would imply marching out a door . . . or climbing out of a window, perhaps."

Ilis thought of her escapade to the mountain cliff after the dance. She suddenly didn't care if she was beheaded; she was insulted by his insinuation.

"Did you have me followed?"

The professor cleared his throat, and the prince whispered, "Hey, stop being so disruptive. Some of us want to learn."

Ilis stared down at the professor, seething.

CHAPTER SIX

As soon as class let out, Ilis jumped from her seat and rushed out the door. The prince shouted her name, but she pretended not to hear it, disappearing amid the throng of students.

No one noticed the new girl who slipped through crowds and made a fast exit through the nearest window. In Ilis's opinion, windows were doors that only the sly and bold dared to use.

She knelt on the roof with her back against the wall of Oros Academy, looking out toward the mountain range beyond. Just past the peaks of the mountains she could see Elgrave Forest, where forest whales swam through the treetops. She wished she were facing the real ocean.

Stars, but she missed the sea. She found tears brimming in her eyes at the thought. Closing her eyes, she pictured the home she had cut herself off from. She could just feel the ship rocking beneath her feet, smell the salty sea air, and hear her crew's rambunctious laughter. All the things she would never again partake in.

She let out a breath and quickly wiped her tears. Now was not the time to be homesick.

Shaking her head to clear her thoughts, she scanned the area. From her current vantage point, she could just barely see the edge of the barracks to her left. Other than that, it was buildings stacked upon each other, little paths winding around the mountainside and through the buildings.

She wondered how the people were able to live up here, so crowded together. Houses were stacked side by side in between businesses and stables and everything else that the mountain needed. Sure, it was a strategic military move to have the capital of your country located on the tallest and largest mountain this side of the Edge; but when that meant you were always on top of each other, was it worth it?

She preferred the open sea, herself.

When she deemed she had given even the slowest of students time to vacate the classroom, Ilis hopped back through the window and slipped into her classroom to explore the hidden tunnel. Now knowing the lock, she hardly had to think in order to pick it and slip through the doorway. She followed her footprints by the light of her glowstone torch to the fork in the tunnel and decided to stay left.

After traveling for about fifteen minutes with her glowstone lighting up the dank stone walls, Ilis realized why they had sealed this place off. Already, she had passed a dozen different intersections, some with as many as five different paths to choose from.

One could get lost in here for a lifetime—a fact proven by the finding of an entire skeleton and several scattered bones along the trail. She kept her path by running her hand upon the left side and taking every left. When she needed to go back, she would merely retrace her steps by staying right.

A few more minutes of exploration led her to a small square door with a brass handle. Ilis tried the knob and it swung open easily, revealing a hallway with white marble floors and open windows. She stepped out into the sunlight, and the door slammed closed behind her. When Ilis turned back, the wall looked just like all the other walls with the exception of a small C carved near the floor.

Musing over her discovery, Ilis wondered where she had ended up. Her eyes scanned the smooth stone walls around her . . . Smooth stone walls which were used in multiple parts of Mount Oros.

She had no idea where she was.

Mentally, she retraced her footsteps in the tunnels. She could have traveled leagues or wandered in circles a mere hundred paces.

Great, Ilis, she thought, bemused. *Way to narrow down your options.* With silent footfalls, Ilis stepped toward the windows. Had her eyes not been hungry for hints at her location, the view would have been breathtaking. The window looked down on the mountain capital of Basileia. She spotted the roof of Oros Academy.

Hearing footsteps behind her, Ilis pivoted to find the prince standing in the middle of the hallway with that silly coy grin on his face—and her satchel over his shoulder.

Inwardly, Ilis gasped. He had stolen her satchel? And she hadn't even noticed?

Outwardly, she tried to look bored.

"Okay, now this whole following me thing is getting creepy," Ilis said, crossing her arms.

"Did you just call the royal prince of Basileia 'creepy'?" the prince asked, in mock astonishment.

"Would you prefer I called you a thief? Because if you don't give me my satchel back, you will be living up to both titles well."

The prince bowed and handed her the satchel. "For the record, I stole nothing. You merely left it in class, and I *did* try and call you as you fled the room."

Ilis chastised herself. She was normally more careful than this. What was it about this prince that made her thoughts feel muddled?

Opening the satchel, Ilis pulled out the prince's watch, medals, and button. She offered them to him.

"Here," she said simply, avoiding eye contact.

The prince laughed. "Keep them. I rather like having you in my debt."

Ilis's eyes locked with his, sharper than the dagger hidden in her boot.

The prince, however, seemed immune to her glares. He held out his arm. "May I escort you to dinner?"

Ilis stood stock-still and mentally ran through the ramifications of saying no to a prince. For the third time that day, she saw herself being led up the stairs to the guillotine . . .

This was getting morbid.

Letting out a sharp breath, Ilis accepted his arm. She didn't enjoy being at someone else's mercy. They walked down the polished stone corridor together—his boots squeaking, hers making not a sound.

"So, enjoying the more hidden levels of our beloved mountain capital?" the prince asked.

Ilis shook her head. "Again, creepy! Be honest: are you following me?"

The prince smirked. "No, not creepy." He pointed to her shoes, which were covered in the gray dust of the tunnels. "Just observant."

Ilis looked at the prince with a bit more respect . . . but just a bit.

"So . . . you know about the tunnels?" Ilis asked, her curiosity getting the best of her.

"Of course." He looked offended that she even had to ask. "They stretch throughout the entire mountain."

"For what purpose?" Ilis asked.

The prince looked at her and smiled. "Oh, none at all! Or, at least, not to begin with. They are the remains of burrows dug by the stone gophers which used to live in the mountain." He scratched his chin, thinking. "Since then, we have widened the ones of use and blocked off those that lead to the maze of tunnels. The Library and Oros Academy's kitchen and dining room are examples of tunnels that have been widened."

They walked arm in arm past a set of guards into a formal dining room, in which sat the royal family. Ilis slid to a stop, inadvertently pulling the prince with her.

The prince chuckled. "Just realizing what level you ended up on?"

Ilis tried to control the heat rising in her cheeks. She was above the academy. The only level above the academy was . . . the palace.

Ilis swallowed, offered a fake smile to the prince, and shrugged her discomfort off, reminding herself who she was: a pirate of *Maribor*, fiercest pirates of the Swallow Seas.

Or . . . at least, she had been. The pang of sorrow hit yet again.

"Malcolm," the middle prince called from across the room, "is this the Royal Thief you've been telling me all about? I thought you said she hated you and was avoiding you like we all do?"

Prince Malcolm ignored the snide comment and said, "Ilis, I believe you have already met my father as well as Magnus." The crown prince lifted his chin but kept his eyes on his food. "However, I don't believe you have met Jasper yet."

Prince Jasper laid down his utensils, stood up, and greeted Ilis with a slight bow. "It is a pleasure."

Prince Malcolm led Ilis to a seat by his own at the grand table. A place at the table was hastily prepared for her by a servant. She took one look at the array of silverware and regretted not paying more attention to Ember's lessons on finery.

"I shouldn't be here." Ilis stated the obvious.

"Too late to run now, *Pirate*."

Ilis stared down at her plate as servants piled it with food, her appetite gone. It was a feast unlike any she had ever eaten, the only exceptions being a few she had managed to steal. But the food was not the problem; it was the company that worried her. Ilis bit her tongue, trying to remind it not to get her into trouble.

She glanced at the king, who acknowledged her with a slight tilt of the head, and then to the crown prince who continued to keep his focus on his food. The memory of the lashings flooded her brain and she felt her chest tighten. The occupants in this room may not be as skilled with a sword as pirates, but they were no less deadly.

"Where are you from, Ilis?" Jasper asked.

"The seas," Prince Malcolm answered before Ilis could.

Ilis glared at the prince, wondering if he was a bigger threat than her own tongue.

"My father is a merchant, so I grew up on his ship," Ilis said, before the young prince could answer for her again.

"Ahh, that would explain your lack of manners," Crown Prince Magnus said blandly.

Ilis took this moment to observe the crown prince in more detail. He had Prince Malcolm's strong chin and green eyes, but his hair was golden blond like his father's. He also held himself with an air that was befitting a prince, whereas Prince Malcolm's air was more befitting a scoundrel. Prince Magnus obviously disliked her, but that was no surprise—she had stolen his crown after all. However, his dislike was something she would have to navigate. She would rather not have the crown prince—and one day king—of Basileia harboring a personal vendetta against her all her life. Such things were rather inconvenient.

Prince Jasper ignored his brother and his rudeness and instead turned to Ilis, curious. "A merchant ship? I've done business with several. I wonder if I know your father."

Ilis cringed inwardly, but looked as cool as a sea breeze while she answered, "We traded wheat for salt with the Sanhildin for many years, which kept us in a steady loop from the valleys to the far shores."

Prince Jasper nodded in understanding, her story being a likely one. "That is a good route, though I admire your courage. I have heard it said that the Sanhildin are a fierce people."

Ilis bowed her head in consent and watched Prince Malcolm to see which fork he used for his salad.

But Prince Jasper was still curious. "Still, I wonder if I met your father. What ship name did you sail under?"

Drat the curious son of a king!

Ilis smiled demurely. *"Naus."* She hated to give such specifics. Specifics could kill an undercover mission.

Prince Malcolm turned to her. "Tell us about the shores. Have they indeed begun to dry up all along the coasts?"

Ilis nodded somberly. The seas of their flat planet had never been too deep, but with the drought, some trading routes were becoming near impossible to pass. "There is talk of abandoning ships entirely as the means of transport around the coast. Soon it will be easier to travel by cart!" Ilis said.

Ilis's brow furrowed at the thought, reminding her of the reason why her mission here was so important. *Maribor* needed seas on which to sail. *Which is why I need the Crown Jewel,* Ilis thought. *Once I have that, I can trade it for their freedom to sail in the Under.*

She inhaled sharply and continued. "But the seas aren't the worst of it, Your Highness. Whole lakes have dried up in the outer lands, along with wells and watering holes. People are being forced inland to escape the heat and find water. And not just people," Ilis said, chewing on the inside of her cheek. "Rumors have it that beasts who have long lay appeased are now waking up again."

Crown Prince Magnus scoffed at this, but Prince Malcolm looked serious.

"What kind of beasts?"

"Sirens, minotaurs, wild griffins, sphinxes . . ." Ilis paused before breathing the last and most feared. "Dragons."

"Oh, come now, child!" said the king, only now bearing in on the conversation. "Yes, reports have come in of beasts having awoken in the outer lands. No one can dispute that. But dragons? The Dragon Age was over a millennia ago, and since then, we have maintained our dominion over all creatures. You cannot expect us to fear an attack of such beasts!"

Ilis lifted her chin, not at all intimidated by the king in all his grandness.

"I do indeed!" she said, only afterward remembering to add a stilted "sir," to her sentence. "We may have done well to banish the dangerous creatures to the uninhabited corners of our land, but in doing so, we have created a great lack of favor in their eyes."

The king laughed at this. "You speak of the beasts as if they had an intelligence through which to bestow favor! What do you suggest we do, find a way to communicate and try to live at peace with them?" The king looked at her and chuckled before returning to his meal. "Ahh, the fancies of youth."

It was not a fancy of youth, and Ilis knew so, having seen with her own eyes a land in which man and "such beasts" lived at peace. But to say so here would put her in more danger than announcing that she was a pirate and not a merchant's daughter.

"Do you think there is someone behind the drought?" the crown prince asked, taking Ilis somewhat seriously for the first time.

"Only if you call the Sun a 'someone,'" Ilis retorted. She took a sip of her drink and watched the different reactions of the princes over the brim of her cup.

Crown Prince Magnus looked oddly somber, Prince Jasper looked slightly amused, and Prince Malcolm looked absolutely intrigued. Though, now that she thought about it, Prince Malcolm had worn a spark of that curious look of interest all through dinner. Ilis mused about trying to be boring just to wipe that look off his face, but decided that her switch in personality would only further his curiosity, which would utterly defeat the point.

"Odd times we live in," said Jasper. "To live in the age that has seen our days grow and our nights shrink . . . Remind me, when did the shift begin, exactly?"

"The same year your mother died," the king said. He gazed out the window in thought. "That was a terrible year."

Ilis tried to remember what her father had told her about the queen's death. If her memory served her right, the youngest prince had been only a year old.

"Some say the world began to die that year," Prince Malcolm said. Ilis watched as the king tensed and the crown prince scowled.

"The world is not dying," Magnus said. "The tragedies we have seen are clearly the works of the Under."

"You truly think that the Under has the power to move the Sun and scorch our lands?" Ilis asked.

"But of course!" defended Magnus. "Why do you think we have devoted our military and funds toward stopping the Under?"

This took Ilis by surprise. "Well, I suppose I did not know that you were doing so."

The king let out a long sigh at his son's words. But Magnus did not stop. "Our full strategy is not commonly known, but I will tell you this: we are doing everything within our power to stop the Under and save our land. They are the reason our world is ending and they *will* pay."

Ilis rubbed the nape of her neck, her thoughts spinning.

"Ilis, what are you thinking?" Prince Malcolm asked.

"That you all are fools! The Under is not the problem! It is the Sun we should be trying to stop, and if something is not done about it, this generation could very well be Basileia's last," Ilis said before thinking. Only after she spoke did she remember whom she was talking to.

One look at the faces of the royal family told her that, this time, she had gone too far.

All three of the princes lowered their heads and did not make eye contact with her. The king slowly pushed back his chair and stood.

Oh, drat her tongue which spoke before she thought! And drat Prince Malcolm for luring her into such a sticky topic! Her cocky self would get her killed if she wasn't careful.

"What would you suggest we do, all-knowing lass?" the king asked, staring her down sternly.

Ilis bowed her head and tried to take on her most humble posture. "Your Highness, I apologize . . ."

The king cut her off. *"Answer the question."* His voice was firm, unyielding. "Do you suggest we fly to the Sun, talk to it, and earn its favor, as you would have us do with the beasts?"

The king spit out his words, and Ilis realized her fault too late. She had insinuated that the Sun would continue on its destructive course unless the kingdom interfered. What could mere men do to change the course of the Great Light?

"No, Your Majesty," Ilis said, head still bowed. "Forgive my foolishness."

CHAPTER SEVEN

Few words were spoken the rest of the dinner. When the final course was finished, the king stood.

"Young thief," he said, "I'd watch my tongue if I were you. It might earn you more lashings than your quick fingers." And with that, he left the room.

The crown prince looked Ilis over disdainfully before following his father. Prince Jasper gave her an encouraging smile upon his exit—and then it was just Ilis and Prince Malcolm.

Ilis knew she should excuse herself, but instead, she just sat there. She felt like she was watching her plan crumble before her eyes. Already, her tongue had made her the enemy of more than one royal and put her ruse on treacherous ground. If they found out who she truly was, it would be a quick trip to the guillotine—and there would be no crew to save her like last time.

Perhaps it was true. Perhaps all her feats were just the work of the crew. Perhaps all her harebrained schemes only succeeded because she had help. Perhaps she should have just stayed on *Maribor* and never attempted any of this. Though perhaps her crew didn't need her to begin with. Perhaps she didn't even contribute to them. Perhaps they truly were better off without her. Thoughts continued to spiral through her head, none of them pleasant.

Prince Malcolm cleared his throat. Ilis realized she had been staring at the table for longer than was proper. She stood, straightened her dress, and said, "Thank you for dinner, but let's not do that again."

"Ilis," the prince said. He paused. "Never mind."

Ilis curtsied and made her exit. Now that she knew where she was, she chastised herself for not picking up on her location sooner. Remembering the glass in her room, she snagged a broom from a closet as she passed through the halls. It was a long walk, so she had plenty of time to think over the day.

Ilis wondered at herself. First the prince had stolen her bag from underneath her nose (either that or she had left her bag at her chair, and Ilis wasn't sure which was more embarrassing). Then she had failed to realize what level she was on, which had landed her right in the royal dining room. And finally, her tongue had run off and brought her plan to the verge of collapse. What had happened to careful Ilis? Her brain felt fuzzy . . . What was this?

Maybe she was just tired. Or maybe her thoughts were confused with the loss of her crew. Maybe there was something in the mountain air.

Or maybe it was the prince. Perhaps he was somehow affecting her thoughts; she did seem to have a harder time concentrating when he was near. That thought frustrated her. She began pushing away the emotions that bubbled up along with it. *Stay focused,* Ilis said to herself.

By the time she got back to her room, she was frustrated with herself and with the prince who seemed to be a blockade to her mission. She leaned with her back against the door and tried to clear her thoughts. Letting out a frustrated sigh, she focused on taking three steady breaths.

One. Two. Three.

"First day of class completed, hidden tunnels found, and my reputation with the royal family nearly ruined—what a fantastic first day," Ilis said with ire. The tension in her shoulders releasing, she gripped her broom, determined to clean up her mess from last night's smashing entrance. And while she swept, she began to plot.

She would not give in to despair. All was not lost . . . yet. No one had figured out who she was, and she could still prove herself. There was still time! Just maybe a little less time than she had thought . . .

When her floor was cleared of all debris, she ventured back out into the hot world and made her way to the Oval Library. In the glaring Sun, the large Oval Window did not glow but instead reflected the Sun's brilliance. It was more than a mere window, being almost too bright to look at and stunningly beautiful as always.

Before entering the Oval Library, Ilis paused to look upon the world of Mount Oros. It was so different from her home on the seas, whose height came only in waves and swells and whose ground was always shifting beneath her feet. Deep in thought, Ilis watched different people walk about her.

A girl of the Speaking Tribe, dressed in gray with a pale pink sash around her hips, walked along while singing a cheerful tune. A young inventor of the Serving Tribe, with mismatched socks, scruffy hair, and a shirt which was not properly tucked in, ran past her in a hurry, a gear or two falling out of his pockets as he ran. Ilis smiled at his blatant disregard of others' approval—but her smile faltered as she found herself locking eyes with a purple-eyed man standing on guard down the street. Ilis bowed her head to the man of the Seeing Tribe and hastily escaped into the Oval Library and out of his gaze.

Despite the fact that, for once, she hadn't been doing anything wrong, she never found it pleasant to be under the watchful gaze of anyone from the Seeing Tribe.

As Basileians loved books above all else, Ilis hoped to find something of use regarding the Crown Jewel in one of their many literary bindings. The Crown Jewel was a mystery of legendary proportions among pirates. No pirate knew where the Crown Jewel was held, or even what the Crown Jewel was. All that was known among pirates was that it was a prize unlike any other.

Myths about the Crown Jewel were abundant upon the seas. Some said the Crown Jewel bestowed powers upon the one who held it; some claimed that it was a fairy who granted wishes; others held that it was the source of gravity. Ilis could hear Ulrich warning her, "Steal the Crown Jewel, me lass, and you just might fall into the sky!"

But no one knew the truth behind the Crown Jewel. So, with purpose in her steps, Ilis slid into the Oval Library to do some research.

Passing once again through the panels in the window, Ilis was surprised to find that the room in which the ball had been held not long ago was much the same. The dais and thrones still sat where they had been, the white banners still draped down from the banisters, and the room was still lit with a magnificent glow. The only difference was the obvious lack of a crowd.

Ilis decided she rather liked it this way—empty, somber, and full of not-forgotten memories. Her footsteps echoed softly as she walked over the marble floor.

Over by the far wall, Ilis spotted a young attendant, perhaps twelve years old, with a trolley of books. The girl—who was of the Feeling Tribe, if Ilis could guess—searched the walls of shelves to restore each book to its rightful home.

Ilis ventured toward her. "Excuse me, miss, but I am new to the capital and was wondering if you could help me."

The girl beamed as if she was born for this moment. "But of course! How may I be of service?"

Her response proved it: she was of the Feeling Tribe.

Ilis let her eyes wander to the halls stocked with books. "How do you find a book on a specific topic?"

The girl nodded, her short brown hair bobbing around her shoulders. "Excellent question! All of our books are categorized by subject fields. Then each subject field has its own hall, and each hall is sorted by date of publication."

With a soft, gleaming look in her eyes, she continued, "There was a great debate over how to categorize them back when Mount Oros was being built. Some thought an author's works should always be kept together, but with so many authors, this proved a difficult task. Therefore, it was decided that they would be organized by topic and then date. However, if you wished to see the entirety of an author's works, one would just consult the Author's Concordance. Each Topic Section has multiple Concordances: one for authors, one for book titles, one for subject matters within the specific field, one for locations mentioned, one for themes talked about, and a few others which I won't mention. My friend Cepher is trying to get them to add one for historical events, for there are many books not housed in the Hall of History that shed light on our history. But to add an additional Concordance would be such a task! I mean, think of the work! Having to go through each of these books and monitor which ones mention historical events!"

The girl paused and cocked her head. "Am I boring you?" She gasped, somehow reading the truth off of Ilis's face, which was devoid of emotion. "I am! Oh, forgive me! Here I am just gabbing away, when you probably have things to do." She thrummed her fingers along her cart, thinking. "If you tell me what Hall you need, I can point you in the right direction, and then you can consult the Concordances for yourself and find what you are looking for, if that would be of help to you?"

Ilis smiled. "Yes, that would be very helpful."

The girl brightened. "Fantastic! Which Hall are you looking for?"

"Let's start with the History Hall."

The girl nearly squealed with joy. "Oh! What a good one! No surprise, that is Cepher's favorite. Personally, I prefer the Hall of Legends myself, as who is to say those legends are not history, written by the Author of Life, that has just been forgotten! But Cepher is always telling me, 'Kat, you can't live among the myths of lore. History is the real key to unlocking our future.'" The young girl, Kat, caught herself and grimaced. "But there I go rambling again." She sighed. "Forgive me for taking up your time."

She stood up straight as if facing an army officer. "The History Hall is on the third floor to the left. If you start by the Oval Window, you will find the beginning of our History Records, and the further inward you go, the newer the volumes will be. There is a staircase right over there which will take you to the third floor." She pointed to a wooden door over her shoulder and then paused, thinking. "Oh! And Concordances are the large yellow books next to the tables at the start of each hall. You can't miss them." She stopped and beamed as if proud of her performance, and Ilis almost laughed.

Ilis inclined her head gracefully to the young firebrand and said, "Thank you. You have been most helpful. I know who to ask should I need help again."

The girl stared up at Ilis in pure joy. Ilis winked at her and made her way to the wooden door young Kat had pointed out.

On the third floor, Ilis spotted the large yellow volumes Kat had identified as Concordances. She looked over the different massive tomes and shook her head in awe. The Basileians' love for books was almost overwhelming. Heaving the Topic Concordance onto the table, for it must have weighed a good forty pounds, Ilis thumbed through the pages until she came to the words starting with C. She followed the listings down the page and stopped at Crown Jewel. There were various titles beneath the listing, but each one had been blotted out and was now unreadable.

Ilis leaned back in the chair, pondering this. She had always wondered if the general population of Basileia knew the secret of the Crown Jewel. If this were any indication, she supposed not. Someone seemed to have gone to great lengths to keep it all a secret. She tried to think of another search she could use to try and find information on the Crown Jewel but came up with nothing. Pushing the heavy, unhelpful hunk of knowledge called a Concordance back into its rightful place, Ilis stood and decided to do a bit of exploring.

She roamed the levels, heading deeper into the heart of the mountain and trying any doors she came across. Most just led to scriptoriums where men and women alike sat copying works, but some were locked (until the locks met Ilis's lock pick, that is) and led to collections of books kept hidden from the public eye. Ilis scanned the troves of hidden knowledge, finding records of shipments and food orders, and lists of those staffed at Oros Stable. Ilis even found recent records which listed schedules and a large workforce of girls for the laundry of a specific sect of soldiers. Basileians and their nonsensical recording of *everything*!

Ilis spent most of the night this way, sticking her nose in places it was not wanted and learning much of little use. She found herself at the other side of the heart of the mountain just as the Sun was beginning to rise. This exit from the Oval Library was rather plain compared with the grand entrance at the other end. All it had was a large wooden door, twice Ilis's height. With a yawn, Ilis decided it was time to catch a few hours of sleep and sauntered out the small entrance, which let out just above Oros Academy.

Ilis got a full five steps down the stairs when she heard a voice she recognized. She was tired, and the last thing she wanted was a run-in with the youngest prince, so she effectively sidestepped behind a large potted plant.

"Do you think we can trust her?" asked the prince. Ilis peered around her flowering friend and saw it was Neil who was walking by the prince's side.

Are they talking about me? Ilis thought.

"Let's continue to gather more information about her. We would hate to move quickly and ruin years' worth of planning."

Years of planning? It can't be me they are talking about then.

"But we are running out of time! In the outer lands, people are dying!"

Neil paused before the door to the library and put his hand on the prince's shoulder. "Malc, believe me, I know. But as a dear friend once told me, 'There are some things that are too precious to be rushed.'"

And with that, they both entered the library.

Ilis's thoughts spun. *Oh, to be able to solve all the mysteries.*

***

The proposed topic for class the following day was the Under. And frustratingly, the class conversation perfectly depicted the general public's consensus on the Under. Every leading and wise Basileian knew that the Under could not be trusted, and thus, the discussion did not venture far from the well-traveled path of anger and distrust toward the other side of their fair planet.

But whether or not the Under could be trusted—a topic Ilis had rather controversial views on—was not the big subject on her mind.

Instead, her mind was set on finding a way to escape sitting next to the prince. She followed yesterday's routine, getting to class first and choosing her seat high in the back by the windows. Only this time, she tried sitting on the opposite side of the room.

The prince, irritating as ever, followed his routine from the previous day as well: coming in late and then claiming a seat right next to her. She pondered getting up to use the bathroom, but then she would have to ask the prince to move so she could get out, which would mean she would have to talk to him. At the moment, that thought annoyed her enough to make her decide she would just have to wait this one out. Maybe he would leave her alone.

She had yet to forgive him for walking her right into a trap with his family. It was as if he had wanted her to share her views on the delicate topic all along. She pondered what benefit he might find in dirtying her reputation before his family, but came up with nothing. She also pondered the conversation she had overheard the night before, but that didn't make sense either. Was it her they were talking about? If so, why did they need to trust her? And what plan had they been working on for years?

Resigning herself to her fate, she listened back in on the class's conversation. The Under, the other side of their flat planet, was considered by Basileians to be the picture of evil. Royal edict stated that anyone found guilty of affiliation with anything Under-related was to be tortured to death.

Several soldiers-in-training—of the Moving Tribe—were engaged in the usual tirade expected of a mindless soldier: "All the Under is evil, and we should smash the other side of our planet into oblivion."

"Our histories hold records of their abominations! It is said that they would fly through the sky as a pack of ravens, land on the shore and shift forms into a swarm of rats, and then scamper through the army lines, only to shift into the forms of blazing dragons and wipe out entire armies in seconds."

Ilis could not help shaking her head and muttering under her breath, "Of all Basileian senselessness . . ."

Prince Malcolm looked sideways at her and then raised his hand. The teacher saw it, paused the soldier mid-sentence, and said, "Yes, Your Highness?"

The student who had been so rudely silenced turned to look back at them with frustration in his eyes. It was then that Ilis realized this was the same redheaded soldier she had met earlier.

The prince cleared his throat and said, "I think our newest classmate has something to add to this topic."

Ilis's stomach dropped.

Prince Malcolm turned to her. "Go on, Thief."

Ilis looked from the prince to the professor.

The professor's eyes landed upon Ilis, and he smiled kindly. "Ahh yes, the Royal-Thief-in-training herself. Ilis, isn't it? Please, introduce yourself and then enlighten us with your thoughts on the Under debate."

The professor settled back with a curious look in his eyes, awaiting her response, and Ilis's throat suddenly felt like a desert.

Looking over at the prince, she saw him watching her with a grin. Ilis could not believe him. Apparently, he not only wanted to ruin her reputation before his family but also before the entire class. What use was a thief with a ruined reputation? What was his goal here? The king had told her the night before to watch her tongue, and here the prince was leading her into another situation that could cause her ruin.

Ilis looked up at the ceiling, trying to decide if she could sputter words of agreement with the fools in this classroom and thereby go back to being invisible. That would be the wise course of action. That would be the course that would lead to her own self-preservation. She opened her mouth to try . . .

"My name is Ilis, yes."

The prince cleared his throat and tried to nod encouragingly.

The little traitor.

Finding the redheaded soldier whom she had sworn to avoid, and who had just been interrupted by the prince, she said, "The points you made were . . ." *Ilis,* she thought to herself, *you are a fantastic liar. Just lie and go back to being unremarkable so you can finish your heist.*

But the words "good," "valid," and "superb" all made her want to throw up. She looked around at the classroom and felt moved by compassion. They lived on a mountain filled with knowledge, yet what they knew about the Under was false. Could she let them continue to believe that the Under was the epitome of evil?

Ilis dragged her hand down her face and groaned. She made eye contact with the soldier again and shook her head.

"They are old and overused! I mean, come on! At least you could have some original thought, but no—you had to go and repeat the age-old arguments of our grand-paps."

Her audience was stunned to silence, and her tongue had effectively been loosened.

Foolishly, she continued: "You probably believe what you do because of your family's stance on the subject, and they got their beliefs from the fact that the government told them that the Under was the source of all of their troubles." She let out a small laugh. "I, for one, don't believe everything I hear."

Her classmates remained deadly silent, but the young soldier clenched his hand into a fist, his face contorted with a snarl.

"Besides," Ilis continued, "the Under is a land not unlike our own." She spread her hands and addressed all of her classmates. "They have royals and cities and children. They cannot all be evil!"

The young soldier finally lost his patience. "That is absurd! They have been trying to destroy us since our country was formed. We were almost wiped out by them!"

"And they were almost wiped out by us," Ilis retorted.

"That's beside the point," the soldier growled. "Besides, how do you know so much about them? For all we know, they could be monsters who eat their children."

"Chaz, you do realize you just quoted a nursery rhyme, don't you? You are not helping yourself," the blonde nurse-in-training of the Feeling Tribe said with a light laugh.

"Stay out of this, Pyra!" the redheaded soldier, apparently named Chaz, snapped. He glared at Ilis, waiting for a response. "Well, how do you know so much about the Under?"

Ilis shrugged. "I'm a decent thief."

Chaz genuinely looked confused. "What does that have to do with anything?"

Ilis sat back in her seat and scanned the classroom, realizing that her classmates had never known a good thief, much less a pirate. While she knew she should bite her tongue as the king had advised and go back to being unnoticed, she felt they deserved to know more about thieves (and pirates, though she *would* bite off her tongue before admitting that to this crowd).

"My father has a saying," she said. "A—" She caught herself before saying *pirate*. "A . . . thief's greatest loot is information. So we stay in the shadows. We keep our ears to the ground, and we steal what information we can."

Chaz laughed. "And you believe your sources? You are contradicting yourself." He threw his shoulders back, confident that he had seized the victory.

Ilis showed a whisper of a smile and let him think he'd won for a moment before replying, "Who's to say I am not my own source?"

There was a moment of silence before a gasp went through the crowd. It was then that Ilis realized her mistake.

She had just admitted that she had been to the Under.

The gallows sounded nice right about now.

Several of her classmates stared at her, jaws dropping. Most looked at her with hostility, as if she had just admitted to eating children—which, to them, she might as well have.

Ilis opened her mouth to take back her words and then closed it. Her words had already been spoken. Drat her wagging tongue! Drat them all for being things she couldn't fight!

Ilis turned to the prince, knowing he needed only to say the word and all would be forgotten. Instead, he looked quite satisfied with the horror he had walked her into. Why he was so bent on her destruction, Ilis did not know. But she was tired of being his pet. She would escape whatever torture he had planned for her, find what she came here for, and leave. Then it would be the prince's turn to look like a fool.

Just as the professor opened his mouth to pronounce her doom, the prince started to laugh. And not just the small chuckle of one who found something amusing, but a deep laugh that was infectious. Soon other classmates joined in, and Ilis stared around in wonder at the change of mood. They had gone from looking like they wanted to burn her at the stake to laughing at her as if she were the royal jester.

On second thought, Ilis wasn't sure which one she hated more.

Finally, the prince calmed his laughter enough to speak.

"You almost had me there, Ilis!"

She almost didn't catch his wink.

The prince leaned back in his seat and turned to their classmates.

"She almost got you too, didn't she?"

He burst forth into another fit of laughter, which they all joined in.

"To think!" The prince gestured toward Ilis. "That this small tot of a girl could have done what our best warriors have not? Ha!"

The class erupted in a roar of laughter, and it took all Ilis had in her not to punch the prince in the jaw and show him what "this small *tot*" could do!

"Oh, now that's a good one!" The prince wiped a tear from his eye. "She got you too, huh?" he said to the professor. "Why, you looked like you were about to call the guards!"

The professor blinked. "Why, that's because I was!" He turned his attention to Ilis. "I am not sure how it is upon the seas, but here in Basileia, we do not use words lightly. Had you truly been to the Under, I would have been duty bound to turn you in. My allegiance is to the Kingdom of Basileia. I would guard your tongue from such tales."

Ilis swallowed hard and nodded. She had received the same advice two days in a row; maybe if she listened this time, she could live long enough to find the Crown Jewel.

***

It was ten o'clock, the Sun had just set, and Ilis was as awake as ever. She was waiting in her hammock for the full cover of darkness before going on her nightly romp.

Ilis rubbed the back of her neck, trying to forget she had almost been discovered today, trying to forget she was now indebted to the prince, trying to forget that if he spoke a word to his father, she would die a painful death. Instead, she tried to remind herself why she was here: to find the Crown Jewel; to buy back her crew's freedom in the Under; to escape the guilt; to prove herself.

But she had yet to even hear a whisper about the jewel. She let out a groan. The stories about the Crown Jewel being elusive were true. What could warrant hiding something so fantastically? Did that mean it was dangerous? Or beyond precious? Or did it even exist? What if she had come all this way for a myth? That thought sent her into a foul mood.

How was she going to track down something that had no written record of its existence? Normally, she would just go out and ask around for information, but that was how Ulrich had lost his hand. Ilis shuddered at the thought. She needed a plan and she needed one badly.

She fidgeted with her glowstone torch, illuminating the ceiling with its bluish glow. How did one find something when one had no leads? Ilis wracked her brain. She wished she had more connections on the mountain. She wished she had someone to ask for advice. But no; she had set out in painfully deep seas to prove her worth alone.

A knock interrupted her thoughts. Deciding to ignore it, Ilis continued staring at the ceiling, only with more ferocity.

The knocker decided to continue knocking—with even more ferocity.

Ilis slipped her glowstone torch back into her stocking. Swinging down from the hammock, she stormed to the door and swung it open.

"What is it?" she fired, ready to stare daggers at whomever it was.

It was the prince.

Shocker.

Her heart began beating faster in her chest, and Ilis scowled. What was going on with her?

The prince opened his mouth to speak but then thought better. Instead, he offered her a wooden practice sword by the hilt. She took it before thinking, and then he was off—and she was following him.

Why she was following him, she honestly wasn't sure. Perhaps she longed for the excuse to let out some steam. Perhaps it was because she wanted to know if he would rat on her. Or perhaps . . . no, she banished the thought before she fully thought it.

He led her to a clearing in the garden, which was lit by the light of several lanterns along the tall, vine-covered fence. The prince rolled up his sleeves and raised his sword in the ready position, but Ilis just stared at him.

The wooden sword felt foreign in her hand. Her fingers itched for *Dawnbringer*. But her sword was at the bottom of the ocean. She scowled at the emotions that thought brought up.

"What are we doing here?" she snapped.

The prince lowered his sword. "Consider this part of your initiation. Father said he would leave the challenges up to me."

Ilis scoffed. "And facing *you* in a swordfight is one of them?"

The prince's grin at her remark said more to her than any words.

"Just how good a swordsman are you?" Ilis asked, her curiosity piqued.

The prince raised his sword again. "Only the best in the kingdom." And with that, he charged.

Ilis raised her sword in the nick of time, but his blow nearly jarred the weapon out of her hand. She jumped back and curled her lip in a smirk. If he wasn't going to pull his punches, neither would she.

Making no noise on the grass, Ilis charged at the prince, feinting right and then pivoting to the left at the last minute, managing to get in a dirty swipe at his calf in the process. The prince, undaunted, charged at her and nearly tripped her. But Ilis was light on her feet, having been taught by Hawk Lancaster, the Swordmaster of the Sea. He had once made her fight with ropes tangled all around her feet, so the prince's swipe at her ankles was nothing. She sidestepped a few of the prince's strikes and then charged and made a few of her own.

On and on they went, a well-set match. Neither was willing to admit defeat, and so the duel dragged on. Finally, when the prince was just about ready to call it a tie, he saw Ilis drop her guard in an attempt to disarm him. The prince dodged her attempt and plunged his sword right through her guard to her exposed neck, stopping just shy of striking her.

Ilis locked eyes with him with a scowl on her face before admitting defeat and dropping her sword. The prince bent over with his hands on his knees, trying to regain his breath. But when he looked back up, he found Ilis gazing at him with newfound respect.

"You didn't lie," she said simply, averting her gaze. She stared at her sword lying on the ground.

"No, but I thought I was about to give up my title to a girl!" The prince laughed and fell to the ground on his back. He looked up at her. "No disrespect."

"None taken."

The prince continued to look up at her, considering something. "You did it," he said, after a long pause.

Ilis put a hand on her hip. "Did what?"

"You are now officially the Royal Thief."

"Just like that?" Ilis balked.

"Just like that." The prince grinned.

Ilis sat down on the grass beside him. Her thoughts ran abuzz. Part of her couldn't believe it had happened so fast. But there had to be a catch. There was always a catch. Her eyes found the dark, starry sky. She gazed up at it, deep in thought.

"Have you truly been there?" the prince asked.

"Where?" Ilis questioned, thinking for a minute that he had meant up to the Stars.

"To the Under."

"Oh." Of course that was what he wanted to know. Everyone always wanted to know what could not and should not be told. To admit such a thing to a royal was to ask for a torturous death—a death that would make beheading look like a mercy.

"I know what I ask you is dangerous," the prince replied, seeing her hesitation. "But I give you my word that I will not tell my father."

Ilis watched the prince. Did she trust his word?

"Why do you want to know?" Ilis asked, avoiding his question.

The prince turned away, and this time it was he who was gazing at the Stars.

"How good of a thief are you?" the prince asked, never taking his eyes off the sky.

"Only the best in the kingdom," Ilis responded, echoing his words from earlier.

The prince turned to Ilis and smiled at this, but then his smile faded. He nodded. "Good, because I need you."

He looked back up at the Stars.

"I need you to steal the Crown Jewel."

CHAPTER EIGHT

Ilis leapt up, her foot snapping a twig as she did. "You want *me* to steal the Crown Jewel?"

The prince smiled up at her. "What, don't think you're capable of it?"

"Oh, it's not that!" Ilis responded. "It's . . ." She realized she didn't want to finish her sentence.

"You don't think I would trust you with our kingdom's greatest prize," the prince finished. He looked at her in startling sincerity. "I wasn't sure if I would either." His eyes again found the sky. "But it is a risk I am going to have to take."

Ilis could not decide if his words disappointed her, or if she respected him more for them. Either way, she could hardly believe her luck! This solved all her problems! Here was the prince, asking her to steal the very thing she had come all this way to steal!

But there was something that still wasn't making sense.

"Do you know where it is?" Ilis asked.

Malcolm simply nodded.

"Then why do you need me? If you know where it is, can't you just walk in and take it?"

The prince's brow furrowed in thought. "It's not that simple."

"Well then, why do you want it stolen? It is the Crown Jewel . . . Doesn't it belong to you?" Ilis asked.

There was a twinkle in his eye as he responded, "Now that, I shall keep to myself." He stood up and gathered his sword. "So are you in?"

"Will I join you in stealing the nation's most prized possession?" Ilis paced under the Stars. Her thoughts ran quickly about. *Could this be real? Is it some sort of trick? Could it truly be that easy? Did he know I came here for the jewel, and he's trying to trap me?* She looked at the prince. If he were lying to her, he was a very good liar.

She shrugged, trying to feign nonchalance. "Why not?"

The prince nodded and then sighed. He returned his eyes to the Stars. "What have you heard about the Crown Jewel?"

Ilis debated about what she should admit, but the legend was pretty well known. "Only that it is the greatest treasure ever discovered in Basileia and that it is kept in the most secret of locations." She then returned the question, eager for the prince's insight. "What do you know about the Crown Jewel?"

The prince looked at Ilis, he too seemed to be debating how much to tell her. "The first Royal Thief gained their position just like you did, by stealing an item of the most value. And the first Royal Thief did more than steal what royals already owned," he added with some ire. "They stole something truly magnificent."

"The Crown Jewel."

The prince nodded.

"Who was it stolen from?" Ilis asked, her eyes eager. "And where is it now?"

The prince looked at her and winked. "I trust you, but not that much."

Ilis pretended to be offended. "What, you don't trust your own Royal Thief?"

"Only so far as I can toss her."

Ilis shrugged in consent. "So what's the plan, Your Highness?"

The prince stuck his sword under his arm. "Call me Malcolm." He cast his gaze up at the Stars one last time before answering. "Meet me after class tomorrow, and I will rally our crew."

"Crew?" Ilis asked. The very word made her uneasy. The only crew she ever worked with she had left on the seas.

Prince Malcolm nodded. "Yes, it will be no easy feat stealing the Crown Jewel, and we will need all the help we can get."

Ilis found her fingers rubbing her scar at the nape of her neck. She pulled them down to her side.

"Who is this crew?" she asked.

Prince Malcolm grinned but made no reply.

"If you tell me Chaz or Dianne, I quit," Ilis said dryly.

Prince Malcolm laughed. "Chaz, yes. Dianne, no. And you and I both know you won't quit."

Ilis growled, unable to argue. "But why Chaz?"

"Because, after me, he is probably the best swordsman in the land, but more than that, I trust him with my life."

"Who else?" Ilis asked.

"Pyra and Neil."

Ilis stopped and stared. She thought back over the past few days. It was no coincidence that these three were among the few people in Oros she had already interacted with. "You've been planning this all along!"

A smile tugged at the lips of the prince. "In some fashion."

"And what, you waited until after I made a complete fool of myself to tell me about it?"

"No," Prince Malcolm said slowly, "I waited until I knew you were the one I had been looking for."

***

Ilis's curiosity was piqued. The prince had mentioned that the first Royal Thief earned their title by stealing the Crown Jewel. If this were true, perhaps in learning more about that Royal Thief, she could discover more about the jewel. Even though Prince Malcolm was about to lead her right to it, he wasn't simply going to let her have it. The more she knew about the Crown Jewel, the better her chances were of making off with it.

Deep in thought, Ilis snuck up the steps of the Oval Library. The Oval Window was lit, as always, its magnificence shining out like a beacon of hope over the mountainside. Once inside, Ilis noticed her little bookkeeper friend sitting at a desk and buried in a thick volume. With a chuckle, she walked up to the girl and knocked on her desk.

Kat's eyes flew up, startled. "Oh! I didn't hear you come in!" Kat pushed her chair back and stood. She cocked her head. "Hey, aren't you the one who was interested in history the other day?"

"That's me."

"Welcome back!" Her eyes flitted behind Ilis and then widened. "Is it dark out already? What time is it?"

"After one."

"My father is going to kill me for staying up so late. I'm afraid I've got a nasty habit of reading past my bedtime," she said, as if admitting her greatest weakness. She stroked the book before her lovingly and sighed. "I'm reading *The Fierce Fledglings*. It's a story about these five girls who have special powers, and they go off and save the world. So I suppose it is no surprise that I'm up past my bedtime. But anyway, since I'm already up, I might as well finish the night off strong by helping one more person. How can I help you today?"

"I'm looking for information on the Royal Thief," Ilis said, trying to hide her grin at the girl's charm. "I figured you'd know where'd be best to look."

"Ahh, so you are interested in Oros Academy's newest student as well, huh?" The girl laughed at Ilis's look of surprise. "Let's just say you aren't the first person who has asked about the topic lately. I've been told that she already has a reputation for disappearing and making things disappear with her. They say her footsteps don't make a sound and that her eyes are as cold as ice." Kat's eyes grew dreamy. "I'd like to meet her. Cepher thinks me silly for this, but I feel like she is a real-life mystery! Is she in your class? Have you met her?"

Ilis laughed. "Uh, something like that, I suppose."

Kat sighed and seemed to melt in her seat. Then she perked up again. "What is she like?"

Ilis smirked. "Black hair, blue eyes, about five foot two, and to get her to laugh is a real feat."

Kat laughed and looked Ilis over. "Hey, she sounds rather like . . ." Kat's face went slack. "Tumbling bookcases! It's you!" she nearly shouted.

Ilis raised an eyebrow. "Astute observation, my friend."

"I can't wait to tell Cepher!" Kat said, bouncing up and down in her chair. Then she seemed to remember her audience and straightened.

"Ahh, well, how can I help you, O Royal Thief?" Kat paused. "Oh right, you wanted to know where to find information about the Royal Thieves, which makes sense considering you now are one. Of course you would want to know more about your job and your predecessors and what it means to be a Royal Thief and how the title came along in the first place . . ."

The young girl thrummed her fingers along the desk. "I've been sending people to the Vocation Hall and History Hall, as those are where our public records on the Royal Thief are." Kat's eyes gleamed. "But I think I can do better for you." She stood, closed her book, and did a little hop. "Follow me!"

"Wait, are you sure you have time? I don't want to get you in trouble with your father," Ilis said, feeling a strange sense of protectiveness over this young girl.

Kat merely came back and tugged on Ilis's arm. "Oh, I'll be fine. Come on!"

Leading Ilis by the hand, Kat brought her up five flights of stairs to a grand entryway. Ilis let out a whistle. Her wanderings hadn't gotten this far up the other night.

Kat jumped up and down. "This is the Council Room where all the royals and council members meet to discuss the workings of our fair country, and it also is where they store some key volumes of knowledge."

Kat began fumbling in her pockets until she pulled out a chain with over a dozen keys. Flipping through them, she found the one she was looking for and inserted it into the doors, throwing them open with a grand gesture.

The doors revealed a large room surrounded by bookshelves but for the far wall, which was made up of the top of the Oval Window. In the middle of the room was a large oval table made of glossy wood, around which sat the crown prince and several other officials.

Kat paled and took a staggering step back. One of the men stood up, his face a mixture of embarrassment and fury. Ilis recognized him from one of the sketches Almanzo had given her to study years ago. He was the Head Librarian and Advisor to the king.

"Kathrine! What are you doing?" the Head Librarian scolded.

"I-I-I'm sorry, Dad! I was just . . ." Kat turned to Ilis and then back to her father. "This is the Royal Thief, and she was . . . and I was . . . and we were . . ." Kat hung her head. "I was just trying to help."

Ilis put her hand on Kat's shoulder. "This is my fault. I do beg your apologies. Kat here was just trying to help me find some information, but I see now that we are in the wrong spot. Please excuse us." Ilis curtsied low and then turned to leave.

"Wait," sounded a voice. It carried the sense of authority that came from always being obeyed.

Ilis turned to find the crown prince staring at her.

After a moment during which Ilis felt Kat tremble underneath her hand, the crown prince turned to those sitting at his table. Ilis scanned the uniforms of those seated, and realized the Captain of the Guard was among them. "We will resume this tomorrow. You are all dismissed." He turned his gaze back to Ilis. "For now, I would have a word with the thief."

The gentlemen stood, gathered their things, and dispersed, Kat's father motioning her to follow him. Ilis winked at Kat as she went, producing the faintest of smiles from the girl. When it was just her and the crown prince, Ilis smiled demurely and bowed her head, saying, "Your Highness."

"What is my brother planning to steal?"

The prince's abrupt question jolted Ilis. Did he know about his brother's plan? No, he couldn't. If he did, he wouldn't be asking her. But still, he was suspicious. And his suspicion made him potentially dangerous.

Ilis looked at him as if he were slightly crazy. "Who says he is going to steal anything?"

The crown prince was unfazed. "Why ask for a thief for his birthday if he had nothing to steal?" he countered.

Ilis just glared back.

Prince Magnus stood and began to walk toward her, his boots clicking on the stone floor as he did. "My father is too trusting of his sons and so is not wary. But I am." He stopped in front of her and glared down into her eyes. "You will tell me what my brother intends to steal, or you will face the consequences."

"You want me to rat on your brother?" Ilis asked, wondering what kind of unhinged family she had found herself in the middle of.

"I want you to inform me of why my brother wants you." He turned to the bookshelves and stroked the binding of a book. "And what he wants you to steal."

Ilis let out a puff of laughter. "Er . . . no."

The crown prince spun and strode toward her until his breath was in her face. On the whole, Ilis would say that Prince Magnus was a handsome man with strong facial features. But there was nothing like anger to take those same attractive features and make them horrid.

"Why not? Because it is immoral?" he taunted.

Ilis didn't rise to the bait. With a slight roll of her eyes, she said, "Sure. As you say, Your Highness."

The prince stepped back, chin lifted and defiant. "You sure do have high morals for a thief."

"And you have very low morals for a prince," she fired back.

He snarled. "I'll make you a deal then. You tell me what my brother is up to and why he needs a thief, and I won't have you beheaded."

Ilis felt like she had just been punched in the gut, but her face wore only her usual smirk. "Excuse me?"

The crown prince turned, pulled up a chair at the end of the table, and sat down. He folded one leg over the other. "I wondered how a merchant's daughter ended up with such skills as your own, and so I went in search of your ship, the *Naus*, only to find that there is no such ship." He leaned back in his chair. "Pirates have been a stench in our civilization for centuries. But fear of them has grown in the past years. You know why? Because it is said they know how to sail over the Edge and are working with the Under to bring us down."

Ilis's heart picked up speed. But she kept control over her face and managed to produce a yawn.

"Tell me what my brother is up to, *Pirate*."

There is that word again, Ilis thought with sorrow. *That title I can no longer claim.*

85

Grief was heavy in her voice as she responded. "I can assure you, Your Highness, I am no pirate. My father keeps his records private and often sets sail under different ship names in order to avoid being targeted *by pirates*. That is why you couldn't find anything on him." Ilis crossed her arms. "You have no power over me."

The crown prince sneered and stood again, his chair scratching the floor as he hastily pushed it back. "Tell me what I want to know, or you will pay."

"Good luck with that."

With a curtsy, she left the room.

CHAPTER NINE

The next day in class, Ilis had a different prince than usual on her mind. She pondered her conversation with the crown prince and what ramifications it might have. Suspicion about her past was rising, and unless she could prove her faithfulness, she feared her stay on Oros would be a short one.

She took a deep breath. All that she needed to do was finish her heist, and then her crew would be free to sail as they wished again—and with the youngest prince's unknowing help, she was almost there.

After class, Prince Malcolm motioned for his crew to wait behind as the other students filed out.

When the class emptied, Ilis, Neil, Pyra, and Chaz all sat in the front row while Malcolm took the place their professor normally occupied. The classroom was dreadfully hot at this point in the afternoon—but then, the classroom was dreadfully hot almost all the time these days.

Chaz let the silence sit for two whole seconds before saying, "So, you ready to tell us what is going on?"

Pyra lifted her eyebrows. "Or are we going to get more vague instructions with no end goal?"

Prince Malcolm shook his head. "I'll explain everything in time. For now, I need your help."

"As if that's new," Chaz grumbled under his breath,

Malcolm threw his shoulders back. "Hear me out on this. I need you to help me steal the Crown Jewel."

Chaz looked at him as if he were crazy, which Ilis considered a viable possibility.

"Haha, good one," Chaz said dryly, his laugh sounding more like a statement than an attempt at humor. "Do you expect me to believe that you want to steal our kingdom's most beloved prize?"

Prince Malcolm was silent.

Pyra laughed nervously. "Okay, forget about the motive—you do realize that it is impossible, right?"

Prince Malcolm grinned almost shyly. "It was, until I found a thief."

Chaz glared at Ilis. "You are putting your trust in this dwarf?"

"Hey!" Ilis reacted in a growl. "I'm no dwarf!"

Chaz raised two red eyebrows. "How tall are you?"

"Five-two," Ilis responded.

Chaz blinked. "I can't believe you just willingly stated that." He looked back at Malcolm. "She is not only a dwarf; she is the worst kind of thief—an *honest* one."

"She is the best thief in the land!" Malcolm said, losing his patience. "And that is all that matters. But I will offer you an out. Each of you will gain nothing personally from our success but could lose your head from any failure." Malcolm took a deep breath. "If you get caught, I will have no qualms about disavowing my knowledge of this quest."

Ilis shivered at his coldness.

"So if any of you want out, you may go." Prince Malcolm looked into each of their eyes, as if daring them to back out. "But if not, then we will gather tonight."

Neil, who had been quiet for the entire exchange, stood, moved to Malcolm's side, and placed his hand on Malcolm's shoulder. "I am with you in this—as always."

Ilis studied the forester. What role did he play in this?

Pyra let out a long sigh. "I suppose we've followed you this far." She let a smile slip. "It would seem silly to give up now."

A struggle seemed to play inside Chaz before he rolled his eyes. "Fine, me too."

Ilis knew why she did not back out—a very selfish reason indeed—but she wondered at the real reason why the others stayed on.

Whatever their motives, they were now bound together by the bond of thieves.

***

In preparation for their heist that night, Ilis explored her room in search of some tools. She was digging through the chest of weapons when she found an old letter crammed at the bottom of the chest.

She unfolded it.

Dearest Anne,

I have a lead on another piece. I may be delayed in my coming back; forgive my long absence. Any luck on your end? I think it is time to reevaluate our strategy. The Quakes are getting stronger. I fear we cannot continue on this path for much longer without jeopardizing our world even more than we already are.

Sending all my love and desperately awaiting when we are together again, Your husband

Ilis reread the letter, trying to decipher its contents. Piece of what? And what did the Quakes have to do with anything? Was Anne the last Royal Thief? What had happened to her? Ilis sighed. More and more questions.

Turning her attention to the bookshelves and maps, Ilis explored her room more in search of information about the previous Royal Thieves. There seemed to be a thick mystery surrounding them. Unfortunately, after an hour of searching, she had found absolutely nothing of use. It felt as if all helpful information on Royal Thieves had been effectively hidden. The letter stuffed in the chest was the biggest clue, but even that didn't make sense.

Still having time in the afternoon, Ilis let her feet lead her as she explored more of Mount Oros. The hot air surrounded her as she walked, and she soon found herself dripping with sweat. Wandering through the gardens, Ilis discovered the greenhouse . . . and the middle prince.

The sight of Jasper sitting in the shade with his back against the greenhouse and a notebook in his hand almost startled Ilis. Had she not known who he was by his face, Ilis easily would have mistaken him for some gardener taking a break.

"Hello," he said, when he noticed her staring.

Ilis bowed her head slightly in response.

"I must say, I am rather offended that I was not included." He continued to sketch, sitting upon a bed of green grass.

Ilis cocked her head.

"You went around stealing everyone's crown except mine. I'll have you know mine is a fine crown, fully worthy of being stolen."

She raised an eyebrow. "Is that so?"

"Indeed. Next time you feel the itch to steal crowns, don't forget it."

Ilis suppressed a chuckle, feeling like this middle prince must make the perfect brother. "I'll keep this in mind."

She came and sat down beside him, trying to escape the Sun's heat. Maybe he would have some answers to all her questions.

"What do you know about the last Royal Thief?"

"Not much." He didn't take his eyes off his sketch. "She vanished when I was about three years old. I've heard she was married and got jilted or something."

"Was her name Anne?"

"It was. And there seems to have been some sort of tragedy with her family . . . See, there used to be a host of Royal Thieves. It was a family trade, so one was born into it. I remember hearing stories about the family of Royal Thieves—they would travel all around the land as the king's spies and come back with the most magnificent tales."

"What happened to them?"

"I don't know." He looked up at Ilis. "There is a lot of mystery surrounding Royal Thieves. I heard that people had started to complain that there were too many of them around the castle, and then all of a sudden, they vanished. Some thought they had all gone on a quest and died in one of the Quakes; others thought they just decided to move and didn't tell anyone. Some even think that the king sent them on a mission to the Under and they died trying to get there. But again, all I know is rumors. No one knows for sure. Well, I'm sure my father knows, and maybe my elder brother as well, but they don't share such details with me."

Ilis processed this information. "You are a prince just as much as your brother."

Prince Jasper raised his pencil. "But I am not the crown prince."

She cocked her head again.

Thinking, the prince dug through his backpack. He pulled out a book and tossed it to her. "Go on, read it. There is only one page to it."

Skeptically, Ilis opened it up. Just as he said, there was only one page with words on it. It read:

I most likely will go down in history as the unimportant middle child in the time of the Scorching Sun. Honestly, history probably won't even remember a middle child in this age. But unlike my elder brother, I don't care to be remembered. And unlike my younger brother, I don't always end up finding myself in the middle of the action. It is just me. So this account may end up being ever dull, but on the off chance that it is not, I ask you to enjoy.

And that was it.

"That's a depressing way to look at things," Ilis stated.

Prince Jasper shrugged. "I don't care to be remembered. I'll make the world a better place in a quieter way. I'll record history through pictures and not words. My culture may not praise me as genius, but I don't care."

"Why trust me with this?" Ilis asked. This was only the second time they had interacted—and the first time, she didn't think she had made that good of an impression.

He flipped his sketchbook around, and Ilis saw he had drawn a picture of her. It was from the night of the prince's ball. She wore her black dress and was juggling three crowns in the air.

"I've got a prediction," Jasper said, handing Ilis the sketch. "I've got a feeling that you will end up giving this kingdom more than you will steal."

"What does that mean?"

Jasper shrugged and began a new sketch. "My brother talks about you nonstop, you know." Ilis did not appreciate his sudden change of topic.

She stood and offered him back his sketch.

"Keep it. Maybe one day you can put it in your book."

Ilis laughed. "As if."

"Every citizen must write one."

Good thing I'm not legally a citizen! Ilis thought. But to the prince, she replied, "Well, then I suppose I'll just have to steal one of those too."

***

They met at midnight, one of the four hours of darkness their world now offered, at the statue of a griffin in front of the academy. Prince Malcolm, being obstinately secretive about the night's proceedings, had told his team only what to bring and when and where to meet.

He had tasked Ilis with bringing a harness she would trust her life to, which gave her hope about the adrenaline that would soon be pumping through her veins. She had found a harness in one of the chests in her room, and while her first instinct was to trust the previous Royal Thief, she decided it was an instinct that deserved to be tested. And thus, Ilis slipped into the harness and leapt out the window of her room as soon as it was dark. That she had escaped without any broken bones was a testament to her harness's security.

Getting there early, Ilis climbed onto the back of the griffin, right between the lion's wings, and settled down to watch her crew arrive. Clothed in a loose black tunic with black leggings, Ilis blended in with the night shadows completely.

Pyra was the first to arrive, and she tugged on her long blond braid nervously as she waited. Her slender face held lines of worry. Then came Neil, who silently greeted Pyra and then stared off at the Stars. Chaz and Prince Malcolm arrived together, each carrying rope over their shoulders.

Prince Malcolm looked around. "Is Ilis not here yet?" he whispered.

"I'm always here," Ilis said, rising from the shadows and relishing the collective jump from everyone but Neil. He merely grinned at her.

"What the blazes, Ilis?" Chaz muttered. He was on edge already for betraying his country.

"You asked for a thief," Ilis said unapologetically.

"And a thief is just what we need," the prince responded. "Are you all ready? It's not too late to back out."

He waited for everyone's silent answer and then nodded. "Neil, you will be our lookout. I want you to station yourself on the roof of the infirmary." He turned to Pyra. "Do you have those candles?"

Pyra nodded and opened a bag as big as herself. It was filled to the brim with candles.

"Good. I need you to take those and light them inside the windows of the library." Pyra made a face, but Malcolm turned to Ilis and continued, "We will be in place above the Oval Window. Once Pyra has lit all her candles, Chaz and I will lower you down from the top of the Oval Window to the middle, where you will pry out the Crown Jewel. Then, when you've got it, we will pull you back up, and the job will be done."

Ilis balked. *The Crown Jewel is hidden in the middle of the Oval Window?* Her mind reeled over this information. No wonder no one had found its hiding place before: it was hidden in plain sight!

"Wait," Pyra said quietly. All eyes turned to her. "If you are having me light candles, does that mean . . ." She could hardly finish her sentence. Her face paled.

"But that doesn't make sense," Chaz said. "The Oval Window is already lit by candles."

Prince Malcolm shook his head. "Yes, but those are just for show. Have you never noticed how few candles there are?"

"Malc, you're not making sense," Chaz said, frustrated that he still did not understand. "How do you explain the constant radiant light of the Oval Window, the largest window this side of the world, if not by candles?"

"It is the Crown Jewel," Pyra said dejectedly. "We are not just stealing the kingdom's greatest prize. We're stealing the light of the Oval Window."

Silence infiltrated the group and hung heavy over them all. Ilis watched as the weight of what they were doing hit Chaz. His shoulders slumped.

The Oval Window was the kingdom's pride and joy. It was the love of all the people. It gave hope to those who saw it, a reminder that the night was not as dark as it may seem.

"Why do you want it stolen?" Ilis asked the question no one else dared to.

Prince Malcolm looked at her, resolved. "I can't answer that. Not yet." He took a breath. "Do you trust me?"

Ilis leapt down from her perch on the griffin and nodded. "Just do me a favor and don't drop me."

She slung the harness over her shoulder. Her brain began to assess the situation as only a good thief can. "You will need a flat and secure place over the Oval Window to drop me down. I would suggest the roof of the Oval Library, but since the library is built into the mountain, it doesn't have a roof."

Prince Malcolm nodded. "I know of a spot; it's a ledge that is situated right above the Oval Window. My brothers and I used to sit and throw berries at people walking below when we were kids. We will have to crawl through some bushes, but it will work."

Ilis nodded, and they all dispersed: Neil and Pyra went their separate ways while Ilis and Chaz followed Malcolm to his spot.

***

They hiked around the mountain to a row of bushes nestled in the mountainside. Dropping to their knees, they followed Prince Malcolm as he crawled through the bushes and led them to a clearing just large enough for three young boys to sit comfortably.

It was slightly less comfortable for three growing young people.

Ilis grabbed onto the trunk of a sturdy bush and leaned out over the edge of the mountain. The wonderful sensation of clarity and panic Ilis always got from heights fluttered in her chest and sharpened her thinking. Her eyes peered down past the seven stories of the Oval Window to the ground below. It was empty, but there was no telling how long it would stay that way.

"Are there guards who patrol around here?" Ilis asked.

"There are guards stationed inside the Oval Library as well as some on the streets around, but none who should be able to see us," replied the prince while attaching Ilis to the rope. He and Chaz had set up a pulley system while Ilis had been taking in the heights.

While they waited for the signal from Pyra that all candles were lit, Ilis began to think like Captain had taught her and look for holes in their plan. She *would* repay him for all he had done for her. He deserved that much.

She tugged on the rope. "Are you sure this rope will hold me?"

Prince Malcolm nodded.

"How much does the Crown Jewel weigh? What if I can't lift it? What if I drop it?"

"You won't," was his only reply.

Ilis thought about returning to her first two unanswered questions, but she was thinking of more. "What if someone sees me? I will rather stick out, what with the glow from the windows."

"Then we will pull you up," the prince replied curtly.

"And if you can't pull me up fast enough?"

"Oh for the sake of my sanity, would you please stop!" Chaz said in a whisper-shout.

Ilis glared at him but kept her questions to herself from then on. She began to form her own backup plans; if she had learned one thing as a pirate, it was that things never went according to plan.

She found herself staring at Malcolm's boots as she thought through her plans. They were rather ordinary for a prince: simple worn brown leather boots. For a minute, she wondered if they were just the boots he wore on heists, but thinking back, she remembered him wearing them at the academy too.

Pyra's whistle interrupted her thoughts. With a shared nod, Chaz and Prince Malcolm began to lower Ilis. She locked eyes with the prince briefly before descending and thought she saw a look of panic in his eyes, but perhaps it was a trick of the Stars.

Any thoughts of plans going awry—or of boots—were soon gone as she was lowered down to the face of the Oval Window.

The edge of the cliff was the trickiest part, but Ilis sat back in her harness and let her feet push off the rocks as the boys lowered her down at a slow but steady pace. Before long she reached the top of the Oval Window. From there the journey was easy, as she merely ran her hand alongside the windowpanes to keep herself from bumping into the surface of the Oval Window as they lowered her down. With a quick look over her shoulder, she saw the view of Mount Oros—its streets lit only by a few lanterns posted like sentries upon the streets. A breeze, hot as always, blew past her cheeks.

The Oval Window was breathtaking from afar, but Ilis wasn't prepared for its magnificence up close. It was utterly brilliant, distractingly so. She had to force herself to remember that she was on a heist and had no time for excessive gawking.

When she reached the center, she let out a Treelick's whistle, and the boys held her position steady.

There it was. The Crown Jewel.

Almost the size of her head, the Crown Jewel glowed a bluish white. It had jagged sides, as if parts of it had been shattered off.

It was magnificent.

It was beautiful.

It was the heist of the century.

Ilis could see why the Queen of the Under wanted it so badly.

She took in a deep breath and reached out her hand, her fingers caressing the Crown Jewel. It was warm like a stone that had been in the Sun all day.

A shock of power went up her arm.

She pulled her hand back, her fingers still tingling. Wonder filled her. A shiver ran through her body, and she had to remind herself to breathe. Something about the Crown Jewel seemed so familiar . . . Shaking her head, she returned to the task at hand.

Reaching into her satchel, Ilis pulled out her gloves and a knife and set to work on removing the mortar which held the stone in place. She figured it would just fit in her satchel.

She placed the knife in the mortar between the stone and the other glass-like panels and began digging the hard clay out. It was slow work, and Ilis had only made it halfway around the stone when she heard a shout.

Ilis peered down and found a guard below.

"Rats!" Ilis muttered. She tried to get through the mortar faster, but it was stubborn and would not be rushed.

Ilis looked over her shoulder and found that the guard was no longer alone—and they had crossbows. Not good.

Thoughts of the heist for the Queen of the Under's crown raced through her brain. They would shoot at her and then Malcolm and Chaz. She had to abort while she could.

She looked back at the glowing stone, her ticket to redemption, the key to unlocking her crew's freedom. Her heart ached, but she knew what she had to do. She couldn't repeat her last mistake.

"Pull me up!" Ilis shouted. She saw Prince Malcolm's head appear.

"Do you have it?"

"No, but we are about to get shot at! Pull me up!"

The prince shook his head. "Not until you have the stone!"

"We will all be dead before then!" Ilis raged.

An arrow whizzed past her head and crashed into the window panel beside her. She was surprised to find that the window did not shatter— but then again, this was no ordinary glass window.

"Get me out of here!"

Arrows began to ping the window all around her. After one more glance up to the boys and finding them absent, Ilis took matters into her own hands. If she kept the focus on herself, at least Malcolm and Chaz would be safe. She pushed off with her feet and swung herself to the right as far as she could. She felt the rope give way somewhat, but the boys still hadn't offered assistance. Her weight pulled her back down, and Ilis swung with it, dodging arrows as she went. When she reached the end of her swing, she sliced the rope. And fell.

CHAPTER TEN

Ilis had time for one brief revelation: *This was not very well thought through.*

Her hope had been to land in a group of bushes, but as she fell, she realized there were no bushes in sight.

The only thing beneath her was stone . . . and a troop of angry soldiers.

Twisting her body, Ilis shoved her knife into the mountainside in a frenzied attempt to find some sort of hold to stop herself from plummeting to her death.

Her body jarred as her knife found a hold and she found herself hanging precariously on the side of the mountain.

She took three shaky breaths.

"I do love just hanging around," she said through clenched teeth.

An arrow clanged as it hit the rock face beside her.

"Me and these guards who have terrible aim, that is."

Her fingers had begun to slip on the knife when she heard her name being called. Suddenly, a rope was lowered down right by her side. Ilis swung her body, released her knife, and grabbed hold of the rope.

As Ilis glared down numbly toward the rocky demise she had almost met, she felt the rope pulling her up. Faintly, she wondered what had made the prince change his mind; but when she was pulled into a nook, Ilis found that her savior was not the prince. It was Neil.

Ilis cocked her head, thoroughly confused.

"How'd you . . ." she began, but Neil hushed her. His eyes were frantic as they scanned the surrounding area and then focused attentively on her.

"You okay?"

Ilis let out a breath and nodded.

An arrow whizzed past them.

"We need to move," they both said simultaneously.

Together they scampered silently up the slope, sticking to the shadows. They passed through buildings tucked here and there in the mountainside until they reached a row of thick bushes. Neil led Ilis along the bushes to a building and opened the door, ushering her in. The humid air and smells of plants gave their location away.

"The greenhouse?" Ilis questioned.

Neil shrugged. "We needed someplace to lay low." His eyes darted to the windows. "There are more than fifty soldiers out there right now."

"I know. They were shooting at me."

Neil smiled at her dryly. "So they were."

Ilis began to pace beside the petunias. "Did you know the truth behind the Oval Window?" Ilis asked.

Neil was silent, somber.

"What did it feel like?" he asked, avoiding Ilis's question.

"The Jewel? It was . . . indescribable."

Neil nodded as if he understood.

Ilis began to pace again. "I can't believe the prince was so foolhardy!" She began to fume. "As if the Jewel was worth more than our lives!" She realized she was being a hypocrite, as that was the very decision she had made in her last heist, but that realization only made her more frustrated.

Neil remained silent.

Ilis spun on him, her eyes like white fire. "Don't tell me you agree with him!"

Neil held up his hands in defense. "I didn't say a word!"

"Your silence spoke for you," Ilis growled.

"Maybe you should just hear his point of view before jumping to conclusions."

Ilis leaned against the wall and let her head rest on the wood. "I wouldn't have had the chance if not for you." She turned her gaze to him. "How did you get over here so fast? Weren't you stationed on top of the infirmary? That is on the other side of the library."

Neil scanned the windows one more time before turning to her. "I'm a fast runner. As soon as I saw the guards, I came running."

She opened her mouth to say that no one could move that fast, but Neil lifted his finger to his lips. The sound of boots and quiet voices came closer.

Ilis scanned the room for a good hiding spot, but there were only flowers. Even she was not capable of disappearing among mere potted plants.

Neil crouched and made his way to the back of the greenhouse, beckoning Ilis to follow him. When he reached the far-left corner, he moved a geranium and felt around on the floor. Ilis watched as he stuck his finger into a hole in the ground and then pulled. A portion of the floor, just large enough for a person to fit through, came up.

With her jaw slightly ajar, Ilis followed Neil through the opening in the floor. She settled the floorboard into place above her just as the soldiers stormed the greenhouse.

The air was musty, a drastic change after the fresh smells from above. Ilis could hear the soldiers stomping around the room above her. She felt Neil place his hand on her arm, and she followed him blindly as he led her deeper into the pitch darkness.

When they had gone twenty paces, Neil stopped and began rustling through his pockets. The darkness was soon illuminated by a single flame from a match, which he used to light a torch. The glow was bright and lit up his face eerily. He motioned with his head, and Ilis again followed.

Neil made turns with a confidence that startled Ilis. Surely, they were in the tunnels beneath the kingdom that she had almost gotten lost in. How did he know them so well?

Finally, they stopped, and Neil looked up. Ilis followed his gaze and saw a rope ladder leading to a wooden hatch.

"After you," he said, his voice sounding loud after their quiet footfalls.

Ilis obliged, scampering up the rope ladder and trying to throw open the hatch. There was resistance, so she had to shove, but she soon found herself pushing up an orange carpet and emerging into a room she knew well.

"Neil!" Ilis gasped, her words laced with both awe and accusation. "How do you know a secret passage to my room?"

Neil placed the carpet back over the trapdoor and grinned. "I got lost down in the tunnels once. Since then, I have spent a good deal of my free time exploring those passages."

Ilis was about to ask what other passageways he knew about when she heard voices in her hall.

"Why would she be in her room?" a light voice asked. "If she did not meet us at our rendezvous point, I doubt she is just hiding in her room."

"She is probably mad at me," said a voice that sounded like the prince. "And I wouldn't blame her."

"She is probably dead," added a gruff voice. "Caught by the guards and . . ."

Ilis opened the door, killing the rest of Chaz's sentence.

Pyra let out a cheer. "Not dead! And not caught by the guards!"

Chaz was harder to please. "But she *was* hiding in her room."

Neil spoke up from behind Ilis. "More like, we just escaped being killed or captured by traversing through secret passageways."

Ilis folded her arms and stared daggers at the prince.

Prince Malcolm bowed his head. "I suppose I owe you an explanation."

She lifted an eyebrow. "Shells, you do!"

He grimaced. "May we use your place for a meeting room?"

Having the prince and his friends up in her room was one of the last things Ilis wanted at this moment, but she was too tired to go anywhere else to meet, so she gave in.

Ilis let the band of failed thieves into her room and could not help but feel a burst of pride at the place which she was able to call her own. It was her first room on land, and therefore, despite the fact that she had only lived here less than a week, it held a special place in her heart.

Her hammock hung above, swinging softly in the hot night breeze coming through the window. Her bookshelves were happily crammed with books she hadn't read but loved to look at. The whole room was clean but not neat, and the effect of it all filled Ilis's heart with joy. It looked *lived in*, and she cherished every corner of it.

Reluctantly, Ilis cleared off chairs and made room for her unwanted guests. Once everyone was settled, Ilis let her sharp glare do the talking.

Prince Malcolm sighed and leaned back in his chair. "I don't even know where to start."

"How about with why you deem the Crown Jewel worth more than our lives?" Ilis asked dryly.

"The world is ending," Prince Malcolm said.

Pyra laughed nervously and then looked at Prince Malcolm, eyes wide. "My, you have a way with announcing the end of life as we know it."

"This is serious!" He stood up and began pacing. "Our days have been getting longer until there is only a sliver of night. The Sun is becoming so bright that it scorches our crops. Drought is spreading and will dry up our entire water supply in a matter of months!" Prince Malcolm struck his fist against the side of Ilis's bookshelf in his frustration. "Beasts have begun to stir, and earthquakes have hit all over the kingdom. In the East, it has been reported that swirling storms of dust—powerful enough to lift a whole cabin off the ground—are appearing and destroying everything in their path! It is even said that a phoenix has been spotted rising from the ashes of a wildfire!"

"Malc, these are all things we know," Chaz said, his voice gruff and somber. "Tell us what we *don't* know."

"My father and brother think it is all somehow the Under's doing. They are strengthening the militia in case of an attack, which is a complete and utter waste of time." Prince Malcolm stared out into the night as if in a daze. "People are flocking to the mountain, hungry and destitute, and we have no hope to give them." He turned and faced Ilis. "So I went out and found some hope."

"What is it?" Pyra asked, sitting on the edge of her seat.

Prince Malcolm shook his head and collected himself. "I guess I should start at the beginning." He took a deep breath. "In the beginning of the First Age of the Kingdom of Basileia, the Moon was the King of the Night."

When Ilis made a face, Prince Malcolm smiled and explained, "The

Moon is the Great Light which ruled the night."

"I know what the Moon is, you wave-washed excuse for a boy. What I don't understand is why you are claiming it as part of history. Everyone knows it is a myth."

The prince let a glimmer of a smile slip. "That's the thing, Ilis. It's not."

A chill settled over her.

The Moon was perhaps the greatest myth of all. Even she, a pirate and lover of lore, knew better than to *believe* in such a fable. But the prince seemed serious about this, which scared her.

Prince Malcolm continued, "The myth of the Moon was created from a history that the kings of old wished to forget. But the truth of history remains true regardless of who remembers. And the Moon is a part of our world's history."

Ilis looked at Prince Malcolm as if he were crazy. Chaz leaned back, seeming unconvinced but not willing to speak up. Neil's face was inexpressive. It was Pyra who urged the prince to continue.

"So in the First Age . . ." Pyra prompted.

Prince Malcolm took a deep breath. "In the First Age, a royal decree was sent throughout the land in search of a thief—one worthy of the title Royal Thief. The king arranged for a competition, stating that whoever stole for him the greatest prize would win the title and thereby serve the Kingdom of Basileia forevermore."

Ilis shuddered at the similarity to her own story.

"Thieves came from all across the land, asking the king what prize he would like best. The king declared that he wanted the Moon. Thus, stealing the Moon became the objective of every thief in Basileia and even beyond. All sought a way to capture the Moon. To this day, no one knows how the feat was accomplished, but someone eventually succeeded in stealing the Moon. On that day, the land quaked as the Moon, in its entirety, crashed to the ground."

Neil groaned, as if it pained him to hear of the fabled Moon's demise.

"A girl of fourteen walked into the palace and offered the king a piece of the Moon. The question arose as to where the rest of the Moon was, but a single piece satisfied the king's craving. The land praised her as a hero, and the king gave her not just the title of Royal Thief but also of Moon Thief.

"However, while the land praised her for her feat, the young girl claimed that the world was in danger and that the rest of the Moon needed to be found. She dedicated her life to putting the Moon back together again. The girl grew, married, and had children, and passed both the title of Moon Thief and the charge of putting the Moon back together to her descendants. But as the centuries passed, the memory of the Moon and its Thieves all but faded away."

Prince Malcolm took a deep breath. He looked each one of them in the eyes before continuing. "I believe the reason behind all of this mayhem—the reason our world is ending—is because the Moon has yet to be completed."

A silence resounded in the room.

"And what exactly does that have to do with us?" Pyra asked.

"Tonight, we attempted to obtain a piece of the Moon," Malcolm replied.

Ilis turned her head to hide her fury at the prince's foolishness. He did not have the right to risk her life on a fable without her consent!

She stood and locked eyes with the prince. "So what, you expected me to go out and just steal the Moon for you?"

"No," the prince said, careful with his words. "Not just steal but also put back together again."

"You put our lives in danger for the sake of lore?" Ilis clenched her fists.

"But it isn't just lore, Ilis," Malcolm pleaded.

"THE MOON IS A MYTH!"

The prince shook his head. "No. It is TRUTH."

In that instant, she saw herself in Malcolm. She heard her own propaganda which she fed to the crew, enticing them to walk into a death trap.

He is just like me, she realized with chilling terror. *Willing to risk lives for his own devices.* Her own guilt began washing over her like a flood. She was furious at him for risking their lives. *Is this how the crew felt?* She shivered, scared of Malcolm . . . and scared of herself.

It was just too much. She shook her head and turned from the group. Throwing the door open, Ilis let it slam behind her as she rushed out of the room, down the stairs, and into the dark night.

CHAPTER ELEVEN

Ilis climbed onto the rooftops and leapt from one roof to the next, trying to calm her thoughts before returning to her room just before dawn. Her emotions from the night before scared her. She resented the prince for risking their lives on a heist. But that was exactly what she had done with her crew. The guilt that had been chasing her seemed to engulf her. She sat and watched the Sun rise and tried to distract herself by musing on the oddity of how the Sun could bring such destruction in its wake and yet still rise every morning in a beautiful display of colors. As it was only around two in the morning, Ilis climbed up into her hammock and closed her eyes in an attempt to get a few hours of sleep before the rest of the world woke up.

But sleep evaded her. She thought about calling it quits right then and there, but where would she go? She had no home.

She did not believe a word of the prince's tale that the Crown Jewel was the fabled Moon, but she was pretty sure the Crown Jewel was made of glowstone, the same material she used in her torch. Glowstone was of high value, mainly because the Queen of the Under would pay an absurd price for any pieces discovered. Knowing that the Crown Jewel was made of glowstone explained why the queen wanted it so badly. But there was another mystery that Ilis could not figure out: how had the Queen of the Under known perhaps the best-kept secret of Basileia? How had she known what the Crown Jewel was when no one else seemed to?

But, in the end, Ilis supposed it didn't matter. All that mattered was how much the queen would pay. And thus, Ilis resolved to spend one more day on this wretched mountain. She would collect her prize and then secure her redemption.

She was done with land and its princes.

The only motivation Ilis had for going to class the next day was that sticking to routine was the best disguise in all undercover missions. She thought about sitting next to Neil to ask him more about the underground tunnels (useful information in her field), but he didn't seem to be in class. Therefore, Ilis once again took up a seat in the far back of the room.

When the prince began his ascent, course set to her, Ilis produced her iciest glare, just daring him to come and sit next to her and taste her wrath. The prince, seeming to understand for the first time that she did not want his company, nodded at her and took a seat in the middle of the classroom. Before he sat down, he looked over his shoulder and winked.

Oh, the infuriating son of a king!

Professor Owlistare began teaching on the History of the Quakes, a history she knew well.

Captain had told her of the seventy-year period when Quakes shook their world frequently, sending quivers throughout the entire country. He told tales of waves as large as mountains crashing on the seas and destroying the coastlines. The catastrophic waves would come out of nowhere, nearly capsizing their ship every time.

Ilis remembered sitting on her father's knee, staring up in awe at his tales. She had asked what she had done when the waves hit, but he merely shook his head and said they had ended right before she was born.

Fiddling with her quill while the teacher talked, Ilis tried to pay attention, but her thoughts continued to return to the night before. The image of Malcolm disappearing was imprinted in her brain. He had left her hanging there with arrows flying all around. How could he? Did he truly care so little for her? This thought brought on an even more painful one: had she cared so little for her crew?

She was shaken from her thoughts when a slight tremor ran through the floor. Then the tremor was followed by a shake.

The world seemed to slow as the ground began quivering violently, escalating rapidly into what could only be a true Quake.

Ilis was thrown from her seat into the wall behind her. She sat there, shocked and unmoving, as she watched the world around her crumble. Walls cracked, creating spider-like webs that crawled all the way up to the ceiling.

There was a brief moment where everyone held their breath, and then it happened.

Part of the ceiling cracked and dropped with a dreadful thud in the middle of the room—right on top of where *he* was sitting.

Students scrambled to get out of the way, panic in their eyes. Figures disappeared beneath the falling mass, and a scream tore through her ears. Ilis lifted her fingers to her lips, only to find that the scream was her own.

Leaping to her feet, she tried to make her way to the ruins. She climbed over desks and chairs in a frenzied haze.

A cloud of dust hung in the air. She coughed.

Students sat dazed all around her. Some lay bloodied, either unconscious or dead.

Ilis shook her head. She needed to think clearly.

Her focus was on the rocks. Move the rocks and maybe she could save them. Move the rocks and maybe she could save . . . maybe she could save him.

She reached the caved-in ceiling and began to shove, push, and pull the rocks away. Frustrated, she yelled at the other students.

"Don't just stand there, help me! They could still be alive!"

A large redheaded figure was one of the first to join in, though she didn't pause to see his face. Getting down on her knees, she continued moving the rocks. Her fingers stung and the sharp edges bit into her flesh, but she continued to tear at the massive heap of debris.

Her breathing came in gasps. She could taste the tears that fell unchecked down her cheeks. It had happened again. She couldn't escape it. This was her fault, and she knew it. He would have sat safely next to her if she hadn't told him not to. Yet again, her actions had brought destruction in their wake. Stone after stone was lifted by her small hands until she found the tip of a brown boot.

She knew those boots.

"O-over here," she managed to choke out.

Figures hurried toward her and began digging the prince out. A medic hovered around and swooped in when he was clear of debris. The medic checked his pulse and then began shouting orders. The world was a slow chaos.

A stretcher was brought in, and the prince laid upon it. His face looked pale, the coy smile she had found so annoying wiped from his lips. Hastily, they took the stretcher out of the classroom. Ilis ignored the cries and chaos around her and followed. They walked through corridor after corridor, not one left unmarked by the Quake.

When they reached the infirmary, they took the prince to a room in the back of the building. A large guard of the Moving Tribe told her she was not allowed to enter.

Ilis balled up her fists, ready to fight her way in there if need be. *I might only be five-two, but just try and stand in my way,* she thought. However, before Ilis could incinerate the guard with her icy glare, he raised his large hand.

"Are you the Royal Thief?"

Taken aback, Ilis nodded.

The guard looked over his shoulder and into Malcolm's room. "The prince mentioned he had a friend in you. Let the doctors do what they must, and then I am sure they will let you in to see him."

***

Ilis sat on the cold ground just outside the prince's door for hours. Doctors scurried in and out with frantic expressions and worried whispers. Half an hour after she had resorted to pacing, a doctor came out, and Ilis jumped in front of him.

"Please," she pleaded, "how is he?"

The doctor looked her over. "Let me guess, you are the Royal Thief?"

Ilis swallowed, not sure she wanted to be reminded of the title she had failed to live up to. "Yes, sir."

The doctor nodded and stuck his hands in his pockets. He was of the Feeling Tribe and therefore had a natural knack for not only healing people but also making them feel at ease.

"Well, I'll be honest with you, young thief, the prince is in pretty bad shape. He has several lacerations that we had to stitch up and a few cracked ribs, but the real thing that worries me is his head." The man paused and scratched his own head. "He is in a coma, and we aren't sure when he will wake up."

The sinking feeling Ilis had felt since the Quake suddenly plunged deeper. "What can I do?"

"Right now, nothing," the doctor replied. He must have seen Ilis's face fall, for he quickly added, "But tomorrow, after the doctors have finished what they need to do, you can come and sit with him. I'll make sure the guards know to let you through."

With a thankful smile upon her lips, Ilis nodded. She considered pacing in front of the door again but decided against it. In the end, she found herself wandering the halls. Her feet eventually took her to the Oval Library: the heart of the mountain.

She stopped in her tracks as she stared up at the Oval Window—or what was left of it.

The entire gigantic window had been shattered by the Quake, leaving a gaping hole right where the Crown Jewel was supposed to be and exposing Basileia's very heart. Men and women were at work boarding off the window, causing it to look even more horrific in contrast to its old majestic beauty.

Tears welled in her eyes, but she willed them away. She raced to the rubble and began searching through it. How long she spent searching, she didn't know. All she knew was that the prince was dying—and that it was all her fault.

"Ilis!" A voice cut through her restless thoughts, but she didn't stop her search.

The Crown Jewel couldn't be gone.

The prince needed it.

She needed it.

"Ilis," the voice said again, softer. Gentle hands wrapped around her shoulders and pulled her back, away from the rubble. She looked into Neil's sparkling blue eyes and briefly marveled at the youthfulness they held. Somehow, after the tragedy of the Quake, he seemed to look younger.

Ilis pushed herself away from him and back to the rubble. "Where were you?" she sniffed. "You weren't in class when the Quake hit."

Neil bent down next to Ilis and grabbed her hands firmly. "Ilis, your hands."

For the first time, Ilis looked at her hands and found them bleeding and raw. She had been digging in the shards of diamond panels, and her fingers and palms spoke the proof.

"I-I-I have to find it." Ilis choked back a sob.

"It is not here," Neil assured her. "I already looked."

Her eyes filled with tears again, seeing the end of Malcolm's hope—and then, with a startled gasp, she realized what it meant for her.

Ilis stumbled backward. She would have tripped over the debris had it not been for Neil's steady hands.

"No, no, no, no," Ilis moaned. "The Crown Jewel can't be gone. I need it to save—" Just in time, she stopped herself before saying "my crew."

The one reason she was here—her mission, her escape from the guilt that threatened to drown her—was *gone*?

Ilis crumbled to the ground in a heap.

"Malcolm will understand," Neil tried to reassure her. He must have thought her sorrow was for the prince.

She just shook her head. Malcolm was dying because of her. His death would be on her conscience. In trying to escape one set of guilt, she had unwittingly fallen headfirst into another. Had she let Malcolm sit where he wanted to sit, he would have been right by her side when the Quake hit, not under a pile of rock.

Not only had Ilis lost her reason for coming, she was losing any reason for staying.

Neil led her to the infirmary, where he sat her down and left her in a hallway crowded with people who were bleeding and sobbing. The Quake had left its mark, not only on the structure of Mount Oros but also on its people.

When Neil came back, he had Pyra in tow. Pyra's tan brow wrinkled in worry when she saw Ilis's hands, but she said nothing. The salve she used eased the pain, and then she wrapped Ilis's hands in bandages until it looked like she was wearing funny gloves.

Pyra put her hand on Ilis's shoulder and said, "I'd tell you to take it easy, but I know that's not in your nature, so just take this salve and put it on twice a day." She handed Ilis a small bottle with a smile.

Ilis nodded and tried to smile back, but she was afraid she only managed a grimace.

***

Mount Oros was in disarray.

It was unfathomable to Ilis that a few seconds' worth of anything could produce such a disaster. Whole structures were crumbled to bits. Gigantic rock pieces had dislodged themselves from the side of Mount Oros and crashed into streets and buildings.

Rubble was strewn everywhere. Some people, hurried and frantic, worked to search through it. Others just sat, crying out in shock and fear. A child stood in the middle of the street, his dusty cheeks stained by tears as he screamed at the top of his lungs.

The devastation was palpable and heart-wrenching.

After walking all day through the desolation, Ilis had returned to her room to try and get some sleep. But when the Sun rose in her early dawn, shining through the window in a glorious splendor that felt unbecoming after such events, Ilis gave up trying to sleep and made her way back to the prince's room in the infirmary. Just as the doctor had promised, she was allowed to enter; but as soon as she did, she wasn't sure she wanted to.

Up against the far wall of the grand room lay the prince, as pale as could be. Ilis scanned the room for family members but found none.

It was just her, alone. With the young man she had almost killed.

There was a lush chair sitting beside the prince's bed, but Ilis figured it was for someone more important than herself. To the right of the bed was a wide window, in which sat a potted succulent. Moving the plant aside, Ilis settled in the windowsill.

Her eyes skirted the prince's room, wondering where his attendants were. The room was deadly silent, and for once, Ilis shuddered in the lack of sound.

"Don't die," she finally gasped out when the silence became too much. "Don't die by my hand. I've already caused one too many deaths. Did you know I killed my own mom? And on my birthday too." Her fingers found the scar on the back of her neck. Out of habit, she rubbed it nervously. "But that's not the whole of it. I also almost killed my entire crew," she said, staring at the unmoving prince. "I deserved to die that day, but Almanzo escaped in time to release us." Her quick fingers brushed her tears away.

She was silent for a moment. But again, the silence grew too much.

"I had grown too cocky. We had gone on heist after heist where we got away with so much. I thought we were invincible. The crew tried to tell me it was too dangerous. They tried to tell me how foolish it was." She looked down at her injured hands. "But I didn't listen. Everyone knows that to try and steal the Queen of the Under's crown is to lose your head. But I thought we could do it. I thought I could do it.

"The trouble began as soon as we set foot on palace grounds. They saw through our disguises, and so we had to run. Ember said we should turn back. But I insisted we keep going. My foolish persistence pushed the crew forward. We lost the guards in the crowds and hastily found our positions. But we didn't even end up making it inside the throne room. Almanzo and I were climbing up the outer wall of the throne room when I slipped.

"*I* slipped. Me! The one who had convinced them all to attempt this foolishness. I lost my grip and fell to the ground, only to be swarmed by guards. As soon as they threatened to kill me, it was over. Almanzo slid down the wall and surrendered, and those hiding on the surrounding rooftops waiting for us to drop down a rope were quickly found by the griffin guards.

"We never even laid eyes on the crown. That is how much of a failure the heist was. They searched us thoroughly, stripping us of our clothes and replacing them with rags, and bound us in chains so tight we couldn't move more than inches. And then we sat in the dungeon for a whole week, separated from one another, awaiting our deaths.

"When they led us up to the guillotine, I moved to the front of the line. It was all my fault that we were dying. I deserved to go first. Captain tried to interfere, but the guard just yanked on his chains and let me go first. I walked willingly up the steps to my doom, each step sounding on the boards in an echo that haunts my dreams. They locked my head in the guillotine, the rough wooden braces on each side clamping down upon my neck. I kept my eyes down. I couldn't meet the eyes of my crew.

"They had tried to tell me not to go. But I had forced their hand. I told them they could either let me go on my own or come with me. I knew Captain wouldn't let me go on my own. That single declaration forced them to their deaths."

Ilis found tears were falling freely down her cheeks. She had never told this story. It was a forbidden topic on *Maribor*.

"I was ready to die. I was ready to accept my punishment. I was ready to get what I deserved . . . and then Manzo saved us. I don't know how he escaped. He never told us. But escape he did. He stole a bow, and with one skilled shot—the sort that only Almanzo Leviathan can accomplish—he pinned the rope of the blade to the wood, stopping the blade just before it chopped off my head. All I was left with was a scar." Her fingers found the back of her neck where a thin line of a scar protruded on the nape of her neck.

"In the midst of the shock of it all, Almanzo released Captain, who let out a roar and fought off any guards who were nearby. The element of surprise is what got us out that day. Manzo came to release me from the death trap after he set a few others free. His steady fingers lifted the blade and he apologized for my neck." Ilis let out a tear-choked laugh. "Ha! He apologized for a little blood after he saved my life." She scowled. "But we both knew I deserved more than just a scrape."

Ilis turned to the prince, who was still unmoving. "I came here to redeem myself . . . or die trying. As soon as we escaped, the Queen of the Under placed a bounty on our heads such that we could no longer set foot on the Under. It is too dangerous. Even faithful old contacts would probably turn us over for the reward. The crew is suffering for my mistakes!" Ilis said, her voice lifting. "They are bound to this side of the world where the seas are disappearing, unable to cross the Edge because of me! So you have to understand . . . this is why I came.

"The Queen of the Under has also set a prize for whoever will bring her the Crown Jewel of Basileia. A prize that is even higher than the price on our heads. I thought that if I stole it and returned it to her . . . I thought I could buy back our heads. I thought I could right my wrongs. I was going to steal the Crown Jewel and then leave. And then you came and messed everything up."

Ilis wiped away the tears.

"Now, to right one wrong would be to create another. To regain the crew's freedom would come at the cost of betraying you. But I had decided to do it. I was going to break your trust and run away with the Crown Jewel. I saw myself in you, you see, and that terrified me. So I wanted to escape you. Better to disappoint you than the crew of Maribor. But now, well, now none of it matters. We both lost. And I am a failure in all senses." Her gaze drifted toward the window.

"There is a part of me that wants all you said to be true. If the Moon does exist, at least that would be something I could do to try and make things right. But I can't just believe it because I want to. I need more proof than your word to believe all this."

Ilis rose.

"I am sorry you have had to discover so painfully that I only ever hurt those who are closest to me."

She left the room more broken than the prince.

CHAPTER TWELVE

The Sun was hot above her, the metal hot beneath her, and her dark cloak soaking in the heat made her hot all over. It was almost unbearable in the bright, scorching weather, but at least it was . . . away. The ground below was buzzing. People rushed everywhere. Some were still searching for lost family members. Others were helping in the rebuilding. Still others were running round in sheer panic, announcing that the end of the world was coming—or, worse, that the Under was on its way to attack them all at that very moment.

It was enough to drive anyone crazy.

Shifting her position, Ilis shook out one of her aching legs. She tried to hide in the shadow of the castle pinnacle she clung to—one of the few pinnacles still standing after the Quake—but with the Sun blazing down on her, she all but failed. Licking her lips, she tasted sweat.

Classes were supposed to resume the next morning, as education was prized only after books in Basileia, so Ilis resolved to attempt the normal life of a Basileian for a few more hot and miserable days.

Ilis looked down on Mount Oros and sighed. She would stay only as long as the prince took to regain consciousness, then she would slip away. Perhaps she could get a job on a merchant ship. She had very little of a plan formed; all she knew was she could no longer stay here.

***

Late that night found Ilis back in the prince's windowsill, staring at the trinkets she had stolen from him the night of the ball. She held them in her bandaged hands. This was all she had to show for her Oathdeath. She had given up everything in an attempt to earn back what was lost. And she had failed, yet again. Only this time, she had no family to buffer her fall.

Her silent self-pity was interrupted by someone entering the room. Ilis froze and watched as the crown prince entered, his eyes instantly drawn to his brother. With slow steps, he walked over to the bed. He looked sorrowful and oh so tired. To her surprise, he sat on the bed and patted Malcolm's hand almost lovingly.

With a sigh, he turned toward the window—and then his eyes landed on Ilis.

She raised an eyebrow. "Why, hello."

"You!" he sneered.

Ilis rose and crossed quickly to the door, not wanting to deal with the crown prince and his accusations.

"Did you steal it?" he demanded.

Ilis's thoughts raced. The Crown Jewel was missing. The crown prince, of all people, would know that.

"Whatever 'it' was?" the prince finished.

With the door handle in hand, her pounding heart settled. Ilis looked over her shoulder.

She shook her head.

"Foolish brother of mine!" he muttered. "Did he tell you what he believed?"

Ilis let go of the handle and turned back toward the crown prince. The fury that he so often wore was dimmed, replaced with a look of regret. He continued, even though Ilis had made no reply.

"He believed that the Moon, the mythical thing of lore, was the reason for our demise. I told him I knew the real reason. I told him I was working to stop it. I told him I would fix this." His face hardened. "But I was too late."

He paused.

"Why do we even try, when even if we succeed, we cannot save the ones we care about?"

Ilis stood hesitant in the doorway.

He stood and turned to face her, his voice firm. "Please understand: I love my brother more than anyone of your kind could comprehend. And I will stop at nothing to avenge him."

Ilis's heart beat in her chest, knowing she was to blame.

He turned once again to his pale, sleeping brother. "The Under will pay for this."

Ilis paused. She released the door handle she had been so desperately clinging to. "The Under?" Ilis questioned.

"Of course the Under!" the crown prince fired. "Who else has the capability to cause a Quake?"

"Why, I don't believe any mortal has those capabilities."

"But that's just it, isn't it? They aren't mortals; they're monsters."

Ilis merely raised an eyebrow.

The crown prince scowled. "But no matter. Soon, there will be none left of them."

Ilis gaped. "You mean to wage war against the Under?"

"They have waged war on us! We will merely be the ones to finish it."

"You cannot seriously think that the Quake was the Under's way of starting a war with us!" Ilis said fiercely.

"Oh, not just the Quake, young thief, but also the Sun and everything that has come with the scorching of our Prevailing Light." He stepped closer until he was towering over Ilis. "Don't you see? The Under has found a way to change the course of the Sun and thus destroy our side of the planet while they remain safe as can be down in their holes."

Ilis laughed in his face. "Why in the world would they do such a thing since it has brought such destruction upon them as well? Why would they risk the cold of unending winter just to scorch a people they have all but forgotten?"

The prince's eyes narrowed. "What do you mean?"

Ilis bit her tongue, which had rattled too quickly yet again. "Nothing," she mumbled.

They locked eyes. Ilis could feel his anger and rage toward the Under and knew in that moment he had put the pieces together. He could have her killed for this.

Her gaze turned to Prince Malcolm, still lying pale and silent, and the prince's eyes followed.

"Leave," the prince said gruffly. And Ilis heard the unspoken words. His brother's admiration for her gave her grace for this moment. But no promises any further.

She turned to the door.

"Good night, Your Highness."

***

The following morning, Ilis found herself once again in Prince Malcolm's room in the infirmary. The prince's condition was unchanged. What if he never woke up? She paced about the room for longer than she meant to. When she finally shook herself out of her worries, a glance at the clock told her she was late for class.

Ilis didn't even hurry through the halls. She was already late. Plus, it felt fitting to take up the prince's role of making a grand entrance.

As their old classroom had yet to be repaired, they met in a different room, which was slightly smaller but with the same layout as their old one. Pyra, sitting on the front row, waved to Ilis and pointed to an empty seat beside her. Ilis merely shook her head and motioned to the back of the class, keeping her bandaged hands hidden within her cloak. Pyra rolled her eyes but nodded, seeming to understand.

From the back of the class, Ilis again took in her fellow students. Everyone seemed to wear a frown on their lips and worry on their brows. Their numbers were down significantly, but the most drastic change was the loss of one specific annoying presence.

However, their wise professor knew how to distract his pupils. Ilis watched with humor as her classmates discussed the exploits of her pirate brethren, trying to decide which were truth and which were tall tales.

"I believe the Lass of the Seas is one of the few tales backed by proof," Pyra exclaimed in the middle of their discussion.

Chaz snorted. "That is because she is a girl, and you believe girls can do anything."

Pyra glared back. "That's because they can." Pyra shook her head and grinned at Chaz, as only a true friend can in the midst of a disagreement.

Dianne laughed shrilly. "But that is beside the point." She turned her fair eyes to Pyra. "Don't tell me you believe that one woman is responsible for the disappearance of all the cattle on the western shore!"

Pyra nodded, considering. "No, I am sure she had help, but I do believe it was all her idea!"

Dianne rolled her eyes.

"Why would someone even *want* that many cattle?" another classmate asked.

Ilis smirked, knowing the answer but keeping it to herself.

"And what about the tale of the Lass of the Seas stealing all the wine from the royals' summer house on the coast, right before the Sunago Festival last year?" a student asked. "I've always thought that one sounded like the perfect excuse for the royals not to be hospitable."

"Ahh, but let's examine the facts, shall we?" Pyra said, merrily regaining control of the conversation. She pointed toward another student. "Renwick, you yourself rode with the caravan taking the wine to their summer housing, did you not?"

The boy named Renwick nodded.

Pyra turned to Chaz. "And you, my friend, were in attendance for last year's Sunago Festival, so you can speak to the king's pure rage at finding his best wine gone."

Chaz merely grunted in assent.

But Pyra kept going, her voice excited. "I, myself, was there and saw with my own two eyes a woman veiled in white walking along the shore the night of the disappearance. Who else could it be if not the famed Lass of the Seas!"

For the first time since the Quake, Ilis truly smiled.

But the conversation and Ilis's smile were both cut short as a warning bugle sounded through the halls.

At first, Ilis thought it was for her—as if, somehow, her smile had given her identity away. She reached for her dagger instinctively. But then the bugle sounded again, and she saw the professor pale to the color of milk.

Ilis realized this was about something else entirely.

An attendant darted into the room and whispered something into the professor's ear. He scratched his long beard and nodded before raising his voice to the class. "Students, I need you all to evacuate single file and head to the lower levels."

The students erupted in quiet chaos.

Ilis stared at the ceiling and watched it crumble again, crushing them all. She blinked—and the ceiling was back to normal, sturdy as ever, with students still rushing out the door.

In her head, she knew crossing the room was safe. She knew that the ceiling would not crash in as it did last time—but panic was nonsensical, and at that moment, her panic was stronger than her sense.

As soon as everyone's attention was diverted, she stepped upon her desk, fumbled with the latch on the window because of her bandaged hands, opened the window, and disappeared without a trace.

She knew she was chancing it. The mountain being put on lockdown meant that there was a threat, and that threat was most likely outside. However, she felt safer outside than running through Oros Academy with crumbling walls that reminded her too much of what she had lost. Ilis swung herself from the windowsill to one beneath her and then began to climb down the side of the academy, toward the main entrance.

Busy in her panicked thoughts, Ilis didn't even think to look at her surroundings until it was too late.

A fiery blast exploded beneath her feet, and she was thrown from the wall.

She barely managed to snag the edge of a windowsill, slowing her fall, before tucking into a roll as she landed. However, she didn't account for landing on an incline, and thus slid down a good bit before coming to a stop on the roof of some building. Her left shoulder appeared to be bleeding, but Ilis ignored it for the moment.

Looking up, she could see the smoldering hole in the academy's side, right where she had been climbing. Stepping out further on the roof, Ilis felt a gust of air blast past her face, stinging her wounded shoulder.

Staring at the scaly beast circling above the castle's walls, Ilis let out a low whistle.

"So that's why they had us all get to safety."

CHAPTER THIRTEEN

Briefly, Ilis remembered all that she had seen in a faraway land where man and beast still worked together in harmony, but she dismissed that thought. Humans had to bond with dragons at the dragon's birth if they wanted any say in the beasts' behavior. Ilis stood there on the rooftop, staring at the winged beast for slightly longer than was probably sane.

The dragon soared over the rooftops of the mountain, its eyes a living fire. Its body alone was the size of a small house, and its wingspan was triple that. It was a deep ashy gray with white talons that gleamed in the bright light. She knew she should find cover and stay safe. That is what she would advise anyone else in her shoes.

But then her eyes fell upon a pair of oxen attached to a cart right beside the East Gate—large, juicy oxen—and an idea began to unfold in her head.

Thoughts whirling, Ilis charged through the abandoned streets. Shutters were barred and locked up tight. The eerie silence was penetrated only by the screeching roar of the dragon above. She was running toward the danger and chose to silence the fear that tried to pull her down. In the past she had thrived in the dangerous . . . surely, she could thrive there again.

By Ilis's analysis, the oxen were about a quarter of a league down the mountain. After running for about a minute, she stopped. She needed to move faster than this.

She closed her eyes and thought. Running along the rooftops would cut some of the distance, but it would also put her right under the nose of the dragon, and she preferred not to be dragon lunch today.

A frantic whinny entered her ears, and Ilis grinned.

Following the sound, she found a horse tied up next to a house. The horse's eyes were white with fear.

"Shhh," she said in a calm voice. "How about we go for a ride?"

She laid her hand on the steed's side and looked into its eyes. The horse shook its mane, as if to say it was up for whatever adventure she proposed. Launching herself onto its back, she set off.

Urging her steed to go as fast as it could, Ilis raced down the mountain streets. Occasionally she would hear the dragon screeching above her, but the buildings surrounding the streets blocked her view of the massive beast until she reached the clearing by the East Gate.

Pulling her horse to a stop, Ilis jumped off. Her feet hit the ground and she whacked the horse on the rump. It let off one sharp whinny before cantering off to find safety.

Ilis turned her attention to the oxen attached to a cart. Their eyes were wide with panic, and they shuffled nervously, pulling at their harnesses that secured them to a post. Past the oxen loomed the East Gate, which towered over the other buildings. The gate was arched, made of wood from Elgrave Forest (the forest whale's domain), and stretched multiple meters above the height of the outer wall of Mount Oros. While it was not as massive as the Main Gate, it still was a feat to behold, as Basileians and their paranoia could leave no entrance to their capital unfortified.

The towering gate was Ilis's focus. She ran toward it, keeping a careful eye on the sky. She knew that beyond the gate was Twin Peaks Valley, a large open field that would be in plain view of the dragon.

The gate itself was locked by a massive beam, a beam that could only be moved by the strength of six men. But thankfully, the East Gate had a wicket gate—a smaller door for everyday use, built into it. Casting another weary glance at the sky and finding it empty of winged beasts, Ilis slipped up to the wicket gate, pulled out pins from her hair, and knelt by the lock. Her bandaged hands hindered her slightly but not enough to keep her from mastering the lock. Pushing the door wide open, Ilis scanned the sky. When she was sure the coast was clear, she ran back to the oxen.

"Need help?" a voice said from behind her.

She spun to find Neil standing in the street.

"Yes," Ilis responded, thoughts spinning. "I need a red cape or something."

Neil looked around, his eyes landing on the Basileian flag flying on a pole beside the gate. It was red with a white mountain upon it. He pointed.

Ilis nodded. "That will do."

Neil climbed up the stone portion of the gate until he reached the flag and yanked it down. He dropped to the ground, did a little bow, and handed Ilis the flag.

Ilis rushed to the oxen, beginning to unharness them from the cart. "Go tell the archers to come to the East Gate with their stoutest arrows."

Neil hesitated, and Ilis shouted, "NOW!"

He nodded and ran off.

When she finished unhooking the oxen from the cart, she led them through the wicket gate. Ilis took a few steps out the gate and into the valley, keeping a careful eye on the sky above. The valley was a sad yellow color, with only patches of green grass. Ilis scowled at the Sun. Even up on the mountain it was scorching the grass.

Tying the red flag between the two oxen, Ilis slapped them on their rumps. Already skittish, the oxen needed no further urging to take off at a panicked trot into the valley, the red flag flapping between them.

She rushed back through the door inside the walls of Mount Oros and slammed it closed behind her. Leaning with her back against the door, Ilis watched with wide eyes as she saw the dragon standing on the palace roof at the top of the mountain. It opened its mouth and a screeching roar echoed down the mountain.

With a mixture of horror and awe, Ilis stared as the dragon spread its massive gray wings, leapt into the sky, and began soaring down the mountain—right toward her.

Her brain told her running was foolish and would only attract attention from the beast, but all her body wanted to do was *move!* Clenching her teeth, she dropped into a ball, wrapped her shaking arms around her knees, and tried to breathe.

She kept her eyes open—figuring if she was about to die by dragon fire, she might as well face the beast eyes open—and watched as the dragon soared through the air and over the buildings of Mount Oros.

The moments seemed to stretch upon themselves. Ilis noticed it all in great detail. She noticed the power of the dragon's wings as the beast flew over the rooftops such that each flap sent roof tiles flying in various directions. She noticed its tail, which swung as it flew like a great whip, no doubt powerful enough to dismember buildings. She noticed its ash gray scales, which shimmered in the sunlight. And as the dragon got mere moments away, Ilis noticed its eyes—eyes which held a wealth of wisdom untapped.

It was a terrifying beast. It was a glorious beast. And she was right in its path.

Ilis sucked in a breath. The dragon was upon her.

But the distraction was enough.

In a moment, it was over. The dragon flew over the East Gate, a wave of wind sent by its wings pulling at her clothes and blasting dust into her eyes.

She heard the dragon roar yet again, followed by panicked noises from the oxen. Her ears picked up the sound of soldiers shouting—hopefully Neil had gotten them there fast enough.

Ilis tried to stand and found her knees so weak she fell back against the door. She laughed softly to herself, took a breath, and tried again.

Her limbs were still shaking, the image of the beast soaring straight at her seared into her brain, but she managed to walk and then run.

She had done her part; now it was time to blend in and take cover.

***

Ilis slipped through the nearest window and found herself in the armory. Leaning against the brick wall, Ilis ripped open her sleeve to see how her shoulder looked. There was a gash about four inches long but thankfully not too deep.

"And that's what you get for disobeying orders," Ilis said with ire, parroting the words Captain had used on her many a time.

Sighing, she turned her attention to the armory and found it utterly empty.

"Hello?" Ilis said.

Silence was her reply.

A sly gleam appeared in her eyes, but no one was there to see it. No one was there to see her explore the ranks of Basileia's weapons nor count the registered guards from the logbook nor unlock the master guard's safe and read its contents. None saw her as she read about a special sect of soldiers set aside for the purpose of *digging*.

Some might say this was a deplorable thing to do when those same guards were out protecting her safety, but Ilis would only retort that it was her sworn duty as the Royal Thief to steal all the information she could about her "beloved" country. They had wanted a thief after all.

When fully satisfied with her plunder, Ilis made her way back up to Oros Academy, keeping a careful eye on the sky. She neither saw nor heard any signs of the dragon anymore. Hopefully, this meant the danger was over. The streets—which were still more rubble than anything else after the Quake—were now eerily abandoned, and she marveled at the efficiency of the city's evacuation system. She walked through the ajar doors of the academy, then ducked through a passageway that led to the academy's basement. That was where she was supposed to be, and for once, Ilis was content to be there.

She easily went unnoticed amidst the chaos, sticking to the shadows with her head down while her eyes drank in the sight around her. Medical stations were set up for any wounded. Hundreds of people were sitting in various corners of the giant mountain basement. Gazes were sharp and nerves on edge as people cowered in fear of the beast who flew freely above.

Ilis recognized a few of her classmates about. Chaz was yelling at a member of the Hearing Tribe who would not let him leave, saying he should be out there defending the city. Dianne was weeping over who knows what. The boy named Renwick was using his Speaking Tribe skills, chittering softly to a group of squirrels that had taken refuge in his coat. Upon further inspection, Ilis wasn't sure if Renwick was comforting the squirrels or if the squirrels were comforting him. It was unnerving to see her classmates, who had just been jovially discussing current events, suddenly brought to such fear.

Ilis slid up to a medical station and swiped some cleaning alcohol, a towel, a needle, and thread. She then grabbed a lantern from its hook on the wall and went to find an empty corner. Finding one, she faced the wall, successfully hiding her shoulder in the corner. The lantern did not offer the best light, but it was enough.

With her hands still bandaged, Ilis poured the alcohol over her shoulder, grimacing as it stung like fire. She wiped it clean. Ilis tried to hold the needle in her crippled fingers, but the movements were choppy and painful. She dropped the needle and sighed.

"Hey," a voice spoke from behind her.

Ilis turned to find Pyra. Without waiting for Ilis to reply, the nurse knelt to get a better look at her shoulder.

She adjusted the lantern, making it shine brighter, and then nodded.

"That's a good one." Pyra reached for the alcohol and poured more, causing Ilis to gasp.

Pyra's eyes grew wide. "Sorry!" Then she shrugged. "But better safe than sorry." She chuckled to herself before getting serious again. "Infection is a nasty business." She took the needle and thread and looked Ilis in the eyes. "Warning, this is going to hurt."

Ilis nodded and let out a small grin. "Wouldn't be the first time."

Pyra laughed, loud and light. "You are right, and if I had to guess, probably not the last either."

With nimble fingers, she stitched Ilis back up.

"There!" Pyra said with a small, satisfied smile. "If I may say so myself, that is some of my best work!"

Ilis looked at Pyra and opened her mouth to say thank you, but Pyra interrupted her before she got the words out.

"Don't mention it," Pyra said with a grin. Hopping up, she left as quickly as she had come.

Ilis stared after the girl for a while before turning and leaning her head against the wall. She sat there for hours, merely watching. She gained a good deal of information from her vigil: which teacher had a soft spot for tear-filled students, which students had a temper, and who could keep their head in the midst of chaos. Ilis watched as a young laundry maid with tear-stained cheeks mumbled about the Under coming up through the tunnels to destroy them all.

After an hour or so, news began to travel that the dragon had been killed outside the gates. An hour after that, people were given permission to head back to the upper levels. Making sure her cape covered her shoulder, Ilis disappeared among the crowd and filed out into the Sun.

Keeping in the shadows to escape the heat, Ilis headed toward the infirmary to see Malcolm. She was stopped dead in her tracks by the sight of a pair of guards standing outside the door. They glared at her icily, and Ilis thought about fleeing. But before she could, two other soldiers came into the hallway behind her, blocking the exit.

"You are to come with us," one of the stern soldiers said.

Ilis lifted her chin. "And if I refuse?"

She felt the tip of a sword prick the back of her neck.

She smirked. "Of course, who would refuse such a kind request as yours?"

Ilis bowed grandly, faking calmness.

"Lead the way."

***

Once again, Ilis found herself standing in the middle of the Council, at the highest level of the heart of the mountain. The king was absent; instead, the crown prince sat in his seat.

She cleared her throat and lifted her chin, wiping all thoughts of doubt from her mind. She needed to be strong. She needed to be resolved.

She needed to be a pirate.

"How can I help you?" Ilis asked the crown prince.

"My father is dead," the crown prince stated, fury in his voice. "Killed in the dragon attack."

Ilis took a step back, her heart pounding in her chest. Malcolm would wake to find his father gone.

"I . . . I am so sorry." Ilis managed.

The crown prince, who was now king, glared at her. "What do you know about the dragon attack?"

She wondered what his angle was. Why was she here?

"I know he blasted a hole in the side of the academy." Ilis thought back to where she had seen smoke from the top of the infirmary. "As well as torched part of the market." Ilis realized she was chewing her lip and forced herself to stop. "I also know that oxen were let out through the East Gate, and while the dragon was feasting, the archers were able to kill the beast."

"With the loss of thirty-eight men, *my father* included," the new king said harshly. "That means that in the past three days, through the Quake collapsing our barracks killing hundreds and the dragon attack, over one-fourth of our army has been wiped out—as well as our king."

Ilis tried to process this information. She had assumed that a few soldiers had been lost during the attack with the dragon, but she didn't know about the collapse of the barracks—and how could she have known about the loss of the king? Her thoughts spun, trying to decipher what all of this meant for her.

The king took a deep breath and continued, "And why would you say that the dragon attacked?"

At this point, the Head Librarian, Kat's father, lost his patience. "Sire, this is preposterous! What validity can there be in anything this . . . thief says?"

Prince Jasper spoke up, his eyes meeting Ilis's kindly. "We are told that a young lass is the one who let the oxen out, creating the diversion. Would that young lass happen to be you?"

But the new king was not to be deterred. "The Royal Thief," he began, using Ilis's newfound title as if it carried weight—which, to these people, she supposed it did— "predicted the beasts waking up just the other day, at dinner in my father's presence, so I want to hear her thoughts."

Ilis's heart beat a little quicker. This had the potential of getting bad. Very bad.

"Well?" The king prodded.

Acting as calm as Captain in the eye of a storm—which was scarily calm—Ilis shrugged and replied, "The dragon was hungry. Are not its actions with the oxen proof of that?"

"Hungry?" The king sneered, his eyes lit like dragon fire. "Wouldn't you like us to believe that?"

Feigning innocence, Ilis asked, "Why, what is the alternative?" Though she knew full well what his answer would be.

"That it was sent by the Under," the king spat.

Murmurs ran through the room. Council members looked at her with horror and fear, as if she had suddenly stepped out of one of their nightmares.

A chill ran through Ilis, but she did not betray it. Instead, she let out a small laugh. "You cannot be serious!"

The king glared icily at Ilis. "We have reports of people passing between sides, and whispers which claim that Unders have found a way to control winged beasts. Those two facts more than warrant our suspicion—which is why we summoned you here. I don't think it is a coincidence that the trouble started once you got here."

Great billows, this is bad, Ilis thought. In her peripheral, she saw guards move to block the exits. *This is very, very bad.*

The king stood. "In the presence of my entire family, you admitted to believing that there was a way to live at peace with dragons."

Yup, this is BAD.

"And just last night, you admitted to me that you've been to the Under."

Mmmhmm, decidedly bad.

Council members pushed back their chairs and stood along with the king, their faces twisted in rage as they muttered curses under their breath.

"We welcomed in an Under spy," one council member said, his voice trembling. "Great Lights, forgive our foolishness."

The king pointed his finger in her face. "You lying, thieving little . . ." He took a sharp breath and composed himself. He locked eyes with her one last time.

"My father was a fool to give you as a gift to Malcolm," he sneered. "Take her away."

***

Ilis was held in prison for the entirety of three hours. She thought about staying there, but they had failed to search her properly; and so, if only to teach the guards a lesson, she pulled out the wire hidden in the heel of her other shoe, unlocked her cell, and snuck out.

Silent and unseen, Ilis snuck to her room to pack her things. Her glowstone torch, her daggers, a cloak, and other items were tossed into a satchel with little care for their well-being. Her only thought was to get off of this wretched mountain. At this point it did not matter where she went, only that she got away from here. She had failed yet again. It was time to simply embrace the fact and live with its consequences.

Ilis paused, closed her eyes to shut out the tears, and took a heavy breath. Guilt over Malcolm's fate haunted her, but her presence here would not change anything. There was nothing she could do to help him now. There was nothing she could do to right her wrongs. She was useless here. Hope seemed to have forsaken her.

She moved to the window and stuck her head out, letting the harsh Sun warm her skin. With a glance to her left, her eyes fell upon the coastline. For the first time, she noticed how much of the coast she could see. In fact . . .

She stepped back in her room and found a spyglass in one of the chests. Lifting it to her eyes, she focused in on one particular bay, a favorite of the crew's. Sure enough, *Maribor* was docked there.

It felt like a punch to the gut. There they were. So close. And yet she had severed any option of her ever being with them again.

As long as breath fills my lungs, hope shall fill my heart.

The familiar words flitted through Ilis's head without warning.

Ilis knew little about her mother other than that she had died giving birth to Ilis, and that these had been her favorite words. While Ilis did not want to find fault in her dead mother's treasured saying, she could not help wondering what reason there was to hope now.

A knock sounded on the door.

She froze. They had discovered her escape faster than she thought. Rushing back into the middle of the room, she began gathering her things.

"Ilis? Hello?" came a whisper-shout from the other side of the door. Ilis turned toward the door and cocked her head. It sounded like . . .

"Ilis," ventured the voice outside her door, "it's Kat! I've found something that you should see."

Ilis paused, considering.

"Oh, Ilis! Where are you?" Kat mumbled, her voice barely reaching Ilis's ears.

Ilis threw open the door, startling the girl and causing her to jump. Ilis scanned the stairway behind her, but it was empty. Kat, and Kat alone, stood before her.

Grabbing Kat by the shoulders, Ilis pulled her into the room and closed the door.

With shaking hands, the young girl handed Ilis a letter.

"Whatever they say," Kat managed to utter, "I don't believe you are evil."

"Thanks," Ilis said dryly.

"Remember the books I was trying to show you the other day? Well, I went back, and . . ." Kat nodded to the letter. "I found this, and I think you should read it. It was written to you."

The letter felt cold and heavy beneath Ilis's fingers. She glanced only slightly at the seal marked with a C before tearing it open. The parchment was old, smudged with years' worth of dust . . .

Her eyes flew over the words, scarcely believing them to be true.

"Oh. My. Stars," Ilis muttered, clutching the letter to her chest.

This changed everything.

CHAPTER FOURTEEN

The beginning semblance of a plan began to form in her mind. If this were true, then there was only one thing to do. But could she dare to even try? It would mean facing her fears. It would mean risking her life—again. And she couldn't do it alone.

She began to pace in her room, heedless of Kat's eyes on her.

I'm going to need help, she thought. *And a lot of it.*

Two ideas popped into her head.

But would they all say yes?

Ilis looked at Kat and tried to smile kindly, chastising herself for scaring the girl earlier. "I've got to go, but . . . thank you."

Kat grinned. "Of course! And I'm going to keep digging. I think there is more to this story than meets the eye. I want to find the last Royal Thief's book. Every Basileian writes one, so she must have had one, but I can't track it down."

Mulling over the letter's contents, Ilis nodded. "I think you're right. Feel free to stay here and check out my room. There are a bunch of books; maybe it's among them."

Kat's eyes widened. "Heaps of books, that's fantastic!" She jumped up and down. "I won't disappoint you!"

Ilis nodded, her thoughts running abuzz. She needed to talk to the others. Checking her watch, she figured she could catch them on their way out of class if she hurried. Ilis smiled at Kat and patted her on the shoulder. Kat, beaming with pride, snuck in a quick hug before heading straight to Ilis's bookshelf.

***

With her hood low, she hid in the shadows and waited for the class to let out. Neil was the first one to exit, but before she even made a sound to try and get his attention, he spotted her in the shadows. He cocked his head and then nodded, seeming to read her thoughts. He paused at the doorway and snagged Pyra and Chaz as they walked out.

He said something to them, and then they all reentered the classroom.

"What is this all about, Forester?" Chaz asked when the professor had left and it was just the three of them standing in the front of the classroom.

"I don't know, but I figure she will clear it up for us," Neil responded as Ilis slid through the doorway.

Pyra gasped, startled, and Chaz tensed. After a long pause, Pyra ventured, "Is it true what they say?"

"It depends on what aspect you are talking about," Ilis answered slowly.

Suddenly, she was questioning her decision to trust them. They were Basileians through and through—and what she was about to ask them to do would be considered treason.

But they were also Malcolm's friends. Surely, they would do anything to finish his quest.

"Have you been to the Under?" Chaz growled, stepping forward and poking his finger in her chest—not the smartest move on his part, considering she was a pirate. Ilis knew he didn't know this, but her temper flared anyway. She sidestepped away from him.

"Yes, I've been to the Under!" Ilis fired, annoyed with his continual pigheadedness. "And you will too if things go my way!"

Ilis regretted her rash words as soon as she said them. Pyra drew back and shuddered. Neil looked at her with wide eyes and shook his head, as if to say, "You just hung your own noose." But Chaz outdid them all by replacing the finger pointed at her chest with his sword.

"Give me one good reason I should not turn you in right now," Chaz said, his eyes a steely gray.

Ilis grimaced and took a breath, trying to calm her nerves. "Stars, I wish Malcolm were here to help me."

"Why would he help you?" Pyra asked with a fire in her voice. Her fingers tugged at her long blonde hair.

Ilis looked into her eyes, fearful that she had lost a friend. "He was right," Ilis breathed.

Somehow, they all understood her meaning.

The Moon was real.

"You believe the Moon is the reason for the world ending?" Neil asked somberly.

Ilis merely nodded.

"What changed? How do you know for certain?" Pyra asked, still skeptical.

"Now I have proof." Ilis pulled out the letter and unfolded it, gathering a gasp from Neil. "This is from the last Royal Thief," Ilis began. She showed it to the others.

Dearest Royal Thief,

> *If this letter is being read, it most likely means that royalty has found at least one Royal Thief to take my place. The royals do seem to love allying closely with us. However, I must inform you that it is all a lie. You are not a Royal Thief but a Moon Thief. Basileia will not have a true Royal Thief until the Moon has been completed. Up to this point, the title of Moon Thief has been passed down, with no need for coaxing, through the family line; but, as I am about to leave and have no child of my own, I felt the need to write this, that you might carry on the legacy.*
>
> *The Moon is not a myth.*
>
> *Mysterious it shall always be, but its existence is very real. And I fear for our world's safety, hope, and peace should I be the last Moon Thief on this side of the horizon.*
>
> *I am taking the power of the Moon to the Under in order to maintain the equilibrium of our world until all the Moon pieces have been found. If I do not, I fear our world will capsize. I grant to you the*

charge of locating the final pieces and completing the Moon. Our world may very well depend upon it.

One Moon Thief to another,
Anne Isilty

Neil held the letter in his hands as if he were holding a piece of the Moon itself. Chaz scratched his chin, his eyes lost in thought. Pyra's face seemed to glow.

"So the last Royal Thief before you . . ." Pyra started.

"Was a Moon Thief," Ilis finished, still in awe at the discovery herself.

"How do we know this letter is real?" Chaz asked, ever the skeptic, though—thankfully—he had re-sheathed his sword by this point.

"It's real," Neil answered, still holding the letter and examining it. "This is the last Royal Thief's handwriting."

They all turned to Neil.

He looked up, his cheeks turning pink. "I . . . uh . . . we studied it in a class once. Since the last Royal Thief disappeared, the king commissioned the Foresters to look for any signs of her throughout the kingdom."

Chaz huffed, seemingly unconvinced.

"What's the alternative?" Neil asked. "That Ilis forged it?"

Chaz glared at Neil. "I didn't say that."

"Boys!" Pyra said sweetly. "Let's try and stay on topic, shall we?"

Pyra turned to Ilis, waiting for her to continue. Only Ilis hadn't gotten this far in planning, and she was suddenly at a loss about how to rally her troops to the cause.

"So the Moon is real," Neil said, trying to help her out.

Ilis nodded. "Yes, and I think I know where the rest of it is."

They stared at her blankly—whether in awe or disbelief, Ilis could not decipher. Ilis took a deep breath and then reached into her satchel, pulling out her glowstone torch. Popping the shining stone out of her reflective contraption, she held it in her palm. She could feel its power radiating in her fingers.

Neil's jaw dropped.

"You've had a piece of the Moon in your satchel?" he said, jaw dropping.

Ilis shrugged.

Everyone stared.

"You've had a piece of the Moon . . . in your satchel!" Neil's words, usually so rare, rushed out like a flood. "Did you know what it was?"

Ilis gave him a scandalized look.

Neil looked at her in disbelief. "Right, who would think this magically glowing stone was part of the Moon?"

"Who would think a mere stone was part of the fabled King of the Night?" She pointed at herself. "Not me."

Neil let a sliver of a smile show before shrugging in defeat. He looked down at her satchel. "Have any more in there?"

Ilis raised an eyebrow. "You are so hard to please."

"Eh, didn't hurt to ask."

She ran her fingers across the stone. "We call it glowstone on the seas, and it is about as precious a gem as you can find, but I had no idea what it truly was." She gazed down at the treasure tenderly before facing her audience. "But here is the thing: there is a buyer out there who, I believe, has bought all pieces other than the Oval and this one. This buyer has paid ridiculous prices for any and all glowstones. My own crew has sold many for such a price. Shells, some marauders even slaughtered whole villages in order to obtain the stones and then sell them to her."

"Her?" Neil asked, his face pale.

Ilis chewed her lip. "The Queen of the Under."

Pyra plopped down to the stone floor, her legs no longer able to support her. Neil paled and started pacing. Chaz just straightened his shoulders and confronted the facts directly.

"The Queen of the Under has the rest of the Moon?" Chaz asked.

"Yes," Ilis said with a deep breath. "She has used the pieces to adorn her crown."

The crown Ilis had failed to steal. Memories about her last heist flashed through her head unbidden. The sound of her footsteps heading up the stairs to her death. The feeling of the wooden brace around her neck.

Hearing the blade dropping, feeling the sting upon her neck, and then finding herself still alive—but burdened by guilt and shame.

Ilis shook her head, clearing her thoughts.

Truth be told, this was the worst idea she had *ever* had—and that was saying something. She looked at those around her. Pyra was sitting cross-legged on the floor, her skirt splayed about her as she chewed on her lip. Neil's face was concerned as he paced. And Chaz looked like he was trying to solve a puzzle.

Chaz stroked his chin. "And supposedly, the only way to save our world is to finish putting the Moon back together?"

"So we have to go to the Under?" Pyra asked, dread in her eyes.

"Beriyth to be exact, but if we are to finish the quest Prince Malcolm set us on, then . . . yes," Ilis responded.

"And you want us to go with you?" Chaz asked.

Ilis looked down, her own thoughts spinning. If she planned on asking them to risk their lives, they needed to know the truth. Ilis groaned. This was going to hurt.

"There is something you should know . . . About the queen's crown . . . Well, let's just say, this isn't the first time I've tried to steal it."

"Tried?" Chaz asked. "Meaning you failed?"

"Abysmally so." Ilis could feel the shame coloring her cheeks. "I led the crew into a death trap, and we got caught." Ilis rubbed the nape of her neck.

"It was a close one, huh?" Neil asked, reading the truth in her eyes.

"Aye, you could say that. We were on the verge of being beheaded when Almanzo—one of my crew members—managed to break out and save us. Only, now the queen has accurate sketches of our faces, and she has placed a price upon our heads."

"How much?" Pyra said softly.

"Around a library," Ilis said.

Pyra gasped. Chaz and Neil simply looked at her in shock.

"Why, you could feed a small kingdom for years off of that!" Pyra exclaimed.

"And you are willing to risk your own safety and try again?!" Neil asked incredulously.

Ilis was silent for a moment before responding. She shrugged. "If Malcolm was right, the fate of the world rests upon the completing of the Moon."

"Hold the Stars," Chaz said. "You are trying to get us to follow you into a heist, *to the Under*—our sworn enemies—to steal something you have already tried to steal and *failed* to do so . . . But you didn't just fail, you failed so utterly that you and your entire crew barely escaped with your lives and not without a ludicrous bounty on your heads." He threw his hands up into the air. "And you think we will follow *you?*"

Her heart sank in her chest. She supposed she had thought too rashly when she imagined they would want to come with her. And who could blame them?

Ilis took a deep breath. "That is up to you," Ilis replied. "You don't have to come. But I am going, with or without you."

"Why?" Neil asked softly.

Ilis turned to him and considered this before responding. "I just have to."

She peered back up at them and found them just staring at her.

Chaz was right. Why should they follow *her?* Hadn't she made the same greedy request of her crew? She was losing hope in even herself.

And what would it even have been for? Prince Malcolm seemed to believe it would save the world, and while she was beginning to agree with him, she could not deny that there was still another motive driving her. She supposed she was *still* just looking for a way to prove herself. And as foolish as this was, this would at least be some sort of redemption. But why would anyone want to come with her on this quest? Who could believe in her if she didn't even believe in herself?

"I'm in," Neil said, hope in his voice. Ilis spun and looked at the young man before her. She wanted to ask him why he was willing to risk so much, but she figured that wasn't the best recruiting technique so merely nodded her thanks.

Pyra took a deep breath, stood, and said, "Me too. If I can do something to help our world, all the risk will be worth it."

Ilis sighed in relief, but Chaz began to shake his head. "No. Pyra, it's too dangerous."

Pyra's grin dropped. "And what makes you think you have the authority to stop me?" she challenged, a temper Ilis did not know the sweet girl possessed flaring up.

Chaz was not daunted by the fire in her eyes. "I don't," he said plainly, "but I am pretty sure you would lose your job in the infirmary if they found out you went traipsing around in the Under!"

"They wouldn't have to know," Pyra said, teeth clenched.

Chaz glared back. "If you went, I would make sure they did."

"Blazes, Chaz!" Pyra fired. "You don't get to make my choices for me! I am going to help Ilis; consequences be burned!" She took a breath and tried to compose herself. "The real question is, are you coming with us?"

Chaz stared at the small, spunky girl for a moment. Ilis wondered how two such different people had become such good friends—but before she could figure it out, Chaz dragged his hand down his face and let out a moan. "Fine, I'm in."

While this wasn't the way Ilis had envisioned rallying her team to the cause, it would have to do.

Chaz began to pace. Ilis could see the wheels in his head spinning.

"But wait," Chaz said, his brow once again furrowed in thought. "Even if all the pieces of the Moon are in the Under, once we get all the pieces, how do we complete the Moon? The other Moon Thieves must have had a place where they pieced the Moon back together, but we don't know where that is."

There was silence in the room.

Ilis's face was stone cold. She had no good answer for this one. Her hasty planning hadn't gotten that far. Though she hated to admit it, even to herself, Chaz had a sound point. She had a pretty good idea where a lot of the pieces of the Moon were, but she had no guarantee that this was the rest of them. Could she ask this new crew to put their lives on the line for this venture when she did not even know if this was where the rest of the Moon was? And then, even if it was the remainder of the Moon, surviving this mission and having all of the Moon pieces in their possession would mean nothing if they did not know where and how to complete it.

Suddenly, Ilis wished she had time to study more about the Moon Thieves. Perhaps Kat, that young book lover, could help her find out more . . . Perhaps there was a book with answers . . . Perhaps . . .

Neil's voice interrupted her thoughts.

"I know where it is," he said.

CHAPTER FIFTEEN

It took Ilis a minute to process the words that came so quietly while she was deep in her thoughts.

Then she spun on Neil.

"What?"

Neil nodded, looking pale but resolute. "I know where the Moon is located . . . or, where the pieces that the Moon Thieves pieced back together are."

"But . . . how?" Ilis asked.

Neil opened his mouth and then closed it, as if he didn't know how to reply.

"Are you a Moon Thief?" Ilis asked.

Neil licked his lips. "Maybe? If so, I am just an honorary one."

"Just an honorary one," Chaz repeated, staring at Neil as if he were seeing him for the first time.

"So when we have all the pieces, you could take us there to finish the Moon?" Pyra asked, her eyes wide with wonder.

Neil just nodded.

They all just sat there staring at Neil.

"Well, where is it?" Ilis asked.

"Somewhere safe," was his only reply.

Who in the world are you? Ilis wanted to ask—but then Neil changed the topic.

"I'd love to just keep chatting, but Ilis, I do believe you are being hunted at the moment."

Pyra turned to Ilis and nodded. "He is right. We should hurry. Also, we are going to have to get you a change of clothes if we want to smuggle you out of the city."

Ilis looked down at her clothes and realized that her dark dress and cape did rather stick out in the daylight.

Pyra grinned and grabbed her hand. "Don't worry, I've got just the thing for you in my room." Pyra turned to the boys. "You two, go gather your things, get us some horses, and meet us out front of the academy in thirty minutes." And with that, Pyra snuck Ilis away.

Pyra's room was pale and bright with yellow curtains and white bedspreads on the two beds. A light oak desk sat in the middle of the room with a vase of sunflowers sitting on top. Pyra gestured to the other bed in her room and explained, "I share a room with Dianne, but she is hardly ever here."

Ilis balked at this information. She could hardly imagine the two girls living together.

Pyra laughed lightly at Ilis's face. "Yeah, that's about how I feel about it too." She dove into her closet and began searching about. Finally, she came back triumphantly carrying a bright pink dress.

"You've got to be kidding me," Ilis said, staring at the monstrosity.

Pyra put a hand on her hip. "You are the most wanted person on the mountain right now. You *need* a disguise."

Ilis threw up her hands. "Then make me an old man! A beggar! Anything but *that!*"

Ten minutes later, Pyra and a lass dressed in bright pink with a large white hat were waiting in front of Oros Academy.

From atop a brown steed, Neil couldn't control his laughter—until Ilis glared daggers at him, that is.

Chaz cleared his throat, trying not to be distracted by the difference a fine dress made in the thief. "So, uh, how are we doing this? All the tunnels to the Under have long been sealed up . . . not that we could navigate them even if they weren't."

Ilis took a deep breath. "By ship," she said. If only they let us, she added to herself.

***

The journey down the mountain to the coast took a whole of two days. Ilis wore the pink dress for only two hours of that time. As soon as they were out of sight from the walls of Mount Oros, she shed the monstrosity and changed into black trousers and a white tunic, her usual garb on the seas. They did not push as hard as Ilis had on her way up and so ended up camping two nights along the way.

They were uneventful days, the kind that seem a blur when one looks back at them. The only noteworthy happenings were when Chaz and Pyra got into a fight about the color of the grass, when Neil started talking in his sleep about "pirate thieves," and when Ilis found herself genuinely enjoying the company of her new crew.

However, through it all, Ilis had a deep-seated unease. She was returning to the home she had reprehensibly abandoned. Few things were worse than evoking Oathdeath, but not honoring it after you had evoked it was hands down one of them. There was only one way she could see this working . . . She began rehearsing in her head what she would say when she faced the crew.

When *Maribor* came into sight, Chaz pulled his horse to a stop. Ilis had led them to a group of trees at the top of a hill that looked down upon one of *Maribor*'s frequent docking places, the bay Ilis had seen from her tower a few days prior.

"Is that what I think it is?" Chaz challenged, pointing to the ship without any clear flags declaring its purpose.

"Depends on what you think it is," Ilis replied, but her pensive look must have answered him.

"*This* is your grand plan? To go on a pirate ship?" Chaz challenged. They all began dismounting their horses.

"Sailing over The edge isn't exactly the easiest voyage," Neil said. "It would take an extraordinary captain."

"Oh, and so just because the thieving pirates can sail, we should trust them?" Chaz retorted.

Ilis looked at him seriously. "No, that is not why I trust them."

"Oh?" Chaz said loftily. "Then why?"

Ilis looked down at the crew who had heard her first words, pulled out her first tooth, and taught her how to swim. She smiled despite the unease inside of her.

"Because they raised me."

Silence struck the group. Ilis turned to see Chaz with a slack jaw, Pyra with wonder in her eyes, and Neil looking like he might be sick.

"You're a pirate!" Chaz accused.

Ilis raised an eyebrow. "Just figuring that out, are you?"

Pyra stared at Ilis, dumbfounded.

"Well, technically I *was* a pirate. And I will warn you, there is a rather high chance they will turn me away. Which, if that happens, I don't know what we will do."

"Why wouldn't they welcome you?" Neil asked.

"Let's just say that in order to leave last time, I had to swear I would never return—and in doing so burnt quite a few bridges."

"So, you want us to follow you onto a pirate ship whose trust you have betrayed? Greaaaaat. This just keeps getting better and better," Chaz said.

"Look," Ilis started, hands outstretched as if to offer peace. "I know this is a lot to take in, and you can still back out. But this is probably your last chance. Just . . . don't make a decision based on old prejudices, okay?"

Ilis turned and unsaddled her horse, slipped off its bridle, and patted it on the side. "Thanks, buddy. Be free." She slapped it on the rump and the horse set off back toward the mountain.

She looked at her friends for a moment. "I will be the first to acknowledge that this is a long shot and probably the first of many long shots. But it's the best plan I've got." And with that, she turned and started down the hill.

Pyra took a hesitant breath and then began unsaddling her horse as well.

Chaz looked down at the band of pirates and muttered, "First I work with thieves, now pirates, and soon Unders . . . This is terrible for my career." Reluctantly, he followed suit. He and Pyra let their horses go free and then began walking down the hill after Ilis.

Neil was the last to let his horse go and head down the hill. He kept looking down at the ship and its occupants with something akin to dread.

When they reached the shore, they found a rowboat left there from a previous heist.

The *Maribor* wasn't far, and the rowboat approached swiftly under Chaz's strong rowing, but Ilis sat perched at the front of the small boat with worry attempting to dig a hole in her belly for what felt like an eternity. She looked up at the *Maribor*, with her majestic dark wood and brilliant orange sails, and saw her former friends silhouetted against the Sun.

What would the crew say? And more importantly, what would Captain say?

As they drew up alongside *Maribor,* Ilis had just one thought. *Please, please just let down the rope ladder. Just give me a chance.*

As if her pleas were answered, the ladder tumbled down, slapping the ship's side with an unfriendly thud.

Ilis turned to her mountain friends. "Uh, maybe just stay down here for a minute," Ilis said to the others. "If they agree to help us, I'll call you up."

While no one seemed thrilled about the idea, neither did they protest.

And so, Ilis climbed up the rope ladder—her movements strong but her heart trembling. She had sworn she would never return, and now here she was, returning—a failure—and with yet *another* request for them to risk their lives.

Even if they didn't step foot on land in the Under, they were still traversing the Edge and sailing in Beriythian waters. It was a risk they had decided was not worth taking after the bounties had been placed on their heads. And yet, now she was asking them to do just that.

Slipping over the ship's railing with practiced ease, her boots hit the deck—the deck where she had taken her first steps, the deck where she had learned to fight, the deck that was *very clearly* no longer her home.

The swords which she had fought alongside all her life were now pointed warily *at* her. The eyes whose intentions she had learned to read with a glance were now hesitant, some even glaring—but all disturbingly hard to read. The forms of her family, ever welcoming in the past even after her most abysmal of failures, were now tense—feet shifting away, grips on swords tightening, and breathing coming in and out in tense gasps as if even just the sight of her made the air hard to swallow. Their lips, which had encouraged, taught, and teased now whispered to one another furtively, and the small snippets of murmurs she did pick up were far from friendly.

A swell of shame burst up inside of her.

What was I thinking? Ilis thought. Who am I to think they would help me after everything I've done? I left them. Abandoned them. Separated myself from them in the most painful of ways. I don't deserve their help.

The seconds felt like slices of eternity, each one weighing her soul down until she thought she couldn't stand it. It was all too much. Their gazes too drastically changed from the family she knew of old. She couldn't ask them for help. This was all a foolish endeavor.

The rampage of her own thoughts, as well as the whispers of the crew, were interrupted by a voice.

"Ilis," Captain said, his booming voice carrying a demand for respect. It was his 'captain' voice—the one he barked orders in; the one he reprimanded crew members in; the one that made you feel foolish for even breathing when it was directed toward you.

There was an eruption of silence.

"You evoked Oathdeath." His words sounded like a death sentence—a death sentence Ilis felt she deserved.

I should just leave right now. I can bow my head, mumble apologies, and jump into the rowboat. We can forget that the world is ending, forget that we probably know how to stop it . . . Anything but face the crew . . . Anything but face my father.

She squeezed her eyes shut. Those thoughts sounded so appealing. Better to flee than face the shame of failing yet again. Better that than facing the damage she had wrought on her relationships here on *Maribor*. Their trust in her had dwindled to dust like the growing shores, and she came asking for help?

But the Captain wasn't done. "What makes you think you can just come traipsing back?"

Great question. What did make me think I could? Ilis found herself wondering.

With every intention of just fleeing and forsaking all responsibility, she opened her eyes. The mumble of apologies was on the tip of her lips, but then she locked eyes with Captain.

And suddenly her plan to flee fell apart.

He stood before her as fierce and intimidating as ever . . . but it was still her Da. And in that moment, she remembered why she came. She remembered why facing them was worth it.

"Oh, Da," she found herself saying.

He didn't know the danger they all were in. She couldn't let her fear of their anger or disappointment keep her from trying to save them all.

She took three deep breaths and cleared her thoughts. She was *still* doing this for them. None would be spared if the Sun kept on her destructive course.

Forcing her voice to be clear, she spoke her well-rehearsed words. "I set off to try and gain back your freedom on the seas. I don't know if you can ever forgive me," she paused. "But I didn't come back asking for forgiveness. I came back asking for help." She stepped forward, hands outstretched and shaking only slightly. "I've discovered something that has changed everything, and I think it's up to me now to do something about it. But I can't do it alone. I was foolish to ever think I could."

She tried to meet the eyes of several of the crew. Ember's eyes were fixed on the end of her long braid. Hawk still had his sword raised her way. Only Almanzo seemed to hold kindness in his eyes.

"I left under Oathdeath to try and help you all, but something greater than Oathdeath has drawn me back. There is more at risk than just one ship's freedom to sail." Even Ember's eyes looked up at this point. Suddenly, she found the entire crew listening intently. She had somehow captivated them. *Now or never!* She thought.

"The world is ending, and I think I know how to stop it."

Ilis watched the emotions that played across the crew's faces. They went from being sincerely attentive to rolling their eyes and chuckling.

Her audience was lost by one single phrase—their lack of belief in her making the words she said like mere fantasy.

And I didn't even get to the part about the Moon . . . Ilis mused somberly.

However, the chuckles from the crew were cut short by a voice.

"She's telling the truth," Neil said, his words somehow carrying both a gentleness and a weighty authority. He hopped over the railing and landed beside Ilis. Grips on swords were tightened and everyone was suddenly on high alert, but it did not seem to bother Neil. "You snicker at her saying 'the world is ending' but you all know it is true. You have seen the evidence of the scorching Sun with your own eyes and know deep down that our world cannot last long under her burning fury."

"Perhaps the snickers weren't at the announcing of the world's end but rather at the claim that the young lass could stop it." The words came from Ember tinged with bitterness and seemed to smack into Ilis's chest. Her leaving left more than one relationship in need of mending, that of her 'sea mother' being one.

Neil looked at Ember and raised an eyebrow with a near-condescending look, "Then I'd say you have too low of a respect for her."

"More like just a respect for our heads . . . Specifically, our heads staying where they belong," Ulrich said. He locked eyes with Ilis and added, "No offense."

"It doesn't matter," Captain snapped. "The oath YOU have made requires me to throw you overboard and demands you stay there."

Ilis thought she saw sorrow in his eyes, but it vanished quickly.

"I am not asking for you to break Oathdeath," Ilis said. "I am simply asking for passage. My sword is at the bottom of the ocean, and there it will stay. I can never again be a part of the *Maribor* crew, but does the oath say anything about not being able to hire your services?"

He glared at Ilis for a long moment before turning his back and walking away.

"We aren't a ferry," Captain retorted.

"No," Ilis said slowly, knowing she truly was on dangerous waters. She stepped forward after Captain. "And you'll never again be my captain, but you are still my Da."

Neil made an odd sound from behind her, but Ilis ignored it, focusing instead on the gruff man before her who seemed to have a war taking place inside of him. Captain paused and then slowly turned around until he was again facing Ilis.

Hopeful for the soft soil that was Captain's heart, Ilis continued, "Which gives me hope that you will hear this request. I think this heist could return the scorching Sun to her rightful place. Please, Da, I have to try. *We* have to try."

His eyes began to tear up ever so slowly, but he held it in well, keeping his look grim and foreboding, making the pirate name proud.

"Ilis," he said, his voice still booming but this time carrying a depth of love that only a father can express. It was his 'Da' voice—the one he told stories in; the one he sang lullabies in; the one that never made you feel foolish, even when you asked the silliest of questions. "Oh Ilis," he said with a slow shake of the head. He turned to Ulrich. "Are her words true? Does Oathdeath simply demand she never again be a crewmate?"

Ulrich scratched his blond beard with his hook. "Technically, I suppose so."

Captain shook his head again, only this time with a small smile. "Ilis, you have the uncanniest knack for . . ."

"Escaping my own noose?" Ilis finished with a wry smile.

"No," Captain said slowly. "Of reminding a person who he wants to be."

In that moment, the entire crew seemed to release a collective breath, and then it was Ilis who found herself on the verge of tears.

Ilis turned and faced the crew. "I have to stand by my decision to evoke Oathdeath and so can't truthfully ask for forgiveness for that, but I do want to ask for forgiveness for any pain I caused you in my leaving." She locked eyes with Ember specifically. "Please, forgive me?"

Before her eyes, she saw tense muscles release and more than one welcoming smile break out upon the faces of her sea family. Ember let out a long sigh and smiled. There were nods all around, followed by Ulrich shouting out, "Ilis, the thief of the hearts of the crew of *Maribor* returns!"

Cheers broke out upon the deck but were silenced by Captain raising his hand. He cleared his throat, crossed his hands over his chest, and tried to look intimidating.

He succeeded, as always.

"The question remains—How are we supposed to help you save the world?"

One step closer . . . Ilis thought.

"Well, now this is where you might think I'm crazy—"

"Because of course no one has ever dared to think you crazy before this," Skinner piped in.

Ilis sighed. "Well, but this one is . . . different." She took a deep breath and fixed her eyes on Captain. "The Moon exists."

Murmurs sprang forth upon the deck.

"Ha ha, riiiiight, good one." Skinner said. "You almost got me." The brown-haired pirate crossed his arms smugly and leaned back against the ship's railing.

"I'm not joking!" Ilis replied, defensively.

"Ilis, everyone knows the Moon is just a myth!" Hawk said.

"But that's just it," Ilis said. "We've all been wrong."

"Claims in fairy tales aside," Ulrich said, "what does this have to do with saving the world?"

"The Moon is the reason for the world ending," Neil said somberly. "If the Moon is not completed soon, we fear even more devastation will come."

Ilis mouthed "thank you" to Neil before continuing. "Pieces of the Moon have been scattered all around our world. They are what we know as glowstone." Gasps and murmurs again rushed from the crew. She motioned to Neil. "Neil here knows where the Moon is and how to complete it when we have the remaining pieces."

A long stretch of silence followed. Neil turned to the captain. "Sir, you know our words are true. You've known it for longer than most."

Ilis looked from Neil to her father, confused. But when Captain nodded, Ilis didn't protest.

"They are right, the Moon does exist," Captain said with a confidence that made Ilis wonder. "And its absence in past centuries has caused much of the world's havoc. I would not be surprised to find it the cause of the Sun's scorching rays."

There was a long pause as everyone seemed to process the information. Skinner's smug look turned to one of utter confusion. Even Almanzo wore an expression of shock. Ember and Ulrich began talking through old stories, trying to see if what she said made sense.

In the midst of their murmurs, Captain's face paled. He locked eyes with Ilis and began to shake his head furiously. "No, no, no! Welcome you aboard my ship as my daughter, sure. But this? Absolutely not!" His voice was tinted with desperation and fury.

The crew's wonderings about the Moon's existence shifted to trying to figure out what the captain was talking about.

"You believe that glowstones are pieces of the Moon?" Ember asked.

Ilis nodded.

"So then that means . . ." Ulrich started, his eyes widened.

"The queen," Skinner whispered.

The captain shook his head again. "You think I would take you back into the lion's den to get eaten alive?"

He turned his back and began stomping away.

Ilis left Neil by the railing and trailed after him. "I know it sounds crazy, and I know it is foolish, and I know I failed last time and so have no reason to hope I will succeed this time, but . . . I have to try."

"I can't risk the lives of the crew again," he said, voice gruff.

"I'm only asking you to sail us there. You wouldn't have to set a foot on land."

Captain shook his head.

"Da, the world is ending, and I think this is how to stop it. Please. Let me try."

"You don't know what you are asking."

Ilis took a deep breath.

Her guilt and shame seemed to rear up again. She didn't deserve to get what she was about to ask for. But she had to ask, and she *had* to be confident. She imagined shoving all the warring emotions behind a door and locking it shut. She threw her shoulders back and faced Captain.

"But that's just it, I think I do know what I am asking this time. And that's what makes this different. I am asking you to risk the lives of the crew by simply sailing over the Edge and landing on the shores of the Under. I am asking you to let me risk the lives of these Basileians as we set out into the heart of Beriyth. I am asking you to let me risk my own life in attempting something that almost got me killed last time, except this time the stakes are so much higher."

"Why do you ask this of me?" Captain said, pained.

"Because as long as breath fills my lungs, hope shall fill my heart."

She knew it was unfair to use her mother's words in such a way, but she said them anyway. She had to move forward. If she gave up now, the self-accusations would drown her.

"If you go, you could die."

"And if I stay, we all will."

He looked at her, and she saw tears in his eyes. "You are so much like your mother." He let out a sad chuckle. "Perhaps too much. Once her mind was set, I could never talk her out of a scheme either." He reached out and cupped Ilis's cheek. "I just . . . I can't stand to lose you too."

Ilis moved forward into a hug, his massive arms enveloping her.

When Captain stepped back, his face clear of the emotions he had shown briefly before, he nodded to the others. Pyra and Chaz now stood on the deck beside Neil. Pyra was hiding behind Chaz, who stood shuffling his feet nervously. Neil stood off to the side, leaning up against the railing, a curious glare in his eyes aimed toward the band of pirates, as if they had already stolen his most prized possession.

"And who might your new scallywags be?"

Ilis turned to look at her mountain friends.

"They are my . . ." Ilis paused and then grinned up at Captain. "My friends."

This was the only affirmation the crew of *Maribor* needed.

CHAPTER SIXTEEN

They set sail with all the speed and efficiency expected of a pirate ship.

Been on land too long, Ilis thought. As the waters deepened and the shore grew smaller, she felt the much-missed safety upon the rocking boat. If only the blue sea itself could protect her from the failures and fears. She shook her head, resolving not to think about it.

Ilis walked along the deck of her home, drinking in the familiar smells and sights. The burnt orange sails flapped about in the wind above her. Her family busied themselves to get out to sea. Each member had their role, and Ilis jumped right into her own. She took the steps two at a time up to the quarterdeck, where Captain stood at the helm.

Ilis stood by his side and began fiddling with one of her daggers. "So . . . you've known the Moon exists for a long while, huh?"

Captain looked at Ilis out of the corner of his eyes and gave a gruff nod.

"How did you find out?"

"We used to help Moon Thieves traverse to the Under," he replied simply.

Ilis's eyebrows shot up. "Oh! Why did we stop?"

"We just did."

Ilis stared at Captain. He had a certain look on his face, one of grief and determination: a look he only ever got when he was talking about her mother.

"It had to do with mum's death, huh?"

Captain's eyes darted to her, and then he looked down.

"Why won't you talk about her more? What secrets are tied up in her death?"

Captain clenched his eyes closed. "Please, Ilis, not now."

"But—"

"Ilis!"

Ilis grimaced.

Captain sighed and reached out to place his hand on Ilis's shoulder. "There are things I've been sworn to secrecy about and trust that I cannot betray. Just trust me, please."

"But this is my story!" Ilis shot back.

Captain shook his head slowly. "It is never just one person's story. Our lives are too intertwined for that."

Ilis opened her mouth to say more, but Captain held up his hand. By the look on his face, Ilis knew this conversation was closed.

He gestured to the main deck, where Chaz was engaged in a duel with Hawk, and let a smile slip. "Go show those boys how it's done."

Ilis let out a long sigh but nodded.

She strode forward until she was leaning against the railing of the quarterdeck, looking down at the main deck. She watched as Hawk with his bright blond hair disarmed Chaz, sending his sword clattering to the wooden boards at his feet. Chaz stared at his sword in disbelief.

"Chaz," Ilis called, grateful for a distraction from the frustration of her father's refusal to share about her mother, "shame on you! I thought you were one of the best swordsmen in the land!"

Chaz's face turned bright red.

Hawk spun his sword in his hand and flashed a bright smile up to Ilis. "Well, my dear, don't we all know that the sea has the best swordsmen?"

Ember spat on the deck and challenged, "Aye, you mean swords*women*?"

Hawk shrugged. "Let's be real, the only swordswomen are on the sea." He smiled charmingly up toward Ilis. "The best of them being our very own."

Chaz snorted. He looked at Hawk with eyebrows raised. "You don't mean to tell me that five-foot-two Ilis is one of your best with a sword?"

Hawk looked offended at this. "Great swallows lad, do you truly know so little of Ilis?" Then he grinned back up at her. "Trained her myself, I did." With a flick of the wrist, he sent his sword flying through the air.

Ilis snatched the sword out of the air, leapt over the railing, and landed right in front of Chaz.

She suddenly looked taller than just five foot two.

Chaz scrunched up his face. "You don't expect me to fight a girl, do you?"

One eyebrow raised, Ilis spun her sword in circles, testing its balance. There was nothing Ilis liked more than a good duel to escape frustration.

"You don't have to fight me," she responded with a grin, "but I would suggest you at least defend yourself."

And with that, she charged at him, knocked his sword to the right, and slid right through his legs. Popping up, she spun around and had her sword pointed at the back of his neck before he even realized what had happened.

Chaz tensed, and Pyra laughed. Ilis glanced around and saw that a crowd had formed. Ten or so of the crew—plus Neil and Pyra—now surrounded them, watching the duel. Chaz slowly turned around, and Ilis found his face once again almost as red as his hair.

She shrugged her shoulders. "Now that you will take me seriously, care to have a real match?"

Chaz clenched his teeth and nodded.

"But first," she said, sticking her sword into the deck and tying her hair back with a strip of leather, "tell me this: between you and Malcolm, who is the better swordsman?"

Chaz's eyes fell, and she remembered suddenly how they had left Malcolm. His pale, unmoving face came into her head, and she had to force herself to stay focused.

"Malc," Chaz replied, then he let out a slight grin. "But only by a smidge."

Ilis nodded, threw back her shoulders, and jumped on the balls of her feet. She tried not to think of the one they'd left behind. She tried not to think of the one who had beaten her in her last fight. She tried not to think of the one she most wanted here. Instead, she focused on Chaz. She watched his movements, looking for weaknesses.

Chaz struck with confident force. His form was impeccable, and his movements were calculated and sure. To each one of her attacks, he had a strong response. And to each of his attacks, Ilis had to make haste in order to avoid and deflect. Back and forth across the main deck of *Maribor* they fought, the crowd of pirates and mountain folk moving out of the way whenever needed. Cheers were often and plentiful, and surprisingly, many were for Chaz. She grinned as the crew of *Maribor* murmured among themselves, studying his moves and stealing them for their own as only a band of pirates can.

"Do you have"—Ilis said between strokes—"some sort of"—their swords locked together, and she looked him in the eyes—"a code of honor when fighting?"

Chaz thrust her away from him and huffed. "What do you mean?"

She inched toward the railing. "I mean, is everything allowed?"

Chaz lifted his chin. "If you are asking if I fight dirty"—he charged at her— "then the answer is no."

Ilis shrugged her shoulder, leapt onto the railing, and fought from there. "I wouldn't call it dirty," she said, their swords clanging with each strike, "but more like using everything to your own advantage." She danced along the railing, never failing to block Chaz's strikes.

Chaz, tired of her games, let out a roar and charged straight at her. Ilis smirked and flipped into the air, kicking Chaz in the back of the shoulders as she did.

Chaz, arms flailing, went headfirst over the railing.

Pyra screamed and dashed to the railing. Ilis turned to Hawk. "I told you that would work!"

Hawk merely shook his head, grinning at his protégé. Ilis leapt again to the ship railing and looked down at Chaz, who was lying in the lifeboat which hung just below the railing.

"You okay?" she asked, reaching out her hand to help him up.

Chaz looked at her, partly in anger and partly in awe, and shook his head. "Now that is what I would call dirty."

Ilis helped him over the railing and patted him on the back. "Eh, what can I say? I'm a pirate."

***

Dinner was a loud affair on the deck of *Maribor*. Everyone talked at once, talked over each other, and switched conversations mid-sentence until it seemed as if everything was pure and utter nonsense.

"Did you see the king while you were on the mount?" Ulrich, the ship's cook, asked Ilis as he heaped more fish onto a platter in the middle of the table.

"See the king?" Ilis retorted. "I had dinner with him! Both of them, now that I think about it."

"He also wrestled a manatee," Hawk said, talking about a thief from the coast.

"Manatee?" Skinner said. "Dem creatures are mere imaginings!"

"Did you hear about the griffin who took off with that old barnacle, Captain Monckton from The Red Ship?"

"Wasn't he in the middle of losing a game of cards?"

"He lost more than his bet," one pirate chuckled.

"What a future," Ember said, stroking her long black hair and referring to who knows what. "Now that's what I call living on the edge!"

"How'd that go?" Ulrich asked Ilis, bringing her back to her current conversation.

Ilis twirled her fork around her fingers. "Eh, let's just say I almost walked myself into a noose . . ." She thought about all her conversations with both kings. "Several times."

"Terrible time it was!" a crew member piped.

"Oh indeed, did you see their table manners?"

"Eh, but that summer festival's wine sure was tasty!" Hawk said.

"Excuse me?" Pyra exclaimed so loudly that the entire table grew quiet—quite a feat indeed. When only silence followed, Pyra repeated, "What did you just say about the summer festival's wine?"

Hawk looked at Pyra. "Eh, that it was tasty?"

Pyra looked excitedly around. "So you drank of it!"

Ulrich laughed. "Of course we drank it!"

Pyra stood up, gaping at Ember. "Then you're the Lass of the Seas! You must be!"

Ember laughed, a deep laugh. She looked up, her dark eyes meeting Pyra's light and eager ones. "No, my girl, I've never had the imagination to think of such things."

Pyra looked downcast. "Oh, I thought I would get to meet her."

The whole crew erupted in laughter at this. Ulrich came over and clapped Pyra on the back. "Why, you already have!" He pointed toward Ilis, who was just sitting there, smirking.

Pyra gasped, and the table again erupted in its usual noise.

"You're the Lass of the Seas?" Pyra shouted across the table.

"Ember, did you ever see the likes of this in the Sanhildin?" someone shouted.

"I'd have never thought he could be so cruel," another person added.

Ilis opened her mouth to speak.

"Quiet, you fool! Only speak if you've got something worth saying!" Captain barked from the head of the table.

Ilis chuckled at his timing and merely nodded at Pyra, who continued to gaze at her in awe.

Captain turned to Ilis, stroking his long reddish-brown beard. "Does it have to be the queen's crown?"

Ilis could hear the concern in his voice. "Any new information on her?" she asked casually, trying to avoid the fact that Captain was so nervous on her behalf—for this was the man who had sent her off to wrestle the sea monster of the North Lagoon, climb the tallest tree in Ocean Forest, and steal the front fang from a sabretooth. But of course, this was different now. This was attempting to do the thing that had almost gotten her killed last time. This was a whole new level of foolishness.

The captain shoved his food around with his fork, making a mountain out of his potatoes. "My informants can't figure out the whispers they hear in the capital. No one has been able to get into the castle in months, not since . . . well, since we got in. And the queen hasn't been spotted outside the castle since then."

"Is she even still alive? Perhaps they are just trying to buy time; the queen has no heir."

"Nah, my girl, she's still alive," replied the captain. "Beriyth wouldn't last without a living ruler. Remember the Blood Oath?"

Ilis nodded. It was an oath Beriythian rulers took upon becoming king or queen. In it, the ruler entered a covenant—a solemn binding agreement—with the land itself. "But how does that prove the queen is still alive?"

"If she had died, the people believe they would only have a short time before nature itself would start revolting and demand a new ruler. Remember the legend about the fire from the mountains that nearly wiped them all out centuries ago? The people seem to think that it all happened because they waited too long for the new ruler to take the Blood Oath. Whether or not them legends are true, the Beriythians believe it to be, so no one would dare pretend that the queen was alive if she was not."

"So the queen is alive but hasn't been seen . . . and the palace is on a form of lockdown. Great."

"No matter what, she will still be the Queen of the Under: the queen who led the battle against the White Wolves of the South; the queen who secured peace for Beriyth from the giants of the valleys in the East by besting a giant in one-on-one combat; the queen who outsmarted the eagle tribes of the Thick Forest; the queen who has continued to lead the Under in peace and thus managed to earn the respect of humans and beasts . . ." Captain turned away. "The queen who almost got your head."

Ilis placed her hand on Captain's arm. "Da, I know who the Queen of the Under is."

"But you've never understood her power on her side of the world! Because of the Blood Oath, all beasts—griffins, centaurs, and even some dragons—bow to her wisdom and leadership. The task that you are setting out on is impossible. It was impossible last time we tried and is even more so now!"

Ilis took a deep breath, trying to calm her nerves. Everything Captain said was true. But they had to find a way. The world just might depend upon it.

"We will be fine," she found herself saying, even though she wasn't sure if she fully believed it.

Captain bowed his head. He looked back up at her and had his usual spark in his eyes. "Sometimes I wonder if I raised you to be too brave."

Ilis smiled. "Ha! As if there is such a thing."

***

That night, Hawk agreed to show the boys to the hammocks below the main deck while Ilis led Pyra to her own quarters in the stern. She let Pyra take her bed and then grabbed a hammock and strode out on deck.

Ilis was deep in thought as she began to hang her hammock, so she nearly jumped when Almanzo Leviathan stepped out of the shadows to help her.

"Hey, Manzo."

Almanzo just grunted and tied the straps of her hammock to the mast. When they were done, Ilis slipped into her hanging bed and watched her mentor in the art of sneaking.

"I learned a lot about the fortification of Mount Oros," Ilis said casually.

He raised an eyebrow.

"Did you know there are tunnels that run all under and through the mountain?"

Almanzo grinned slightly and nodded.

Ilis huffed. "And you never told me?"

He merely inclined his head, but Ilis understood his meaning.

"Aye, aye, the best teacher is not words but experience. That seems to be your excuse for everything."

Almanzo leaned against the mast. Ilis could tell he was about to speak by the look of concentration3 that came across his face. "I can come," he said slowly, using his seldom-uttered words. And she knew just what he was offering. The only reason she still had a head was because of him. He was offering to risk his life to keep her safe.

Ilis shook her head. "The crew from Mount Oros are not known. They will be less likely to draw suspicion."

Almanzo raised an eyebrow and opened his palm, their sign for "what's the plan?"

Ilis took a deep breath. "I have no idea. But I'm going to go to the Damarises this time. I know it is risky, but . . . I can't think of anyone else that I can trust."

He looked thoughtful for a long moment before tugging at his mustache and nodding.

"Eh, good night to you too," Ilis said. She sighed and sank deeper into her hammock. As she watched, Almanzo slid through the shadows and across the deck, making not a single sound as he disappeared into the hatch.

***

The next morning, Ilis awoke and lumbered downstairs to help Ulrich cook breakfast. The one-handed pirate had the greatest knack for cooking but also for making a mess. If Ilis were honest, any time she helped him, she spent more time cleaning up after him than anything else.

"Morning, Ulrich," Ilis sang as she swung into the kitchen galley.

"Morn, Lil Star," Ulrich replied, using her pet name from childhood. Ulrich Buckley and Captain had grown up together, and as Ulrich was perhaps Captain's best friend, it only seemed right that Ilis view him as her uncle.

"How can I help?" Ilis asked, wiping up some batter from the floor before Ulrich slipped in it. She sniffed the air. "Fresh biscuits and sea sausage?"

Ulrich grinned and pulled out a bottle with bright orange liquid inside.

"And orange juice!" Ilis finished with a sigh, and they both laughed over their shared love for a mainland staple. She found herself overwhelmingly grateful for each moment with the crew. They were moments she thought she had lost forever.

Ilis held the bottle lovingly in her hands. "Steal this from that shop off of Baker Street?"

"Nope," Ulrich said, mixing batter and causing half of it to fly out of the bowl in his excitement. "Stole the oranges from an orchard on the coast and then made the juice myself from a recipe Capt's little sister once gave me." Ilis had only ever heard stories about her aunt. She, along with so many others, had died in the Quakes.

Ilis gasped, uncorked the bottle, and sniffed the freshness inside. She closed her eyes and let out a long sigh. "Mmmmmm."

Her eyes popped open mischievously, asking a silent question.

Ulrich laughed and tossed her a glass. Ilis was sitting on a table, a glass of orange juice in hand and an expression of complete contentment on her face, when Neil walked in, looking seasick. He saw her and chuckled.

"Enjoying that, are you?"

Ilis beamed. "Neil! You've *got* to try this!" She shoved her glass of orange juice in his face. Neil grimaced and stepped back, closing his eyes and trying to wave off a bout of seasickness.

"Blazes, how can you enjoy that when it smells so musty down here!"

Ilis glared at him, her hand still outstretched. "Taste it," she ordered.

Shaking off his nausea, Neil let out a small laugh. He took it from her eager hands and sipped it.

"Isn't it the best thing you've ever tasted?" Ilis asked, her eyes bright.

Neil looked at her. "Ilis, have you ever had orange juice before?"

Ilis looked offended. "What kind of question is that? That's like asking if I've ever noticed the Stars in the sky."

Neil shrugged.

"Are you telling me this is not the best orange juice you've ever had?" Ilis asked with a huff.

Neil nodded. "I once had a friend who could make an orange juice that tasted as if it was sunshine in liquid form." Ulrich looked at Neil oddly at this line, but Ilis just screwed up her face and stole her glass back from him.

"Fine. Ulrich, don't give this ungrateful lad another drop of your glorious orange juice. I will not let anyone who does not appreciate its greatness have a single drop of it." Ilis smiled wickedly. "Even if that means I am the only one who gets to drink it."

Ulrich chuckled and pulled the biscuits out of the oven. As he shook them to cool them off, several of the biscuits went flying in the air. With the grace of a dancer, Ilis placed her glass on the table, leapt up, and caught seven of them before they landed on the ground. As for the two forsaken biscuits that had not been so lucky, she picked them up, inspected them, brushed them off, and then placed them on the platter with the rest. Ilis bowed. When she straightened, she found Neil looking at her with the strangest look upon his face. But then he blinked, and the look was gone.

Ulrich picked up the platter of biscuits and took them above deck, leaving Ilis alone with Neil. She realized that this was the first time it had been just the two of them since boarding *Maribor*.

"Neil?" Ilis started, remembering that she had so many questions for him.

"Yes, Ilis?"

"I don't even know where to begin!" Ilis sat back down on the table.

Neil chuckled.

"How are you a Moon Thief? And where are all the others? And why did you never tell us that you were a Moon Thief? Why didn't you tell us before that you know where the Moon is? Where is the Moon? Did Malcolm know?"

"Ahhh." Neil paused. "Well, to start off, I'm not technically a Moon Thief because the Moon Thief title is passed down through generations."

When it did not look like Neil was going to continue, Ilis prompted again. "Then what are you?"

"Someone who's trying to do the right thing."

"You are speaking in riddles."

Neil smiled. "I suppose I am." He took a seat across the table from her. "I do believe that there are some Moon Thieves who are still alive, though most of my ideas are speculation at this point."

Ilis raised a brow at this.

"How big is the place where the Moon is kept? I suppose they have been able to piece together most of it at this point if we are just missing a few last pieces. Is it huge?"

Neil chuckled. "It's surprisingly smaller than one would think."

"How do you even know the location of where the Moon is being put back together?"

Neil let out a small huff of laughter. "That is an interesting question. I suppose you could just say I always have?"

"I don't understand."

"My whole story is one of those things that makes perfect sense until you think about it."

"That makes absolutely no sense."

"Only because you thought about it!"

Ilis blinked. "That is utterly unhelpful!" She grew quiet. "I suppose the bigger question is how am I supposed to trust you when so many secrets are involved?"

That question seemed to pain him. "Ilis, I am sorry. I know this doesn't make sense, but it will soon. Just give me more time."

"More time for what?"

Neil considered this. "I can't say, but . . ." He paused. "Malcolm trusted me."

Three words. Those three words hit like a cannonball to her chest. And Ilis found that was all she needed.

She stood, tired of the confusion that was Neil. "Fine, I suppose if you are trusting me in attempting this heist, I can trust you with your secrets. But tread lightly. If I find a reason to distrust you any more, I'll show you the plank myself."

***

The next few days went by in a blur. At first, the seas were open, and the whole world again seemed to be there for Ilis's taking. The wind whipped in her ears, her guilt and shame remained mere whispers, and she could almost forget the pale young man who was not here with her. Plus, with her new friends on board, it seemed as if the best of her two worlds had collided.

Day three of the journey was when the seas got rougher, but that was expected as they entered the East Seas. After two days of rough sailing, Captain's face grew grim, and he began barking orders to maximize their speed. They began to near the Edge.

"Why exactly are we trying to go faster toward the world's edge?" Pyra asked. She currently wore trousers and a yellow blouse with her hair braided back, looking like a full-fledged pirate lass—that is, until she picked up a sword. They were on day five of her sword training, but her improvement was small to say the least. Not that this fact affected her cheerful resolve to learn. "I would think it would help it if we slowed down near the Edge."

"Go too slow and you don't clear the Edge . . . which means you get bashed to pieces." Hawk said nonchalantly.

"Ah, I do believe I do not understand at all." Pyra said, trying very hard to keep her cool. "How exactly does this work?"

"You fall off the side of the world," Ember stated blandly. Ilis rolled her eyes at her foreboding sea-mother.

"Not exactly," Ilis amended. She wiped sweat from her brow. The air was hot and humid. "We will reach the Edge of the sea and then be pulled by gravity until we emerge out the other side."

Ember looked at her dryly. "We fall off the side of the world."

"So the ship just . . . tips over?" Pyra asked.

"Rather, we sink and then do a drastic flip when we reach the end," Ilis replied.

Pyra stared at her blankly.

Ilis pulled out a coin, a Basileian letter, and held it up. "Our world is made up of two sides. On one side is Basileia and the countries that surround it. On the other, Beriyth and its neighboring kingdoms. The Edge is just like the edge of a coin—its existence is what holds the two sides together and, at the same time, what keeps them apart. It will be a bit of a wild ride, but it's perfectly safe."

Chaz huffed behind her. "'*Perfectly safe,*'" he said in a high-pitched voice.

Ilis looked over her shoulder to find him gripping the rope attached to his belt.

"If that were true, you wouldn't have given us leashes," Chaz said.

Neil came and patted Chaz on the back. "Don't worry. I am sure that, once we go over the side, you will thank Ilis for her precautions." Neil winked at Ilis.

The more time she spent with the forester, the less he made sense. He had the worst seasickness Ilis had ever seen, and yet he seemed so familiar with the workings of a ship. And then he would make comments—

comments about the Edge, comments about the Under, comments about the Moon—that continued to hint he knew more than he was letting on.

Ilis watched him stride across the deck and settle before Hawk, who was in the middle of spinning a daring yarn about the Quest of the Emerald while spinning real yarn out of seaweed. She was thinking about going to ask Neil again what some of his comments meant when she felt something shift under her.

They had reached the Edge.

CHAPTER SEVENTEEN

To the untrained eye, nothing looked amiss—granted, to the trained eye, nothing looked amiss either. That was the secret of the Edge: you never knew what was coming until it was too late.

One moment the ship was sailing along full speed ahead across the waters, and the next moment, the water beneath them was replaced with air. *Maribor's* momentum sent them out over the Edge just enough to clear the side before plummeting downward with sickening speed. A wall of water and stone whizzed by as they fell, the boat in utter chaos as it plunged down off a cliff that no one had seen coming but everyone expected.

Ilis counted the seconds in her head.

One.

"HOLD ON!" Ilis screamed as she watched the pirates grip for dear life and her friends flail about, held only by the leashes she had made them wear.

Two.

Ilis had taken this trek enough to allow herself to enjoy the crazy rush of the wind in her hair and the saltwater all around as the ship continued to drop.

Three.

She locked eyes with Captain. They plummeted to the symphony of Pyra's screams and Neil's moans for what seemed like a slice of eternity.

Four.

They moved toward the ropes connected to the sail made for these occasions. Ilis had named it the Flippy Sail . . . at the age of four.

Five.

Ilis and her father began to untie the sail. Fail here and—well, no one fully knew what would happen if they failed to release the Flippy Sail. But Skinner's theory was that they would stay suspended in the void of the Edge and never again see land. Ember's theory was that they would crash into the rocks and die.

Six.

The Edge of the beginning of the Under appeared just beneath them.

Seven.

They loosened the ropes and a large purple sail unfurled into existence at the bow of the ship, immediately filling with air. The ship lurched forward, beginning to flip.

Maribor creaked and moaned underneath them, but she was built for this. Her masts were thick, made of the wood from Elgrave Forest, where the forest whales dwelled. Her keel was coated with a tar from the steaming pits of Kapar, the most durable tar on both sides of their fair world. The pressure that was being put on *Maribor* at the moment was tremendous, but she would not break.

It happened in one stomach-twisting moment. They flipped through the air and soon found themselves facing the Under and her ocean—and yet not quite there.

They perched precariously, the front half of the boat in the waters of the Under and the other half dangling over the Edge.

"Loose the main sail!" Captain roared.

They only had one shot at this. Lose their momentum, and they would fall backward and discover the fate of those lost to the Edge.

The sails filled with air and caught, jerking the ship yet again, only this time it was a relief. The wind pulled them safely onto the water of the Under's ocean and away from the Edge.

Chaz rushed to the railing and promptly threw up. Pyra collapsed in a heap and started sobbing slightly. Neil had his eyes closed and a death grip on the railing. He took a few deep breaths before slowly opening his eyes and relaxing his grip.

Ilis offered Pyra a hand. "It's quite the ride, isn't it?"

Pyra gulped, her eyes wide and wild and wet with tears. She opened her mouth and then closed it. In the end, she just nodded and wiped the tears away.

Ilis helped Pyra up and then joined Neil and Chaz at the railing. They were confronted by an icy blast of wind. Ilis shivered.

"So this is the Under," Pyra said, a mixture of awe and reserve in her voice, though in truth, they could see little in the dark but city lights off on the horizon and a spattering of Stars in the sky above them.

"It's very dark," Neil observed.

"It's very . . ." Chaz rubbed his side where the rope had cut into his skin.

"Normal?" Ilis finished smugly.

He rolled his eyes but made no remark . . . until he noticed the Stars. "Wait, that is Varos? And Canthares!" Chaz's jaw dropped. "How is that possible?"

Ilis held back her grin. "We share the same Sun and Stars. They revolve around us, or us around them—depending on which centaur you listen to."

"The Under has Canthares too," Chaz chanted under his breath. His eyes looked glossy.

"To be clear, where we are going is the country of Beriyth. The Under is merely what those on our side call it."

"How often have you been here?" Pyra asked, her voice quiet. The waves lapped at the side of the boat.

"Often enough to know that this degree of coldness and darkness is not typical," Ilis said, distractedly glancing at the sky. Pyra's teeth began to chatter.

Ember came out from below the deck, her arms full of coats and scarves. She made a face as the cold breeze affronted her. "You'll be needing these," she said, dumping them at Ilis's feet.

Ilis nodded and then looked back out toward land. There was the Wharf of Engledurn on the coast and the city lights of Qirya, the capital of Beriyth, in the distance. She pointed to the left of Engledurn. "We will anchor there, at Dagger Tooth Cove, like we did for the Heist of the Bumbleburg Seeds."

Almanzo nodded and turned the wheel to adjust the course.

Captain came up beside her. "It's not too late to turn back."

Ilis looked up into his dark eyes. "What if this is the only way to save our world?" *And the only way to redeem myself?*

Captain bumped her on the shoulder. "Ahh, but we both know that's not true. There will always be multiple paths you can take, sometimes it's just that there is only one path we can see."

Ilis pondered this, wondering if there was another path she could choose—one that wouldn't lead her friends straight into the land of their sworn enemies or herself back onto the path that nearly cost her head.

Ilis threw up her hands. "If there is another way, I truly can't see it."

Captain nodded. "Are you sure you don't want anyone to go with you?" he asked softly.

Ilis's heart broke. She shook her head. "No, it's too dangerous."

The captain chuckled. "Ha, says the lass going herself." He tapped his fingers along the railing, his rings making a sound that reminded her of her childhood.

Ilis just shrugged and placed her hand over his large one. His nervous fingers slowed.

"Mind waiting for our return?"

The captain, with flushed cheeks, managed to call up a smidge of his ferocity. "What do I look like, your cabin boy? I'll be there only if it suits me."

Ilis grinned, knowing that it would indeed suit him. "Thanks."

***

Ilis, Pyra, Chaz, and Neil, bundled up, loaded their packs and themselves into the rowboat, and set off toward shore. They rowed through the dark, wintry night, the cold and sharp wind swirling around them and seeming to whisper foreboding secrets. As they neared shore, Pyra broke the silence.

"Didn't you say there was a wharf nearby? Why aren't we going there?

This place does not look . . . often used?"

"That's an understatement," Chaz said gruffly. They reached the coast and began pulling the rowboat onto the land. The shore was frozen and barren. "This place looks as abandoned as it gets."

Ilis nodded. "Exactly. Why else do you think we use it?"

Pyra nodded and shouldered her pack, the others following suit.

"So, where exactly are we going?" Chaz asked, eyeing the city lights on the horizon with disfavor.

Ilis looked him over before responding slowly, "To Qirya, the capital of Beriyth. That is where the palace is."

Chaz dragged his hand down his face. "Lovely, right into the heart of the Under."

Ilis raised an eyebrow at the soldier.

"Hey, where is your sense of adventure?" Pyra cheered. She hopped up on a snow-covered boulder and swung her new sword at a tree. Snow fell off its branches and gave her a snowy cap, but she wasn't paying it much mind, as her sword was firmly stuck in the trunk. Putting all her weight against it, she managed to get it free while also managing to fall on her rear. She looked to Chaz and shrugged.

"It just fled for its life at the sight of your swordsmanship," Chaz replied dryly.

The world was black about them, lit only by Ilis's glowstone torch and the lanterns they carried in their hands, which cast an eerie glow on the snow. They marched to the sound of snow crunching beneath their feet and Chaz's constant cheerful comments:

"You do know that the Under is the worst of all humanity!"

"What if they find out who we are and boil us alive?"

"What about the beasts that roam freely?"

Or Ilis's personal favorite: "Are you sure they won't eat us?"

But, thankfully, other than Chaz's many encouragements, the trip through the countryside to the capital was uneventful. They traipsed through snow-covered grasslands down a well-worn road. Every once in a while, they would pass a tree whose branches were frozen solid. Ilis worried about what effect the sudden winter had brought upon the harvest. Harvest shouldn't have been for another few months! They had skipped from summer to winter. Without the harvest . . . Ilis didn't want to dwell on the food shortage that was bound to follow.

The capital of Beriyth was flat—very flat when compared to Mount Oros—and surrounded by a river that wrapped itself around part of the large city like a moat. The river also shot through the city at multiple points, making up the majority of the streets. Twelve of the thirteen entrances into Qirya were waterway entrances, which Ilis would have used gladly—if they hadn't been frozen. As Ilis had yet to commandeer a vessel, and *Maribor* was too large to sail upon the river, Ilis and her crew headed toward the only land entrance to the capital, which was located on the Eastern side.

As they got closer to the gatehouse, Ilis turned her back to it and faced her crew.

"Okay, look," Ilis said, her hands outstretched as if she were trying to brace them for something. "A great deal of what you have heard about the Under is false." Ilis paused, not sure how they would take this next bout of information.

"But?" Pyra said, her slender eyebrows raised.

Ilis cocked her head. "But . . . some of what you have heard is true." Ilis took a breath, closed her eyes, and decided to just get it over with.

"Uh, Ilis?" Neil ventured. "If you are about to tell us that the tales of beasts living in the Under are true, well, I think we've already gathered that."

Ilis opened her eyes to find Pyra gaping, Chaz looking like he might pass out, and Neil looking . . . well, like his usual confusing self.

Pivoting on her heel, Ilis turned to find a cloud of glowing beings, about the size of hummingbirds, flying out of the gate.

"Are those . . ." Pyra started.

"A herd of pixies," Ilis finished with a grin. "And they are neither the strangest nor the most marvelous beasts you will encounter in Beriyth."

And with that, they began again their course to the gatehouse. Ilis tucked her glowstone torch into her pack and pulled out a scarf and a large-brimmed hat. She wrapped the scarf around her neck and let it cover her nose. Then she placed the hat on her head and let it sag to hide her features. She figured it would be enough of a disguise to walk through the city without being recognized . . . as long as she didn't let anyone get too close.

The gate was made of bronze and currently covered by a thick layer of snow so that it gleamed oddly. Man and beast alike traversed through the gate, which was guarded by several soldiers armed with swords, spears, and axes—depending upon the guard's preference.

An ogre brushed shoulders with them. A gnome trotted to their left. A cyclops stood as one of the guards of the gate.

Chaz's breaths started coming in ragged gasps.

"This is a bad idea. This is a *very* bad idea." He stared openly as a wind nymph solidified from her wind state into her humanlike form.

"Cool it," Ilis replied in a hushed tone. She lowered her head and led her troops through the gatehouse, hoping to pass as a nobody.

"Hail!" cried the cyclops guard in Blood Tongue, the Under's national language.

Ilis paused and turned to him, barely peeking out from under her hat to look up into his one massive green eye.

"What is your business?" the cyclops asked.

Ilis motioned to her companions. "We were shepherds before the cold came. We are looking for work," Ilis said in perfect Blood Tongue.

The guard nodded and motioned them through. It was a common enough fate these days.

They passed through the gatehouse and entered into a city of white. Roofs that looked like dewdrops topped each structure, making the city a picturesque sight that was a marvel to behold.

Chaz seemed to be panting. "You . . . you speak their language?"

Ilis shrugged, still keeping the hat pulled low. "We spent a few seasons on this side of the world."

Neil looked at her in disbelief. "You say that so casually."

Ilis turned to him. "It was my life."

An odd look came across Neil's face that Ilis could not decipher. She added it to the list of mysteries about him.

They walked through the snow-covered streets, and Ilis could not hold back her grin at Chaz and Pyra's reactions. The two walked around staring openly at the creatures around them. Ilis had to remind them often to close their jaws.

Pyra and Chaz meandered around for nearly an hour, trying to inconspicuously gaze at beasts they had only heard about from bedtime stories, while Neil and Ilis hung back and watched. Feeling safe from discovery under her hat and scarf, Ilis had wanted to get the scope of the town again, and she rather enjoyed the spectacle of Pyra and Chaz gawking over the sights.

A girl with long white hair rode through the streets on the back of a white caribou whose antlers stretched out so wide that man and beast alike had to step aside for them to pass. What looked like a normal man walked by, but any time he blinked, raindrops fell from the sky and landed on his shoulders. It was a city full of oddities.

"Wonder is a beautiful thing," Neil said at one point.

Ilis turned to him. She had almost forgotten he was there.

"You've been to the Under before," Ilis said, piecing things together.

Neil gave her a crooked smile and pointed back up ahead where Pyra was about to pet a griffin pup. Ilis quickened her step and grabbed Pyra by the elbow, apologizing in Blood Tongue to the mother.

They walked the snow-covered streets alongside beasts of all shapes and sizes, weaving past shops and houses alike until the cobbled streets stopped. Ilis stared at the frozen water street before her and cocked her head.

Chaz was at her shoulder immediately. "What's wrong?"

"Normally, this is where I would steal a boat and row down the canal," Ilis whispered back.

Chaz looked at the ice stretching out before him. "Well, you aren't going to be rowing anywhere."

Ilis's eyes drank in her surroundings. Since her last trip to the Under, the temperature had dropped significantly. Even in the winter, temperatures rarely got below freezing at the capital. Now, everything was frozen. The Upper was burning while the Under was freezing . . . Their world was perilously balanced.

Ilis shook herself out of her thoughts as a boat glided across the frozen surface, running on two metal skate-like things attached to the keel. The man in the boat propelled himself using a long staff with a metal tip.

Ilis motioned her head to the gliding boat. "Stay here, I'm going to find us one of those."

Ten minutes later, Ilis appeared in the exact same boat she had pointed out to Chaz. Chaz looked offended, but Ilis just laughed. "Don't worry, I paid him for it."

What she didn't mention was where she had gotten money from.

Appeased, Chaz helped Neil and Pyra on board. Ilis navigated over the frozen river and through the town. Buildings two to four stories high sat stacked side by side along the river. They passed shops that smelled of spice, streets where human children played and laughed alongside beast children, and houses where women knit before warm fires.

Ilis watched her friends as their eyes took in their surroundings. Chaz was on edge, his fingers wrapped around the hilt of his sword, Pyra had a slight smile on her lips as if the entire scene amused her, and Neil looked lost in thought.

Ilis slid them to a stop before a broken-down brick building. It was three stories high, made of gray bricks, and was the sort of building that easily went unnoticed because of its sheer normalcy.

Tethering the boat to a tall wooden post, Ilis climbed up the side of the building and disappeared through a window.

Pyra stared up after Ilis. After a few minutes she said, "Surely she is coming back for us, right?"

"No," came Ilis's voice from inside. She opened the door. "I thought I'd leave my crew out in the cold all night." She gestured for them to come in. "Welcome to one of the *Maribor* crew's many landaways."

Chaz cocked his head in a question as he entered through the broken-down entryway into an abandoned house. He was about to ask what in the world a "landaway" was when Neil answered it for him.

"I think it is like a hideaway on land."

"Ohhhh," Chaz said, nodding. He gave another long look around the building. It had chipped plaster walls, broken wooden flooring, and a ceiling that appeared to be leaking. "I always imagined hideaways as much . . . nicer."

Ilis raised an eyebrow. "Too nice, and we become conspicuous." She reached down and pulled at a broken floorboard, revealing a stash of weapons and supplies. "But this little place has everything we need."

CHAPTER EIGHTEEN

Leaving her crew to settle in, Ilis ventured back out into the frigid air. Her boat-turned-sled skated across the ice, producing a sound that was a sharp contrast to that of the waves crashing against *Maribor*.

She glided past houses, businesses, and everything in between. Everyone was doing their best to stay warm in the freezing winter. Ilis passed several bonfires, and each time, she was tempted to enter and enjoy the warmth promised within—but she was on a mission. There was no time to enjoy the comforts of dillydallying.

Sliding up to the round clay house she knew well, Ilis secured her boat-sled, stepped up to the doorstep, and knocked on the wooden door frame. Upon the frame was the engraving of *pass vi shekhikh*, which meant "pass through light" in the Blood Tongue. This was the door that only the hoofless used, so it was solely for the house's guests. The door was a simple red curtain, such that Ilis could have easily walked right in, but no one in their right mind intruded upon a centaur.

The sound of hooves clipping upon the hard clay floor of the house inside met Ilis just before the curtain drew back. Landra Damaris stood before her, her long brown hair framing her face and falling down to her hands, which were placed squarely upon her hips.

A scampering of hooves sounded just before a second, smaller figure appeared. Young Arline was about ten years old and already as tall as Ilis with her long horse legs. She beamed at Ilis but made no sound. Trotting in place beside her mother, she awaited her mother's permission to greet

Ilis.

Landra appraised Ilis. She cocked her head and then nodded.

"Malchus," Landra shouted over her shoulder to her husband, "we have a visitor. It's the Star-Eyed One. Tell Caiacus we will have to meet up with him another time."

Landra held the curtain open for Ilis to step inside, but before Ilis could move, Arline had charged through the door and nearly tackled her. Ilis chuckled and melted into the embrace of the young centaur.

"Arline," the mother centaur scolded, though in her eyes were tears. "Let our guest enter."

Ilis's presence was always one of joy and solemn reminder interwoven because of the memories connected to her.

Her thoughts flitted back to that night. On a heist to steal a map from the Nahiru Archive, Ilis had been tasked with sneaking into the Damarises' house in order to obtain a key. Silent as the night, she had rowed a small canoe up to their house but found an odd sight before the *pass vi shekhikh* doorway.

Splashing in the water was a young Arline of six years old. Ilis locked eyes with her for one moment, panic overflowing from the young centaur's eyes, just before her head submerged under the waters.

Ilis paddled her canoe up to the spot and dove in. Grabbing the girl around the waist and dragging her upward, Ilis reached the surface and shouted for help.

Malchus was there in an instant and fished both of them out. The Damarises welcomed Ilis into their home with open arms that night.

"Your daughter did not cry out for help," Ilis had said all those years ago. She sat by the fire with a blanket around her shoulders and her wet clothes sticking to her skin.

"She is not yet of the age of speaking," Landra replied, wiping tears from her eyes as she lay on the cushions with Arline by her side.

Ilis realized in that moment how little she knew of the centaurs' ways.

"When is the age of speaking?" Ilis could not help but ask.

"It varies for each centaur." Landra replied, stroking Arline's hair. "The journey of finding one's voice is never the same, but once one finds it, you are considered a full member of the tribe, and your voice will hold weight in the councils. However, often times those who find their voice the latest end up being the wisest among us. We do not despise the journey of finding one's voice."

In this moment, Malchus had come over to Ilis, still shaking. "You saved our daughter's life. How can we ever repay you?"

Ilis chuckled. She considered lying for a moment but thought better of it. "Well, I came here to steal your key to the Nahiru Archive."

Malchus stiffened at this. "The Nahiru Archive is a sacred place to my people. I would not dare send you there to trespass. However, I will accompany you and shall give you as a gift whatever you like."

And thus Ilis, Lass of the Seas, managed to obtain more through telling the truth than she could stealing. The Damarises never approved of Ilis's heists, but this did not stop them from inviting her over again and again into their household. She had ended up accepting those offers often over the years, simply because she enjoyed their company.

However, on this day, she would be asking for help.

Ilis entered the house which held so many memories for her. The Damarises' house was one level comprised of a massive round room lit only by a large fire burning in the center, around which all other furniture had been arranged. There were cushions of bright colors to lounge upon on one side, a desk with papers and quills on another, and a table on another wall.

Malchus moved to stand by his wife. They both were strong intimidating sorts, but few centaurs were not. Their jawlines were sharp; their hair fell long and loose and was a deep dark brown. Malchus wore an open vest of olive green, while his wife wore a beige loose blouse. From their stomachs down, their horse coat matched their hair, the only exception being that Landra had one white sock upon her left front hoof and Malchus had four black socks. Upon Malchus's side was strapped his sword, *Gilindruor*. Ilis had heard the tales of this sword. It had been passed down Malchus's line for centuries and was said to have slain more than one dragon.

But the most tantalizing aspect about the couple were their eyes.

Landra's left eye was blue, while her right eye was brown. Malchus was the opposite—his left eye was brown, while his right eye was blue. Such was the way of married centaurs. Upon entering the covenant of marriage, the two were made one. With centaurs, this had the physical representation of swapping one eye color for that of their spouse. It was a beautiful loss and gain all at once, and some said that married centaurs had the ability to see through their spouse's eyes in moments of dire need.

In centuries past, centaurs had considered it an affront to marry someone of a different eye color than them, but few still held to such old-fashioned ideas.

Arline held the same dark coat and hair of her parents, with no socks. Her eyes were a sparkling green, and though she was not yet of the age of speaking, she found other ways to communicate her wisdom.

Malchus motioned toward the cushions along the wall. "Won't you sit?"

Ilis nodded, made her way across the room, and sank into the cushions. Arline came and curled up next to her, laid her head in Ilis's lap, and closed her eyes. Malchus stood over by the desk, flitting through various papers.

"Would you like some tea?" Landra asked.

"Yes, please."

Landra placed a kettle over the fire and then turned to Ilis. Waiting.

Ilis took up a portion of Arline's thick dark hair, began braiding it in small braids, and—for the first time in a while—allowed her thoughts to run free.

"I think I might have set out on an impossible quest."

Landra raised an eyebrow. "Well, that is not new. Though I am surprised you have come back. I thought we would never see you again after your last heist."

"I thought the same."

"Three hours," interrupted Malchus; he had a reputation for having the timeliest of interruptions. "We only saw the Sun's face for three hours yesterday."

"Wait, that can't be right!" Ilis said. The last night she remembered upon the Upper was at least four hours long, so the Under's day should have been the same . . . It could not have changed so drastically in such a short period of time.

Malchus looked up from his writings. He raised an eyebrow as if to say, *Do you truly want to challenge a centaur?*

"Exactly one hundred and seventy-four hours ago, there was a tremor that ran through our land. It was felt from here all the way to the Sparkling Seas. That day, the Sun was precisely two minutes late—few noticed. The next day, the Sun was four minutes late. The day after that, eight, and then sixteen, then thirty-two. Yesterday, the Sun was sixty-four minutes late, and only showed her face for less than three hours. Today, if my calculations are correct, the Sun will be one hundred and twenty-eight minutes late and will only shine for less than two hours."

Arline lifted her head from Ilis's lap so that she could look her in the eyes. Her green eyes were focused on Ilis. It felt like the young centaur was reading her very soul. Arline turned to her mother and nodded, some unspoken message being conveyed.

Landra cocked her head. "Ilis, you know the cause of this."

It was not a question. Ilis knew better than to deny truth to a centaur. It all was connected. The Moon's lack of presence in the night's sky was bringing about their end.

Malchus began to pace. His hoofbeats became rhythmic, like a setting of a beat for a great symphony. "But it is not just time that has changed. The position of the Sun also has changed. She is further and further away from us each time she shows her face. And according to my estimations, that means she is also closer and closer to the Other Side."

Ilis took a shaky breath. She asked the question she did not want to know the answer to: "How much time do we have?"

Malchus turned to face her. He straightened his vest. "Unless something shifts, we have sixty-two hours until the Sun is so far away that we freeze on this side and the Sun is so close that the world burns on the other side."

It took Ilis a minute before she could breathe steadily again. She had to blink back tears. She took three deep breaths. One. Two. Three.

She couldn't think of a single witty thing to say.

Landra gasped and turned away from Ilis, tears in her eyes. "Not only do you know the cause, but you have been tasked to be the solution." The mother centaur moved to kneel beside Ilis. She stroked her cheek, tucking her hair behind her ear. "Why does changing the course of the Sun rest upon such a young one? You have always been more than you seem, yet . . . I wonder." She tilted her head. "Young one, I do not know why such a task has fallen upon you, but I do know this. You hold a fire that may be just what we need."

Ilis shook her head. It wasn't supposed to go this way. The fate of the world wasn't supposed to have such a dire countdown. Malcolm had known he was trying to save the world, but had he known that time was running out? She honestly just wanted to cry.

The kettle began to sing, but Landra didn't move. She just continued to sit beside Ilis in silent comradery. Arline nestled herself even deeper into Ilis's lap.

Malchus put down his papers and moved toward the kettle. He poured three steaming glasses of tea and brought them over. Ilis accepted hers gratefully, and then Malchus joined them on the cushions. Arline sat up and sipped from her parents' glasses, as was their habit.

Multiple long moments of thoughtful silence followed, during which Ilis tried not to lose all hope.

Her course had not changed. She would steal the queen's crown and complete the Moon . . . now, the entire fate of the world just rested upon her shoulders, along with a death curfew. Lovely.

"I need help," Ilis admitted. This was why she had come here in the first place.

"I should hope so. If you thought otherwise, I'd have to give you a lecture upon humility and right seeing of yourself," Malchus said. He stood and moved back to his desk, where he again riffled through his pages.

"What is your plan, young one?"

"Er, I am assuming you mean other than saving the world from the Sun?"

Malchus looked up and gave Ilis a brief smile, amusement in his mismatched eyes. "Yes, other than that one."

Ilis took another long sip of her tea, delighting in the warmth that filled her body. "Well, my plan is to put the Moon back together. And in order to do that, I need to steal something." Ilis paused. She did *not* want to admit this next part. "I need to steal the queen's crown."

A slight shiver ran through Landra's frame. She stood back up to her hoofs and moved to the fire again. She placed a pot on the fire and boiled water. There was a small table beside the fire upon which she chopped vegetables and meat and began tossing them into the pot.

"You already tried that," Landra said, stating the obvious.

"But not with your help," Ilis added with an apologetic smile.

"You almost died," Landra stated. She turned to Ilis fiercely. Tears were in her eyes. "I was in the crowd. I . . . No! We will not help you risk your life for such a dangerous task!"

Malchus considered this. "We may not have a choice."

"Starsbound, we do!" Landra said.

Malchus remained calm. "Our other option is to let our land freeze without interfering." He nodded. This seemed to decide it for him. "Hindrances?" Malchus asked, his eyes perusing various books and papers on his desk. Arline slipped Ilis's mug from her fingers, took a sip of her tea, and then gave it back with a sly smile. Ilis smiled, nodding her head at the young one.

"Well, the castle defenses . . ." Ilis replied to Malchus, "unless we stole it off the head of the queen; in which case, the queen and her guards."

"Do you *want* to lose your head?" Landra asked.

Ilis spread out her hands. "The only other option is to steal it from the throne room, where it is kept while the queen sleeps. But that is what we tried last time, and we got caught."

Landra took a deep breath and sighed. "You will need a creative mode of entry." She moved to her stew and began adding spices.

"We tried that last time . . . and it didn't work."

Landra looked at her and raised a brow. "Giving up?"

"No," Ilis groaned. "How many guards are at each entrance again?"

Ilis asked.

"Seven at all but the main, which has fourteen," Malchus said.

"Men or beasts?"

"Whichever can do the most damage," Landra replied.

Ilis groaned. "And we can't sneak in under a guise because they have a guard whose sole purpose is to read your intentions as you walk through the gate, right?"

Malchus nodded.

"Any secret tunnels I don't know about?"

"The only tunnels are within the castle grounds, leading to various parts of the castle. None lead outside." Malchus looked to his wife and shrugged. "Well, one does, but it is guarded by a dragon, so we would not suggest that route."

Ilis sighed, exasperated. "Well then what would you suggest?"

"Finding a very creative mode of entry, Star-Eyed One," repeated Landra.

Ilis flopped onto her back and stared up at the dome ceiling stained by the fire. A hole of a chimney was in the middle of the roof, and through it, Ilis could see the Stars to which Landra likened her eyes.

After a full thirty minutes of staring at the Stars—during which Arline had braided Ilis's hair—Ilis said, "If only I could fly, I could create a diversion, fly in, land on the roof, and steal the crown. It would be easy."

Malchus and Landra exchanged glances.

There was a long moment of silence.

"We would be betraying the trust of a friend," Landra said.

"In order to save the world," Malchus replied.

Another long stretch of silence passed between them. Then they nodded and turned to Ilis.

"A dragon is to be born in fourteen hours, upon the next rising of the Sun."

Ilis's jaw dropped. The birth of a dragon was an event of monumental importance. Her thoughts spun.

Malchus nodded again, as if affirming to himself that this was the right thing to do. "But you will need a gift of trust to give the Elder

Dragon." He scratched his head in thought.

Arline stood up from Ilis's side and clomped over to her father. With doe eyes, she placed her hand upon *Gilindruor*.

There was a moment of struggle in Malchus's eyes before he nodded. He patted his daughter upon the head. "My daughter has a wisdom that is untainted by wealth or possessions." Malchus unstrapped the sword and gave it to his daughter, who brought it to Ilis.

Ilis accepted *Gilindruor* with reverence. She looked around at this family, tears forming in her eyes. This family had adopted her, and that was an honor she did not take lightly.

***

Ilis returned to the landaway with dinner and a plan in tow. She found Pyra and Chaz engaged in a thumb war and Neil pacing nervously. They all started when she burst through the doors.

"The world is ending," Ilis blurted out. She set down a pot of stew, given to her by the Damarises, on the table with a bang. "Malcolm was right. And . . . well . . . I just found out that we have sixty-two hours to save it."

"Oh," said Chaz.

Pyra blinked. "You are even worse than Malcolm at breaking news to people."

"But I have a plan!" Ilis added.

Neil let his head fall into his hand. "Are you sure we have so little time?"

Ilis nodded. "It came from a centaur."

"What does that have to do with anything?" Chaz asked.

"I forget your education is limited to the Upper." Ilis rubbed the back of her neck. "Centaurs are known for their wisdom and insight. They watch the Stars, they count the days, they keep careful records of the times. They also read truth in people's eyes."

"Like an Understander?" Pyra asked.

"Something like that."

"Sixty-two hours?" Neil asked.

Ilis nodded.

"I don't like you going off on your own like that," Neil grumbled.

Ilis chuckled despite herself. "Neil, all I did was skate up to some very old friends' house and ask for advice and some food. Trust me, when I do put myself in danger, I promise to give you a front-row seat."

This did not seem to make Neil feel any more comfortable.

Pyra sniffed the air and then sighed. "Oh, food!"

Within minutes, they had the feast spread out before them.

Chaz took one large slurp of the soup, and his eyes began to water. "What is this?" he managed to choke out.

Ilis held back a laugh, tore off a chunk of bread, and dipped it in her own soup. "The Beriythians value spice in all things, especially their food."

Pyra sipped daintily at her soup and then asked, "Are they truly that different from us?"

Ilis leaned back and thought on this. "They have different values, and different ways of doing things, so in a way . . . yes. But in other ways, not at all. They are all mothers, fathers, brothers, or sisters, just like us. They have hearts that beat and long for things, and minds that ponder, just like us." Ilis smiled as she thought about the Beriythians. "They are fiercely loyal and have such strong family values that the husband and wife are considered to have committed a scandal if they are apart for more than a week at a time—which makes a few things tricky, as I am sure you can imagine."

Pyra pulled her legs up to her chin and wrapped her arms around them. "I think it is sweet."

Chaz gaped. "But this is the Under we are talking about!"

Ilis nodded, thinking about Chaz's rant against the Under in class not long ago. "It's not what you thought it would be, is it?"

Chaz was silent for a long moment. The sound of slurping soup suddenly seemed loud.

"Wait, what about the shapeshifting?" Chaz said. "Is that true too? Can they really shift from rats to birds? Or any form to another? I kept watching for it, but I didn't see it on the streets."

Ilis raised an eyebrow and chuckled. "I don't know where you got that idea, but that's the biggest load of rotten seaweed I've ever heard."

"But no!" Chaz protested, "Our histories record it, and we are *very* good at keeping records."

Ilis just shook her head and began gathering dishes. "I've never heard of such a thing."

Long after Neil and Pyra had fallen asleep, Ilis heard Chaz get up and go out the front door. Curious, she got up and followed.

She found him sitting on the front steps, just looking out at the frozen world. Ilis went in, got coats for both of them, and then sat down beside him. They sat like that for over an hour in silence. Ilis had a pretty good idea what he was thinking but, at the same time, knew that he would bring it up when he was ready.

While she left him to his own ponderings, Ilis's thoughts ran in another direction. She tried to visualize her encounter with the queen and ready herself for whatever may come. The queen was known to be a warrior so would be skilled in combat. If they happened to cross paths, she would need to be ready to fight. The queen was rumored to be part beast, so Ilis would need to be ready to face anything. The queen had a reputation of being the mightiest in the land—there was no room for Ilis to make mistakes.

Her thoughts scampered about this way and that until all the scenarios were covered. She imagined the worst possible outcomes and then created plans of attack. She took a deep breath. She would be ready.

The next morning at breakfast, Chaz hardly ate; he merely played with his food and wore a look of deep brooding. They sat at a sturdy wooden table that held many a scar from the *Maribor* crew.

"Why the long face?" Pyra asked, biting gingerly on the spicy hunk of bread Ilis had procured for breakfast.

Chaz shook his head, as if to clear his thoughts. "All night, I've been thinking about our plan . . . and, well, I'm just not sure we have one."

Ilis took a deep breath. She waved for him to continue.

Chaz stood up and began to pace. "We are here to steal the pieces of the Moon, pieces that the Queen of the Under has collected, all in order to complete the Moon and save our world, correct?"

Ilis nodded.

"But how do we know that the queen's crown holds the rest of the pieces? We could take the queen's pieces and Ilis's stone to the place where the Moon is being put back together, and it could still not be enough!"

Ilis faced Chaz, "You are right. It very well may not be enough. But we've run out of time. All we can do is try and hope it is enough."

"But what about the Oval?" Chaz challenged. "We lost that Moon piece." He turned his back on Ilis and stared out into the frozen world. "Ilis, you've led us into a mission that has already failed."

Ilis took a shaky breath. She had known this moment was coming. Chaz was not one to follow blindly, so of course he would see the flaws in her plan.

"But we don't know that. Failure would be refusing to even try. You might be right: we might be risking our lives for nothing; but if we are correct, then we are about to die anyway. Or, you might be wrong, and the pieces that we do have just might be enough to stop the Sun from her destructive course. Therefore, if you want us to fail, go ahead and quit. As for me, I'm shooting for the Stars, expecting to succeed."

Chaz stared at her. She was small. She was confident. And somehow, she had become their leader.

He bowed his head and nodded. "Here's to shooting for the Stars then."

It was a somber moment. Each person seemed to be counting the cost and yet, at the same time, realizing that death was close either way.

"Well," Pyra said, "now that we have that settled, what's the plan?"

Ilis took a breath and thought over her conversation with the Damarises. "Two of us will cause a diversion at the palace gates while the other two will sneak into the castle."

"Well, obviously you will be one of the two going to the castle," Pyra said, nodding to Ilis.

"And me," Neil said, as if he was daring anyone to challenge him on it. "Chaz and Pyra can create a diversion to help us slip past their notice."

Ilis nodded and looked to Chaz and Pyra. "Does that sound good to you two?"

Pyra laughed. "It sounds perfect!" She beamed at Chaz. "Unless I'm mistaken, Chaz has a whole book full of ideas stored up just for these kinds of things."

Much to Ilis's surprise, Chaz blushed.

Ilis raised an eyebrow. "Well good. I suppose you will need supplies?"

Chaz stood and began to pace again. "Yes," he said gruffly.

"Give him an hour or so to think," Pyra assured Ilis, "and he will have it all figured out."

For the next forty-three minutes, Ilis, Pyra, and Neil watched as Chaz paced back and forth across the floor. The squeaky boards announced his every step as he rubbed his hands over his furrowed brow. Occasionally he would stop, pull a notebook from his pocket, and scroll through its pages, making notes along the way. Once or twice, he asked Ilis about the layout of the entrance to the castle, where the guards were stationed, and other questions.

"Do they have any unique fears?" he asked.

Ilis leaned back in her chair. "Fire. Deep in the bones of every Beriythian is the fear of fire; that's why they build in brick and stone and have roads of water."

"Why are they so scared of fire?" Pyra asked, leaning forward with her elbows on the table.

"Centuries ago, the mountain exploded and sent balls of fire raining down on the land. The houses were made of wood and went up in flames instantly; the whole capital was destroyed."

"Wait . . . what mountain?" Chaz asked.

Ilis stood and opened a window, frowning when it was still dark outside. "Estenbur. Even when the Sun is out you can hardly see it, but there is a mountain on the horizon."

"How far away is it?" Chaz asked.

"Over five leagues."

"And the mountain shot fire all the way down here?" Pyra looked aghast.

Ilis nodded.

"Terrible day," Neil muttered.

Ilis turned to him. "What?"

He cleared his throat. "That must have been a terrible day."

Ilis felt like there was more to that statement but didn't even know what to ask. Instead, she continued with the story. "Most Beriythians believed it was an attack from the Upper—that somehow, they had caused it to happen to destroy Beriyth. Either way, the fires burned the capital to the ground and killed thousands. And thus, the people fear fire to this day."

"I'd fear fire too if I had that history," Pyra commented. She turned to Chaz. "Can you use that fear?"

"Of course," he replied, deep in thought. "Fears are very useful things."

Pyra cocked her head. "I don't think I like that statement."

Chaz didn't seem to hear her, for he replied, "Pyra, you would fly pretty far if we catapulted you."

Pyra threw up her hands. "And I like that statement even less!"

Chaz shook his head. "Sorry, bad idea."

"You think?"

Neil let out a small chuckle.

Chaz picked up his pacing yet again. Pyra stood and began to do the dishes, and Neil followed. Ilis watched as they worked: Pyra washing and Neil drying. They worked well together. She wondered if they had been close before the heist for the Crown Jewel.

Her thoughts were interrupted by Chaz letting out a big sigh.

"I'll need a good deal of gunpowder, wood, thick wool, and a few foxes."

Ilis raised a brow. "And what do you plan to do?"

Chaz smiled mischievously, almost mimicking the look Ilis often wore. "Give them their worst nightmare."

***

"Ilis!" Pyra whispered while pulling on Ilis's sleeve. They were in town shopping for supplies for Chaz's diversion. Ilis looked over at her friend, who was currently gripping her arm for dear life.

"Hmm?"

Pyra nodded her head toward a large frost-white creature prancing next to them.

Ilis grinned. So as not to be overheard, she leaned close to Pyra's ear and said, "It's a unicorn."

Pyra spun and leaned into Ilis's ear. "I know it's a unicorn! But it's walking right next to us! And it's . . ." She stole another look at the beast, who was carrying on a conversation with a man. "It's not wild!"

Ilis led Pyra through a few streets and away from the crowds of people before responding. "There are a great many beasts who would be gentle if we only gave them the opportunity to be so."

Pyra shook her head and looked back among the streets. A dragon with large green wings that shimmered in the night sky flew overhead, mounted by a rider. "It's just so different." A man-child and a griffin cub wrestled over a wooden sword across the street from them. Pyra let out a laugh. "And yet at the same time, exactly the same."

They rejoined the boys, and Pyra shared about all that she had seen. Chaz, eyes wide, described how they had bought the gunpowder from a minotaur by using a note written by Ilis and then pretending to be mute.

"Everything our side has banished, this side has embraced," Pyra said in awe.

Ilis nodded. "And everything this side has forgotten, your side has diligently recorded for preservation."

"What a world that exists! And we didn't even know it," Chaz said thoughtfully.

"What a world that exists—and we wanted to destroy it!" Pyra said solemnly.

"Both sides are so rich, imagine what life would be like if they worked together instead of fighting each other," Neil said. All eyes turned to him, but he seemed to be in a daze. "Each side has wasted so much time fighting the other. Thousands of lives have been lost in the pursuit of destroying that which they don't understand. I dream of an age where there is peace between the two sides of our fair world, where battles are replaced with celebrations and deaths are replaced with marriages. What a beautiful thing that would be."

"Neil, you talk like you've been here before!" Chaz said with a gruff laugh. "That kind of talk would get you hanged on the mount."

Neil seemed to shake himself out of his daze. He laughed with Chaz. "Which is exactly why you have never heard me speak like that before." He clapped his hands together. "Now, I hate to rush us, but considering the dire predictions about how little time we have left, shall we go?"

Ilis stared at Neil for a long moment before shrugging. He was making less and less sense the more she got to know him.

When they got back to the landaway, Chaz readied his supplies. He measured out the gunpowder into separate leather pouches. He cut strips of wool and laid them out on the tables. He even fed the foxes to "make sure they had plenty of energy" for the upcoming task.

He completed one mysterious task and was deep into another when, suddenly, he looked up at Ilis. "Wait, how do you plan to sneak into the castle?"

Ilis grinned wickedly. "Why, steal a dragon of course."

CHAPTER NINETEEN

Ilis had only heard rumors about the Dragon Nest—rumors that were carried by the Mesheisar, the group of Dragon Riders.

The bond created between a dragon and a "fireless one," as the dragons called all other beings, was a bond so unique and unexplainable, that the Blood Tongue had to create a new word for it. Qasar has ancient connotations of the verb "to knit," as that is what happens when a dragon and a fireless one bond—their souls are knit together in a connection that is thicker than blood.

Over a millennia ago, when the country of Beriyth was formed, the dragons had made a covenant with the fireless saying that they would allow twelve of their kind to be soul-knit with the fireless and become Mesheisar Dragon Riders. Never more than twelve, but anytime one pair died, another bonding could happen to take its place.

Therefore, the Mesheisar were an elite group and currently only consisted of two humans, two large pixies, two minotaurs, two griffins, a dryad, a troll, and a phoenix (a powerful combination). The hatching of a dragon's egg only happened around once a decade, so the fact that one was happening tonight *and* that there was an open spot in the twelve— right as Ilis needed a ride into the castle—was a coincidence Ilis couldn't help but wonder at. Perhaps the Stars were on her side.

Ilis had heard that the Mesheisar Dragon Riders would never tell what happened at the nest, or even what it looked like, other than that it was guarded by an Elder Dragon, so to approach without a gift of trust would be asking for a fiery death. But the location of the Dragon Nest *was* common knowledge. Follow the stream that flows south from Qirya for three miles until you see a hill to the east—at the top of that hill is the Dragon Nest. But other than that, Ilis had no idea what she was getting herself—or her team—into.

Bundling up, Ilis and her crew set out from Qirya and followed the river that flowed south. They carried lanterns with them to light up their path through the darkness. Their conversation was sparse, and Ilis indulged in little of it. Her thoughts were spinning. The weight of the world seemed to press on her shoulders, and she found herself focusing on her breathing to keep her thoughts from running too far off. This would work. It had to.

When they saw the hill to the east, they ceased following the river and found their way through the snow-covered fields toward the hill. As they got closer, Chaz voiced the obvious.

"There is nothing there."

The hill was indeed void of any visible structure. From where they stood, it looked like a completely ordinary hill; the only thing that set it apart from other hills was that it had a path marked out by stones that led to near the top.

"It's up there," Neil responded.

"Oh? What is it then, invisible?" Chaz challenged. His boots were wet and frozen from stepping in a puddle, and they had not improved his mood.

"Maybe," Neil responded with a shrug. "These are dragons we are talking about. I wouldn't put it past them to guard their young with some sort of deep magic."

Ilis shrugged and began the hike up the hill. Their boots crunched in the snow, and as they hiked, the Sun made her appearance on this side of their world. She peeked over the mountains in the distance and cast an eerie glow through the frosty air all around them.

Pyra let out a huge sigh. "It is good to see you, dear friend."

As they hiked, following the path of large gray stones marking out the way, Ilis watched with horror as she witnessed how lopsided the Sun's course was—as well as how small the Sun was. Malchus was right—she truly would only grace their side of the world for less than two hours today. Ilis gulped. The rising of the Sun marked the hours they had left— they were now at forty-five hours until the end.

As they neared the top of the hill, the path came to a sudden stop. The group halted.

"Well, now what?" Chaz asked.

Ilis looked at the rest of the hill. From this point on it was much steeper. They would have to climb up the rest if they wanted to go any further, but somehow, climbing didn't feel right. There was an ache in her chest that Ilis didn't know how to describe. It felt as if they were walking on holy ground.

"To gain the Elder Dragon's trust, you must bring a gift that proves your desire is partnership and not dominion," Ilis said under her breath.

Because of the Damarises, she knew that tonight was the night the dragon was to be born. With a few whispers in the right ears, the dragon's previous qasar-to-be had been detained from the birth.

The dragon elders did not let just anyone bond with their young. Whoever had planned on bonding with the dragon tonight had, no doubt, already proven their trust; but for Ilis to show up and take his place, she would have to prove her own worthiness of this sacred gift. Thankfully, dragons cared little for the squabbles of the fireless, so they would not find Ilis's theft of the role to be wrong . . . as long as she was accepted.

Ilis pulled *Gilindruor* from its sheath and thrust it into the dirt at her feet. "I give you *Gilindruor*, who brought death to your people, as a sign of my loyalties to your kind."

Those words evoked a change upon the hillside. The top of the hill seemed to unwrap and unroll, uncurl and unfold. When they realized what they were truly looking at, Pyra stumbled backwards, Neil let out a low whistle, and Chaz began muttering things under his breath.

The top of the hill was a dragon.

Ilis gulped, realizing what this meant. The Dragon Nest was not just guarded by an Elder Dragon, the Dragon Nest was an Elder Dragon. The eggs must lie beneath the folds of its wings! This made so much sense! Ilis had heard tales of how Elder Dragons were stationed all around the world guarding places of rich heritage—this must be how they did it! Elder Dragons were such large beasts, their bodies could easily be mistaken for landscape.

The Elder Dragon's head had uncurled itself from being wrapped around his body until it was raised above Ilis and her friends, looking down upon them as the great beast had every right to do.

His scales were a dark gray, a gray that melded perfectly into the landscape of the hilltop. Pocketed in his massive skull were eyes that gleamed with a depth of emotion that Ilis could not decipher. It almost looked like rage, but not an evil rage. Smoke blew from his nostrils in great columns and leaked from his lips.

"I would like to officially voice my opinion that I think this is a terrible idea," Chaz said, his voice quiet.

"And the other five hundred times you have said so were not official because . . ." Pyra said, never taking her eyes off the dragon.

Chaz gulped as he looked up at the dragon. "Because they were not said while staring at the beast."

The dragon's eyes fixed upon Ilis. It took all her resolve not to squirm. The dragon lowered his head and poised it so that he was eye level with her.

Ilis found herself breathing in ragged gasps. Her thoughts found their way back to Mount Oros and the dragon that had brought such destruction upon the mountain capital. If this dragon wanted to, he could kill all of them right where they stood. One blast of his breath, or even one swipe of his tail, and they were goners.

The dragon opened his mouth and sent forth a blaze of fire. Ilis jumped back, but she was not the target. The dragon engulfed the sword with its fiery breath until the sword bore the semblance of a silver puddle. The dragon lifted his head and let out a roar that shook their bones.

The gift was enough.

The hillside shifted yet again. The dragon lifted one of his wings, and precisely where the path had ended, a space appeared for them to walk forward. The path continued underneath the dragon's head and neck and between its leg and what appeared to be part of his tail. It looked as if a tunnel had opened up in the hillside, but it was a tunnel that traversed under the wings and around the body of the Elder Dragon.

Ilis lifted her chin and walked forward, hoping that her team would follow. She heard their boots shuffle along behind her and let out a sigh of relief. They walked into the cave of the dragon's body. When they had passed through the opening the dragon had created, there was a ragged rustling of his wings rubbing along his scales, and the opening closed behind them.

They were engulfed in darkness. It was in that moment that they realized they had left their lanterns outside.

"I knew it! This was a ter—"

"Hush up, Chaz," Pyra said.

Ilis pulled out her glowstone torch from where she had it stowed in her left stocking and used its light to take in their surroundings. It looked like they were just in some sort of tunnel, but the sides of the tunnel were made up of the unmistakable gleam of dragon scales. The heat from the dragon's body was a stark contrast to the chill of outside, and Ilis found herself wanting to take off her coat. She had a hard time deciphering what part of the dragon was what, but there was a very clear path that it seemed they were to follow.

"Well, I suppose we go forward," Ilis said.

They walked with quiet footfalls. Chaz didn't even seem to be in the mood to bemoan their circumstances. They followed the path underneath the dragon's wings until they found the nest. If Ilis was reading her surroundings correctly, it appeared as if the space was created along the side of the dragon's belly, with the dragon's leg and tail each forming another wall. The ceiling must have been its wing. In the center of the space were several different nests made up of rocks. Inside the nests, eggs of various sizes were nestled.

Ilis knew the one they were here for immediately. Most of the eggs were small and, therefore, still years away from being ready to hatch. But one stood out above the rest. It had a golden sheen and stood as tall as a large horse.

Ilis walked over to the nest and paused.

"This is a terrible idea," Chaz muttered yet again.

Ilis took a deep breath. Little did Chaz know how right he was.

The reality of the situation was that this truly was a terrible idea. Ilis seemed to have a knack for embarking on such things. But to understand why this was such a terrible idea, one had to understand the way the fireless and dragons bond.

The moment a dragon breaks forth from its shell, its soul is open, vulnerable, and willing. There is just a moment, the smallest of moments, when it is able to completely trust a fireless one. If one misses this moment, the opportunity to bond is gone, and the honor of gracing a dragon's back will be forever out of one's grasp. The dragon may choose to work alongside other creatures, but never closely, and always with suspicion. The dragon will only ever truly trust another dragon.

For you see, dragons can read each other's thoughts and intentions. Nothing is hidden between them. Therefore, they know with absolute certainty that they can trust one another. A dragon is physically incapable of deceiving a fellow dragon.

But the fireless beings are a mystery to dragons. Their thoughts and emotions are hidden behind several layers of words and actions.

The only moment when a dragon can see a fireless being clearly is right at the dragon's birth, when the whole world is breaking open for the newborn to see and explore. In that moment, if a fireless being enters into the dragon's reach, and the dragon finds the fireless worthy of trust, then a bond is created. While the dragon cannot read the thoughts of the fireless as it can a fellow dragon, it will be able to sense the intentions of the fireless's actions and, therefore, trust them.

Now, an astute observer would question this, saying, 'If there is no risk involved, is that even trust?' And therein lies the difference between the fireless and dragons.

To the fireless, trust is a choice. To dragons, trust is a reality of kinship.

For a fireless being to enter into that brotherhood is the greatest of privileges.

Passing off her torch to Pyra, she chewed her lip. She only had one shot at this. She tuned out Chaz's comments, dismissed her own fears, and focused on the dragon egg.

She took a shaky breath. Doubt filled her body. The dragon would see her, perhaps like no one else ever had. The dragon would discover her thoughts, her memories, her dreams . . . and her failures. In a single moment, the dragon would know her. And what if the dragon did not trust who she was? What if she was not worthy of the dragon's trust? What if . . . What if . . .

Their mission genuinely rode on the back of this dragon. To fail here was to fail the world. Beriyth would freeze while Basileia would burn.

Ilis climbed up into the rocky dragon nest and stood before the egg, craning her neck to look at the top. Its golden appearance almost gleamed like true gold in the faint light of the torch.

Oh foolish daughter of the sea, Ilis chided herself, *you have placed the fate of the world on the chance that a dragon trusts you. And why should it?*

Tears sprang up in her eyes.

Suddenly, all she wanted to do was abort the mission. All she wanted to do was run away. She did not want to be seen. She did not want to be rejected.

But somehow, she took a step forward. Somehow, she found the courage to lift her hand and place it on the egg's shell.

A sound like glass being shattered filled the air as the egg began to crack.

But Ilis stayed firm.

A thousand memories flooded her brain. All of her failures flashed before her eyes. She saw them all so keenly. She saw each moment she let her father down, each moment she lashed out with her words against her crew, each moment she was selfish and proud. The heist where she almost killed her entire crew flashed through her thoughts in painful detail, followed by a replaying of Malcolm being crushed. All the things she tried to keep pent up and hidden suddenly leaked out. They leaked and then spilled and then turned into a flood. Her worries, her fears, her greatest mistakes were all laid bare before the eyes of the dragon.

Ilis's heart sank in her chest. The dragon would never trust her now.

Their mission was lost, and it was all her fault. As always, she was the reason things fell apart.

Ilis felt tears streaming down her cheeks. Sobs began wracking her body. And just as Ilis was about to pull her hand away from the egg's cracked shell, she felt something meet her hand.

She couldn't open her eyes. Not yet. She wasn't ready to see the eyes of the one who had seen her so truly.

But then she felt the breath of the dragon beneath her palm, and an understanding struck her.

The dragon had seen her and had not turned its back on her.

The dragon had seen her, and it had chosen her.

Suddenly, Ilis understood. A dragon's trust was a choice too—but a deeper choice. It was a trust that knew the depth of one's untrustworthiness and somehow still managed to make the leap.

Why hello human, the beast spoke in Ilis's thoughts.

CHAPTER TWENTY

Ilis gasped and opened her eyes to find a scaly, slimy beast the color of sunset and the size of a horse standing before her, looking deeply into her eyes.

She staggered back toward the edge of the nest, attempting—and failing—to open her mouth to form words. She had *heard* the dragon in her thoughts. That was not supposed to happen. That was impossible.

She tried again to form words, but nothing was coming out. After multiple tries, she squeaked out the dragon greeting of "Ka'oth bonkur."

The dragon seemed to chuckle. *Your accent is abysmal, but I appreciate the sentiment.*

"How is this possible?" Ilis said aloud, marveling at the mystery she hadn't known the existence of. She stepped away from the beast and watched as the dragon did a quick shake of her limbs and was freed from the remainder of her birth cage. *You tell me. I was just born.* There was no animosity in the dragon's words, just intense curiosity.

Ilis stumbled back and fell on her bottom into the hard rocks. The dragon strode forward, placing her great head almost in Ilis's lap.

The dragon sniffed at Ilis and then purred. *There is nothing in my mother's memories that indicates she ever communicated this way. She had a bond with a fireless, but they could never . . .*

Ilis couldn't help herself; she interrupted the dragon. "You have your mother's memories?"

Of course! Don't you have yours?

Ilis shook her head.

Hmm, what odd creatures humans are. The dragon cocked her amber head, eyes glistening. *Perhaps our communication link has to do with your ancestors. Are they connected with the deep magic?*

Ilis shook her head again.

Hmmm, the dragon replied deep in Ilis's thoughts. *Well, never mind then.* The dragon nudged Ilis and managed to pick her up until she was again standing. Then the dragon faced Ilis so that they were looking eye to eye.

My name is Kanaph, and I choose you, the dragon spoke. *Not for what you have done, or what you will do, but who you are. You are now my qasar.*

Ilis felt the tears stream again down her cheeks. She took a faltering step back, the reasons she did not trust herself prominent in her thoughts. "I don't deserve this."

Exactly. Is that not what true trust is?

Eyes locked with the dragon who saw her deepest depths, Ilis saw a truth she hardly dared to believe—she had been fully seen, fully known, and fully chosen, even with all her mistakes. Taking a shaky breath, she realized she had two paths before her. She could continue to carry the guilt of her past or release it and accept that it did not define her.

You are not defined by your mistakes, the dragon said. *But will you believe it?*

After a deep breath, Ilis nodded.

Good, then shed your guilt like I just shed my shell, and let's get on with this adventure.

Ilis took a deep breath and felt the weight of her guilt begin to lift. A smile crept upon her lips as she wiped at her tears.

Stretching out her limbs, Kanaph crawled about the nest. The dragon extended her wings. A thick slime dripped off of them. Kanaph curled her lip. *Lovely experience, being born,* the dragon said with thick sarcasm.

She stretched out her wings again, this time flapping them.

There was a loud whoosh. Ilis felt her hair lift off her shoulders from the force.

Kanaph craned her neck and let out a roar, albeit a rather squeaky one.

Pleased with the sound, Kanaph turned again to Ilis. *What is your name?*

She took a deep breath to compose herself. Wiping her nose on her sleeve, she cast a quick glance at the others who huddled well out of reach of the dragon. Chaz stared at them with wide eyes. Neil had his head cocked. Pyra smiled encouragingly.

Turning her attention back to Kanaph, she replied, "Ilis of the Seas."

The dragon seemed to purr. *And who are those cowering behind you?*

"My friends," Ilis replied.

"Uh, Ilis? Do I need to question your sanity? You do realize you are talking to yourself," Chaz said.

Oh, he's a fun one, Kanaph commented.

Pyra placed a hand on Chaz's arm, wonder in her eyes. "No, I don't think that is what is happening."

And she's a bright one!

Ilis chuckled. And then let out a pent-up breath.

The dragon read her thoughts. *You need help.*

Ilis nodded.

Well then, let's see how these things work.

Kanaph let out a screech—and the Elder Dragon's body responded. Ilis cringed at the sound of the Elder Dragon's wings rustling alongside its scales as the wings withdrew, revealing the open sky above. The light of the already setting Sun flooded the nests.

Ilis's heart sank, the Sun's setting light a somber reminder of why they were here.

Kanaph took three large steps, reached the edge of the nest, and then launched herself in the air—only to face-plant on the ground right next to Chaz. Dirt flew in all directions, and Chaz ended up covered with a good bit of it.

He wiped at the dirt on his face, causing it to smear and eliciting a giggle from Pyra. "I was right. This is a terrible idea."

The Elder Dragon's head appeared above them. His long neck stretched until he was perched to where he had a good view of the youngling.

Kanaph looked up toward the Elder Dragon. It took Ilis a moment before she realized that they must be talking in their thoughts.

Kanaph huffed, smoke trickling from her nostrils, and stretched out her wings again.

"What did he say?" Ilis asked.

He told me not to launch myself as if I were attempting to dive off a cliff but to use my wings instead.

Ilis tried to hide a smile.

Kanaph poised herself, neck raised and wings extended. She beat her wings once, twice, and then took a stride forward and jumped with a third solid flap of her wings.

They all heard the air catch beneath her wings and watched as Kanaph flew up. She let out a high-pitched roar and flapped about above their heads. She managed to stay in the air for about thirty seconds before crash landing back in the nest.

Ilis rubbed the back of her neck, and Kanaph read her mind once again.

I'll be able to fly you wherever you want to go, the dragon said confidently. She cast her cat-like eyes to Ilis's cowering friends. *Are they coming too?*

"Only two of us," Ilis responded. She moved away from the winged beast to face Pyra and Chaz. In a rush, she gave Pyra a hug. As she released, she whispered, "Thank you . . . for everything."

Pyra smiled. "This is what friends are for."

Ilis faced Chaz, suddenly at a loss for words.

"We will meet you back at *Maribor,*" Chaz said, reminding them all of their decided upon rendezvous point.

Ilis blinked back an odd set of tears and nodded. She and Chaz knew better than the others that their chances of surviving the night were slim. Ilis tried not to dwell on the fact that the world's chances of surviving the next forty or so hours were even slimmer. Their world was being destroyed by the Sun, and it had somehow landed on their shoulders to stop that from happening.

Ilis lifted her chin and turned to Neil. He was facing the dragon.

"She won't eat me, will she?" Neil asked.

I could, Kanaph said in Ilis's thoughts. Kanaph let out a puff of smoke from her nostrils.

Neil turned to Ilis. "Was that a yes or a no?"

Ilis approached Kanaph and laid her hands on her warm scales. They felt like jewels under her fingers, and Ilis wondered at the honor she was about to partake in.

Kanaph read her thoughts and chuckled. *Ahh, if you think riding me will be an honor, we will get along well.* Kanaph turned her head toward Neil. *Tell him I won't eat him as long as you like him.*

Laughing, she turned to Neil. "She says as long as I like you, she won't eat you."

"Great," Neil said dryly, though Ilis thought she saw a glimmer of a smile on his lips as she turned away.

***

Ilis and Neil climbed onto the back of Kanaph, and immediately, Kanaph launched herself into the air.

Neil, being unprepared for the sudden motion, fell and landed solidly on the ground. He sat up and rubbed his head. "Fantastic creatures, dragons. Humans just seem to be prone to injury around them."

If humans weren't so fragile, perhaps that wouldn't be the case.

Ilis extended her hand and helped Neil back up. He patted Kanaph on the side. "Mind going a bit slower for me? My bones aren't as young as they once were."

Kanaph huffed and paused. *Is everyone ready?*

They grabbed on to Kanaph's neck.

"Yes."

Kanaph beat her wings and lunged forward. The dragon's body heaved upward until they were in the air. They lurched to one side, and Ilis found herself slipping. Neil, who had somehow managed to keep his seat, pulled her back onto Kanaph's back. Ilis gripped the dragon with her knees and breathed steadily.

You okay back there? Kanaph asked.

"Well, we are still back here!" Ilis responded, trying to sound positive.

They flew around the Dragon Nest for over an hour, giving Kanaph time to figure out her wings as well as Chaz and Pyra time to get to the gates of the palace. When they had waited long enough, they flew down the hill toward the city gates. Wind whooshed all around them. Kanaph flapped her wings harder, angling her body upward, and they soared high over the walls and toward the center of the city. Ilis's breath caught in her throat.

Qirya, the capital of Beriyth, was beautiful from the skies, especially in the light of the setting Sun. The rivers carved through the city in graceful strokes. The castle sat to the side, surrounded by a wall with a tall gate and a river that arched around it like a moat. Lights gleamed on the waters.

The sight of the castle brought up memories like a surge. She heard the echo of the crew of *Maribor*'s pleas to abandon her scheme to steal the queen's crown last time. She heard her own promises of success. She saw the looks of doubt and fear upon their faces as they attempted to break into the palace, followed by the looks of despair and hopelessness as they were caught. She rubbed the nape of her neck.

This time would be different. It *had* to be.

If they failed here the world would end, and everyone she loved would either be burned to a crisp or frozen solid, depending on what side they were on. Everyone—her classmates back in Basileia, the Damarises, the crew of *Maribor* . . . Malcolm—would die if they failed to complete the Moon. They *had* to succeed.

Taking three slow breaths, she let a smirk grow upon her lips. "They say insanity is doing the same thing twice but expecting a different result," she said as they neared the castle enough to see its purple hue, "but I prefer to view it as persistence."

Neil chuckled behind her.

Who is this friend of yours? Kanaph asked in Ilis's thoughts, causing Ilis to jump. The sudden thoughts in her head felt jarring.

Not wanting to reply aloud, Ilis tried to respond in thought as well.

Neil, a Forester from Mount Oros. Ilis willed her thoughts to be communicated and found them to be heard.

Kanaph was silent for a moment, but Ilis could feel her thinking.

There is something odd about him, she finally said. It is as if he is hiding himself or is not fully himself or . . . Ilis could feel her dragon searching for words *. . . I don't know.*

Ilis thought on Kanaph's words. There was much about Neil that did not make sense, but she had begun to believe that this was just part of his personality—like a faraway light that shines but is never understood.

"What are you thinking?" Neil asked, startling Ilis out of her musings.

"Uh," Ilis muttered, trying to think of how to answer.

Just be honest and ask him! Kanaph prompted.

"Well, I was thinking about you," Ilis stated.

She felt Neil chuckle behind her. "Is that so? And what about me?"

"That you are a mystery to me," Ilis said plainly. She craned her neck so that she could better see him. "Who are you truly?"

Ilis watched as a mischievous grin crossed his face. "What makes you think that I am any more than just Neil the Forester, friend of Prince Malcolm, and now, friend of you?"

Ilis turned forward again, her eyes barely seeing her surroundings. She hardly registered the snow-capped houses of the Under, hardly registered the glistening frozen rivers below, hardly registered that they were nearing the castle.

Finally, she answered, "Because you are too much of a person to be 'just' anything."

Ilis turned to see his face as he replied, but his eyes were down at the land beneath them. "There is the diversion," Neil said, pointing to bright flames which danced about by the gates of the castle.

They watched as the courtyard before the gates erupted in pandemonium. Guards of all shapes and sizes scurried about chasing after foxes whose tails appeared to be dragging some sort of small fiery contraptions. Small bursts of explosions appeared in the wake of the foxes. The griffin, which was set to guard the skies, dove down to see what was going on.

"It's time," Neil said.

Kanaph needed no urging. She dove right into the castle grounds, past the guard stations, silent and undetected. In three long strides, she slid to a stop in the snow on the roof of the castle.

Slipping off the warmth of Kanaph's back into the cold of the snow was shocking. Ilis paused and placed her hand on Kanaph's amber snout.

Wait for us, if you will, Ilis said.

Kanaph lowered her head in answer. *Try not to die,* her dragon replied.

Ilis and Neil trudged through the snow-covered rooftop until they reached a small door. The door was locked, but Ilis had it unlocked in moments. The door opened to an interior balcony that ran all along the ceiling of a circular room.

Ilis let out a breath. They were in the throne room. This was further than she made it last time.

Her eyes scanned the perimeter, taking in guards, exits, and weapons. The throne room was an enormous dome with vibrant sash curtains lining the walls. In the center of the grand room sat the throne. Twelve guards were stationed at various exits around the dome. Half of the guards were facing outward—toward the exits, and the other half were facing inward—toward the prize in the center of the room. Not one guard looked the same. There was a girl with butterfly wings, and so many more. But Ilis's attention was drawn to what sat in the middle of the room. On the throne sat the crown, adorned with more Moon pieces than Ilis could count.

Ilis took a deep breath. This could be enough! Maybe these were indeed the last of the Moon pieces! All they had to do was get the crown, and then Neil could take them to the rest of the Moon. And if Ilis had to guess, she would say that the rest of the Moon was hidden in the Under, which would explain why Neil acted like he had been here before.

But she shook her head. First things first. The crown.

With Neil on her heels, Ilis snuck around the interior balcony at the top of the room until she reached the curtain in the line of sight of a cyclops. Cyclops, while fierce in battle, were not known to have the best eyesight. Then, grabbing a fistful of the curtain, Ilis slipped in between it and the wall and began to slowly lower herself downward. The curtain rustled gently, but Ilis was skilled in the art of going unseen. What was a surprise was when Neil began to follow her and made almost less noise and movement with the curtain than she did. Yet another mystery to solve—if they survived the night.

Hand over hand, Ilis lowered herself down the curtain. The thrumming sensation of adrenaline pounded in her veins, but she paid it no mind.

All she had to do was steal the queen's crown, and their world would be saved.

Her feet touched the ground, and Ilis took a breath. Neil landed beside her and put his hand on her shoulder. She looked back at him, but he merely brushed past her, motioning her to wait. She wondered at his nerve, but he peeked out from behind the curtain before she could challenge him.

Ilis watched as Neil's form went rigid. He threw out his arm, as if instinctively, to protect her.

A chilling voice rang through the room.

"I knew one day you would find me."

CHAPTER TWENTY-ONE

Ilis peeked from behind Neil. Over his shoulder, she found the queen, a woman in her early forties, sitting on her throne. Her black hair fell into her lap in long locks and was a stark contrast against her pale skin. She looked like she hadn't seen the Sun in a very long time—and upon thinking about it, Ilis realized, she probably hadn't. This whole side of the world was Sun deprived.

The crown was sitting upon her head.

How had she gotten there so fast?

The queen's eyes landed on Ilis. Her lips formed a small O as she raised a single eyebrow, surprised.

"Well, well, well." The queen gasped, "I see it is not just me you have found. She tried to steal my crown, you know, and I couldn't have that. So I had to kill her. Only, she didn't die." The queen leapt up and began to dance about to the beat of a song she hummed softly under her breath.

After dancing in a full circle around her throne, she collapsed back down, lounging in it as one would on a sofa.

She grinned openly at Ilis, either completely oblivious to the awkward silence filling the room or relishing it. "Pretty little thing in a pretty little dress, witty little thing in a witty little mess," the queen sang softly under her breath, her eyes never leaving Ilis.

Neil stood dumbfounded.

Laughter, like that of a child, filled the room. It took Ilis a moment to realize that the laughter was the queen's. This was the queen who ruled the Under? This was the woman who garnered the respect of both man and beasts—including dragons? The queen Ilis knew was legendary. The queen Ilis saw was . . .

The queen sat up and put her chin in her palms. "Tell me, my dear child, how much has he told you?"

Ilis's eyes flitted to Neil, confused. She wanted him to explain. But all Ilis saw was Neil's rigid back.

"Ahh," the queen cooed, reading the truth in her eyes, "then he has lied to you."

This seemed to shake Neil out of his haze. He took a step out of their hiding place and toward the queen.

"The world is ending, Anne." Neil spoke with a quiet power.

Ilis turned to look at Neil. How did he know her name? And why did he speak to her as if he knew her?

The queen stood and laughed. "Oh, the world has been ending for a long time!" She flopped down to the floor and sat cross-legged before her throne. "Why should I take notice now?"

The queen cocked her head. With a face devoid of expression, she lifted her hand, palm upward. Suddenly, the energy in the air shifted. Ilis's cape began floating. She stared at it, her jaw dropping. It just began lifting off the ground, though not as if caught in a strong breeze . . . It was more like it had just been freed from the confines of gravity. With a quick glance around the room, she noticed that she was not the only one affected by this strange occurrence. All around the room, people's clothing, the curtains upon the walls, and even people's hair had begun slightly falling upward. Had it not been something controlled by a mad woman, the sight might have been humorous.

Then the queen flipped her hand, her palm facing Neil, and jerked her hand back toward herself.

The unseen force leaking from the fingertips of the queen jerked Neil forward, the toes of his shoes leaving trail marks on the marble floor until he stood within arm's reach of the queen.

The queen looked almost sad as she faced the young boy before her. "How dare you come here, after all these years?"

Neil, unaffected by the shocking force which had just dragged him across the room, simply continued to stare into her eyes. "This was always the plan."

She rolled her eyes. "Stars, what is it with men and their plans! Oh, wait." She let out a burst of giggles. "I keep forgetting, you are not a man."

Neil's eyes grew somber. "If I don't get the final pieces by tomorrow, the Sun will crash into the brink, and then the whole world will burn."

"Burning timber all around, burning embers to be found, burning herds here to find, burning words in your mind," the queen sang with a brash smile into Neil's face.

"We . . ." Neil started. He threw his shoulders back, trying to be resolved. "We don't have much time."

"Oh, my dear!" the queen scolded. "We still have more time!" She patted Neil on the shoulder. "Time is the one thing you've always had." Her face turned bitter, as if the words had tasted sour. But then with a shrug, the look was gone.

Ilis's head spun. She understood Neil had been talking about the Moon, but *nothing* else was making sense.

The queen rubbed her eyes and slowly made her way back to her throne. She settled down and, for a moment, looked as if she were going to fall asleep. Then she said, "Why so suddenly?"

She yawned, and Ilis found herself yawning too. The queen tapped her fingers upon her crown—her crown studded with Moon pieces.

"I remember . . ." She paused and blinked a few times. "I remember you saying we had at least another century."

Suddenly, the queen jumped up and stood upon her throne, her face scandalized. "Am I that old already? They don't look too wrinkly," she said, throwing out her hands and inspecting them. "BRING ME A MIRROR!"

A guard, who had been standing in stoic silence, rushed forward and held up a mirror to the queen.

The queen smiled and preened at her reflection. "Oh my, don't you look *good* for near on a century."

Her head snapped up and, she looked at Neil, understanding.

"Oh," she said dryly, "it hasn't been a century."

She sat upon the back of her throne, looking like a bird on a perch. "Then why, oh why, does the old time fly? Why, oh why, does the . . ." The queen's jaw dropped. "You didn't?"

Neil was silent.

"Oh."

It was one word from the queen's lips. She seemed to understand something in his silence that Ilis did not.

The queen seemed to understand a great many things Ilis did not.

Neil shrugged. "It was worth a shot."

The queen blinked. "Worth a shot?" Laughter bubbled out of her small form. "Oh honey, even I wouldn't have attempted such a *foolish* deed!" She laughed again. "It honestly is quite funny when you think about it!"

In one fluid motion, the queen leapt from her throne and grabbed Neil's hands. "Dance with me, my sweet!"

But Neil stood rooted, unmoving.

The queen let go of his hands and pouted. "Oh, why won't you dance?"

"Anne, this is serious!"

"And you think I don't know that?"

"You're acting . . ."

"What?" taunted the queen. "Like one drunk on wonder?" She picked up his hands again and tried to pull him into a dance.

"No." A single tear fell down Neil's cheek.

"Oh, my dear, don't squabble! There are far better things to do than waste your breath arguing with me!" She reached out her hand and used her mysterious powers to force Neil to move. They were jerky and uncoordinated, but soon the queen and Neil were dancing around the room.

Ilis watched in horror. She had been prepared to fight a warrior queen or face a beast queen or beat a mighty queen. Foes of all ferocity, Ilis had been prepared to manage. But an insane foe?

When the queen had her fill of dancing, she released Neil from her grasp, and he fell in a heap at her feet. She skipped up to her throne and sat back upon it, clasping her hands together as she did so.

"Let us recount, shall we? You have set off the end of the world, and knowing the mind of those brilliant and yet so foolish Otherlanders, they will undoubtedly think it is my fault." The queen pulled off her crown and threw it up into the air. It spun end over end before she caught it in her hand and placed it back upon her head. "Because everyone thinks they should smash the Under to smithereens." She rolled her eyes, clearly disgusted. "They will think it is my fault. They will blame me for the wreckage of the Sun." She let out a shrill bark of laughter. "And then they will attack."

The queen looked at Neil and said, "If you led them here, I am going to be impressed at how such a steady block as yourself has learned to change."

Neil shook his head. "I am trying to stop a second war between sides." He looked at her as if he felt betrayed by her doubt in him. "I have always been trying to do so."

The queen huffed. "Believe what you want," she smiled demurely at Neil. "But you forget how well I know you."

Neil's shoulders crumpled at this. But the queen wasn't done. She got up off her throne and moved toward Neil.

"Remember the forest whale? Remember how we tracked it down for months in search for the Moon piece it swallowed? That was ME you did that with!" The queen spoke in frantic gasps, as if pleading with Neil—or maybe even herself—to remember. "Remember our sail to the Isle of Ee? Remember how you fell in that pit and broke your leg? I am the one who pulled you out! I am the one who nursed you back to health!" She knelt down beside Neil. Tears sprung in her eyes. "Have you forgotten our nights under the Stars? Have you forgotten the dreams we shared?

Have you forgotten . . ." The queen turned her head and scowled. "Why do I even ask? I know the answer." She stood, dusted off her dress, and faced Neil. In a moment, her face was controlled, lacking all expression. "You forgot me."

Neil shook his head. Tears fell freely down his cheeks. "No, I never forgot."

216

"How could you not?" the queen lashed out. "How could you have left me here if you did not forget me?"

Ilis could barely follow their conversation. In fact, she had given up on following the conversation and decided that the best plan for fighting insanity was to charge. All she had to do was charge at the queen, steal the crown, and then make a very hasty exit.

That is a terrible idea, Kanaph spoke in her thoughts.

Well, I'm open to options! Ilis shot back.

Don't die, was her dragon's only response.

A quick glance around found all exits properly blocked. And leaving the way they entered would most definitely be too slow. So even if she did manage to get her hands on the crown, escaping would be a problem.

"Teedel dee, teedel dum, teedel DIE," chanted the queen. She cocked her head. "Oh, how unfortunate for you, but when you think about it, it isn't that bad of an idea! I wonder if it is even possible. But wouldn't that be a kicker, that the way to save the world is to kill you!" She giggled.

"She's insane," Ilis commented, throwing up her hands.

"Oh! Why, thank you for noticing! I worked hard to get here . . . no . . . I worked hard to . . ."

An odd change came upon her. For a brief moment, it seemed like there was an echo of joy and wisdom in her eyes—but then, it was gone.

Her face grew solemn, and she began whispering, as if reminding herself. "I am bound to protect my country. Bound to do what is best for my people. I am bound by blood. My will is not my own." She stroked her own hand, as if comforting herself. "If you were your own, you'd let them live." Her eyes grew cold. "But you're not, so . . ."

A crazed smile spread across her lips.

"Kill them."

The queen gave Ilis one quick look, as if considering keeping her as a captive—or a pet—but then, with a shrug, she said, "Both of them . . . Ahh, but then what?"

The queen turned to Neil. "Oh, before I kill you, do those Otherlanders have a proposed time of attack? No doubt they have just been waiting for proof that the Sun is our fault . . ." The queen waved her hand in dismissal.

"Never mind, I don't want to hear your thoughts. It doesn't matter when they are planning on attacking. We will just have to move faster than them, and seeing how I know the route through the tunnels and they don't . . . At least not yet." The queen paused and looked intentionally at Neil. "And no, we haven't used it but just have held onto its knowledge until it might come in handy. Meanwhile, those Upper soldiers have been digging around trying to forge their own way to our side. Ha!"

The queen turned to one of her guards. "Bring me my sword and ready my troops." Her voice dropped low. "It is time we gave Basileia the war they have been longing for."

Ilis's heart sank.

War was coming to Basileia—and a war with men and beasts that the kingdom could not even fathom. Ilis's thoughts went to those she had met on the mountain: her fellow classmates, Kat, the professor, and Malcolm . . . She had just brought war to their doorstep.

The queen clapped her hands. "Chop, chop! Like I said, kill them."

Guards from all around the room moved into action.

Ilis pulled her daggers out and stood, ready to fight. Neil, however, seemed to have a different idea. He swung his arm toward the guards, and they were all sent flying backwards up against the walls.

Ilis's jaw dropped.

Neil had powers too?

He dashed to Ilis's side and grabbed her by the shoulders.

"I'll explain everything later." He cast a furtive glance at the guards. Some lay knocked completely unconscious, but others were slowly pushing themselves up again. "I was a fool not to tell you sooner." He looked at her desperately. "I need you to get your dragon and fly back to Mount Oros and warn them of the attack. You need to tell them that she will come through the tunnels—she knows how to navigate them."

A dwarf, shaking his head as if to clear it, let out a low growl and charged at them. He lifted his club, but Ilis was ready. She swung her dagger, slicing open his leg. The dwarf crumpled to the ground, clutching his limb. Grabbing Neil's hand, she pulled him away from the dwarf.

Neil's eyes didn't leave Ilis's, drinking her in as he spoke. "You need to stop them, and to do so, you will need the help of Basileia. You need to fly back and warn the kingdom, and after you've warned them . . . you need to steal the crown."

Ilis's thoughts ran amok. They came *here* to steal the crown. And now she was going to leave before they had it?

"Wait . . ." Ilis started.

In her peripheral, Ilis saw a human guard get close. She spun to her left and found him standing before her wide-eyed and blinking, with blood dripping from a wound in his head. *What had Neil done to them?* Ilis thought. In one movement, she swung her leg and tripped the dazed guard and then turned her attention back to Neil.

"Stealing her crown should slow her enough for you to be able to subdue her," Neil continued.

"This isn't making sense! Shouldn't we try and steal it now?"

Another guard, who was also moving with slurred movements, got close. Ilis threw her dagger at his leg.

"Ilis, look around you. I'm afraid we've run out of time."

"Neil," Ilis pleaded, not understanding any of his ramblings. "What is going on?"

Neil reached out and stroked her cheek with an odd mixture of pride and grief in his eyes. "You are about to save the world."

Then Neil closed his eyes.

Ilis gaped at him, wondering if he had gone utterly senseless. They needed to escape, and now! Her eyes flitted to the guards surrounding them. More of them seemed to have regained their wits and were coming close. She readied her dagger and envisioned her next move. She would fake to the right, slice to the left, and in doing so, steal the guard's sword, which would give her an advantage with . . .

Her thoughts were cut off as she felt her body drift upward. It was the same sensation she had felt earlier with the queen, only stronger this time, enveloping her whole body. She felt weightless, as if gravity no longer existed, and her body was acting as such . . .

A noiseless gasp left her chest. Eyes wide with wonder, she gaped at Neil, who now stood a few feet beneath her. His hands were lifted toward her. An energy radiated off his being, causing her to rise off the ground.

The queen looked like a child having a temper tantrum as she screamed in rage. "KILL HIM!"

The guards ran toward Neil, but he made no move to defend himself. Instead, he used some power unknown to Ilis to lift her back up to the balcony in the ceiling. Just as Ilis was safe, she saw Neil's eyes open and lock with hers.

At that moment, a guard thrust him through with his sword.

Blood.

So much blood.

Neil crumpled and Ilis's hand clamped over her lips to hold back a scream. *Not again. Not again.* Ilis felt her legs give way, and she clung to the railing. Neil's form fell to the ground: motionless and wet with blood.

Trembling, Ilis watched as the Queen of the Under danced up to her prey. The queen reached Neil's lifeless body and turned to look up at Ilis—but Ilis was gone.

She threw open the door to the rooftop and barreled out into the wintry night. Her feet rushed over the cold, frozen ground toward Kanaph.

Two sets of footprints marked the way she had come. The lone set of returning footprints shouted of the one she had left behind.

She paused before Kanaph. The dragon read her thoughts, saw her memories, and asked no questions. For a moment, Ilis felt a warmth surrounding her thoughts, like a long draft of hot tea to her frantic soul. And then came the tears.

Ilis flung herself upon Kanaph, gripping her scales and finding comfort in the pain of the hard edges against her soft palms. Her tears fell unchecked as Kanaph took to the sky, the cold wind kissing her cheeks and howling a song of lament along with her soul.

CHAPTER TWENTY-TWO

Her heart thick with sorrow, Ilis hardly registered the flight over the Under. She barely noticed when they dashed past the deck of *Maribor* or when gravity swung them over the Edge and to the Upper. It was an occasion of momentous proportions—her first crossing of the Edge on the back of a dragon—but all significance of it was dull to her. Sights of the Upper in all its brightness were lost on Ilis. She squeezed her eyes shut and let them slowly adjust to the Sun.

Suddenly, Mount Oros was on the horizon. The hundred league journey felt like a moment.

She lifted her chin and took a shaky breath. Her father had taught her to control her feelings before a heist. Normally those feelings were nerves or fear; today, it was sorrow. She took another deep breath. This time it was steadier. She took a third breath and scowled. "I'm not in a mood to be witty," she grumbled. Kanaph tried to comfort Ilis, speaking peace and courage to her heart, but she ignored it. She didn't want to be comforted.

Her thoughts spun as she planned out her words, her actions, how she would go about accomplishing Neil's last charge. All sorrow and exhaustion were pushed to the side. There was no time for such things now.

Zipping past Mount Oros's defenses, Ilis urged Kanaph toward the Council Room's window. Alarms blared, but Ilis hardly heard them. Her thoughts were focused.

Any glass of the Oval Window that had withstood the Quake was broken under the force of Kanaph's wings as she tore into the Council Room. They landed, Kanaph's talons scraping on wood, in the middle of the Council's table—right before the young king.

The room erupted into chaos. Council members were either shaking or screaming. All had brandished their weapons. Multiple had taken stances around their young king. Chairs were knocked over and the table on which Ilis stood now had holes from Kanaph's talons.

Ilis slipped off her winged beast, telling her mentally to find a safe spot. With a flap of her massive wings, Kanaph flew out the way she had come.

"The Queen of the Under plans to attack from the tunnels before sundown." Ilis let out her rehearsed words in a gasp. "She will bring with her the royal crown, made of the missing pieces of the Moon. If we do not steal her crown and return the pieces to the Moon, the Sun will crash into the ground, and the whole world will burn."

In the midst of the cacophony, the king had not even risen from his chair. He blinked slowly, seemingly unfazed. "Why, you make it sound as if the world is ending," he said, sounding slightly amused.

Ilis looked at him. "That's because it is."

And then, whether from sheer exhaustion or sorrow, she fainted.

***

Malcolm watched in awe as a dragon landed on their table and Ilis shared her desperate news. He saw the wobble in her step and knew what was about to happen. He leapt up and caught her just as she fell.

Holding her in his arms, Malcolm's thoughts ran abuzz. He had been awake for the entirety of four hours, and in those four hours, he had almost decided that the empty haze of unconsciousness was better than the nightmare he had awoken to.

His father was dead, the kingdom was in near ruin, and Ilis had been accused of the deepest treason.

Nothing was as it should have been.

Malcolm looked up at his brother. He had tried to explain that things were not as they seemed. Ilis was a threat, not even Malcolm could dismiss that, but she was also perhaps the only one who could save them.

He looked down at Ilis in his arms, knowing she had done this for him.

The king gathered the attention of his nobles. "Let us not be distracted from the task at hand. We had anticipated an attack was coming soon. Now we know the timing, as well as the location of her exit. All of the deepest tunnels let out on Mount Eros, just on the other side of Twin Peaks Valley. That is where the army will emerge. We shall continue to ready our forces."

"With all due respect, my lord, if what this girl says is true, we must change our tactics! Our world is at stake!" the Head Librarian said.

The king laughed. "Oh, and now you want to believe her? Has your young fable-loving daughter taught you to believe in fairy tales?"

He paused and looked into the eyes of every one of his council members. King Magnus knew his quick rise to the throne was not gladly accepted by them all, but he needed each of them on his side for this. Instead of explaining all he knew, which would lead to a long and strenuous debate, he chose to drag the young thief through the dirt.

"Or have you forgotten she is the pirate and thief? What pirate ever tells the truth? Have you forgotten that she is in league with the Under? What Under spy has ever had our interests in mind? Have you forgotten that *she*," the king sneered at the unconscious lass in Malcolm's arms, "is responsible for my father's death?"

Malcolm's face darkened. "Brother," he warned.

The king ignored him, dismissing him as merely the annoying younger brother once again.

"But if you won't believe me," the king said, "perhaps you will believe an Understander who is known for being able to read the truth in people's statements." The young king turned to Dianne. She stepped out from the corner she had scampered to when the dragon had entered and raised her chin loftily. When the crown-prince-now-king had called her to aid him in his newfound kingship, she had sworn her undying allegiance to him—her own path to power clear in her mind.

"For those of you who did not notice the way her pupils dilated or the quiver in her step, take my word as an Understander: her words spilled forth false poison! No doubt she was sent here by the Under to distract us from their real means of attack!"

The king nodded at Dianne and then stood.

"I will not allow the Under to have the upper hand by making us believe in a fairy tale. Continue to ready the troops." He nodded to his men. "You know your orders."

Malcolm looked at his brother, shocked. Still holding Ilis in his arms, he waited until it was only him and his two brothers alone in the room. Before Malcolm could speak, however, Magnus looked to Jasper and said, "Go make sure everyone is doing as they are told."

Jasper looked at Malcolm, as if wondering about the safety of leaving the eldest and the youngest alone together.

"Go on now!"

Prince Jasper patted his brother the king on the shoulder as he left, whispering, "Go easy on him."

"What are you doing?" the youngest asked the eldest, once they were alone.

"I am going to win the war," the eldest responded.

"At the cost of the world?"

"You don't know what you speak of!"

"The Moon is real!" Malcolm shouted. He looked down at the girl in his arms, pride growing in his heart. "She risked everything to tell you that."

"It doesn't matter if the Moon is real or not," his brother said quietly. "What matters is that we do not allow the Under to take hold of what is ours." The king suddenly looked very tired. He moved to look out the broken window at his broken kingdom. "If I am the king who is overcome by the power of the Moon, history will forgive me. But if I am the king who is overcome by the force of the Under, history will have no kind words to speak of me."

Malcolm looked at him in disbelief. "You would risk the fate of our world so that history might be kind to you?"

The young king growled. "You say that as if I had a choice! If the Moon is the cause of the scorching Sun, then I have no power to stop it." He looked into his younger brother's eyes, pleading with him to understand.

"But if the Moon truly is a myth, and I risk the salvation of my country in pursuit of a fairy tale, my legacy will be one of scorn and mockery." He shook his head. "And I cannot allow that to be my story."

***

When Ilis awoke, all she heard was the sound of something clomping against stone. She groaned, hating land and its abominable rocky form.

"You're awake!" came a voice that she recognized. It was the voice she kept hearing in her dreams—the dreams that were teasingly blissful in the moment and then painful when she awoke.

"Arrr, why must my land-dreams continue!" Ilis groaned.

"Uh, Ilis?" came that dream voice again.

"Stop talking to me," Ilis grumpily replied. "I'm just dreaming."

The voice laughed. "Dreaming of what?"

"Of you!" Ilis said, jerking her head, but even the slight movement caused her head to throb. "Oohh," she moaned.

"Hey, careful!" The dreadful clomping stopped. "The doctors said I should let you rest, but there wasn't any time. And to be honest, they told me to rest too . . . I didn't listen then either."

Ilis opened her eyes to find herself cradled in someone's arms—Malcolm's arms. Staring at Malcolm, Ilis realized that she was not dreaming.

It took all her pirate training not to blush.

"You're alive," she said breathlessly. Staring up into his eyes, she could feel his breath on her cheek. It was warm and smelled of oranges.

He grinned. "Sorry to disappoint you."

Ilis shook her head. "Malcolm, I . . . I . . . ." She couldn't seem to get the words out, but Malcolm understood.

"No apology is needed," he said softly.

"But I almost killed you!" Ilis blurted out, pushing herself out of his arms so that she might stand and look him in the eyes.

"Not intentionally . . . at least, I hope not," he added jokingly.

"Of course not!" For the first time, Ilis noticed her surroundings and changed the topic drastically. "Where are we?"

They stood in what looked like a cellar, with a large wooden door before them. "We are currently standing inside Mount Eros before the entrance to my brother's secret project. He has had a group of soldiers set aside to clear out the tunnels to the Under—the tunnels discovered nearly a millennium ago and then destroyed because of how dangerous they were. Granted, he has yet to actually find a path that makes it all the way to the Under, but he has gotten close. And thankfully, their thorough notes on the project say that any and all of the deep tunnels must come this way."

Ilis's thoughts ran abuzz. She remembered her findings of the group of laundry girls set aside to wash a specific set of soldiers' clothes—that must be this group of soldiers! And the laundry girl who was so petrified that the Under was attacking—she must have been one of them! One who had accidently figured out the task of the soldiers whose clothes they were washing.

Malcolm grabbed a lantern from the wall and led Ilis through the wooden door. It banged closed behind them.

Ilis's head bobbed. "We are in the tunnels." She scanned the area looking for an army and found none. The tunnels of rough-cut stone stretched before her, branching out in various directions. Their lantern lit up the path before them for about ten feet before the darkness beyond seemed to swallow all the light up. "And we are all *alone*." She squeezed her eyes shut. "Please be a dream, please be a dream, please be a dream."

"Uh, Ilis?" Malcolm ventured, his voice sounding rightly concerned.

Ilis's eyes snapped open, and she faced him with all the ferocity of a pirate. "What are you THINKING? She is coming through the tunnels! I came to warn you so that you could rally your army and stop her, NOT go and try and stop her all by yourself!"

"Uh, Ilis!" he repeated, his eyes fixed on something behind her.

Ilis gritted her teeth. "If she is right behind me, I am going to punch you so hard."

She pivoted on her heel and found herself face-to-face with a gray scaly creature twice as tall as she was, filling up the space of the tunnel. It snorted, and she felt its breath in her face. It was musty and smelled like mold.

226

"Uh, Malcolm?"

"RUN!"

She needed no further prodding to sprint as fast as her legs would take her down one of the branches in the tunnel. The creature lumbered behind them, thankfully not faster than they could run, screeching a scratchy call all the while.

"What is THAT?" Ilis shouted as they ran for their lives.

"Stone gopher," Malcolm panted.

"*That's* a stone gopher?" Ilis yelled.

"What did you expect?" the prince replied between gasps for breath. "Cute—and fuzzy—and the size of a rabbit?"

"YES!" she yelled back.

Suddenly Malcolm jerked Ilis to the right, pulling her inside a small crevice in the wall of the tunnel, which effectively tucked them both out of sight. He blew out the lantern, and they listened as the gargantuan stone gopher rumbled past.

Ilis panted for breath and slapped Malcolm in the arm. "Blasted blow horns! Have you gone bonkers? What are you thinking?"

He placed his hands on his knees and gasped for breath before answering. "That we should probably try and stop the queen before she gets to the Upper."

"Oh? And us dying by the hands of the stone gophers is a real great way to do that!"

"Well, at least it will give the queen a good welcoming party."

Ilis listened as a herd of stone gophers responded to the first one's call and followed it.

"It might buy us some time," Malcolm added. He relit the lantern.

Ilis stared at him a steely moment before nodding. But then she slapped him again. "And why in shell's name didn't you bring a whole army with you?"

The prince rubbed his arm where she hit him. Ilis had a strength to her that was shocking in her small form. "Do you mind hearing me out before dealing your punishment?"

"Do you mind explaining why you dragged me down here *alone* to almost get trampled by beasts?" Ilis responded, not missing a beat.

Malcolm grinned his coy grin that Ilis suddenly found quite charming. When had that happened? Did she want it to happen? Did she have any control over it happening? These thoughts and more swirled through her head, but she didn't have time to sort them out.

"My brother the king decided that staying in our fortified mountain was the best defense against the Under."

Ilis groaned.

"So that left you, me, and a hairbrained scheme. Think you can steal a little something for me?" he asked, his eyes alight with mischief.

"You do realize I'm a pirate, right?"

"Oh, that's old news."

Ilis smirked. "What would you have me steal this time, my prince?"

CHAPTER TWENTY-THREE

Crowns. Why did she continue to find herself stealing crowns? At this point, this was attempt number three for this specific crown. Not insanity. Just persistence. Right?

Ilis and Malcolm sat tucked away in a crevice in the ceiling of the tunnel. Ilis had thanked the Stars that Malcolm was a proficient climber. He truly would have made a great pirate. He scaled up the side of the tunnel alongside her, gripping small handholds with ease, climbing until they reached their current hiding spot—a crevice in the top of the tunnel. The crevice was just large enough for both of them to sit without being pressed up against each other and was located just high enough to be able to look out upon the rest of the tunnel and have a prime view of things— at least, when there was some light. However, upon the extinguishing of their lantern, they entered into pitch darkness. They sat in silence for a long time, each lost in their thoughts.

The air was musty and dank. There was a constant dripping of water off of a stalactite that seemed almost annoyingly loud in the otherwise starkly silent space.

Ilis's thoughts found their way back to the day of the Quake.

"I am sorry," Ilis said quickly, trying to get the words out of her mouth before she clammed up again. "I-I . . ." Her head fell to her chest.

"Sorry for what?" Malcolm asked.

"In class . . . the Quake . . . you almost died because of me," her words came out in a rush.

"Oh, Ilis, don't apologize. It was not your fault."

She shook her head. "You wouldn't have been sitting there if not for me."

There was a brief silence before he replied. "And you wouldn't have almost died the night of our heist if not for me."

"At least it was because you were doing something you believed in," Ilis said. "All I was doing was being . . . selfish."

"Yes, but I expected that much would come along with the Lass of the Seas."

It was a moment before the meaning of his words sank in. Ilis's jaw dropped. Had he known who she was from the beginning?

Prince Malcolm laughed, guessing her shock, though he could not see her face. "The announced search for a Royal Thief was all to draw you in. If I'm honest, I had no idea if it would work. But it was worth a try."

"But I don't understand. If you knew who I was, then why in the world would you want me to be your thief?" Ilis asked.

"I suppose because I like to keep my enemies close," Malcolm quipped.

This line brought a brief smile to Ilis's lips as she thought of the day she had been made his thief.

"Also," Malcolm added, "Neil was pretty set on having you on the team. Where is Neil, by the way? And Pyra and Chaz?"

Ilis took a shaky breath. She kept on seeing Neil's face right before the life went out of his eyes: calm and accepting, with a quiet smile upon his lips as he saved her and left himself wide open to attack. There were so many questions about him that would now remain unanswered.

Where had he gotten such a strange power? The Under was filled with people who could do things Ilis didn't understand, but this was something different. There had been a power that radiated from him. She had felt it resonate in her bones. It felt strangely familiar . . . Why had he kept his powers a secret? How had he known so much about the Moon? And how had he known the queen? The queen was old enough to be Neil's mother; only, after their interactions, that seemed unlikely. They seemed to treat each other as . . . as equals. It was as if they had some sort of past together . . . but, since the queen had ordered him killed, Ilis supposed it was an ugly past. Ilis grimaced, remembering the blood.

"Ilis?"

She realized numbly that he had said her name several times.

She pressed her palms into her eye sockets, trying to erase the constant mental replaying of Neil's death. She swallowed hard.

"You okay?" Malcolm asked.

"He died for me," Ilis said. As she said it, Ilis realized that this was what bothered her the most. Why would he think her life valuable enough to trade his own for it? She had done nothing to deserve it.

"Neil?" Malcolm's voice faltered.

"Yes," she whispered. She wondered what Malcolm's face looked like. She could see it in her head—disappointment in her, grief for his friend, and regret for ever asking Ilis to be a part of his team.

"What about Pyra and Chaz?" Malcolm asked.

"I don't know," Ilis said soberly. "I can only hope that they made it back to *Maribor*."

Before Malcolm could respond, a faint tread of marching footsteps began to float down the tunnel.

This was it.

Ilis rubbed the back of her neck, trying to calm her nerves. She feared this was their last chance at getting these Moon pieces.

"Malcolm, how many hours has it been since I arrived?"

"Six?"

Ilis thought for a moment. Her flight over the Edge and to Mount Oros had taken almost twelve hours. "I think that means we have twenty-two hours until our world catches fire by the Sun's heat."

Malcolm paused and cleared his throat. "Oh lovely, there is a dire countdown now. Well, then let's steal these Moon pieces, shall we?"

Yes, steal these and then die. Because the only one who knew the location of the rest of the Moon is now dead, Ilis thought. *We can't save the world if we don't know where to return the Moon pieces to.* She blinked back tears.

For the sake of everyone she ever loved, the Moon needed to be completed today.

There has to be a way. Neil told me to steal her crown. There has to be a way.

She took a deep breath, rolled onto her belly, and pushed herself forward so that her head was peeking out of their hiding spot—a hiding spot that conveniently let them rest right above the middle of the tunnel. Malcolm grabbed onto her legs to steady her.

Ilis thought back to the first time she had tried to steal the queen's crown. Oddly enough, that failure had been what started this whole journey. Had she not been so desperate to prove her own worth and escape the guilt she felt over her failure, she never would have ventured to the mountain, never met Chaz, or Pyra, or Malcolm . . . or Neil—the one who had given his life for her.

Silent as a mouse, Ilis watched and waited until she saw the approach of soldiers below. She noticed with no small amount of pleasure that the ranks appeared to be a bit roughed up by their run-in with the stone gophers. The army of men and beasts marched rhythmically through the tunnel, but there were many who already were bloodied and dirty. Banners, which proudly bore Beriyth's signet of a golden dragon, were already torn. Not a bad start.

At the moment, all Ilis saw were infantry, but she had no doubt the queen had brought all of her best soldiers with her. Heads of both man and beast began passing under her gaze. Griffins marched soft pawed, dressed in thick leather armor—so as to not be too heavy in flight. Trolls, cyclops, dwarfs, minotaurs, and men all marched dressed in armor of silver steel.

The fiercest warriors from the Under were now marching upon Basileia.

Malcolm's grip was solid around her ankles as she eased out and uncurled herself until she was hanging. Briefly she had the memory of the last time she let this particular boy lower her down into a risky situation—their failed heist for the Crown Jewel—but she dismissed the thoughts. Somehow, she had grown to trust him despite what happened that night. The tunnel was dark, lit only by the soldier's dim torches, and her dark tunic and leggings blended in completely with the shadows.

Ilis waited, watching for the queen and her entourage. She had to hold in a growl when the queen finally came into sight, the image of Neil's death replaying again in her head. The queen rode upon a large, muscular gray steed whose thick mane and tail both almost dragged upon the ground, marking it as an Ethledyr. Ethledyr steeds were said to have courage and wisdom that rivaled a dragon's. The queen herself was dressed in bloodred armor, as was customary of Beriythian rulers. Her black hair fell down her back in a long, thick braid, and upon her face was a look of sheer determination. She was surrounded by her guards, each of whom wore a red helmet marking their service to the queen. At the rear of the queen's entourage were two soldiers who were pulling a cart with a trunk upon it. Ilis wondered briefly what the trunk held before turning her attention back to the queen. The crown lay lopsided upon her head, just waiting to be stolen.

As the queen neared, Ilis slipped out even further from her cleft. She blocked off all thoughts of her past failed and deadly attempts at stealing this crown, and instead focused solely on the task before her. Malcolm had secured himself with a rope so he could extend as much as possible, giving Ilis two hands and enough reach. And thus, Ilis—with a blow dart gripped between her teeth—dangled above the queen's entourage.

Right as the queen reached beneath the cleft, Ilis lifted her finger to the blow dart, aimed at the annoying dripping stalactite, and fired.

Please work, Ilis thought desperately.

Her upside-down shot was remarkable. She hit right what she was aiming at—a small crack in the stalactite. After three long seconds, during which the queen moved right into position, the stalactite cracked and fell to the tunnel floor, shattering into a million pieces.

The queen and her entourage halted, hands on their weapons.

It was in that moment—that moment when every eye was on the object which just fell from the ceiling, when every muscle was tense and every thought focused on what was obviously the greatest danger—that Ilis made her move.

She stretched out her hands toward the crown. Just as her fingers were almost touching the prize, Malcolm's grip slipped on her ankles and she jerked downward ever so slightly. Ilis grimaced, but Malcolm managed to regain his grip.

Ilis swallowed and took a quick, shaky breath.

With the nimble fingers of a desperate thief, Ilis lifted the crown off of the queen's head. She held her breath, holding the prize in her hands with a mixture of shock and relief. She had done it! She had finally done it! She had stolen the Queen of the Under's crown!

The queen continued marching along with her army—one step, three steps, seven steps away. Just when Ilis was about to breathe easily, the queen lifted one of her slender hands. A sharp command rocketed through the tunnel, and the entire army thudded to a stop.

The queen halted her horse and twisted in the saddle to look up at Ilis, who was dangling from the ceiling held only by her ankles.

"Well, you just won't give up, will you?" she drawled with a mix of mockery and bemusement. "I suppose the old saying is true: like mother, like daughter."

The queen laughed as Ilis's thoughts spun. *What did she just say? What did THAT mean?*

The queen clapped her hands together in glee. She playfully smacked one of her guards beside her, "See, Jonis! I told you we had yet to see the last of her!" The queen slipped off her horse and did a merry jig right there in the tunnels between the two worlds while Ilis hung above her head.

When the dance was finished, the queen looked back up at Ilis.

"Oh! Excuse me! I suppose it was rude of me to leave you hanging up there."

The queen lifted her hand, and suddenly Ilis felt heavy. Her bones, her skin, her entire body seemed to increase in weight to such a point that Ilis felt herself slip from Malcolm's grasp. Malcolm let out a garbled cry as Ilis began plummeting toward the mountain rock ground, but before she could even twist to adjust herself to the landing, Ilis felt the heaviness lift as an opposite sensation filled her body.

She felt weightless. The sharp change made Ilis's head spin. She looked down and tried to control her breathing. She *was* weightless. She was levitating—inches above the ground and just a few paces from the queen.

This was not good.

However, the most unnerving part was not the impressive display of the queen's powers but, instead, the fact that her and Neil's powers felt so similar. They had to be connected!

"Oh, don't look so terrified! It is not becoming." The queen cocked her head, plucked the crown out of Ilis's fingers, and then set it upon Ilis's head.

"What do you think, Jonis? How does she look?"

The guard beside the queen made no comment.

"Well of course she does not look as good as me, but . . ." The queen laughed and, with a twist of her fingers, sent the crown flying off Ilis's head and into the air.

Ilis tried to reach for it, her last hope, but she found herself pinned by the queen's power. The crown, with the final pieces of the Moon, floated through the air until it landed upon the queen's head. The queen dropped her hand and Ilis fell to the floor in a heap.

"I'm supposed to take the head of anyone who would try and take my crown," said the queen, considering. "But since I've already tried that with you, I think I'll let it wait for a little while. Besides," she said, gesturing to her red armor, "I would hate to get blood on this before the battle has even begun."

The queen pivoted on her heel and began marching again. "Oh," she added over her shoulder, "and we mustn't forget your little friend."

Ilis heard a thud behind her and found Malcolm on his knees. He looked up at the queen with both fury and fear in his eyes.

The queen halted and clapped with delight. "I know! Give them the cart to push." She laughed. "That will keep their thieving hands busy."

Ilis couldn't keep it in anymore. She pushed herself to her feet. "Did you know my mother?"

"Did?" The queen looked back at her and shook her head. "Oh, my darling, I assure you . . ." She shrugged her shoulders and continued to march. "I still do."

***

The world was ending.

Within the next twelve hours, the Sun would crash and burn one side of the world to a crisp while the Under would freeze solid from lack of exposure to the Sun. There was no escaping the devastation that was coming. Their entire world was about to die. Her thoughts found their way to her crew—her family aboard *Maribor*. She recalled the countless nights sailing under the Stars in glorious silence with the whole ocean billowing before them, the tall tales told in whispers, the boasts shouted across the deck, and laughter . . . oh how she missed their laughter. She could almost hear their voices now.

An ache to be with them arose in her heart. At least then they could have died together. The Damarises had wondered why the task had been left to Ilis. They should have intervened. No one should have trusted the fate of the world to her. Who did she even think she was, to try and save them all? She couldn't even save herself.

Ilis looked up at the queen's crown, just paces away from her. She was so close, and yet so far.

She shifted her grip on the handles of the cart. Something shifted inside the trunk upon the cart, sending a shiver down Ilis's back. She suddenly wondered what vile creature they were bringing with them. Probably snakes. That would be appropriate. Because snakes would make the end of the world so much more enjoyable.

Ilis looked beside her and locked eyes with Malcolm. He tried to smile at her reassuringly but failed. Silent tears were falling unchecked down his face. Ilis felt as if a knife had struck her heart. In that moment, she realized that he must feel the weight of her failure as keenly as she did. She had failed him too.

That fact pierced her more than a million weapons ever could.

The tunnel they were marching through was narrow at parts (forcing the army to slow and walk single file), and then other times wide (allowing soldiers to walk five abreast).

Just as Ilis's arms were beginning to cramp from pulling the cart, there was murmuring from the front of the line. Ilis craned her neck to see over the shoulders of the tall soldiers, trying to glimpse what was ahead. She saw nothing more than the backs of man and beast.

The queen straightened. "What is it?" she asked tentatively.

No one replied.

"Your queen asked a question!"

More murmuring flowed through the crowd, and Jonis bent his head. "It appears that we have reached the end of the tunnel."

"Ah," replied the queen. She nodded to a pair of large trolls. "Markus, Algerius, would you be so kind as to remove the boulder ahead?"

With a grunt of response, the trolls lumbered through the frontline infantry. Jonis followed.

A sharp burst of light, followed by screams from the front line, cut off their conversation.

The queen gripped her spear, her focus forward. "What is it?"

Jonis walked back to them. Ilis took the moment to study him. He was of average height, but his arms, legs, and chest were all heavily set with muscles. He was clean shaven, had a small notch in his left eyebrow from a scar, and had eyes that seemed to glow orange in the lantern light. His form was human, but something felt oddly unhuman about him, though Ilis couldn't decipher what.

Jonis stopped by the queen's side and explained the commotion at the front of the line.

"It appears as if the men who opened the exit are now blinded by the Sun, my queen."

The queen relaxed, realizing her opponent was the Sun. "Oh, well, it has been a good bit since we saw our dear Prevailing Light in such force, hasn't it?"

The crowd of men and beasts parted for their queen as she moved to the front of the line, dragging Ilis and Malcolm along with her. A wave of warmth hit Ilis in the chest. It felt like they had just walked into a wall of heat. She looked back at Malcolm.

"Malc," Ilis whispered. "The Sun, she is burning our land!"

Malcolm's face was distraught.

The closer they got to the opening of the tunnel, the greater the heat and the more they had to squint against the brightness of the Sun. When Ilis reached the opening of the tunnel, she covered her eyes from the blinding light—and truly, it was blinding!

Desperate to assess her surroundings, Ilis peeked out from her fingers and attempted to look around. Her efforts were rewarded by a white haze being seared into her eyes and tears dripping down her cheeks. A panic began to fill her; a pirate was only as good as her attention to her surroundings.

The soldiers around her began to cry out, no doubt feeling the same sting as Ilis.

Another wave of heat hit her. She felt sweat begin to drip from her pores and ooze down her skin. *And we haven't even gotten outside yet!*

Ilis let go of the cart, wiped at her mixture of tears and sweat, and waited for her eyes to adjust. Suddenly, Malcolm was by her side. She couldn't even fully see him, but he grabbed her hand and whispered into her ear.

"There is still hope. It is not over yet."

Ilis wanted to scoff and tell him he was being ridiculous, but it was at that moment that Ilis realized her eyes had adjusted enough to see more.

Peeking from behind her fingers, she stood and moved to stand beside the queen's horse so she could have a better view. The sight before her shook her to her bones.

"We are doomed."

The Sun was twice its normal size.

CHAPTER TWENTY-FOUR

Wars seem like pointless things, and yet filled with so many pointy things, Kanaph thought. *Death is imminent for mankind, so why run to it? What could be so worth dying for?* The dragon shook her head and let out a blast of smoke and flames. The sight pleased her exceedingly, so she did it again. When her thoughts found their way back to the senselessness of this war, and perhaps all others (though this was the only one which she personally had experienced), her concluding thought was, foolish fireless beings.

The young dragon was perched upon the tallest remaining spire of the mountain castle. She was rather surprised that none of the mountain people had spotted her yet—especially considering she had just blasted fire into the air . . . which, upon thought, was perhaps not the wisest of ideas—and tried to kill her, but she supposed with the Sun and impending war with their sworn enemies, they were a bit preoccupied. Kanaph glanced idly around. To her right sat a valley, the other side of which held her Ilis. She could feel Ilis, even faintly hear the thrum of her thoughts, though Ilis was separated from her by rock and mountain. Kanaph's chest swelled with pride. In not one of her ancestors' memories did she find a connection as deep as the one she had with her qasar.

The dragon focused intently, trying to see how deep the connection was. She closed her eyes and followed the string of her heart, now knit together with Ilis's. There was a glimmer into Ilis's thoughts. Her qasar was doing that math, trying to figure out how many hours they had left according to some centaur's prediction.

The connection snapped before Kanaph could hear Ilis's conclusion.

The dragon huffed. Perhaps she was too far away. She unfurled her wings and stepped off the spire, letting herself plunge down the side of the mountain castle before spreading out her wings and letting the air catch.

Shouts filled the air from below—she had finally garnered the attention of the mountainlings—and soon arrows peppered the air around her. Kanaph easily swooped one way, then the next, and avoided the arrows, as they were not the arrows of one prepared to shoot a dragon—just the "Oh no! There is a beast above me! I should shoot it!" arrows.

The young dragon escaped the castle mountain premises, flying over a gate that held the recent marks of dragon fire, and then over the valley. The valley was filled with dead grass. It was not a pretty sight. On the other side of the valley the mountainside peeked up again. This second mountain's height was pitiful in comparison to the mountain castle, but outside of comparison, she felt it held worthy height of its own. Inside that smaller sister of Mount Oros sat the opening to the cave in which her qasar was.

Stretching her wings wide, Kanaph flew up the smaller mountain's side, and landed perhaps sixty paces above the opening through which the queen's soldiers were beginning to flood out.

The soldiers saw her but ignored her presence. They probably thought she came to fight with them—as if she would dirty even one claw on behalf of the fireless. Her mother's memories told her that as soon as the next ruler of Beriyth was crowned, she would have to swear her allegiance in order to be welcomed in Beriyth, but until then, she had no such constraints. Looking around, she realized there were no dragons at all on the battlefield. The queen must not have thought them necessary.

Shrugging her wings and trying to fold them into a comfortable position on her back—a harder thing than one would expect—Kanaph settled down to try and connect with her qasar's thoughts yet again.

She followed the connection, only this time found it so much stronger. Suddenly, the dragon found herself seeing things as Ilis did!

Her qasar was at the opening of the tunnel. She tried to take in her surroundings but only got a glimmer of Mount Oros in the distance before the light of the Sun blinded her and she had to clamp her eyes shut.

Don't blind yourself, Kanaph spoke to Ilis's thoughts.

"Kanaph?" Ilis said aloud. Her eyes snapped back open and then blinked away at the light.

Hush child! No need to announce to the queen that you have a dragon on your side.

The dragon watched through Ilis's eyes as her qasar looked back at the queen.

She looked fierce and strong in her red armor but did not seem to have noticed Ilis's slip of words.

Kanaph? Where are you? Ilis clenched her eyes closed and willed her thoughts to be heard.

The dragon chuckled at her qasar.

Above you on the mountainside.

Kanaph saw through Ilis's eyes as she tried to look back out of the tunnel.

Where are we?

You just came out of the other mountain, Kanaph replied.

What mountain?

My mother's memories do not hold its name. There is a valley between the castle walls and where you are.

She listened to Ilis's thoughts as she tried to figure out where exactly that was. When Ilis thought of a memory of a dragon dying outside of a gate, Kanaph grimaced.

So that's how he died. That looked like my great uncle. But yes, that is the one. The gate on the other side of this valley is burnt by dragon fire.

Uh, Kanaph?

Hmm?

Are you reading my thoughts?

Oh, not just that, young one! I can also see what you are seeing. This connection is quite fascinating!

Quite a few thoughts went through Ilis's head, none of them excited about the fact that the dragon had access to her mind.

Woah there! I'm sure I can disconnect it.

The dragon reexamined the connection between them, trying to focus solely on what Ilis was seeing.

The cacophony that was Ilis's thoughts subsided.

There, now your thoughts—other than the ones you speak to me—are your own, Kanaph said.

Until you decide to enter again, Ilis remarked.

Well, yes . . . But perhaps we should revisit this topic at another time, say when the Sun is not about to burn our world to a crisp? Did you ever figure out how many hours we have left?

If my calculations are right, then . . . eighteen, Ilis replied.

"Ilis?" Malcolm's voice came from beside Ilis. She turned and found him looking at her with a worried expression on his face. "The queen ordered us forward."

Ilis bobbed her head and began pulling at the cart they were dragging.

Kanaph, you can't distract me like that!

It's not my fault you can't focus on more than one thing at a time.

This remark did not seem to sit well with her qasar. Ilis felt angry for a moment before her emotions changed and the anger was replaced with despair.

Kanaph opened her eyes, thus severing the link to Ilis's sight, and found she could still feel her qasar's thoughts subtly. What a strange thing!

From her perch on the mountainside, the dragon watched as the queen exited the tunnel into the bright sunlight, followed shortly by Ilis and Malcolm with their odd chest on a cart.

With an odd mixture of curiosity and yet disinterest, she watched as a bright red tent was set up for the queen. Malcolm and Ilis were allowed to enter with her and rest in the shade while the army took their places in the field. And it was a good thing too—even from her perch, Kanaph could see her human beginning to burn and get drenched in sweat from just minutes of exposure to the Sun.

On the other side of the valley, she saw archers lining up on the wall.

The wall was about as tall as a middle-aged dragon so—it took Kanaph a moment to convert that to fireless metrics—five stories tall. The top of the wall leveled out for archers to sit and fire down upon the armies as they approached their walls.

Every once in a while, the dragon would listen in on what was happening in the tent by connecting to Ilis's thoughts.

The queen lounged upon a throne and gave orders about her army. She wanted the infantry to go out with the siege weapons and amass just out of the archers' range, then her knights and archers would form ranks, with the cavalry flanking the sides.

Kanaph snapped the connection and grew restless. *What foolery is this! The dragon looked up at the Sun. How can they not see the senselessness of such plans?*

She unfurled her wings slowly, so as not to have them tangle up with one another, and then set to fly off around the mountain and come upon Mount Oros from behind and hopefully go unnoticed again. Because all of the army was located on the south side with the East Gate, she found it almost too easy to go unnoticed and land again on the spire.

From here she could see all the more clearly the workings of both armies.

Beriyth was indeed gathering in the valley as the queen instructed. The infantry was now sitting in the baking Sun, just outside of what they thought was the Basileian archers' range. Behind them, the knights and archers were still lining up. Their numbers were staggering.

Basileia, however, held the high ground. Hundreds of archers dressed in olive green lined the walls, their longbows aimed at the army down below. Soldiers were ordered to brace the East Gate to withstand the queen's mighty siege weapons using thick wooden beams. The King of Basileia had walled himself in behind the impenetrable stone fortification that was Mount Oros.

Kanaph watched the armies amass for hours. It took an extraordinarily long time for them to get themselves in order.

While they marched around to get in formation, the dragon appraised the mountain castle with admiration. Being as most of it was carved out of the mountainside itself, it would take the force of a grown dragon to even make a dent in it. The outermost wall was almost twice as thick as her qasar was tall. Such space created room for multiple rows of archers to stand as well as multiple tents under which she figured the high-ranking officials were stationed.

She saw the king, arrayed in full battle armor, enter one such tent alongside a man with a long white beard. The two humans seemed to be arguing. Though they went out of her sight, she wondered if she could still hear them. The dragon tried to focus her hearing on what he was saying and was delighted to find that she could pick out bits and pieces.

Being a dragon was a fantastic thing.

"I don't care about the Sun!" the king shouted, "All I care about is the army of our enemies that is amassed outside my doorstep!"

"But your majesty," the white-bearded man protested, "the Sun will destroy both sides of our land if we do not stop it."

The king seemed to take a deep breath and composed himself. "Dear professor, I hear what you are saying. And you sound very much like my younger brother. But I have chosen my course. I will ask you to join me on it or leave me be."

Kanaph huffed out smoke. This was nonsensical. She did give the king credit though. Even though his thought process was foolish, he was sticking with it and had managed to rally the entire kingdom behind him. He would have made a good king. Too bad it looked like today would be his last.

The professor bowed his head and stepped back out in the blaring Sun. He walked along the wall, behind the rows of archers in green, and then took a set of stairs down to the courtyard below.

The courtyard held the rest of Mount Oros's fighting forces. Based on the lack of proper fitting armor and confident stances, Kanaph estimated that perhaps only one third of the numbers stationed behind the castle wall were truly trained soldiers. The rest were probably pulled from their villages in a desperate attempt to gain numbers—poor souls.

But why were their numbers so low? She resolved to ask Ilis about this one.

Kanaph looked back over the wall at the Beriythian forces, and then back at Basileia's. *The wall is the only thing saving them from pure desolation,* she mused.

And then her gaze settled upon the Sun, who was looming above them like a giant in the sky and blasting down upon them with unhindered fury. Kanaph growled, smoke curling up from her lips. Today was going to be all of their lasts if something did not change. For a moment, she wondered if she could fly up and push the Sun away. But she quickly dismissed the thought; her mother's memories warned her of flying too close to the Sun.

The heat was debilitating for the armies. The dragon watched as soldiers on both sides just dropped from dehydration. This was going to be an interesting battle.

She was pulled out of her own thoughts by an emotion being sparked up in Ilis.

This is curious, Kanaph thought. Even though she was now across the valley again, she still could pick up on some things from Ilis. Perhaps the connection was stronger now that Ilis was out of the mountain.

She tried to focus in and see what was going on with Ilis.

At first all she got were emotions—shock, fear, anger. But then she was able to tap into her sight again.

Ilis was still in the tent with the queen, and she was staring at the chest—the chest Ilis and Malcolm had carted all the way through the tunnels. A soldier had just opened the chest, and inside were two humans—Chaz and Pyra!

Chaz was drenched in sweat and looked sickly but conscious. Pyra however, was slumped over in the bottom of the chest, unconscious. Her dress was drenched through with sweat and clung to her frame.

"Water!" Ilis shouted. "Someone! Bring water!"

Ilis whipped her head around to see the queen nod to one of her attendants. They stepped forward with a water skin.

Suddenly the connection was severed—whether it was because of the distance or the fact that she sneezed at that moment, Kanaph was not sure. But by the time she was able to see through Ilis's eyes again, Pyra was awake and sitting up. Kanaph felt Ilis's fury.

Ilis stood and faced the queen.

"How dare you! You almost killed them!"

The queen studied Ilis. "And? They will die in a few hours anyway."

This only infuriated Ilis further. "The world is ending! Why have you declared war on Basileia? You should be trying to stop the Sun! Otherwise, there will be no Basileia to rule!"

"Oh, I don't want to rule Basileia. I didn't even want to rule Beriyth. That is not what this is about."

Ilis threw up her hands, exasperated. Kanaph felt what Ilis was feeling. She was hot. She was sweaty. The world was ending because the Sun was crashing into it, and the two sides of the world had decided to wage war on each other. This was senseless!

"Then please, enlighten me! What is this about?" Ilis exclaimed.

The queen smiled at Ilis's display of temper.

"Do you know about the Blood Oath, child?"

Ilis nodded. Her thoughts went to what she knew about the oath: it was the oath that the rulers of Beriyth took on their coronation day, the oath that was said to bind a ruler to the land.

"My blood is mixed with the land of Beriyth. It is now impossible for me to act in a way that would harm the land of my blood. I am sworn to protect my home. If we did not attack Basileia, they would attack us; therefore, I am obliged to protect my land."

"Oh, and the freezing lack of a Sun does not garner your attention?" Ilis rebuffed. Kanaph found herself nodding with her qasar. She was making good points.

"The Blood Oath does not pay heed to the Prevailing Lights; it knows mankind has little say in such matters. Therefore, the Sun is not my problem."

Ilis wanted to scream. The queen was insane. Her logic was senseless!

"Are you saying you are only interested in the betterment of our land because of the Blood Oath?" Ilis challenged. *My young one is growing bold, Kanaph thought,* but kept her thoughts to herself. *She thinks she is about to die, so has nothing to lose.*

246

"Are you truly telling me that there is no part of you that realizes how senseless this is?" Ilis continued. "Is there no part of you that wants our world to survive?"

The queen's eyes softened for a moment. A tear fell down her cheek. "There was once a time I would have done anything to stop a war between our two sides." Her eyes hardened. "But now I have chosen my side. I will not let Beriyth fall to these Otherlanders."

Jonis entered the tent. "My queen, they have begun firing down upon us."

"And?" said the queen, shaking her head as if to clear it from Ilis's words. "We are out of range."

"Their bows have more force than anticipated," Jonis replied.

Kanaph watched as Ilis's thoughts went to the Foresters and their arrows, which could fly to impossible lengths.

"Ahh, yes, the Foresters. Send out the griffins," said the queen.

Kanaph opened her eyes, and thus cut off the connection to Ilis's sight, but kept an ear tuned to her thoughts. Their connection was leaps and bounds beyond that of Kanaph's ancestors, or at least the ancestors on her mother's side—as those were the only memories a dragon gleaned.

Down in the valley, just as Jonis said, the Beriythian army was being fired upon. And, just as Ilis had thought, it was all the Foresters' doing.

By order of the queen, the griffins took flight. They were armored with some form of leather breastplate. Kanaph wondered why they needed such things until she remembered that griffins did not have scales. She pitied the fireless beasts. How could they live with themselves, so unclothed?

The Foresters saw the griffins coming, so shifted their targets. One griffin fell. Then two. But then the griffins were upon them. The winged lions began plucking up the Foresters upon the wall and throwing them down.

From down in the valley, the queen had stepped out of her tent into the blaring Sun and joined the ranks of her army on the back of the Ethledyr. "Forward!" she commanded, and the rest of her army charged.

Ilis, Malcolm, Chaz, and Pyra were bound but still in the queen's company.

Her infantry, now almost unhindered by the arrows of the Foresters, marched forward. A team of twelve trolls pulled a battering ram larger than Kanaph herself. Kanaph appraised her size, and realized with pride that, even as a newborn, she was of an impressive size—such an impressive size that she accurately compared a massive war machine to herself. The trolls made it to the gates and disappeared from Kanaph's direct sight, but due to the wood shaking on the other side of the gate, it was not hard to guess what was going on.

The young dragon watched curiously. She glanced back up at the Sun, whose descent ever increased. Were they going to just fight a war while the Sun destroyed them? *Oh, how easily the minds of the fireless are deceived by greed, pride, and power.*

She watched as a young man with mismatched stockings ran through the courtyard filled with militia, up the stairs to the wall, and then along the wall until he found a captain. In the hand of this young man was a glimmering contraption in the shape of a large bowl. She cocked her head as it glimmered from the Sun; it appeared to be a contraption made of mirrors.

The young man explained something to the captain. The captain nodded, and the young man stepped forward and tilted the bowl-like contraption toward one of the griffins. It reflected the Sun—whose rays were beyond strong—and the effect was immediate and visible. Suddenly, the griffin's wings burst into flames.

Kanaph huffed. *Well, that's new.*

The Foresters beside the young man turned and cocked their heads. The young man tilted the contraption again, catching the Sun's light, magnifying it, and then sending it to another griffin's wings. This one too went up in flames. Both griffins plummeted to the ground.

The Basileian army erupted in cheers.

It was at this moment that the queen raised a blue flag. The dragon searched her mother's memories but had no recollection of what a blue flag meant.

What does the blue flag mean? Kanaph asked in Ilis's thoughts.

Kanaph felt Ilis jump at the sudden words in her brain, but her qasar did not comment on it. *It is a request to talk about peace. Once the flag is raised, no further attack can be made until the flag is withdrawn.*

Kanaph closed her eyes and connected to Ilis's vision. She was standing behind the queen's gray steed. Ilis looked over her shoulder at her friends. Their arms were bound behind their backs.

"How does she know what a blue flag means?" Chaz asked. "Is it the same in Beriyth?"

He is an astute fellow, that one, Kanaph commented. *And you can tell him no. Beriyth's symbol for a peace treaty is the ruler cutting off their hand and sending it to the other army.*

Ilis gagged, her thoughts going to the rumors she had heard about that tradition. "No," Ilis responded simply. For some reason, she left out the part about the hand.

You have to admit; the hand is a much more serious show of one's desire for peace.

Ilis ignored Kanaph and turned her attention to Chaz. "I don't know how she knows our customs."

"Maybe she has been to the Upper?" Pyra asked.

"But how?" Chaz asked. He was drenched in sweat. They all were. And their skin was beginning to turn the angry red of being exposed to too much Sun.

You guys look terrible, Kanaph commented.

What a helpful remark, Ilis replied, though it was said with a smile.

We need to get you out of the Sun.

Ilis looked up at the Prevailing Light. *Well, not sure how that is going to work.*

Kanaph felt the fear and despair fill Ilis. *Don't go there. There is still time.*

Orders were shouted, and bowmen on both sides ceased firing any more arrows. The blue flag had to be honored.

The dragon opened her eyes and saw that the king had moved forward on the wall so that he could see the queen.

"King of Beriyth, I wish to speak to you!" yelled the queen.

There was silence. The king stood, back straight, glaring down at the queen.

"If you are afraid this is some sort of trick, I swear by the blood of my country that I will not try and attack you during our conversation. After we talk, I will make no promises, as we are—after all—in a war."

"And I should trust your word? The word of our sworn enemies?" yelled back the king.

The queen seemed to smile at this. "Is dear old Professor Owlistare still around?"

Kanaph watched the line of Beriythians from her perch on the spire. The soldiers whispered among themselves. The old man with a long beard, who had been arguing with the king earlier, stepped forward. He climbed up the stone steps to the top of the wall beside the king and peered over the wall.

The old professor squinted in the light. He cocked his head and muttered something under his breath before shouting, "Anne? Is that you?"

The queen bowed her head. "It is indeed." The dragon noticed idly that the queen was dripping with sweat and yet looked completely collected.

"Your Majesty," the professor said, turning to the king. "This is Anne Isilty. The last Royal Thief of Basileia!"

Kanaph felt Ilis's thoughts erupt in a fury. The young pirate was trying to make sense of this. The Queen of the Under was the last Royal Thief?

The dragon watched as the king moved to get a better look.

The Queen of the Under waved chipperly at the King of Basileia. "Why, hello young king! You were just learning to walk when I left this rock of a mountain."

"What sort of trick is this?" asked the king.

"No trick!" the queen replied. "However, I have come to destroy you before you destroy us. So, I would like to ask: will you surrender peacefully? If you lay down your weapons now, we won't have to kill you."

"Excuse me?"

"You are clearly outmatched. It is only a matter of time before we win. But we would win with less casualties if you surrender."

The king remained calm. "Your thought process is faulty. We have the tactical advantage of the higher ground."

The queen seemed to consider this. Then she shrugged. "I take that as you saying you do not want peace?"

The King of Basileia threw back his shoulders. "If your definition of peace is surrender to you, then yes. But, before we go back to trying to kill each other, would you care to fill in the gaps of my understanding? I am so curious . . . If you truly are Anne Isilty, the last Royal Thief, how did you become the Queen of the Under?"

Kanaph leaned forward. She did not know this tale either. Her mother had known only that the past few rulers of Beriyth had been human. Before this family line had been crowned, her mother's memories informed her that a line of centaurs had ruled; before them, her grandmother's memories informed her that a line of griffins had ruled. But when each line dwindled until there was no heir, the line adopted a child of another race—this is how Anne's family had come to rule. But how Anne, who had once held a full life here in Basileia, had become queen—this was unknown to the dragon.

The queen looked off to the horizon, her gaze distant. "If you want to know the truth, I honestly don't remember." The queen giggled. Her eyes snapped to the king. She gripped the blue flag in her fists and tore it in half. "Let the war recommence."

CHAPTER TWENTY-FIVE

Ilis wanted to scream.

She had watched as the rulers of two nations attempted to talk about peace, and not once did they mention the fact that the Sun was about to destroy them all. Could they not see that their doom was upon them! Did their pride truly blind them so completely?

The Foresters began to fire down upon them again. Malcolm motioned with his head, and their small crew took cover behind a cart that held weapons. Ilis watched with wide eyes as the queen dismounted from her horse and just stood out in the open, right in front of the tall walls of Mount Oros, but not one arrow found its mark. Ilis's jaw dropped as she realized what the queen was doing. The arrows around the queen were falling to the ground with small thumps.

"Your Majesty!" the queen shouted in a sing-song voice. "Remember how you said you had the advantage as you had the high ground? Well, let's see what we can do about that, shall we?"

While two griffins swooped in to provide cover, the queen spread her hands out wide and threw her head back, eyes closed. The light from her crown burst and streamed out all around her.

Ilis felt the power surge through the air. For a moment, she felt weightless, as if gravity had lost its hold on the land. Panicked, she looked toward the others and saw that she was not the only one. Every man and beast around the queen now hovered a few inches above the ground.

Then the queen swung her hands forward, and they all fell to the ground. Ilis watched in wonder and horror as the queen's power was focused directly before her. A portion of the castle wall, about thirty paces long and made of the strongest of mountain stone, began to crack at its base and rise up.

"What in the name of all that is recorded," Chaz muttered.

Pyra let out a gasp.

Malcolm moved so he was standing shoulder to shoulder with Ilis. Their hands were still bound, but his presence was a comfort.

"She will destroy them all," Malcolm said, his voice somber.

The queen's head snapped up, her entire form now sparking with white light. She let out a shrill scream and thrust up her hands. The hunk of the castle wall flew up into the air and then crashed back upon the Basileian army.

Pyra screamed.

Ilis fell to her knees, trembling.

The queen stumbled to the ground. "You should have chosen surrender," she growled. Then, with a war cry that raked Ilis's very bones, the Queen of Beriyth rallied her army.

The impenetrable wall of Mount Oros now held a cavernous hole. Ilis found herself gaping at the sight, her mind struggling to wrap around the facts. There was now an opening in the wall thirty paces wide, and behind it, a huge portion of the Basileian armed forces had been smashed by the wall where the queen threw it.

Ilis's stomach turned. Chaz was shaking with fury. Malcolm's face was pale and distraught. How many of his friends lay under that rock? How many of his associates, guards, and mentors had just died by the queen merely lifting her arms?

The Beriythian army charged past Ilis and her friends toward the now exposed mountain city.

What was left of the Basileian army scrambled to find order and stand in the gap. They formed a hasty line in the opening of the wall just in time to be met by the Beriythian army of man and beast.

Ilis watched the two armies meet in a bloody clash that was bottlenecked in the gap in the wall. The Beriythian weapons met with the Basileians' swords in a chilling ring. A cyclops used a club and took out two men in one blow. A griffin flew above the armies and swooped down, plucking men up and then dropping them on their fellow soldiers. Trolls pushed through the forces, causing havoc. The two armies were pressed up against one another, their battlefield the space of fifteen paces. The Basileian archers continued to fire down, but one by one, the griffin plucked the Foresters from their perches until there were few left. The one mirror contraption wasn't enough to stop the swarm of griffins.

As for the queen, she pushed herself to the middle of the action and fought like a crazed animal. Her sword found its mark time and time again.

Ilis found she was having a hard time breathing. The air was scorching hot. The world was ending, and she was watching the two sides kill each other in their final moments. She closed her eyes, trying to close out the screams of war that were her current existence.

She wondered what the queen had meant by saying that she still knew her mother.

That was impossible. Her mother had died giving birth to her. For so long she had believed that her birth foretold the anguish that poured forth to those nearest to her heart . . . Maybe it wasn't true after all.

Ilis looked up upon the Sun which was waging war on both sides. She had been sent to save the world, and she had failed.

There is still hope, Kanaph spoke to her thoughts. Ilis had lost track of where the dragon was, but their connection felt strong, so she couldn't be too far.

Ilis shook her head numbly. She could see no way for them to stop the Sun.

Who did we think we were? Ilis thought. *A pirate, a prince, and a rag-tag team setting about to save the world.*

Ilis, there is still *hope,* Kanaph repeated.

"No!" she shouted, panic rising. The battle was so loud she doubted anyone could hear her anyway. "You don't understand! We lost! We've failed! And the world will now burn because of it."

That is not true.

The battle continued around them. But Ilis just crumpled to her knees unnoticed. Everyone was focused on the demolished wall of Mount Oros which was now surrounded by a blood bath.

Young one, hope, Kanaph said.

"As long as breath fills my lungs, hope shall fill my heart." The words that had once flowed from her mother's lips resounded in her mind like Captain's voice in the midst of a storm.

Ilis closed her eyes and focused on her mother's favorite words, blocking out the sights of battles being lost. And in that moment, Ilis saw she had a choice: hope or despair. Which would she choose?

To hope meant to risk being disappointed, and she wasn't sure she could handle that anymore. Ilis let out a sob, a new wave of sorrow crashing, as she realized perhaps the real reason she was terrified to hope.

The sight of Neil sacrificing himself for her again came to her mind. He had thought she could do this. He had been so certain she could save them all that he paid with his life to give her the chance. If he thought so highly of her, maybe she could risk thinking the same.

"To hope is dangerous," Ilis said. Taking a deep breath, she steeled herself. She let out a huff of laughter and smirked. "But when have I ever let danger stop me?"

In that moment, Ilis made a choice. And it would be a choice that changed the world.

Her eyes snapped open, the sparkling blue holding a fierceness few would dare cross paths with. She would *not* quit. That would not be the end of her story.

In the gaping opening of the mountain wall, the opposing armies continued to meet in a gut-wrenching cacophony of metal and screams.

Ilis glanced about. Whatever guards were supposed to be guarding them were either dead or lost in the battle. Her eyes landed on a knife a few paces from her. She flopped to the ground and rolled over to it until her fingers grabbed it behind her back. With slow and careful movements, so as not to cut off her fingers, Ilis maneuvered the blade and cut off her bonds.

With a smirk on her lips, she rushed up to her friends. "I don't know about you, but I choose hope."

Malcolm let out a whoop as Ilis cut his bonds. Pyra looked like she was going to cry.

Chaz looked . . . well, he looked like he was ready to charge into the battle with his bare hands.

"What's the plan?" Malcolm asked when all of them had been cut free.

Does one go out and find hope, or does it just rise on its own?

A shadow flew overhead, and Kanaph landed beside them in the battle.

Like I told you, Kanaph said. *There is still hope. And he's on my back.*

Seated on the dragon was a young man . . . A young man who looked a lot like Neil.

CHAPTER TWENTY-SIX

Ilis did a double take, the memory of Neil being stabbed still fresh.

"Neil???" she asked, shocked.

Neil slipped off Kanaph's back. He smiled softly at Ilis. "Indeed."

He gazed up at the Sun, his face worried. The Sun now took up a quarter of the sky. Their skin was blistering. The heat made Ilis's head spin.

The armies continued to wage their war. The Beriythian cavalry had come in from the side and assisted the attack. The battle was bottlenecked in the span where the wall was destroyed, but Ilis could see that the Basileian force was already beginning to dwindle, while the Beriythian army seemed to have unlimited numbers.

Neil's eyes, however, were fixed on the Sun. "We are running out of time." He shook his head, somber. Then he turned to Ilis. "My dear, I need your piece of the Moon."

She looked at him, confused, but pulled the glowstone from her stocking and gave it to him nonetheless. The moment their fingers touched, she felt the spark rise up through her entire body again. Hope. All was not lost. Ilis watched as the stone gleamed—and then disappeared into his palm.

Her jaw went slack. She looked into his eyes, youthful and sparkling.

And, somehow, he seemed . . . shorter.

He caressed her cheek, then turned and walked through the battlefield—straight toward the queen.

Hope blossomed in Ilis, though she hardly understood why.

Neil seemed to have no fear of the queen as he walked toward the middle of the battle.

"He doesn't even have a weapon," Chaz remarked under his breath.

Ilis lifted her chin, picked up a sword from a fallen minotaur, and said, "We are his weapon."

And with that, she charged.

"You heard the pirate!" Malcolm said, picking up a sword of his own and following. Chaz grumbled something about death wishes while Pyra laughed and chose a shield over a sword.

The four of them guarded Neil as he made his way to the queen. They fought off cyclops, griffins, men, and other beasts, all while making their way to where the fighting was most intense.

And then the queen noticed them.

She finished off the victim before her, rose up, and flew through the air, landing before Neil. Her power was terrifying.

Malcolm shifted so that he was standing in front of Ilis, and for once, she didn't mind someone stepping in to protect her.

Not that she needed any protecting.

"My darling," Neil said, staring up at the queen.

The queen gripped her sword in her slender fingers. She pointed it toward him. "Come to die again?"

Neil just shook his head. "You have the power to control the fate of this world." He stretched out his hand. "Choose to let its fate be a beautiful one. Don't choose destruction."

The queen scowled. "Choose?" She pointed to the crown she wore upon her head, power radiating from the final Moon stones. "This was never my choice," she spat. "It was always yours."

Neil bowed his head. "Which is why I must make this right." He looked back up at her, eyes pleading. "Please, give it to me."

Snarling, the queen pointed her sword at Neil's throat. "You gave it to me. If you want it back, you are going to have to take it."

Neil's shoulders stooped, as if her reply was his greatest fear. He stepped back and raised one hand, palm facing up. A sphere of white light formed in his palm. It looked as if he were holding a living Star.

"Don't make me do this, Anne," Neil pleaded.

"You died last time. What makes you think you will win now?"

A tear rolled down Neil's cheek. "Because last time I wasn't willing to pay the cost of winning. Last time I wasn't willing to kill you."

Waves of emotion flickered over the queen's face—understanding, sadness, fear, and then anger. The queen let out a roar and charged at him, weapon raised and ready to strike. Ilis and Malcolm both raised their swords, ready to fight should Neil need them.

Even with the sphere of light in Neil's hand, it seemed like an unfair competition. Ilis could now see that her eyes had not been playing tricks; Neil truly was shorter, and the queen towered over him. She held her weapon with a skill and confidence that came from years of practice. Neil stood looking like a child, with no armor or weapon other than a sphere of light.

With the roar still ringing from her lips, the queen charged, but Neil didn't move.

In seconds, the queen was only five paces away. Her feet hardly seemed to touch the ground. The sphere in Neil's hand grew.

Four paces away. Her red armor glimmered in the Sun, each scale reflecting and making her look like a ray of Sun. Neil lifted his chin.

Three paces away. The crown upon her head glowed, its radiance bright even in the brightness of the Sun. Neil took a deep breath, steeling himself.

Two paces away. Her eyes were fierce, determined, and cold. A tear rolled down Neil's cheek.

One. Her sword began to fall in a savage sweep.

Ilis opened her mouth to cry out, but the sound never escaped.

Neil stepped forward, ducked the blow of her sword, and shoved the sphere of light into the queen's heart.

In a burst of light, the fight was over.

Shocked, Ilis watched as Neil knelt by the queen's fallen frame. Her crown rolled away from her, but it was not to the Moon stones that Neil went.

Neil stroked the queen's cheek with the caress of a lover. The queen's eyes fluttered open, her gaze drifting around as if she were in a daze. Her eyes locked with Neil's, looking confused before understanding softened her features.

"So, you've found the rest of yourself, have you?" she asked, in a shockingly kind voice.

Neil shook his head, his eyes wet with tears. "All but a few final pieces, my dear." His eyes flitted to her crown, and she followed his gaze.

"Ilis, do you know what is going on?" Malcolm whispered. Ilis shook her head. They stood only paces away from Neil and the queen.

Anne's features contorted, distraught. She struggled to lift herself, taking in the wreckage around her. "I . . . I . . ."She looked down at her hands, tears falling down her face. "I did this?"

Neil hushed her, staring at her chest, which was gushing red with blood.

"I—I am sorry," Neil managed. "I never should have given you my power. It was too risky."

"We both know it needed to happen." Anne, too, looked down at the blood before smiling and placing her hand upon his cheek. "Don't worry. I am a mere mortal. I always had an end."

Neil blinked away tears. "As long as breath fills our lungs," Neil started.

"Hope shall fill our hearts," Anne finished.

Suddenly, as if just remembering something, Anne looked around, searching.

"Where is . . ."

Her eyes fell upon Ilis, before turning back to Neil.

"Ilandere?" Anne asked.

Neil nodded.

Tears sprang again in Anne's eyes.

Malcolm cleared his throat and stepped forward. "Uh, pardon me, while I hate to ruin whatever is going on . . ." He paused and glanced back up at the Sun. The heat was unbearable, and the Sun was taking up far too much of the sky. "I do believe there is still a world to save."

They all were sunburnt and blistering, even the King of Basileia, who had somehow managed to make it through the battle fray and now stood red skinned on the outskirts of their group. Not that the king seemed to be paying his skin any mind; he seemed much more interested in the odd scene before him.

Malcolm continued, "So, in order to not be crushed by the Sun, I've got a feeling that we need to get the Moon back in place . . . Neil, if you could just reveal the secret location of the Moon, we can go and put the final pieces in place and breathe easily."

Ilis stepped forward and picked up the crown, prying the stones out with her knife. She held the stones for a moment, feeling the buzz of their energy, before locking eyes with Neil.

A rush of memories concerning Neil that had never made sense swarmed in her head. His odd sayings and behaviors flew through her brain only to be conjoined with what little information she had gathered about the Moon. Different moments and facts started clicking into place to form a startling realization.

Could it really be?

Kanaph read her thoughts and seemed to huff in surprise. *That would make sense why he felt so different upon my back.*

It would explain a great many mysteries about him, Ilis replied to her qasar.

"You are the secret location, aren't you?" Ilis said, more as a statement than a question.

Neil grinned, his mouth pulling to one side with that mischievous look in his eyes.

She shook her head in disbelief. "You are the Moon!"

"I always knew my daughter would be a smart one," Neil replied with a wink.

He leaned down and planted a kiss on Anne's lips. When he pulled away, they both had tears in their eyes.

"What a kiss, that brings each other to tears," Neil whispered.

The grass around them suddenly burst into flames from the Sun's force. Kanaph began patting out the area around them with her wings.

Neil sighed. "I do believe that is my cue." He gave Anne's hand one last squeeze, wiped the tears from his eyes, and stood.

He stepped up to Malcolm and extended his hand. Malcolm looked at the young boy before him, who was not truly young at all, and then wrapped him up in a hug.

"It's been an honor to be your friend," Neil said, his voice oddly young and high pitched.

"Says the Moon." Malcolm laughed and shook his head. "No, the honor has been all mine." Malcolm cast a worried glance toward the Sun. "We are sure this will work, right?"

Neil laughed. "Let's hope so! I've caused enough Quakes for my lifetime."

Ilis's brain raced, trying to decipher that statement. "The Quake last week . . . that was you?"

Neil grimaced. "Unfortunately. I took the Crown Jewel and then thought maybe that would be enough. So I tried to go back up . . . only things did not go as I hoped."

Malcolm rubbed his head. "That's one way of saying it."

Neil moved toward Ilis, his eyes full of care and love. "Oh, how I wish there was not a time limit upon moments like these."

Ilis offered him the Moon pieces.

He took a deep breath and looked at her intently. "Remember this, when night is at its darkest, remember who you are." Then he stood on his tiptoes to plant a kiss upon her forehead and accepted the pieces. They dissolved into his skin . . . and he changed yet again before their very eyes.

He stood before them as a seven-year-old boy, with a mischievous look glimmering in his eye. He winked at Ilis, cast a heartsick look at Anne, and then looked up. He jumped into the air, clicked his heels, and then shot into the sky in a column of light.

That column of light rose up and up and up through the sky until it met the Sun—and began pushing the Sun back in a sparkling embrace.

Sparks of light, like shooting Stars, flew across the sky away from the bright pair of Sun and Moon. Ilis wondered for a moment if that was how Stars were born—from the embrace of Sun and Moon. But then her attention was caught by a cool breeze that wafted against her skin.

As the Sun shrank in the sky, the mountain cooled. The fires in the valley died down.

When the Moon had pushed the Sun back unto her rightful throne, where she could warm and not scorch and share her rays evenly between the two sides, there was yet another flash, and the Moon disappeared to hide until nightfall.

Off in the distance, she heard the king mutter, "Reigning Lights . . . they . . . they *live*."

Ilis stared up at the sky for a long while, attempting to process. Finally, she turned her eyes to Anne, the Queen of the Under, hoping to find an explanation.

Anne lay on her back, looking up at Ilis. Blood gushing from her wound, she managed a small shrug. "Your father always was one for the mysterious."

"What?" Ilis hurried to the aid of the bleeding woman. Ilis's hands pressed against her wound to staunch the flow. "But Captain . . ."

Anne smiled and nodded. "Is my brother and adopted you when I told him I needed him to."

Ilis shook her head, looking back up at the sky where Neil left. "But he can't be . . ." Ilis started. "He is MY age!"

"Well, my dear, that is because he ages backwards. Every piece of the Moon he regained made him younger." Anne smiled softly. "I met him when we both were around twenty."

Ilis looked down at Anne in awe, finally putting all of the pieces together. "Wait . . ." Ilis went forward and knelt before her . . . mother?

Anne reached up and stroked her daughter's cheek. "Oh Ilandere, I'm so sorry . . . for everything."

A tear fell down her cheek, and then Anne—Queen of the Under, wife to Neil the Moon, and mother to Ilis the last Moon Thief—died in her daughter's arms.

CHAPTER TWENTY-SEVEN

Ilis closed the door to her room behind her. The lock clicked into place. She walked over the thick orange carpet toward the hammock and stood beneath it, staring up at the hammock for a long moment before deciding she didn't have the energy to climb up.

She was shaking, she noticed with some surprise. She held her hands out before her—they were still stained by blood. Moving toward the water basin, her mind in a fog, Ilis began to scrub at her hands. But the blood wouldn't come off. It was stuck between the creases of her hands, as if refusing to let her escape reality.

Anger and grief boiled over in her, and she threw the basin against the wall. It shattered to pieces and Ilis sank to the carpet in the midst of them, arms wrapping around her knees.

She had just watched her mother die.

Her *mother!*

All these years, her mother had been alive, and she hadn't known! Her mother hadn't died giving birth to her. Ilis hadn't been the cause of her mother's death!

Tears began to fall down Ilis's cheeks unbidden, and yet once they started, she couldn't stop. Her whole body began to rack in sobs.

How had this happened? How had her mother ended up in the Under? Why had she abandoned her? And then there was Neil! He was truly her father? Ilis loved Captain dearly, but why had they all lied to her? Why had no one told her that Neil was her father?

Questions swam in Ilis's head.

Her father had killed her mother. That reality hit and sent yet another wave of wracking sobs. And yet, could it have been prevented? Was there another way?

There was a knock at her door. Ilis didn't move.

"Ilis?" Kat's voice came from the other side of the door. "I know you are probably feeling overwhelmed, but . . . Well, I found something you should read."

Something slipped underneath the door.

When Ilis heard Kat's footsteps recede, she stood and moved toward the door. There was a small brown leather journal on the floor. Wiping her hands on her leggings, she bent to pick it up. She fingered the worn leather. There was a thin C shape on the cover.

She leaned against the wall and slid down until she was sitting. With still shaking hands, she opened the journal. The first page said:

Property of Anne Isilty, Royal Thief of Basileia and the final Moon Thief this side of our fair world. Started in the year 1,049 of the Kingdom of Basileia, in the time of the Scorching Sun and upon the discovery of the Moon.

Ilis turned the pages and discovered her mother's story.

All my life my family has told me the history of why we do what we do.

In the First Age, the king declared he wanted the Moon, and all thieves scrambled to bring it to him and thus obtain the title of Royal Thief. Only, things did not go quite as planned, for it was not an accomplished thief who stole the Moon, but a young girl. How the girl managed to steal the Moon from the sky is a mystery, but what is known is that the girl mourned the loss of the Moon and so did not accept the title Royal Thief. She chose instead to bear the title Moon Thief, and took upon herself the quest of putting the Moon back together again.

That girl is my many greats' grandmother.

My ancestors took on the quest of dispersing among the various lands to search for the lost jewels of the Moon and put the pieces back where they belonged. It was an extravagant task that took centuries. And just when they thought they had gathered almost all of them, they realized that there were pieces on the Under as well.

This was an important time among us Moon Thieves, for we realized that our work was far from finished. The realm of the Under held a whole new harvest of Moon pieces. All but one Moon Thief family, my great-grandfather's, moved to the Under in search of these pieces. However, as the Under Moon Thieves gathered up their findings and gave them back to the Moon, Quakes came upon the land in great force. Many have wondered if these two events are connected; I have my suspicions.

I grew up knowing this was my history. I myself have been out hunting down Moon pieces with my parents and grandparents. But I didn't understand how important this task was until after all but my brother and I died in the Quakes. My brother set out upon the seas to search, thus making me the lone Moon Thief in Basileia. It was then that I met the Moon himself.

The Moon is a person. His name is Neil.

And this is our story.

Ilis devoured the story of her mother, reading the quests and adventures with tears ever streaming down her cheeks. Her parents traveled for years in the Age of Quakes, looking for missing Moon pieces, and their life was made beautiful by each other's presence. Then came some journal entries that were more somber.

Three years after their wedding, Anne wrote:

Neil is beginning to worry me! He wants to try and go back into the sky, for he believes that the Quakes are his fault, but I don't believe we have all of the pieces. And I fear that even worse consequences than Quakes will happen should he try and return prematurely. Also . . . I am not ready to lose him.

Ilis's thoughts drifted back to the Quake that had almost killed Malcolm . . .

Later that year, Anne wrote:

The Quakes continue, and Neil grows restless. We have not found a Moon piece this side in over a year. However, a new batch of pieces just came from the Under, and as soon as they passed over the Edge, the greatest Quake yet recorded hit, killing hundreds—including the Queen of Basileia. This was the final proof Neil needed. Something has to change, though I fear what the change will be.

Ilis flipped through the journal, reading as fast as she could.

Five days after that, Anne had the following entry:

Neil and I just had a long and rather heated debate where I learned a great deal of things about our history that I almost wish I didn't now know. I hardly know what to think now. History is supposed to be a trustworthy thing, especially in Basileia. But now, there is nothing to do but move forward. I am being sent to the Under while my husband stays on this side. It would not be so terrible if only we could stay together, but I am the only one he trusts with this burden. He will teach me how to harness the power of the Moon, and then I shall take all of the remaining Moon pieces to the Under to maintain balance. He believes that the Quakes will end when I go over with the Moon pieces.

I tried to tell him that this was just a temporary solution, for the world is waning because of his lack of presence in the sky. He is the rightful Ruler of the Night, and until he regains his throne, our lands will suffer the consequences. But he says he cannot bear the suffering caused by the Quakes, and that if we do not restore balance, he will resort to trying to return to his throne prematurely—which I fear would be the death of us all.

She flipped to the final pages, her fingers brushing upon them. They were stained with tears.

Neil has taught me the secrets of the Moon, and I can do things that would have made me marvel once, but now, I can only think of leaving my love. To the Under I go, never to see my husband again. Unless, that is, he can find all the remaining pieces.

Ilis sat back, trying to understand. Her parents had separated themselves in an attempt to stop the Quakes. And it had worked. Her mother had sacrificed herself for the sake of their world.

But then the Quake that happened recently . . . If Neil had tried to go back up, then Anne was right! His trying to do so had been the catalyst for the Sun almost destroying them all! In his attempt to save the world, he had almost doomed it.

There was one final entry.

I leave tomorrow, but I just discovered something that has brought me both immeasurable joy and indescribable pain.

I am pregnant.

I cannot tell Neil, for he will change his plans if he knows. He will say we cannot separate for the sake of our child. And while that is all my heart wants, I now understand that this needs to happen. The Quakes must end. Too many lives have been lost already. And I see no other option than to continue on with the plan. We must do this to create a safe world for our child to live in.

I will leave the child in the care of my brother, Captain of Maribor. I dare not take the baby with me, as the power of the Moon running through my veins scares me. I already am not myself. The child will be safer with my brother.

I pray there is a day we can reunite. But I know not if that day will exist.

To my darling child, if you ever find this, know you are loved. Know you are cherished. Know you are ours. And forgive us for not being there for you.

The journal entries ended there.

Ilis wept. She wept for her mother, who she never knew. She wept for her father, who for years had not even known she existed. She wept for what was lost. And she wept for joy for what she did have. Grief and joy intermingled in her tears as she found herself overwhelmed by the love of her parents, who had sacrificed their very lives that she might live.

EPILOGUE

Ilis peered over Kat's shoulder, reading as she wrote. When the king had told Ilis she would be pardoned of all claims against her and reinstated as the Royal Thief on one condition, Ilis had feared he would ask her to do something terrible. When he had told her his condition was that she record every detail of her past few weeks, Ilis could not decide if she would rather face the lashes again. Kanaph chastised her for the thought and reminded her that she had just completed the Moon.

Completing a book could hardly be a task greater than that.

The problem was that Ilis, as educated as she was, wasn't a very good writer—which is where Kat came in. The young girl had jubilantly offered her services. The rules would have to be bent slightly, as each citizen of Basileia was still expected to have written their own work, but it would do for now.

"Kat," Ilis ventured, "you aren't going to just end it like that, are you?"

Kat turned to Ilis. "Why not? Tears are not something to be ashamed of. Cepher always says that tears are the mark of trueness to one's soul."

Malcolm chuckled.

They had been holed up in Ilis's room for almost a month, working on this project. Chaz and Pyra had helped too; everyone was willing and eager to help Ilis regain her rightful status on the mountain. Ilis had tried to tell them that even if she regained the title of Royal Thief, she would still travel often with Captain. But the others did not seem to mind if she was gone occasionally.

They only wanted to ensure that she would come back.

At the moment, Pyra and Chaz were off looking for more C markings around the palace. Ilis had a gut feeling that they had something to do with the Moon Thieves, but what the connection was, or why many of them marked the entrances to tunnels, they had not yet figured out.

Malcolm, who refused to leave until the project was finished, had tried every seat in the room before proclaiming that Ilis had "a great lacking in comfortable seating" and promptly left to bring a chair from his room. He sat in the chair now, *The Art of Letter Writing* in his lap and a smile upon his lips.

Ilis turned to him, raising an eyebrow. "What, you think that my book should end with me sitting on the floor of my room crying?"

Malcolm threw up his hands. "Last time I tried to disagree with you, I got crushed by rocks, so I'm tapping out of this fight."

Ilis glared at him. "Oh, that's cruel." She turned to Kat, "Also, who *is* this Cepher you keep talking about?"

Kat smirked. "My grand-paps. You know him as Professor Owlistare."

Ilis raised a brow. "Your grandfather is Professor Owlistare?"

Kat nodded and grinned. But her grin quickly turned into a pout. "But wait . . . did you just say your book?"

There was a loud whoosh, followed by the scraping of tiles on Ilis's roof.

Ilis pulled a rope and opened the roof panel for Kanaph to stick her head through.

Kat has a point. This is not truly your story, Kanaph said in Ilis's thoughts.

"Fine! It is all of ours. But I am the one the king asked to write it," Ilis said, exasperated.

Kanaph cocked her head. *Are you calm?*

Ilis took a breath and nodded.

Good. I've brought news from Beriyth.

The dragon pulled her head out of the opening, shifted positions on the roof, and lowered her claw, which had a small leather pouch tied around it.

Untying the pouch, Ilis opened it to find a letter.

Ilis read it quickly. Her jaw dropped, and the letter fluttered from her fingertips.

Malcolm jumped from his chair and picked up the forsaken missive. He, too, read it speedily, his face paling.

"The Under can't just . . ." Malcolm didn't seem to have the words to finish.

"What does it say?" Kat asked. She plucked the letter from Malcolm's shaking hands. Kat's eyes moved quickly over the lines. When she was finished, she handed it back to Ilis and turned back to her pages, pen in hand.

"Well, now that has the makings for a more dramatic ending."

***

Anne's journal entries made no sense until you coupled them with what Ilis had learned on her adventures. The Moon and his wife Anne found a way to delay the crashing of the Sun long enough for all of the Moon pieces to be found, but with the transference of the Moon's power into a mortal frame, Anne's heart turned dark like the night sky. Neil unintentionally made his own wife into his deepest, darkest enemy.

Somewhere along the way Neil apparently found out about Ilis, which explained his dislike for pirates: to him, pirates were the thieves of his daughter—a crime he would not forgive lightly.

And thus, Ilandere, daughter of the Moon and Anne Isilty, became Ilis the Lass of the Seas. And that is the end of our story.

However, when the truth is told, this isn't the end. It's just the beginning. And Ilis's next story has much to do with fixing the Moon, becoming Queen of Beriyth, and saving the world yet again.

***

Ilis gasped as she read the new final words Kat was writing in the book. "KAT! That is an even worse ending!"

Kat shrugged. "What? We all know it's true." She gestured to the window, where they could see the night sky. Even though night had regained its claim to half the day, and the Moon had regained his claim as King of the Night, things were not right.

The Moon was bloodred.

It had happened the night of the battle. The whole crew—Ilis, Malcolm, Pyra, Chaz, and even Kat—were up on the rooftop of the castle, awaiting the Moon's first rise in over a millennium.

They cheered when they first saw the Moon rise into the sky. But their cheers grew silent when his light faded from a sparkling white to a bloody red.

"Neil isn't supposed to be red, is he?" Chaz asked.

Ilis paled, dread filling her . . .

Kat's voice brought Ilis back to the present.

"At the very least, something is wrong with the Moon, and you must help him," Kat stated. "As for the rest, is that not what the letter said?"

Ilis felt Malcolm's eyes on her. She didn't know what to think of the message. Her heart quickened in her chest at the thought of an adventure she did not want to take. She did not want to be queen. She did not want to have to try and save the world again. She wanted the adventure to end right here.

"But there is never a real ending anyway," Kat continued with a shrug of her shoulders. "Every story's end is truly just the introduction to another story."

Ilis moaned. "We are terrible at writing endings."

ACKNOWLEDGMENTS

Once upon a time, I read someone's acknowledgements, and they were actually fun! I wish I could do that too . . . I suppose you will have to be the judge of that.

First off, I just have to thank my Creator and Savior who gave me a knack for stories and was oh-so present as I discovered this story.

Then I have to thank Ruth Nelson (AKA R.A. Nelson. If you don't know about her, go check her and her books out!). Ruth, Moon Thief would not be published if not for you, so thank you for helping me birth my book child. Thank you for the many hours you put into editing and polishing this book and encouraging her author.

Jacques, thank you for helping me to bridge the gap between my imagination and the words I had on paper. And thanks for being a critic and a fan all at once; this is perhaps the greatest combination a writer can ask for.

Then there are my first readers—Maria and Angel. Thank you for reading and loving Moon Thief . . . even when Ilis smirked every other line.

Daniel, thank you for reading and rereading and rereading Moon Thief and offering key input at every turn.

Emily, thanks for being a staunch supporter of Ilis, to such an extent that you being you brought Kat into existence.

Thanks to my parents who homeschooled me through high school and let me spend hours upon hours just writing and exploring the worlds of my own imaginings.

And thank you to you, my dear reader, who just read all the way to the end of my acknowledgments. Thank you for joining me on this adventure. Cheers!

ALSO BY FUTURE HOUSE PUBLISHING

We appreciate your purchase of this book. We hope you enjoyed it, we had a lot of fun making it! To help us keep telling great stories, we'd love it if you could take a few minutes to leave us an honest review. Thank you in advance!

If you love *Moon Thief,* then stay tuned for the next book in the series! Until then, you might also like other books published by Future House Publishing.

The Method to Infinite Things by Madison Boyer
Mortalkind: The Heavenly Heist by Alexander Harrington
The ATLAS Project by L.M. White

And many more! Look for your next read by visiting
www.futurehousepublishing.com

ABOUT THE AUTHOR

Rachel Shinnick was born in Minnesota, considers North Carolina "home", but has her favorite memories from living in Hawaii, where she would run to the ocean to swim with dolphins and hear whales sing. She is a Jesus-follower, an avid tree-climber, a spikeballer, a chocolate connoisseur, an accidental-intruder-of-shark-caves, and was an honorary coach on her father's college football sideline when they won the national championship (she even got a ring to prove it!). Currently living in Italy, she spends most of her time training young people to be launched into ministry through an organization called Youth With A Mission. When she's not out adventuring the Tuscan countryside, you will often find her tucked away doing one of two things: either reveling in the world of someone else's magnificent imagination or putting words to the fantastical worlds of her own. She stands giddily excited to be able to read these stories to her future children—but hopes the rest of you enjoy them until then!

Check out her website: rachelshinnick.com and follow her on instagram: @rachelgraces

GET IN TOUCH

Interested in having Rachel Shinnick come visit your school? Have a question about the series or want to talk with the Future House Publishing team?

We'd love to hear from you! Follow us on social media, visit our website, or send us an email.

For more information visit us online at
www.futurehousepublishing.com or contact us:
books@futurehousepublishing.com

Please join our mailing list for new releases, exclusive offers, and our best deals. You can join by visiting www.futurehousepublishing.com!

Made in the USA
Las Vegas, NV
09 February 2024

85536655R00163